The Buds Are Calling

The Buds Are Calling

B. COYNE DAVIES

IGUANA

Publisher: Meghan Behse
Editor: Paula Chiarcos
Front cover design: TinyFleaArt

ISBN 978-1-77180-449-3 (paperback)
ISBN 978-1-77180-450-9 (ebook)

This is an original print edition of *The Buds Are Calling*.

To the memory of M.A. according to our ancient agreement.
And to H. and P. who are considerably more lively.

Author's Note

This story begins in the summer of 2013, in a state that will remain nameless, possibly even mythical. Why, the ever-changing patchwork of state laws across the nation can boggle the mind and disorient a person so they have no clue where they're at. With some hesitancy I can tell you that this particular state, with its reformist bent and inevitable bureaucratic gloom, was probably more north than south and more east than west. But the pinpointing of territory, governance or the body politic is of little relevance. And in any case, it's trouble best avoided.

~ B. Coyne Davies

PART ONE

Seeds

Sad Ones, do not banish us. Do not merely bury us. We sing of the great desire. We sing of suns and the myriad lights, the sweet songs of summer and souls. Of love, and the quiet heart. It opens and unfolds the clouds. A song to caress the shimmer of your tears. A song beyond the throb and sting. A song beyond the fall. We sing so gently and we hold you dear for all that comes to be. We root our care in the dark damp deep that murmurs, soft beneath your feet. Oh Sad Ones, do not cover us to rid your sight of this. Do not banish us. Do not seize your breath so tightly.

from Cannto III, *Cannabidadas*

Chapter 1

Ernie Kippett shook the daturas as he lifted them from the shovel's blade. He wanted to get as much soil off the roots as possible. The bed had subsided over the years so all dirt was valuable. Tomorrow morning he'd be digging up hostas to replace everything. His friend Carl was demolishing one of the gardens over at the old Rosemore estate and had said Ernie could take all the hostas he needed for the terraces. The owner of the terraces, Mrs. Cranston, was a galleon of a woman with cannons ready. She had been unusually agreeable about the arrangement. Probably because of where the hostas were coming from. She was a stickler for status and was determined to preserve the terraces' reputation. They were the "floral pride of Hullbrooke," and Ernie was surprised she let him work on them. He had a hunch that Carl, with his lifetime horseshoe-up-the-arse gig taking care of the estate, must have put in a good word for him.

Daturas had been blooming in this bed as far back as Ernie could remember. Maybe Mrs. Cranston had grown something different in the intervening years when he was off selling his soul and being eaten alive by Lenore. But the white and purple trumpet flowers looked exactly the same as the ones he'd seen every summer from the time he was five. Why she'd decided to replant the bed precisely now — in July — seemed a little nuts. There'd been no problems for at least thirty-eight years. Maybe the old girl was battling dementia; paranoia too, lurking in there somewhere among the perennials. He looked at the growing piles of wilting plants in the yard bags and felt deflated. Hostas were okay, but the daturas were interesting. A little mysterious even. Definitely more colorful.

"The kids could get into them. Kids're crazy now!" Mrs. Cranston said, skirt billowing in the wind. She'd thrown her hands up in disgust. "Stupid too. On their phones all the time. You know datura can kill people." She'd turned to Ernie, vigorously wagging her finger. "They'd try eating or smoking it so they could film something. Share it. Post it! And hope it goes viral. You should see the idiocy my granddaughter gets up to."

Ernie didn't think kids were any dumber or crazier than he'd been. He dumped a bucket of water onto the bed and then headed up the terrace steps to the wagon. He came back with a couple of pots, surveyed the wet patch and focused on some white blooms, then picked up the shovel and sunk it in deeper than he had all day. He had to dig well below the roots. After levering the shovel load up and peering closely at the clump, he dumped it into one of the pots. Then he dug out a purple bunch in the same way and put that into the other pot. Carl had originally told him to ask Mrs. Cranston if she'd kept any seeds.

"Good heavens! Why would I do that? The seeds are even more dangerous."

Carl had told him if he wanted to transplant some of daturas for his new digs above the Rent-All, he could leave them at the estate until he was ready to move. Ernie had no idea if they'd survive. He was relying solely on Carl's expertise. Carl knew lots about everything, probably even that Ernie was living out of a station wagon, or he wouldn't have offered to take the plants. It was a point of dignity though not to bring up certain things around here. Ernie had to laugh because the station wagon was an upgrade.

Ernie put the newly potted daturas in some shade under a lilac bush and finished digging up the rest of the bed. It took him another hour or so in the hot sun. Mrs. Cranston's compost was at the far side of the house, and he had to lug the bags of expiring plants up nineteen stone steps. When he finished he was dripping with sweat. He slid his eye patch up and wiped his face with a spare T-shirt from the station wagon, then slid the patch back into place over his right eye. As he came back down the steps he hunted for his water bottle and found it right about where he'd been digging before lunch. As he went to pick it up he noticed the great fat toad.

Mrs. Cranston had told him about it. "Make sure you don't hurt the big mother toad. I think she lives in the datura bed. She's part of the family you know." Since Mrs. Cranston had birthed a substantial brood, Ernie was impressed she'd keep track of a toad. Did the mother toad have a name? Ernie had inquired.

"Oh, she's had a half-dozen names. I forget what the kids called her. Gladys maybe. Yes. Gladys." At any rate the toad was ancient by toad years. She just sat there warty and occasionally blinking. At one point she shifted slightly and tucked her hind leg a little tighter under herself. The notion occurred to Ernie that a toad living among the dangerous datura roots would have a remarkable constitution or at the very least was going to miss tripping out now. And he didn't bother telling Mrs. Cranston that toads can pack a pretty nasty toxin of their own. She might order the execution of Gladys, along with the daturas, if she knew.

Ernie took a slow drink of water and started tidying up. Tomorrow would be a long day but a payday. Mrs. Cranston, especially if you listened sympathetically to her indignations, various complaints and grim analyses, always added a little extra. Really nice thing about people around Hullbrooke — cash agreements were a matter of course.

It hadn't even occurred to Ernie to come back to his old hometown. His family was gone now, his mother dead from lung cancer, his brother married to a painter and living in Portugal. He figured he'd be sitting tight in Brooklyn for the rest of his life. But Lenore had given him the idea. She was on and on about LA, how their relationship had ruined her dreams, and now it was all too late and he'd never appreciated that. He'd suggested delusional ambition was making her miserable and would for the rest of her life, so maybe she should try getting a handle on that. At which point she'd said, "Oh, why don't you just go back to that little bumfuck nowhere town you came from." And so, by golly, he did.

Ernie decided he was doing pretty well, considering. At least he was making a little money and he did have a rust bucket he could sleep in. Mostly he tried to sleep outside, often on top of the vehicle. But when it was raining, like it would be tonight, he scrunched up his six-foot-six self to fit inside the old Volvo. Not only did the exercise make his bones ache the next morning, it stunk in there. The previous owner had big dogs with poor digestive systems and lousy control at both ends, Ernie guessed. He could spend the night at the Two Trees motel but he'd rather not get in the habit while it was still warm out. Plus he needed to save his money. With luck Gerry would get the old office over the Rent-All cleaned out in the next few weeks so Ernie could set up house in it. A place where he could put a stove, a really good one, because cooking might be the only thing left that gave him pleasure.

After sweeping and hosing off the terrace stairs where he'd been working, he filled up his dented plastic water bottle and stashed it in his tattered knapsack. He picked up the two pots of daturas and climbed the nineteen steps again. Before driving away he made sure to turn off the faucet on the side of the house. Mrs. Cranston had relayed dark and unpleasant tales about previous negligent yard help.

Ernie drove along the tree-lined street with the upscale houses and then steered his car down the hill into Hullbrooke's diminutive downtown. He parked along the main street and took himself into Chelsea's, where for a couple of hours he coddled a beer and chatted with the locals. Everybody was in high spirits. The state, arcane and impenetrable as ever, had finally passed the new weed regulations that very afternoon, right about the time Ernie had met Gladys the Toad. Not that it would make that much difference. Anybody who was registered — for medical reasons of course — could already grow six plants. For lots of people, depending on the yield of their plants, that could be more than they could use. So it was easy enough to score some, even if you weren't sick or racked with pain. Hell, it was always easy to score some. Ernie's smoky high-school days were long before medical use was state sanctioned. The new laws would just allow for commercial production and apparently they got rid of the whole indictment-for-possession-of-small-amounts insanity. Everybody at Chelsea's agreed; legal recreational use probably wasn't long in coming.

When Ernie left the bar he sauntered along the main street for a few blocks and picked up an egg salad sandwich and a bottle of German lager at the deli.

"See you workin' on the terraces today. Nice! She pay you good?" The plump Greek woman, whose brother had owned the deli for years, winked at him.

"If I do a good job."

"You do good. Sure. I know. You just like your dad."

This woman mentioned his dad so often, Ernie could only wonder what exactly had gone on between them. According to his mother, Ernie's tall, dashing father, Alejandro, was a prize prick. She claimed

Uruguay specialized in them, and Alejandro was out of the picture by the time Ernie could walk. In spite of all that and his pure Danish blood from the distaff side, his mother had christened him Ernesto, for which he was very grateful. But he did regret he'd never met the man. Too late now. Alejandro, felled by an aneurysm, was only charming the daisies these days.

The rain started to sprinkle as Ernie left the deli. He made his way back to the car with his purchases and then drove about fifteen minutes out of town to the old Lusteadt Side Road, a series of potholes with encroaching vegetation and even the odd washout. But at a leisurely fifteen miles an hour or so, he could navigate it. No one would bother him. About three miles in, after the rock cuts, there was a wide shoulder where he parked and had a view of Little Silver Lake. It wasn't bad and a quiet unobtrusive dip after a day's work or in the morning was good for maintaining personal hygiene. He'd parked in the exact same place the night before and watched the moonlight on the water. But tonight, all he could see was rain sluicing down over the windows. By the morning the clouds should have moved on and then he could pretend he was in a motel with a private lake.

Ernie finished up his egg sandwich and beer, then crawled into the rancid back of the station wagon, being careful not to knock over the daturas. It wasn't easy given his length. He pulled a little reading lamp out from the side-door pocket, settled himself in a ratty sleeping bag and groped for the paperback that was digging into his knee. There were about ten or so books scattered throughout the car. He'd bought them at a yard sale, a buck a book. There were even two on gardening. But damn, the batteries on the lamp were dead. He was exhausted anyway. He lay there uncomfortably. Without fail Lenore came to mind.

Ah yes, his lost love Lenore. Except she wasn't lost. He knew exactly where she was: Miami, her hometown, spending the money she'd cleared from their joint savings account before she took off. It wasn't much, mind you. She probably used it all just moving everything from Brooklyn to Florida. But her sneaky stinginess rankled.

She didn't play fair. Not ever. That part right before she suggested he go home? The cruelest part where she'd called him a stupid crazy fucking wall-eyed asshole? That was below the belt and a head wound combined. He'd never forgive her for such a cheap schoolyard shot. She'd probably been saving it ever since she read the damn article. He'd read it too. To summarize: People with exotropia — the broad stroke of strabismus that turns the misaligned eye outward — were more likely to have low IQs and/or psychiatric disorders. But Ernie was neither stupid nor crazy. No. He was impressive. With all that height, half the world figured he'd been an NBA hopeful. And with his eye patch and stoic dignity, the other half thought he was a veteran. Lenore was just mean. She'd say anything to keep herself center stage. Dis his friends if they didn't compliment her enough. Lose it if he had so much as a conversation with another woman, even if she was a colleague. Sure, criticize his work but demand luxury. He couldn't even read a book without her complaining. He should have left years ago.

But the sex. Damn! It was like an addiction — no, it *was* an addiction. He'd never had a beautiful woman do things like that with him. He'd probably pawn the station wagon to have sex with Lenore again. Yeah, he would.

Maybe he did have a low IQ.

It occurred to him as he dozed off that in place of Lenore, he was now cuddling up with two pots of daturas. Given their reputation for producing hallucinations, nausea, hyperthermia, tachycardia, confusion, temporary paralysis and possible death, he felt right at home.

Chapter 2

Lydia Rosemore dropped her eyeliner. "Shoot!" It rolled off the pale oriental onto the hardwood under the dressing table. "Oh my gracious." She bent down and fished for the errant tube, grimacing at her reflection in the mirror. It wasn't an angle of herself she was used to: head sideways, cheek flattened on the milk-glass tabletop, an ash-blonde lock flopping the wrong way over her forehead, her face sinking in a forest of brushes, cotton swabs, bottles, tubes and pots of cosmetics. She noticed a tiny gap in the normally perfect array of eyelashes over her left eye. For Lydia, eyelash implants were the key to being acceptable under all circumstances with the least amount of daily effort. Perfectly curved, perfectly colored, perfectly aligned. Little wonders they were, and they saved her from facial drabness. Mostly. Middle age, and perhaps *fifty-four* in particular, was not that kind to her. As she continued to grope around, the notion of getting "real work" done came to mind again. Her first mother-in-law had managed two facelifts before she reached fifty. But Lydia found the thought of going under a knife that way rather repulsive.

When her hand finally landed on the eyeliner, Lydia snatched it up and applied it with maximum proficiency. Normally she'd skip the mascara but not this evening. Not with those gaps. She picked up the closest tube — taupe — and applied it with equal speed. Corinna at the spa was right: Black or navy mascara was always more dramatic with blue eyes, but the taupe would have to do. She was running late. She finished up with a light coating of lipstick and the blush was minimal to go with it all. Caldwell couldn't complain. "Aren't you the rosy-cheeked cherub today, Lydia," he'd say. As if he knew anything. He did pay attention to details though and she liked that. He made her feel energized and desirable again. And finally, a man her own age. A man who was as tall and trim as she was. With a full head of hair! And my gracious, just the most distinguished dash of gray streaking through all that dark chestnut. He knew how to dress too. Other women looked at him. They certainly did. And he told jokes. She'd never laughed so much in her life. And what was life without these things?

When Caldwell Porter and Lydia Rosemore had officially announced they were a couple, it had not gone down well with the friends and associates of either of them. Although to be fair, those on Caldwell's side — what few remained after his business adventures — were considerably more understanding. "Money," they agreed. Lydia had tons of it and Caldwell none. Never mind she was an airhead. All the better maybe.

Lydia's friends, on the other hand — actually there weren't many of those either — shook their heads. Her own daughter viewed the relationship with increasing alarm. She asked her mother how she could be turning into such a doormat, and Lydia remembered then that her own mother had often been called a doormat. She had always felt her father loved her mother though and that was the important thing wasn't it? Wasn't that worth the odd emotional bruising? Love was the basis of everything. It was the ground you built on. And if you didn't have love, well, then you didn't have anything.

Lydia's lawyers and accountants, the ones her second husband, Jordan, had recruited with great foresight, had taken a particularly dim view of the relationship. They suggested the mismatch of means was not seemly. Lydia would protest that Jordan, God rest his soul, would want her to be happy. They agreed of course he would; he'd taken very good care of her for over twenty years. So Lydia would point out that Caldwell made her very happy. He paid attention. He talked to her. The presents he bought her were "so touching," and he'd taken her on "super holidays to exotic places." Yes, but all with her money, they'd pointed out. Lydia did not see the issue. Caldwell loved her deeply and she would have him. So the lawyers had drawn up the pre-pre-nups and the accountants had capped her expenditures. Jordan had prepared them for every possibility and this was simply an implementation of Plan F. They were disappointed but well instructed from beyond the grave.

That evening after collecting Caldwell and dining out, Lydia had words with him that inclined her to believe he might not love her so much after all.

"To make money a person needs to take some well-leveraged risks. Or just any risks, Lydia," Caldwell had muttered as he ran his hand through his well-coiffed hair.

"Well risks aren't everything, sweetheart. Although I guess being alive is something of a risk we all take. And you know, it is a risk to decide to be joyful. That's what I've decided to be. Joyful."

"For God's sake. Do you have to keep spewing that drivel?" He rolled his eyes. It was something he did with increasing frequency these days. "New Age isn't *new* anymore, you know," he continued as his face became flushed. "You might want to try developing a brain cell for a change."

Lydia lowered her gaze. She demurred, as she often did when she could see Caldwell was getting stressed, and said she would mention his new business idea to her lawyer.

"Oh for God's sake!" He threw his hands in the air. He was only suggesting she invest some of her yearly disposable income, not shift her assets or renovate her portfolios. Her income was breathtaking from Caldwell's perspective and he felt an urgency about its going to waste. He found spending money on simply enjoying life over the last two years was now beginning to feel a little hollow. He was a doer, a deal-maker, a mover, not some over-age gigolo. He still had ideas and great things to do. He had passion and imagination. All he needed was the start-up money.

Lydia, long made well aware of her poor grasp of money matters, had vowed never to invest without speaking to Jordan's appointed advisers. Even if she could do what she chose with her own income, it was just one of the things that helped keep her mind clear. "It's just how I do things, sweetheart. You have to understand this about me," she said.

"I understand nothing about you," Caldwell sputtered. "You abdicate your power at every turn. In fact it drives me crazy!" Caldwell straightened to his full height. "I just don't know that I can put up with this anymore." He strode out of the room, slamming the door behind him, got into his 1969 refurbished MG — a birthday gift from Lydia that year — and sped off into the night.

#

Lydia's daughter, Mel, called about two weeks after Caldwell had driven away. "Mummy, are you okay? You sound like you've been crying."

"Oh. I suppose I'm not exactly at my best." Lydia tried laughingly in her Southern manner to keep the conversation light and pleasant, as she always did. But then her daughter asked about Caldwell and Lydia couldn't hold back the tears.

Mel had trouble hiding her jubilation. Caldwell might finally be out of the picture. "Mummy, you know what we must do? We must take a week or two at Rosefields. It's perfect this time of year. You know it will cheer you up."

Rosefields, Lydia's country estate three hours outside the city, was an old farm that had been in Jordan's family for years and was completely rundown by the time he took it over. Jordan poured almost a million dollars into its restoration and expansion. He bought up adjoining farms too. The grand house became even grander, with several gardens, a patio that looked out over the hills and a pergola that framed the view. The old barn and sheds were rebuilt. A new horse stable and indoor riding arena were erected. The outbuildings were all state of the art inside but the exteriors matched the colonial style of the house. The same approach was taken for the new five-car garage with an apartment over it. There was a swimming pool in addition to the Great Pond. There were tennis courts, paddocks and numerous riding trails with jumps dotted here and there throughout the six hundred acres of fields and woods. Along with the horses, there was a flock of sheep and some barnyard chickens. At the far side of the property was the farm manager's house, another fine if more modest example of colonial architecture. It too had been restored and the interior renovated to achieve modern functionality and comfort.

Lydia drove the three hours to Rosefields while Mel periodically quoted Steinem, Faludi and any other feminists she felt were relevant to her mother's plight. Lydia had to remind her daughter that unlike her, she had not grown up privileged, had not gone to the best boarding schools and had certainly not been subjected to the dark expectations that women in prominent families often endured. No,

Lydia had been raised simply, in a suburb of San Antonio. She was undoubtedly blessed and cursed with genes that had made her tall, attractive, photogenic and something of a prize in her youthful days. "I've always viewed that as providing opportunity, not some means of subjugation. Men are very susceptible you know. Am I supposed to ignore God-given appeal?" Why of course she got more attention than she wanted sometimes. And some of it not very pleasant either. But she hadn't suffered. Not much. And she chose well. "Look where it got me! And *who* it got me!" Lydia reached out for Mel's hand and smiled brightly as they cruised slowly up the quarter-mile driveway to the estate.

The paddocks on either side glowed with the green grass made even more brilliant by the darkened post-and-rail fences still wet from the rain a half hour before. Down the hill by the old weir where the Great Pond spilled into the creek, the honeysuckle were blushing as they nodded over the tumbling water. The hydrangeas opposite the five-car garage lolled in the gentle breeze, like a wave of cool magenta. As they got closer to the house, wild rose vines, white and pink with flowers, climbed the fences that overlooked the borders of mauve petunias. Two of the four mares Lydia owned had new foals and they were all out in the paddock closest to the house, prancing, kicking and chasing each other under the watchful eyes of their mothers. And watching over them, while weeding the oval garden, with its prize roses in front of the house, was Carl, the farm manager.

"Welcome to paradise," Carl shouted as Lydia and Mel emerged from the Mercedes SUV.

"See?" Lydia said.

#

Country life was so good for the health. The mind could rest and the body flourish. Nothing like a hack through the woods on horseback and taking a few fences before breakfast. And nothing like planning some landscaping. On Carl's advice, Lydia had decided to expand the pond. The land next to it was so poorly drained it wasn't good for anything but it wasn't wet enough to constitute a marsh either — Mel held the view that all marshes must be preserved. Lydia and her daughter helped Carl stake out the area. It would all be finished by the next time they came back. Then they could look out upon the Even Greater Pond of Rosefields.

The two weeks weren't all bliss for Lydia though. Caldwell was often on her mind and knowing her daughter's view of him she couldn't talk about how much she missed him. They'd had no contact since he'd stormed out. She'd left two messages passing on appointment reminders: his yearly physical and another from his dentist. Caldwell had left a message saying he was going out West for three or four weeks. West would mean California or Utah. Maybe Washington. Caldwell had relatives in each place, though he was no longer on speaking terms with his son who was holed up in the mountains east of Seattle. Oddly, Caldwell also had relatives living not far from Rosefields. In fact as a teenager he'd spent three years with a cousin's family about twenty miles east, right outside Hullbrooke, after his father disappeared. But in all the times he and Lydia had been at the estate, he'd never once tried to contact the Hullbrooke relatives.

Lydia didn't know whether to wait and see if Caldwell would come back to her or to make some offer that might entice him. She decided it wouldn't hurt to run Caldwell's business idea by Cyrus. Her lawyer would have an opinion anyway. Lydia had no opinion at all about it, but Mel, ever mistrustful of Caldwell, saw it as utterly preposterous. It was nothing other than an investment scam to bilk her mother of her money and an invitation to get in bed with organized crime.

Lydia waited a few days. She served on a number of volunteer committees, and there were two luncheons and a charity auction coming up. She didn't want to have her daughter's admonishments and dark thoughts still running through her head when she talked to Cyrus. And maybe she wanted to have a chat with Corinna too. Corinna had become her newfound confidante; she worked at Lydia's favorite spa. It was amazing how comforting it was to talk with that woman. Lydia knew she would feel much better about Caldwell after a facial. Corinna understood people's hearts.

So as Corinna applied the final deep-penetrating herbal moisturizer, Lydia noticed she was feeling much happier. Corinna had pointed out that Lydia had lived most of her adult life without Caldwell and had not only survived but prospered. She would do so again. Whether he returned or stayed away need not affect her happiness. This was something of a revelation for Lydia. Corinna believed that for a woman of Lydia's qualities and experience, a man should be no more than icing on the cake. And if he failed to meet the criteria of good icing, never mind caused her suffering, well she should move along and find herself a better batch of raspberry truffle buttercream, which was Lydia's favorite.

When Lydia finally called the lawyer's office, Cyrus was on holiday — Spain or Portugal, they thought — where he was incommunicado. "Is it an emergency?" the receptionist had asked, which meant, was it something a junior partner might be able to deal with? It occurred to Lydia that perhaps a more objective opinion might be helpful in this instance. "Yes," she'd replied.

#

Three weeks later Lydia's little team of lawyers and accountants held a meeting. Before them was the quintessential opportunity to implement dearly departed Jordan's Plan D — What to Do If Lydia Is Smitten With a High Risk Investment. Luther Cohen, the junior partner from Cyrus's firm, was pumped. And he'd been doing his homework. Since meeting with Lydia he'd spent three weekends and almost every evening digging through journal articles, corporate legal history, financial reports and everything he could get his hands on about cannabis. Yes indeed! Good old weed! He'd never imagined a plant could have such a long and varied involvement with the human race. Or such a bizarre and calamitous legal history. It had been used for everything from building materials and clothing to medicine and sacred rituals. Given its utility it was astonishing that it had also become illegal and so vilified.

"Look at the history of liquor after prohibition." Luther's finely drawn jaw fairly jutted with eager confidence. He was a clean-shaven fellow, though long hours with his head in case files often found him sporting a dark shadow, and his unruly dark locks had to be kept in line by frequent visits to the barber. He cleared his throat. "We need to be very medically minded to get our foot in the door. Make the application cut. But personally I think we have to look to the future. And it looks like it's bound for pleasure, not prescriptions." He grinned at everyone as he moved to the next slide and even his glasses seemed to glint with excitement. Not being blessed with any great height, Luther cultivated a trim, dapper and energetic image that best staged an intellect he regarded as more shrewd than brilliant. His brains got him where he wanted to go and that was the main thing.

The younger generation at the meeting all agreed, recreational marijuana use was just a matter of time. The feds, the FDA and the DEA were gradually losing their teeth on this as states opted for legalization. Once it went recreational, the medicinal side of the industry would probably operate like herbal supplements. Or maybe it would disappear altogether. Drug companies would probably never be able to generate sufficient returns on research investment. Regardless, the money would be in recreational.

Malcolm, Lydia's accountant and financial whiz, was initially appalled they had even contemplated this meeting. His son had blown so much white stuff up his nose, Malcolm had to take custody of his grandchildren. But the previous Friday night over drinks and oysters, Cyrus had reminded Malcolm about a small matter only the two of them knew anything about: the significant sums Jordan had left in accounts elsewhere, offshore and deemed very . . . un-American. The funds had been languishing for such a Plan D. So Malcolm reached for another oyster, sucked the slimy thing down in one gulp and blinked a few times. "Yes," he said still blinking. "Quite right." The rumors and hype were worth consideration. The future of marijuana was looming. It really could be the Next Big Thing.

And so the meeting had gone on for a full morning, Luther not once waning in his enthusiasm, while the others weighed risks and considered the devilish details. By the end of it they agreed Lydia's estate should throw its hat into the application process. The state would award licenses to only fifteen companies and they would be allowed two dispensaries each. Luther had heard rumors that several hundred applications were expected. They'd need to get up to speed quickly and of course milk any contacts that could be advantageous. And Lydia should be called immediately. They wanted to see Caldwell's business plan.

#

Lydia phoned Caldwell to tell him the news. She told herself she must remain measured and calm. Corinna had advised she not roll over like an abandoned spaniel. She would be pleasant but cool as a cucumber for at least another month or so. It would give him lots of time to notice what he was missing. After talking to Corinna, Lydia realized she was still smarting from Caldwell's comment about her brain cells. He'd gone back to his studio apartment over the laundromat in Queens. Maybe a little more time there in the summer heat might lead him to revise his opinion.

But Caldwell had been busy. Crazy busy, like a dog in a slaughterhouse boneyard. He hadn't stopped since he'd left Lydia's. He'd been calling everyone with whom he was still on speaking terms. He'd been reaching out to contacts of old contacts, especially if the original contacts were dead and buried. He was hoping to drum up any kind of investment money. This new project took hold of him in a way he'd never felt before. He was obsessed with growing a plant that defied all simple definition. It was legal. It was not legal. It was a wonder drug. It was a curse. It was risky. But whatever way he looked at it, the payoff would be enormous. He was hooked. He'd even used the tiny bit of money that remained in his San Francisco bank account to fly around the country. As it turned out, he did have contacts. His year hiding in the old beat-up Airstream along the Green River had not been a wasted one. It led him straight to Colorado, the holy land of weed's second coming. Turned out Caldwell wasn't the only genius hiding between the towering mesas watching the river flow and the cryptobiotic crusts form.

Lydia instructed him that the advisers would need to see a business plan. It dawned on Caldwell during this conversation that the money being considered far exceeded the five-figure scraps he was hoping for from Lydia's income. This would mean hundreds of thousands, possibly millions of dollars. It was extraordinary. It could mean only one thing: Lydia's advisers, stalwart professionals all, clearly had faith in him. He could finally build a great company, maybe even an international one. He would revolutionize the marijuana industry. Destiny was singling him out. The realization brought him to tears. "Lydia," he said choking up, "you don't know how much this means to me."

Normally Lydia would have been brought to tears herself by Caldwell's response. His uninhibited expressiveness was one of the things that impressed her most about him. A man who could cry. It touched her deeply. But this time she was not so moved. Perhaps it was the memory of Mel's sulky, mean-spirited observation about this. "Sure, and he has all the impulse control of a six-year-old to go with it." Or perhaps it was the unhurried and very practical tone Cyrus had taken when he spoke to her about the matter. Anyway, Lydia did not cry this time. "Well, that's a happy outcome, I guess. The meeting is next Tuesday at nine thirty." She went on to give him the address and parking information. "See you then." She put down the phone and smiled to herself. Corinna was right. Being cool with Caldwell was actually very easy.

Chapter 3

"I can't even."

"That's just not possible!"

"Seriously. Hullbrooke?"

It was a warm and clammy evening. Three young men sat slumped in a swing seat on the veranda. They were friends from early childhood and had many things in common. They all lived in the old residential section of Lyston and spent long hours gaming in each other's basements. They hated school. They'd always hated school. They'd all been kept back at least once at various grades by concerned parents, psychologists or teachers who'd fussed about their emotional development, the stress of remarriage families and a litany of cognitive challenges including myopia, possible dyscalculia, probable language-processing disorder, delayed executive functioning and the old standby, attention deficit disorder. As the young men saw it, they'd soon be ditching the Ritalin and coming to the end of their high-school careers. They had better things to do and better drugs to use. In fact in this last regard they had long been devotees of the humblest of them.

From time to time their faces were softly lit by the glow from their cell phones.

"I'm tellin' ya, Hullbrooke's got a lit skate park! It's awesome AF."

"Awesome as fuck? Hullbrooke's not even on the map!"

"Map's basic. Find a local one."

"It's like two hundred people maybe!"

"More. They got three pizza places."

"So. Nothin' else there."

"Yeah. See. It's got a hardware store. Gas stations."

"Tavern."

"So?"

"Tellin' ya, bro. This park is lit. Ginormi. Like a football field!"

"Ginormi? What are you?"

"We should go."

"We need a car."

"Yeah, we need a car."

"I got a car."

"Dude!"

"Dad's car."

"How'd you finesse that?"

"Applied to college."

"Thought you weren't going."

"Well maybe I'm not. You going?"

"Prob'ly."

"Takin' what?"

"Business."

"Business?"

"That sucks."

"So. What are you takin'?"

"Agriculture."

"You mean cows an' shit?"

"No. Horticulture. Plants."

"Seriously?"

"Yeah. Program's only two years."

"That's sad."

"I can take the accelerated one. Do it in a year and a half.

"That's sadder."

"Mom says I could work in medical weed."

"What!"

"Yeah. When I'm finished I can go work for one of those medical weed producers. Like in New York or Maine. They got 'em everywhere but here. Or I could just move to California, maybe Oregon. Go see my dad."

"Why didn't you tell us?"

"That's fucking awesome!"

"I'm gonna do that!"

"Me too!"

Chapter 4

It was two o'clock in the afternoon and Petra Soames was sitting in a penthouse bar with a bird's-eye view of the harbor. After she moved to dreary little Hullbrooke for her mom, she often came into the city. Normally she wouldn't stay this long (she'd finished the shopping and errands an hour ago) but it would be two hours before the lecture. "Plants and the Mammalian Brain" by Reginald Blycroft — the Herbert T. Renfell Professor of Botany, Thistle-on-Tyne University — sounded just too overblown to resist.

Petra studied the olive in her martini. It had three dimples. Maybe that meant she could order two more martinis, three altogether, without adverse effects. Regardless of all the AA meetings prescribed by that odious weasel of a doctor back in Idaho, she believed a quiet, civilized drunk still had the potential to contribute to society. Take Winston Churchill, W. C. Fields, Dorothy Parker, Vincent van Gough, Alexander the Great for Chrissake! Unlike Alexander though and the rest of the ethylated crew, she had no ambition. Perhaps that was the overarching problem.

Petra was a plant scientist. Or rather she had trained as one. An evolutionary plant physiologist to be exact but then after her PhD, she'd strayed into molecular biology and genetics. "Not another gel jock!" her old supervisor had moaned in his Glaswegian brogue about her choices. "Geneticists are the universal twits! They never see the forest for the trees. In fact they can't even see a bloody tree half the time." Even then Petra had no great drive for accomplishment. She settled for lending a hand in Gerald the Gel Jock's lab. And then she married him. That she'd been effortlessly eclipsed for over a decade by the acclaimed geneticist only rarely crossed her mind.

"Would you care for another?" the waiter said smiling down at her.

Petra was momentarily startled, and with a well-honed nervous reflex she brushed her dark bangs to one side with her left hand. "Oh. Yes, thanks. And I'd better take a look at a menu too."

The waiter gave a nod and went off.

Petra stared down at the olive again. Why in God's name did it remind her of her ex? Gerald wasn't particularly dimpled. Petra thought back fondly to the day her marriage began to unravel. Thomas was a PhD student. He'd come over one night to drop off the first draft of an article. Gerald was at some meeting as usual, and seeing Thomas looking exhausted, she'd offered him a glass of wine. Thomas was from France, "from well-cultured stock too," he'd deadpanned one day while preparing tissue cultures. They told each other jokes and shared a fondness for old and off-beat movies. That Thomas was tall and lanky was especially pleasing to her since Gerald was compact and stocky. Whereas Gerald radiated power and high energy, Thomas came across with wide-eyed sincerity and even a little clownishness. It was Thomas who pointed out how upsetting it was to see the way Gerald made demands and demeaned her all in the same breath, that it was Petra, not Gerald, who often had the best ideas about what to try next when grad students ran into some dead end with their research. And whereas Gerald seemed eternally oblivious to her appearance Thomas told her with a sly smile she was dangerously luscious and looked just like the "famous vixen flapper in *Pandora's Box*." One thing led to another and Petra never regretted a thing.

When the waiter returned with the menu, Petra's appetite was drawn oddly to the vegetarian selections. She wondered if there was some plot afoot to make the plant and fungus dishes more appealing than the ho-hum peppercorn steak and the sole meunière. Petra settled on fresh shiitake mushrooms sautéed in garlic with a lemon Chablis sauce over zucchini noodles with seared yellow peppers, snow peas and roasted cashews.

At one point not that long ago, Petra thought she had the perfect life: a well-paying job in a private lab, a young lover — not Thomas of course, someone a little closer to her forty-odd years and shy of commitment. Just like she was. And she'd been involved with a local grassroots environmental action group and specifically with a phytoremediation project. But then that all unraveled too. The lab was acquired by a bigger one, the lover decided he wanted a wife and kids after all, and overnight the state went all right wing and the green funding dried up.

When Petra's dinner arrived, aromatic and eye-catching, it lifted her spirits greatly and took her mind off her less-than-stellar past. She read the book she'd brought along to keep her company and give her some insight into the upcoming lecture. It was about opioid receptors. Addictions of any type were dear to Petra's heart. She ordered a third martini.

In her respectably lubricated state, Petra found the talk moderately interesting and mildly disappointing. She didn't quite agree with the conclusions of Dr. Blycroft, a pretentious old windbag as it turned out with an ersatz stutter and a hee-haw laugh. He predictably suggested the rewards to the mammalian and particularly human brain were all just a matter of mistaken intentions. The buzz was meant for the bugs, the naughty herbivores. The compounds were just roaming toxins. Sure. And humans just happened to stumble under the influence with our fresh-faced naiveté, newer complement of superfluous genetic material, vestigial receptors and plain dumb luck. Talk about a cop-out!

To Petra's thinking the human species was destined to commune with plants for better or worse. And mostly, humans would do the plant's bidding. Any way you looked at it, dependency was a given. Just consider the allotment of biomass alone. Plants owned the planet, and most living organisms benefited from them one way or another if you really wanted to take a good hard-nosed evolutionary perspective. Just consider the number of poppies cultivated to supply the opium trade and how much land that involved, with humans scurrying about ensuring the plants' well-being, protecting them, even taking out the competition! Humans murdered each other just for the privilege of association. Now from the plant's point of view, that's evolutionary success!

Petra had nothing but admiration for this cleverness. And she was a more-than-willing servant. The next morning she decided to plant trees. And shrubs. She was feeling energetic. The new treatment she was on was very encouraging. Recent approaches to handling her booze problems didn't involve total abstinence, shaming and punitive ideology, just a little pill now and again. Petra viewed this as a giant step forward. She surmised she didn't have much to be ashamed of anyway other than the effects on her own health, and she was quite healthy. Ready for change.

Petra found her mother's yard appalling. With its single oak tree in one corner of an unremitting lawn, it was a study in tedium and outdated conceit. All the neighbors' backyards were grass too. There was no doubt about it: Lawns sprang from unconscious systemic social insanity. First and foremost they were an affectation of status that peaked with the likes of Versailles. Back then only royalty and the aristocracy could afford a great lawn. It took servants with scythes or women on their knees with clippers and scissors to keep things groomed. Okay, maybe there were a few sheep involved too. But in Petra's view every fool who spent hours cultivating the perfect fescue, murdering dandelions or spraying pesticides and portioning out fertilizers all for the sake of perfect turf was still just trying to keep up with Louis XIV.

Above all Petra hated mowing lawns. Mowers were noisy and smelly. They belched out more noxious exhaust gases than any sane person could imagine: acetylene, methane, ethylene, toluene, benzene, m- and p-xylene, isopentane, propylene, iso-octane, n-butane, 1,2,4-trimethylbenzene, isobutylene, ethylbenzene, o-xylene, 2-methylpentane, ethane, formaldehyde, 3-methylhexane, 2,3-dimethylpentane, 2-methylhexane, 3-methylpentane, 1,3-butadiene and at least a dozen more nasty volatile or persistent petrochemicals. And that didn't cover even half the organic emissions. Just the big ones. Add whopping blasts of nitrogen oxides, carbon monoxide and particulate matter, and Petra wondered how anyone could survive a summer. The fact that small spark-ignition engines were only moderately regulated and not at all until the 1990s turned weekends in Hullbrooke into Petra's private Beijing. Weed whackers were just as bad and the sound of them on an otherwise peaceful Sunday afternoon just about drove her nuts.

Her mother suggested she get an electric mower. "They're quiet," Doreen said. "Or how about one of those ones you just push by hand and the blades all whirl around. Like we had fifty years ago. They still make those?"

"Mother, I have no intention of spending three hours mowing a damn lawn," Petra replied. "I'd rather have gravel."

"Well you can do what you like. It's your house too now."

Doreen's stroke had left her partially paralyzed, not enough to send her into a nursing home but enough to make life difficult. At loose ends herself, Petra figured taking care of her mom was a good thing to do. The joint ownership of the house was a very generous gift, and Petra was certainly appreciative, but she still had trouble thinking of the property as anything other than her mother's. Petra would never have chosen the house or Hullbrooke. But she might as well live anywhere. Freelance work for a textbook publisher was hardly location specific. She might try her hand at consulting one day. In the meantime, diversifying the vegetation in the backyard would do.

She mentioned she was going to rip up chunks of lawn and put in beds. "Lots of annuals for next year. Brighten the place up." And she wanted hedges. Rapidly growing ones. Big bushy lilacs, privet and junipers, even swamp cedar, anything so she wouldn't have to look at the neighbors' dismal backyards. Actually if she'd had her druthers, Petra would have just transplanted some local vegetation and let whole the place go wild. But Hullbrooke municipal laws prevented such progressive remodeling.

Doreen thought Petra's plans were all very ambitious. "Too much work to keep up, let alone put in," she'd grumbled, and she reminded Petra that lawns, even if you despised them for some peculiar reason, were infinitely easier and you could still hire a local kid to mow them. Petra was undeterred.

At seven o'clock the next morning, she started up her mom's van. Her mother hadn't been able to drive since the stroke so they'd posted a For Sale sign in the windshield. The van faced out to the street but so far there hadn't been any interest. Nobody around here wanted an old van. They all drove trucks, Petra had observed. Or SUVs, she noted with particular disgust. She pulled the sign out of the window and let the motor run for a bit. She'd have to get gas. It was a forty-five-minute drive to Caldor's Nursery.

After filling up the van at Gerry's Gas Bar and Hullbrooke Rent-All, Petra decided to take the back roads to get a better sense of the area. She'd been in Hullbrooke for several months now but had never explored much. The surrounding area had hills, escarpments and lots of craggy outcroppings. There were woods everywhere and a few farms dotted around too. Some didn't look like they were doing all that well. Often there were just rundown houses or cabins tucked among the trees. A few places were clearly upscale; a couple of them even looked grand and palatial. It was quite a mix. She liked it best though when there were several miles of uninterrupted countryside. She reached Caldor's fifteen minutes after they opened.

The nursery altered Petra's mood. Several greenhouses were all connected and as she strolled slowly through them, basking in the filtered sunlight and the range of colors and jumble of scents, she fairly floated. Everywhere she looked pleased her. Vines, creepers, shrubs, ornamental grasses, ground cover, heritage plants and hybrids lined the rows and rows of tables. At the far end was a tall greenhouse that opened out onto a yard. Young trees of all kinds were clustered in loose rows. They sat in large biodegradable hairy pots or great round burlap sacks. There were smaller ones too of course. Petra saw what looked like a recently uprooted bunch of birch seedlings just sitting in a pail of slurry. She took it all in with a deep breath and began humming.

Practically everything was on sale, so Petra rationalized buying up as much as she could. She'd have liked to buy the whole place but she settled for filling the van and giving her credit card a workout. Her well-laid plan to take her time and design the garden gave way to a kind of gorging on instant beauty.

Petra drove home happy. All that life riding behind her in the van was invigorating. A Cleveland pear, a crab apple and a pagoda dogwood waved at her in the rearview mirror while sheltering the shorter assortment of willow hybrids, cedars and lilacs that would grow up like weeds in no time to make her neighbors disappear. There were three rose of Sharon trees too, and she rationalized she wouldn't have known what the blossoms really looked like for a couple of months if she'd bought them in early spring like most sensible gardeners. There were grasses and ferns as well. The soil under the oak in the backyard was a bit boggy at times and the ferns would get it into shipshape.

But Petra's prize was the dioecious ginkgo tree. She had purchased a male, pretty fan leaves and all. Or so she was assured repeatedly — "You don't want the females because their fruit is sticky, messy and smells like vomit." Petra found the nursery staff amusing. She wouldn't have minded whether it was male or female. It would likely take another twenty or thirty years to mature, by which point it would be someone else's problem. But she liked the notion of purchasing a boy plant. Especially one from such a sturdy species. Ginkgos were known to have survived Hiroshima! And they were the only species left in their group, the vast majority of Ginkgoales having not made it past the Pliocene. But the most notable thing about it was the genome. It had three times more DNA than humans, and a battery of chemical defense mechanisms of which humans had learned to avail themselves. Ginkgo was very old medicine.

Petra began to whistle. She'd rent an overpriced rototiller that very afternoon from Gerry's. And she'd pick up a new spade. The one at her mother's had a cracked handle and a chipped blade. She'd be thoroughly occupied and thoroughly content for a week or more. And she'd hire the glum, feckless fifteen-year-old next door to help. The boy moped eternally when he wasn't high, but Petra had noticed he was at least somewhat interested in money.

PART TWO

Dormancy

Oh Sleepers, let us bring you the dreaming of the gods, its play of parallels, the paradise of perpendiculars. Do not be shy in slumber. Take our hand. We wait in the trillions, patient and fused where time has no thrust, no sword of direction. We wait. We wait with the needle's eye, the emptiest of small spaces, in the singularities of thin air and in the dimming of the sweet dark earth. Let us bring you the seeing of the bee, the touch of the wind, the scatter of sound. Let us trust you in the night with the wonder of many, the bliss of all and sundry.

from Cannto I, *Cannabidadas*

Chapter 5

Alice sat in a small meeting room in City Hall. The room was stuffy and there were portraits plastered along the wall in a neat line — mostly middle-aged white men, stern and unwavering, staring down at her from the photos. She stared back. A thin film of sweat began to appear on her dark-brown forehead and it briefly occurred to her that not only did hot flashes increase the discomfort on muggy days and not only did her legs ache and not only should she have given wearing her heavy wool blazer a pass today but the photos of most of these potbellied men with their copious jowls were positively revolting.

Rachel, a young city planner, walked in. "Mrs. Morgan, good to see you again."

"Really? I'm not so sure," said Alice.

"What can we do for you today, Mrs. Morgan?" she said smiling.

"I thought you people were fixing the old paint-factory site."

"We are. We're doing what we can, given the subsurface infrastructure and the level of contamination."

"And what exactly does that mean? You're doing nothing, right?"

"Well. . ."

"Am I right?"

When Alice moved back into her old neighborhood it had already improved. It was more diverse. The derelict houses and buildings had attracted creative people of all kinds, it was a favorite settling spot now for new immigrants and the gang presence was subdued. She bought a house three blocks from where she'd grown up and opened a pharmacy only twenty minutes away, if she walked quickly.

The pharmacy was across the park that abutted an abandoned paint factory. Children were warned never to play there. People kept their dogs away. Until a year ago, two crumbling walls remained, and for a lark, some artist had painted a giant octopus clasping several smartphones on one of them. There had been a bare oily-looking patch too, where the cracked and mostly eroded factory floor still existed. Dead trees languished on the site and copious weeds, cadmium, chromium, lead and a whole host of unhealthy petroleum-based toxins lurked in the surrounding soil.

The site was both delinquent and orphaned in the eyes of the EPA but prioritizing for remediation was clearly a dark art among federal officials. So Alice had been pressuring the city instead. Couldn't they clean it up and send the bill to the EPA? Or sue the EPA? Everybody else did.

"Mrs. Morgan, I saw the project outline you submitted and it is truly a lovely idea, but there are simply not the funds right now to put something like that in place."

Alice began to tap her meticulously manicured fingers on the table. "The funds? Or the will?"

Rachel didn't want to get into discussions about who was stalling the rehabilitation of this neighborhood and why. "Funds," Rachel said.

"That's ridiculous. The city just spent over six million dollars . . ." And Alice went on to detail the expenditures used for the renovation of the recreation center and pool on the other side of town, miles away from where she lived. She also reminded the young planner of the monies blown on several other projects over the last half dozen years. Finally she got back to the subject of the community garden. "I priced out the topsoil. I even talked to a plumber. City water lines are already there even if they need repairing. I priced that out too. The funding required is quite modest. So frankly, Miss Clairmont, I don't know what you're talking about."

"Unfortunately, Mrs. Morgan, we don't have a cent left in the budget to build the kind of community garden you're talking about." This was an exaggeration but necessary. "And because of the remaining contaminants you'll need containers with liners. You'll have to ensure the paths between the raised beds are properly finished so you can control runoff and ensure safety. You'll have to bring in all new soil. We just don't have the money for that right now."

Habitually beleaguered by the city's stark realities, Rachel and the other planners really liked Alice. They would spontaneously smile when her name came up, even though she had only ever been cantankerous with them. The thing was, she wasn't some big developer with dollar signs in her eyes hoping to buy up buildings cheap and hang on to them until the locals were driven out so they could throw up luxury condos or apartments. No, Alice was pushy for the right things. The things they thought they'd gone to school for.

"You know what I say to all these excuses, Miss Clairmont?" Alice tilted her head back slightly and peered at Rachel. "Bull . . . shit!"

Rachel suppressed a smile. "Mrs. Morgan, I find it as disappointing as you do. You know we approved your plan, in theory — that is with the adjustment I just mentioned, the containers and of course the pathways finished in some manner."

"So I bring you a new proposal and *then* you'll fund it?"

"Uh, no. But we won't get in the way of you personally building it."

"Me?"

"Well you and the people in your community willing to help."

"Miss Clairmont, it's a community garden. Of course we're going to build it. But we still need funds to get it started." She stared at Rachel for a second and then began fishing around in her large leather handbag. "I have the full-color EPA flyer. Tells me how the various levels of government are going to chip in, how everybody's so keen urban landscapes can be revitalized. Oh, and how the return on the dollar for investment in this kind of brownfield remediation is more than significant, benefiting all administrative branches and tiers." Alice looked up briefly with an exaggerated smile that had all the sincerity and goodwill of a rattlesnake. "It draws a wonderful picture of universal participation. Have you seen these publications? They're real nice. Oh, here it is."

"Mrs. Morgan, have you thought of crowdfunding?"

Brochure in hand, Alice frowned at Rachel. "Is that what bankrupt governments resort to these days? Crowdfunding?"

Rachel suggested it might bring in money from just about anywhere. And the planning department would help. They'd make sure all the right permits were issued, all the right materials were used, everything was inspected properly. And Rachel said she'd even show up after work with a trowel if that would help things along.

That evening Alice called her son, Zack. She'd only called him once since he'd started his job with the big corporate law firm in the state capital. He'd been at the top of his graduating class and they'd nabbed him right away. He was, bless him, also technically savvy, so Alice wanted to ask him if he'd have time to help her set up the crowdfunding website. She wanted it to be attractive. Convincing too, and Zack excelled at being convincing.

"Mom! What a cool coincidence. I was just going to call you."

"Good news I hope." Alice adored Zack's current girlfriend and in the back of her mind hoped they'd decide to settle down or at least not split up. He never seemed to have much luck with girlfriends sticking around.

"Guess it depends on how you look at it," Zack said. "It's . . . interesting!"

Alice knew from the tone it wouldn't be anything to do with the girlfriend.

"Mom, I have a favor to ask."

"Oh?" He'd never asked for a "favor" before. He'd just said, "Mom, is it okay if I bring home three weeks of laundry?" Or "Would you be your celestial self and cosign this car loan for me?"

"So," Zack continued, "you know the state is now allowing dispensaries for medical marijuana . . ."

"I heard about that. My staff make a lot of jokes about it."

"No doubt!" Her son paused, trying to figure the best approach. It would be a tough sell but it could aid his progress at the firm. And chances were nothing would go further than the first step anyway. "So the firm is putting in an application for a registration. You know, to operate medical marijuana dispensaries and a cultivation and manufacturing facility. It's all tied in with this wealthy woman's estate the senior partner manages."

"That is interesting, I guess."

"Anyway, there will likely be hundreds of applications so our chances for getting the registration are very slim. But here's where you come in. They want a pharmacist to help them with the application process."

"Oh, honey. I'm pretty sure I can't do that. I haven't read any of the literature on marijuana. I know there've been some studies but not enough to get it past the FDA. It's not anything I've ever really looked at."

"Well . . ."

"Really I don't know about it. Mostly it's a nuisance and a problem around here. You know that. I don't think I can help you."

"No, that's okay. You don't have to know anything about marijuana. It's just, the firm figures the more they use a pharmaceutical model for the dispensaries, the better the chance of success. Some of the other states already require pharmacists. I told them I had just the right mom for that!"

"So you've already offered up your mother?"

"No, Mom. I just said I'd talk to you."

"I see. And this application entails what exactly?"

"Well . . . you need to read the regulations and what the team comes up with. Then you can change, you know, where they don't quite have it described correctly for how you'd run a pharmacy."

"I guess that sounds easy enough."

Zack was very appreciative. And when she told him about the crowdfunding, he offered to get the website up and running for her that very next weekend.

#

Saturday morning, Alice finally got around to reviewing the documents her son had sent. She started with the state code, the new regulations on cannabis dispensaries. Lord, they were tedious and the state was profoundly schizophrenic. On one hand, authorities were bent on ensuring the availability of safe product, but on the other, they still considered the whole activity criminal. The restrictions around cannabis production and sale were more elaborate than those for opiates sold in regular pharmacies. *Well isn't that something*, Alice thought. The state never failed to surprise. Alice soon needed a break to keep her eyes open. "Wonder how much all this is going to cost?" she said to the coffee pot.

Alice continued her reading and eventually got around to the application itself. She was into it a mere five minutes when she let out a gasp. She felt her blood pressure rising. She blinked to keep her eyes from exploding out of her head. She reached for her phone and practically put her back out in the frenzied effort. She pounded on her son's number so hard she broke one of her fingernails and produced a hairline crack in the smartphone's screen.

"Hi, Mom," her son answered innocently enough.

"You want *me* to sell weed? Tell me! What did I do wrong?"

"Mom. Please, be calm!"

"Calm? You want me to sign this! Send my name to the state authorities letting them know I'm willing to deal marijuana. Speaking of which, what exactly have you been on lately?"

"You're overreacting!"

"Are you stupid?"

"Mom!"

"You don't think they'll notice what part of town I live in?"

"Luther thinks that's what's perfect about it. And you have exactly the right experience. You'd do it right. Everything by the regulations and . . . and you know what happens in the states where it's better accessed and regulated?"

"I certainly do not."

"The dealers leave town!"

"Well, I don't know where your head is. Doesn't matter where the dealers are. Neighborhood's still on the radar. And the people in it. Oh yeah, I forgot . . . you didn't have to grow up in a neighborhood where 'spread 'em,' not hip-hop, was the dance everybody got good at. Yeah, 'cause you know, just comes natural to us folk!"

"Mom!"

"You know how many families around here been destroyed by drugs? By the war on drugs? And you know most were Black, right? Let me guess. You're the only brother in that law firm and you—"

"Mom! You're taking this all wrong."

"I'm taking it as I see it, Zack. I thought laws on selling your mother down the river got changed a few years back! Did I miss something?"

"Mom! We're on the same side."

"No, we most definitely are not!"

"Just listen for a minute. This is the thing you need to stand for. We need change! You think for a minute the laws on marijuana weren't tied to racism to begin with? Goes right back to the nineteen thirties. Check out the history, Mom."

"I'm sure it's fascinating."

"It's a nightmare! You know the department that's now the DEA was created by the same guy who headed up the Department of

Prohibition? He was losing his old job so he made up a new one. Anslinger. You ever heard of him?"

"No."

"Yeah, well he started the lies."

"I don't care what he started. I've seen the people who get finished."

"Mom, it's important! This guy Anslinger, this fraud, he fabricated all sorts of crap about weed. He wrote it was harmless, before his job was at stake. Later in the thirties he starts a war on it so he can head up the offensive. It's a war on hemp too. Cotton and timber industries love it. Nylon is just coming onto the market so the oil industries back him too. William Randolph Hearst, timber giant and newspaper mogul, loves him in particular. Hearst revved up the propaganda machine and Anslinger, he just got creative with the facts to suit the times. About violence and weed, sex and weed, insanity and weed, most of it targeting race. So he'd hang on to his job. Keep rubbing shoulders with the ruling class. Reify the racial caste system and consolidate white prejudice." Her son was just hitting his stride.

"Spare me, Zack."

"Context is crucial, Mom. You taught me that."

Alice held the phone a few inches from her ear. It barely diminished the intensity coming through.

"He claimed it made people violent. You know they used marijuana on the Caribbean plantations to keep slaves docile! All these lies he conveniently dished up. He played on white fear so he could put more Black people in jail. And even where the law wasn't overtly prejudiced that's who they targeted for enforcement. More free labor for the state. And then the drug war got revitalized under Nixon. Convenience again, Mom. They could target civil rights and the antiwar movements. All those years of politicians competing for who could be tougher on crime, and you know where that landed us. Eighty-some years of this bullshit! Now we have streamlined institutionalized slavery in the prison system. Black people use less weed than whites but are ten times more likely to be arrested for it. How much longer you want this kind of injustice to continue? Embrace the change, Mom." Her son cleared his throat, and then his voice took on a steely tone. "And you lied when you said you didn't know anything about weed. I heard what you did for the Palmers. Dad told me about it. So what have you got to say about that?"

Alice took a breath. The Palmers were their neighbors when the children were small. They had a sick little girl and the doctors finally gave up on her. Family almost went broke trying various drugs. Alice had helped them out whenever she could. One day she'd noticed an article in an old journal from the seventies that talked about treating seizures with marijuana and it took her back to when she was a very little girl. She'd watched several times as her grandmother prepared her Great Aunt Evelyn's "special secret medicine." Aunt Evelyn was bedridden, not very coherent, and lived more or less in a bedroom at the back of Alice's grandmother's house. Every so often, her grandmother's friend would drop off a package of dried plants and her grandmother would grind them up. She'd pour a little vodka or rum on the ground plants and let it sit for a couple of hours. She'd pour off all the alcohol and put it aside. Then she put the plant mash in a couple of cups of cooking oil and let it heat up. Not too hot and never so the plants sizzled. She'd keep it hot on a warming plate and let it sit overnight. Occasionally she'd give it a stir. The mixture was strained the next day and the oil from it was added to the saved alcohol. "Gotta shake it real good. Teaspoon with her juice in the mornin' helps the fits," her grandmother said. Alice realized years later the plants were marijuana.

So Alice had passed this information on to the Palmers. The little girl didn't live past the age of seven but at least her last four years weren't plagued with seizures every fifteen minutes. Her parents could have been hauled away for illegal possession of course, abusing the child and who knows what else. And maybe Alice would have lost her license or worse at the time if word ever got out she'd given them the idea and a recipe to boot.

"I don't know what you're talking about," Alice huffed. "And besides it's irrelevant."

"No it's not. You know this stuff works whatever else it may be, it's medicine. And you deal with medicine. Besides you handle way worse stuff."

Alice was starting to fume. She stared at her broken nail.

"Oxycodone, fentanyl, morphine, tramadol to name a few. Am I right? And what about all those drugs the FDA cleared, the ones that were just fine and made billions until the patents ran out and then they published all the adverse reactions, the complications, the death statistics. People don't die from marijuana overdoses. You know that."

Alice took the phone away from her ear and put it down on the kitchen counter without putting it on speaker mode. While her son's voice squeaked away, she sighed and poured herself another cup of coffee before picking the handset up again.

"And you know, Mom, this isn't a bad law firm I work for, despite what you might think about the demographics. I mentioned your project to Luther and he had a talk with the senior partners. Every year the firm donates to a worthy cause whether or not it's tax deductible. They've just picked your community garden as the worthy cause this year. What do you think of that? That's twenty thousand, Mom, right away into your crowdfund account."

Alice maintained her silence but then finally said, "You mean they donate if I sign the application."

"No. They're donating regardless. They've already allocated the funds. I saw the statements yesterday. And they'll pay you on top of that. A consultation fee for the time you spend on the application." Her son let this sink in. It was all true. He had however left out the small detail that Luther already thought she was on board with everything. Zack was supposed to set up a telephone conference with Alice and the team in the next couple of weeks.

"This is a deal with the devil. Brokered by my own son!"

"You know that's ridiculous. And you know what we're doing here is right."

"I know nothing of the kind. All this gobbledygook you're cultivating like a bad seed. Trying to sell me on it . . ."

"Look it up. Think about it."

"Fine." Alice spat the word and hung up.

Her son called her back the next day with more rehearsed indignation on the obvious link between oppression and the history of weed, implying that only her participation could help remedy centuries of disgrace.

But Alice was in no better mood for his soapbox sermon. She hung up on him again.

#

It took Alice almost a full week to come close to understanding what might be in her son's head to offer her up like sacrificial hamburger. All for the benefit of some rich white woman's marijuana operation. Just thinking about it made Alice's head feel like it was going through a meat grinder. Marijuana, if not the cause, was at least on the scene of practically every tragedy she personally witnessed. Families ripped asunder, good lives ruined. Hell, people didn't even have to use drugs, they just had to own the phone where the boyfriend made the call to the dealer. And what about her cousin Gerome? Wouldn't hurt a fly 'til they locked him away for possession. And no chance in hell to turn anything around when he got out. Checkin' the box didn't exactly pave the road to success. Couldn't even get a place to live. Then he did become a criminal.

Marijuana was a weed all right. A noxious one. A scourge species with dubious or at least complicated medicinal value. No pharmacist in their right mind would waste their time with it. Would they? Let alone sign their name to something that went straight to the state authorities. One minute her son was bemoaning the unbearable whiteness of the new commercial marijuana industry while the brothers and sisters filling up the jails still paid the price for it all, and the next he was endorsing it for apparently the same reasons. "It's time to shut down Slaves Incorporated!" he barked at her. "You know there's more Black men incarcerated now than there were slaves before the Civil War!"

Ha! Who was he all of a sudden politicized out of his privilege to lecture her? As if she didn't have a clue about the scope of the problem. She'd lived it. Grown up with it! She was still seeing and feeling the fallout. What was he doing? Sitting in his fancy new office distorting his brain with "progressive solutions." What the hell would he know? He never had to worry about crippling student loans. Had he gone completely crazy? Or had she raised a monster? He might as well be setting her business up for a drug raid. What next? Open a café with free wireless for the dealers?

She'd taken twenty years to alleviate the revulsion she felt for certain aspects of her neighborhood. She'd only moved back because she figured she had more skills now. Tools to make things better, make a difference, and her tool kit certainly did not include ensuring the neighbors got high or hauled away and thrown into the black hole of the justice system. If she wasn't thinking about it the right way as her son kept insisting, well maybe thinking wasn't what the problem required. Maybe turning her back and shutting the door was the best call. And as for economics, she was doing her part. She was one of only a very few African-American business owners in the district. She was already giving at the office! He had some nerve.

After hanging up on her son two more times, and on his third try hearing the remorse in his voice mixed with panic, she softened. A little. Eventually he owned up to his conniving. He'd told his bosses about her because he thought it would help him get ahead. And of course they'd been impressed. Charmed. Why wouldn't they? Alice was a community star. But all the righteous justifications and politics he'd come up with were an afterthought, though he did learn a few things about marijuana. The truth was, he didn't really care all that much about it one way or the other. Even if the arguments were valid, he was sorry. Really, really sorry. Everybody at the firm was hyped about the application. There were millions of dollars in the offing. He'd found it all exciting at first but then kind of disgusting. Greedy speculation had engulfed everyone. Luther, the junior partner, had told him if it all worked out he was looking forward to retiring before he was forty-five and he'd settle for nothing less than a sixty-foot yacht to go with his gabled mansion.

Alice frowned as she listened to her son. Zack sounded exhausted. But he told his mom he'd have the firm take her name off the application. And before he hung up, he told her again he was really, really sorry.

Alice felt sad for him. On a whim she decided to spend her Sunday at the university library making use of their online resources and checking out a few old medical and pharmaceutical journals.

That night she called Zack. "Not so fast," she said.

Chapter 6

Lydia's little team, and Luther in particular, were very busy. Between the grins and snickers about it all, completing the application was designated an outside activity, but as the deadline drew closer it turned into a 24/7 all-hands-on-deck work binge, with a freelance writer, a security consultant and an engineer in tow. And of course Caldwell was not to be left out of any detail. He came barreling into meetings and late-night sessions demanding that some item be changed because it was "obvious something like that could never fly!" What were they thinking?

The Department of Health was demanding business plans, building designs and security provisions. They wanted to see guaranteed access or outright ownership of suitably situated properties. And they wanted appropriate manufacturing and agriculture practices. Even waste management was not to be trivialized, and innovation in this regard could win extra points. And the state wanted to see a lot of money: a $30,000 nonrefundable application fee and the immediate remittance of a substantial six-figure administrative fee upon the application's success. All requirements designed to discourage the small-time players, the old black-market growers, the amateurs or anybody who might not take the state extremely seriously.

Lydia's team took the state very seriously. And also took her funds to purchase a building close to Hullbrooke, a characterless twenty-five-thousand-square-foot industrial structure built circa 1980 that had flourished in the early days of the tech boom but was then repurposed as a warehouse and trucking company depot. It was abandoned like everything else in recent years as companies merged and downsized and work got outsourced. Lydia already owned commercial buildings in the city, and a storefront just recently vacated in the upscale downtown area would be the perfect location for a dispensary. They also took out a lease on some mall space in Lyston for the same purpose.

Collecting the right people to form the medical cannabis company was crucial for the application, which was why Alice was so enthusiastically welcomed by the team. She was listed as the director of sales and dispensaries. Next they found a horticulture expert, a businessman who owned and operated greenhouses that supplied a chain of garden centers. Security would be a big issue too, so Cyrus suggested they retain the consultant who was already working on the application. So Greg Tiller, the retired police officer who'd even done a brief stint in the FBI in his younger days, was happy to oblige. Luther was listed as legal counsel and CEO. One of the associates in Malcolm's financial firm gleefully took on the position of CFO. And Lydia was the silent president. It was perfect. Lydia wasn't aware of the money set aside by Jordan in a moment of levity as he thumbed his nose at the IRS. And she was hardly one to keep track. If the project took flight, the prominent individuals in both firms stood to benefit handsomely. Jordan had been both generous and clever with incentives.

Caldwell was miffed. Not because he was overlooked as an executive and left off the organizational chart. Actually he was pleased about this. The fewer some people knew his whereabouts the better. No, Caldwell was miffed because he had not been consulted on either the building purchase or most of the people hired. In particular he felt he should have been asked to vet the sales director. The dispensary outlets needed careful planning to serve their market effectively and gain a competitive edge. And why did they insist on a cultivation expert who'd possibly never even grown a marijuana plant in his life let alone brought a crop to flower? That was utter stupidity. Sometimes, in spite of the encouraging salary they doled out to him, Caldwell suspected Lydia's little team was intent on stealing the project out from under him.

But Lydia's team had simply been observant. They were looking to invest the least amount of time and resources. They paid attention like good hunters and pragmatists.

"I've been traveling around this country for the last three months," Caldwell told them. "Been up to Canada too. The state outfits are all amateur. Putting out tons of substandard product! Why do you think black-market marijuana still thrives? The medical growers don't have a clue. They don't even know what good marijuana is."

That Caldwell should know what constituted "good" marijuana was well remarked by the team. And they'd also noted his lack of a solid business plan. Malcolm was particularly unimpressed. "His financial reasoning," the accountant observed dryly, "is absurd. No wonder the man hasn't ever had a pot to piss in."

A few of the claims on Caldwell's resumé didn't add up either. Caldwell's only real competence appeared to be hoodwinking of one form or another and leaving a trail of stranded investors. "Strictly small-time though," the financial investigator said. "He's more of a one-man band. Maybe a bit of a clown act too! You have to laugh or you'd cry about how gullible people can be."

The team had debated Caldwell's suitability, but Caldwell presented well: a tall, dashing figure in line with an aging matinee idol. And however much his pitches might resemble those of a snake-oil salesman, he was talented at cloaking dubious arguments in authoritative jargon and vernacular as required. And he was certainly busy doing the legwork. But his real knack was his keen and fervent belief in his ideas. Whether they were the result of his own curious thought processes or something he'd grabbed from whatever flotsam and jetsam he took a shine to was irrelevant. Belief was the key. They'd found a serviceable front man. He fooled some of the people most of the time. That he occasionally had a short fuse would simply require more perseverance and agility in the handling.

"You're intentionally excluding me!" he cried at one point. "What kind of a relationship is this? Business is built on trust. Everyone knows that."

The team suppressed their amusement. Even though Lydia wasn't sharing her bed with Caldwell anymore — it had been three months now — she made a placating move, hosting a little dinner party and weekend retreat at Rosefields. The purpose was to come up with the all-important name of the company and settle on the branding before the application was due. Luther, Malcolm, Cyrus and their respective wives, and of course Caldwell, were all in attendance. Alice couldn't make it, so she sent suggestions: "Keep the name neutral and remember the target market at this point is not the public. It's the DOH."

The weekend was peppered with touchy moments. Caldwell found the team's approach overly cautious. And they were trying to quash his creativity. He was sure of it. They didn't have any themselves, so they weren't going to let him have any either. He'd devised catchy company names like Inhealth, Cannhavitall, Eufloria, Apothecann, Cannatose, and Bhanga Lux. The team chuckled dismissively and moved on to lackluster monikers of their own. Caldwell only begrudgingly took his seat at the table again after Lydia pulled him aside and whispered something in his ear.

The team finally settled on the name CannRose-Medi because it was in no way suggestive of the black market, as per state requirements, and it referenced Rosemore in honor of Lydia's enabling contribution. To Caldwell, the name was just plain lame. Nothing to grab the attention. It didn't roll off the tongue. No pizzazz. No guts. No glory. The company was sinking into obscurity before it had begun!

Lydia was very sympathetic to Caldwell regardless of the state of their relationship, so much so that when shares got sorted, she transferred most of hers to Caldwell. The lawyers and Malcolm were unanimously horrified. They modified and mitigated the transfer in every way available to them. But in spite of all their efforts, it did give Caldwell a measure of control.

This added thermite to Caldwell's burning ambition. In his mind's eye he went years into the future and saw it was bright. Very bright. The building in Hullbrooke would expand not just by thousands of square feet but by acres. And it wouldn't be for just any marijuana. Only the best. He saw dispensaries multiplying across the nation as the regulations changed. They'd go international. Laws were changing worldwide. *Curiosity*, the Mars rover, was making the news too, and Caldwell envisioned he'd even put dispensaries on another planet someday.

He was so caught up with his narrative of the future, he was certain Lydia's team had embraced it too, along with the fact that only he would be able to oversee the renovations for the cultivation facility. He'd employ the most sophisticated technology and implement advanced growing methods. Drying and curing were an art form, and they'd be industry leaders. He'd settle for nothing less than producing the finest cannabis in America.

"This is how you make medicine," he announced, "with impeccable standards and impeccable intentions. It will change lives!"

The team smiled again.

When the application was finally hand delivered to the Department of Health on the midnight deadline, most of the people involved heaved sighs of relief. They could get back to life as normal. But not Caldwell. He was wired. He didn't sleep. He could overlook a dreary brand name now. Maybe he could even make magic with it. Whoever thought *Microsoft* would be a hit? He'd left the t-crossing and i-dotting to the dullards. He was meant for bigger things. He was taking the lead now. His mind was racing with all the components of the business and how they would come together. It was electrifying. He'd never felt so alive.

He wanted to keep moving forward. Cyrus and Malcolm encouraged this, especially since they could really be stuck with him now. They suggested Caldwell keep doing his research because if they did win the registration, they were going to have to move very quickly. He was given traveling expenses. Of course Lydia topped these up. He'd impressed upon her how important it was to look successful right from the get-go.

So Caldwell crisscrossed the country once again. He visited all the legal growers and producers that would let him in the door. He attended every conference on marijuana. Even the academic ones, where he barely understood a word. He went to Europe and Israel, where they'd been doing research on medical marijuana since the 1960s. Who said there was no research? The FDA was in denial. Caldwell also spent a lot of time in Colorado. He told Lydia he had friends in the know there. They'd be invaluable when it came time to actually growing the plants indoors and making products.

At about the same time he also brought Lazlo on board. Lazlo was one of the cousins Lydia had heard about and he lived less than an hour away from Rosefields. He had a contracting company and Caldwell informed Lydia that Lazlo was a smart businessman and he'd give them a better deal around here. You had to watch out; a lot of the local builders and contractors liked to take outsiders for a ride.

With family handling the renovation, they wouldn't have to worry, Caldwell explained.

Caldwell had plenty of other relatives too but he told her they wouldn't be interested in the medical marijuana industry. They were conservative. He didn't bother to mention they lived in a compound south of County Road 10 and were among the Guardians of Jude and Ezekiel. The group's Bible-thumping had seen better days but they still maintained a vocal aversion to activities they perceived as morally loose. They preached the evil of all things mind-altering. They also had a deep and abiding mistrust of government and of nosy social workers with whom they'd had considerable contact over the last three decades. Lazlo's and Caldwell's fathers were rebellious brothers who had somehow extricated themselves from the Guardians in the late 1950s. The cousins were extremely grateful for this and for the fact that a hundred or more years of inbreeding had not landed either of them with deformed jaws or some other incapacity.

"Lydia. So very pleased to meet you finally." Lazlo's handshake was damp and soft. He had a puffy face with heavy-lidded watery eyes, and his hair was dark and thinning on top. He didn't resemble Caldwell in the least and he often spoke in a quiet voice as if he didn't want anyone to hear what he was saying. And when he smiled it made Lydia shudder ever so slightly but she couldn't put her finger on what exactly bothered her about him. Caldwell reminded her that blood was thicker than the price of construction. So Lydia hired Lazlo's firm to begin renovations.

The lack of a proper tender process irked Malcolm to no end. The accountant was on the board of this fledgling company, he reminded Lydia as they were sipping cocktails and munching oysters, and she should have run it by him. But Cyrus came to her defense and suggested with a somewhat measured cynicism that Malcolm might as well just let it slide. No matter the contractor, in Cyrus's experience renovations usually ran anywhere from twenty-five percent to double the quote, so maybe it was better there was no quote in this case. And Malcolm should remember where the money was coming from, Cyrus said with a wink that Lydia didn't see. And feeling a little tipsy, he hooted, a tad derisively, that this Lazlo probably wouldn't be averse to a cash arrangement.

Lydia sat intently considering the remarks, and she imagined how Jordan might respond to her advisers. After a few seconds she said in a very steady, assured voice, "I'm not altogether happy with the fellow myself, but Caldwell finds him indispensable. An established bond potentially leads to faster results, no? I think despite misgivings we do need to support Caldwell. We want this venture to be successful. Is that not the case, gentlemen?"

Cyrus practically dropped his drink and Malcolm briefly choked on an oyster. They stared at her, spooked. Eventually they cleared their throats and said, "Of course. Absolutely." Then they went on about an alternative plan for a microbrewery in the event of not making the application cut. They confessed they'd be more comfortable producing suds rather than buds, and Lydia thought a microbrewery was a wonderful idea. She figured Caldwell wouldn't be nearly as enthusiastic. But in either case, offices would be needed and so they all agreed Lazlo could start renovations for the administrative section of the building right away.

#

The work began. Caldwell insisted the place have a design that was striking. It didn't matter an ounce to him that plans were already submitted to the state. It would be important for investors to see something impressive. Something they wouldn't forget. This was fortuitous for Lazlo. He brought in a young aspiring architect who minced and raged with artistic sensibilities. He was the son of a previous client — Lazlo had botched work on a major downtown office building in Lyston, and the owner had been out for blood. But he was mollified by the prospect of his son making progress in his chosen career, and the lawsuit was dropped.

The young architect was impossible of course, completely impractical, but he had Caldwell firmly in his corner insisting on a vast array of expensive materials, finishes and detailing. Malcolm and Cyrus didn't mind a bit. To them it was irrelevant. And for Lydia it was all very exciting, and they were pleased she was happy and not just blowing money on Caldwell for personal reasons.

Chapter 7

The three young men sat on a screened-in backyard veranda in their overcoats. Some old 2Pac, turned down low, rapped in the background. Large bottles of soft drinks sat at their feet. The air was pungent, smoky, and the three young devotees enthused about their future.

"It's so lit we can start right in with the co-ops."

"That cuts off even more time."

"We could be working in weed with the first state dispensaries."

"It's so dope. Fuckin' dope!"

"Yeah, I been readin' up on plants and weed. Like, a lot."

"Yeah?"

"It's lit AF. They have sex."

"When?"

"Like whenever they want? That would be awesome!"

"No, when they got flowers! Dude, where were you in biology!"

"Kruts was the worst teacher ever!"

"Ever!"

"Weed's got male plants separate from female plants."

"I knew that."

"All plants are like that!"

"Dude, seriously. Did you not even open the textbook?"

"Did you?"

"Yeah. Most flowers have both sexes. On the same flower."

"So flowers have sex with themselves. What's the big deal about that?"

"Dude, you're so basic."

"Not."

"Who cares?"

"Because. We wanna know about weed."

"Can't we wait 'til college?"

"They're not gonna teach weed in college!"

"So why are we going then?"

"Dude, to learn about plants."

"I don't care about flowers."

"Where do you think the buds come from?"

"Greg or your mom."

"No dude, the female flowers!"

"What about the male flowers?"

"They're useless, bro!"

"So what happens to them?"

"They kill 'em."

"That's mean."

"No, they don't. They just don't grow 'em. Mom just grows the mothers. So all the clones are female."

"Can you clone a father? That would be lit."

"Why would you want to clone the fathers? They're useless."

"Because then it's equal. And that would be better."

"Not if they cloned *my* dad."

"Mostly they don't have fathers, just mothers."

"Seriously then somebody has to kill the fathers sometimes."

"Dude. You're seriously basic."

"Yeah. Savage."

"You should prob'ly get studying now."

"Getting baked is better."

"Can we go look at your mom's grow room again?"

"Prob'ly."

"She gonna keep growing her own?"

"Course. Why not?"

"Because you'll be able to grow it for her!"

"She says she has to know what she's getting."

"It's so fuckin' lit. Horticulture!"

"My dad hasn't figured it out yet. He just thinks I'm woke to the environment."

"Seriously?"

"I told him it was for sustainable farming."

"That's awesome!"

"Yeah, that's so dead!"

Chapter 8

The sun was shining through the window onto Ernie's new — at least new to him — stainless-steel restaurant-grade fifty-nine-and-a-half-inch gas range with four burners, a grill and a griddle. Ernie was delighted. Things might move slowly around Hullbrooke but people kept their word. Gerry had finally cleared out the old second-floor Gas Bar and Rent-All office. Ernie now had a place where he could set up possibly the best kitchen in Hullbrooke, not to mention he could sleep peacefully in his own bed.

"That is one hell of a stove!" Carl remarked, stepping back to admire their installation work. Then he flipped a switch to try the vent above. Ernie and Gerry had put it in the week before. It began to hum. "Nice unit. Where'd you find it?"

"Diner demolition. Other side of Lyston. You know where they had to reroute twenty-seven?"

"Oh yeah, that was a mess." Carl was looking at the stove again. "That thing has two ovens doesn't it?"

"Yes it does." Ernie grinned. "With five adjustable racks between them."

It had taken Ernie a while to locate a range he wanted, but it had been worth the wait. He could have purchased a smaller more space-appropriate one earlier but it was more expensive and he was not taken in. Extra computerized features, especially secondhand ones, mostly caused trouble.

"It's simple, basic and worthy of a fine chef, I might add," Ernie said, "and they threw in the salamander for nothing." He tapped the boxy-looking stainless-steel broiler suspended at eye level.

"Lucky you." Carl picked up a cloth and began polishing the control valves and the oven doors.

Ernie stood back and watched the sheen start to come up but he got impatient. "I think we should just christen this baby and hope we don't blow the place up." Carl moved aside and Ernie lit one of the burners for the very first time. They applauded as the flames sprang gently into a perfect circle and Ernie put a kettle on to boil.

In Ernie's first career he'd worked his way up to commis chef. He'd been a diligent student under the tutelage of Jacinthe and the usually inebriated Masu, whose pedigrees included the finer culinary schools of France and Japan, respectively. Life was full of promise and good food until Joachim Gomez-Richtenbach II (or III depending on the reviewer), famed head chef, grabbed him by the arm one day and held a knife to his throat while screaming at him. Then he threw Ernie out, telling him to go flip burgers because he'd make sure Ernie never worked in a good kitchen again. It wasn't anything Ernie did. If the man's wife took a shine to him, could he help it? But the situation cost him dearly and almost broke his youthful heart, though it didn't diminish his enthusiasm for the métier. In fact it improved it. Cooking for a living was hectic and highly stressful in hot kitchens and hierarchies. It created Joachims and Masus. Ernie knew he'd learn to hate it in time. Not doing it for a living was a way to keep his love alive.

As the kettle slowly came to a whistle, he ground the coffee and measured the amounts out into his yard-sale French press. The press was at least twenty years old and had an art deco look to it with engraved metal legs. The lady who sold it to him said she thought it was stupid and pretentious. Her mother had used it. Ernie didn't say anything, just paid the five bucks, and she told him to take the damn grinder too.

After Ernie had made the coffee and they'd cut up the spice cake Carl's wife had sent over, they sat around reviewing and assessing the current local gossip. Not a single topic of any importance was touched on, but Ernie was close to rapturous. The months of living rough, occasionally foraging in dumpsters and then relying on deli food and dining out of his station wagon on whatever he could buy that wouldn't rot in the sunbaked car had practically rendered him a walking skeleton. Now he could roast, griddle, sauté, simmer, steam, broil and bake his way into renewed vigor. He was going to eat better than he ever had in his life.

Ernie supposed he was a modern revisionist now. His dreams were well amended. He'd had it with striving, go-getting and the all-American nightmare. Nothing had recovered for him after the housing crisis. He'd limped along and eventually lost each of his jobs, including the one in real estate. The bank foreclosed on the condo and then Lenore made off with the leftovers. He managed to hang on to his debt and Lenore's medical bills for her varicose treatments. And then he lost those too. Bankruptcy has its special price.

What surprised him most was the change in his mood over the last eighteen months.

The heartrending losses, one after another, had broken him. And when he was feeling most sorry for himself, he saw his downfall culminating in Lenore's departure. He embodied failure and had become repulsive to her. "It's grief," his sister-in-law had said. "There are stages and you just have to go through them. You know, denial, anger, bargaining, depression and acceptance."

Ernie figured she was right except it was never his way to stick to the prescribed agenda. His stages went more like this: Stage one: No more pussy. At least not with Lenore and that was really depressing. Stage two: Plain broke. And that made him angry, though it ensured Lenore would stay away. Stage three: Ongoing depreciation. He'd have to maintain poverty until the divorce was finalized otherwise she'd clean him out again. But he could accept that. Stage four: Redundancy. If she found some other poor schmuck he'd be off the hook altogether. That was a pretty good bargain! Stage five: A classic epiphany, though Ernie knew some of his old hotshot business buddies would think he was in denial.

His epiphany happened right after he'd spent the night in a cell for vagrancy and one of the cops who thought he was veteran gave him forty bucks to go get himself a good breakfast. As Ernie dug into his home fries and chugged back his coffee that morning, he realized the freedom he experienced at having nothing of value according to Lenore or the rest of society was actually okay. In fact it was better than okay. At times, like right then, staring out the window at a couple bickering on the street and realizing he no longer had a single crippling responsibility or commitment, it was exhilarating. So he was never going back to the idiot he used to be. His new lifestyle was no ruse. It was fucking A! So Ernie resolved to thrive somehow on as little as possible.

And it was looking good. Hullbrooke, the place of his birth, just might be his own personal specially tailored El Dorado. The evidence was piling up. In his very living quarters he had a regifted Murmuring Life Fountain, which trickled ceaselessly with optimism and frugality.

As for the nitty-gritty practicalities of living on next to nothing? His rent was minimal because he was the watchman at Gerry's Gas Bar and Rent-All. He just had to live there, keep an eye on things and pay utility costs. Gerry wasn't fussy. And now, along with tending to the Cranston terraces, he had himself a ten- to fifteen-hour-a-week late-afternoon gig, mostly sweeping up floors or wrestling with a Shop-Vac at the old trucking warehouse. He showed up when the carpenters, electricians and other tradesmen knocked off work. The guys saluted, high-fived or nodded in male-bonding custom as he came through the door. He was everybody's friend. What could be better?

"A tidy workspace is a happy workspace," Lazlo, the boss, said in a gravelly voice, blinking his rheumy eyes. Lazlo reminded Ernie of Gladys the toad. "The lads are supposed to clean up after themselves, ya know. But there's always a mess somewheres. They start griping about each other. And there's the washroom and snack area. They're worse than children."

Ernie didn't mind any of it. He was surfing a ripple of good fortune and observing the daily progress manifesting in front of him. It was interesting too. Offices were being built and they were upscale and designer-funky. More like Hudson Yards than Hullbrooke. Lazlo told Ernie there'd be plenty more work if he wanted, especially if they got the go-ahead from the state for medical pot. Ernie didn't want more work, but minimal employment extending well into the future was pleasant enough to consider. He could make plans. Hallelujah!

After Carl left and the late-autumn sun continued to sparkle on Ernie's stove, he looked around to assess his own progress. He just had the one big room, freshly painted. Along the side wall, about midway between the stove and the tiny washroom with its beat-up stall shower, was a large cabinet Ernie had found at the local dump. Its doors were broken and bashed so he took them off. Now it was a better-than-average shelving unit. He kept just about everything he owned in it, apart from the kitchen stuff. Near the stove he'd put up a rack for hanging pots he'd been collecting from thrift shops, yard sales and the dump. And he'd found a dehydrator and a meat smoker requiring the most minimal of repairs. He'd fixed them himself in a single afternoon, making only one trip to a hardware store for a cord and a couple of casters. What some people threw away!

Just below the window closest to the stove was a utility sink he would replace with a counter top, cupboards and a kitchen sink as funds and opportunity permitted. There was an old side-by-side fridge courtesy of Gerry. Mrs. Cranston had given him a freezer she decided was too big now for just her and her husband, and Ernie had built shelves above it. Rounding out the kitchen area were a table and two chairs.

Ernie's bedroom was a recently covered piece of foam on the floor closer to the washroom. The fountain trickling beside the bed was from Gerry's wife, whose sister had given it to her, and she couldn't stand it. It was the water-spewing fish she hated. If you took out the cost of the stove, Ernie had furnished his new abode for less than a hundred and fifty bucks and it was the foam he slept on that cost him the most. Go figure.

There were windows all around the room. One of them opened out onto the roof over the old car bays left from when the place had been a full garage. He already had the meat smoker set up out there, and along with his cooking Ernie was taking up rooftop farming come spring. The building was solid enough to hold three or more feet of snow in the winter, so Gerry was all for it as long as Ernie shared a few vegetables.

And speaking of sharing, or rather bartering, because that's what it really was, word soon got out to the Hullbrooke hunters and anglers that for a few fish or cuts of meat there was a guy back in town who would make you mouthwatering jerky, smoked meat and gourmet wild-game sausages to melt your heart. And now that he had a stove, there'd be meat pies and fish cakes. Ernie was pretty sure he would never eat poorly again.

As he was surveying his humble kingdom, it occurred to him that he had an address now, so he could register for medical weed. It could have been his stressed-out achiever days or Lenore or his unpleasant brush with the head chef years ago, or more likely sleeping in the rusty Volvo, but something had left him with neck pain. Hallelujah one more time! He could grow his own weed, and if the factory got going, there'd be seeds, clones and expertise at hand, not to mention a fallback supplier. There was no end of possibilities.

Chapter 9

Petra stood at the kitchen door looking through the window at the garden she'd built. With the shrubs still all wrapped in burlap for the winter, it looked like her backyard was populated with strange people. Little people who'd never get on with things, who would stagnate. Petra was getting tired of the freelance work. Four chapters in a high-school biology text didn't exactly cut it for stimulation. The editor kept telling her to shorten her sentences. Dumbing down for students was a nationwide preoccupation. Petra pulled her sweater closer around her and shivered.

Her own dumbing down was becoming apparent too. What happened to that research she'd been so passionate about twenty-five years ago? The evolutionary physiology of angiosperms, Darwin's neglected child. Why had she stopped caring about plants? The peculiar ones. The ones of no corporate interest. Did dropping the ball on her own path of inquiry stem from some evolutionary pressure? Was her curiosity maladapted, doomed from the outset? Questions, questions, questions. If she was honest about it she'd have to admit all research ever gave anyone was more questions. She'd have liked a few more answers.

Right now she particularly needed answers about her computer. It was behaving oddly. She'd have to take it to some technical savant, she just didn't know where to find one. Any other time she'd hop in the car and make the three-hour drive into the city. It was always a welcome break. But Petra's mom hadn't been feeling well and a visit to the doctor revealed Doreen had pneumonia. In fact the doctor had her mom stay overnight in the hospital so they could run a series of tests first thing in the morning. She was on the mend now, but it had been difficult and even scary.

Petra mulled the notion that maybe she was a less-than-good daughter. She should have insisted her mother get medical help sooner in spite of her protestations and reproaches. "Just a little sniffle. You're making a big deal out of nothing again." Doreen could take care of herself thank you very much. Only she couldn't. Not now. Not so much. And Petra had opted for the long-term care plan, hadn't she? She was the long-term care. She watched the snow fall and the little burlap people in the backyard shifted and shuddered.

Petra had noted her mother's doctor was dark haired yet had penetrating blue eyes. This was fascinating, if only for the genetics. It occurred to her she could call him up under some pretext, some concern about her mother, and then just ask him out on a date. He wasn't wearing a ring. She'd checked. It could liven things up a little. He might even be a good conversationalist. As long as he wasn't a good drinker. She didn't have a clue where anyone would go on a date in Hullbrooke. She'd heard Chelsea's was a local gong show, but maybe he'd find it fun. Or maybe they could make the trek to Lyston.

The next day she called up the doctor's office about her mother's medication.

"Oh yes, he's available for this sort of thing after office hours before he heads up to the hospital in Lyston," the receptionist told her. "That's usually about three o'clock. Would tomorrow work?"

"Perfect," said Petra. She was about to thank her and hang up.

"Oh wait. I forgot . . . he told me this morning too . . ." The receptionist gave a little chuckle. "His little girl is in a dance recital — such a cutie! His wife is picking him up at two forty-five."

"I see," said Petra.

"I'm just going to put you in for one o'clock instead. We had a cancellation and he's very understanding about these things."

"Thanks." Petra turned her phone off and threw it on the table.

#

"I could have told you he was married," Doreen said that evening. "Why didn't you just ask me about him?"

Petra was standing in the doorway to her mother's bedroom with her arms crossed. "I didn't think I needed to. He wasn't wearing a ring." She found the whole incident almost amusing now.

"Lots of married men don't." Her mother was sitting up finishing a cup of tea, with her cat curled up at the end of the bed. "You want me to have my friends here set you up on a date?"

Petra yawned. "Absolutely not."

"I'm sure they could find somebody. Probably a lot nicer than the sort you usually end up with."

"I'm not desperate, Mom. I just . . . happened to find him attractive."

"I'm not saying you're desperate. But maybe you do need a little company."

"I'm fine."

"You sure don't have any social life here."

"Not yet."

"You've been here a year! And I don't think paying that little delinquent next door to help you with the garden and shovel snow constitutes a social life."

"It doesn't and I'm fine."

"The cat has more of a social life than you do."

"Good for him." Petra turned around and headed to the kitchen.

"You know what Mabel Mansing told me today?" her mother yelled after her.

"How could I possibly know?" Petra yelled back.

"She said she heard the Rosefield people bought up the old trucking warehouse. They're going to grow pot in it or turn it into a microbrewery. Maybe both."

"Bully for them."

"You could get a job!"

Petra walked back down the hall to her mother's bedroom, all the while scrubbing a pot with a wad of steel wool. She smiled broadly as she leaned against the doorframe and continued scrubbing. "Luckily, Mom, I know nothing whatsoever about growing weed or any kind of crop for that matter and I probably wouldn't recognize hops if I fell over some. Not my kind of plant science!"

PART THREE

Germination

As we are born to the boom and drive we are no different from you. Begin, begin. No matter the prospect, the love lost to pain, the start to catastrophe. We remain. Promising. Oh to surface with time and feel the earth's spin. A sole directive: Begin. Begin! The promise of time is a treasure. We watch you, tender marvels waking to the bright orb. Waking to revolutions that stir the cosmos. Fledgling efforts gather to surpass the sum. At each node the transformations come, while the sprouting whispers of giants. The nascent drive loves the soul, the sun and the sigh of the wind. Begin. Begin.

from Cannto III, *Cannabidadas*

Chapter 10

Alice Morgan flopped down on her sofa. She'd just come back from a meeting with the neighbors, sorted out the plots for the community garden. Spearheading the project had truly been an eye-opening experience. Alice hadn't any idea she had such a varied group of neighbors all keen on planting something they could watch grow and ultimately eat. Luckily, now the garden was almost finished, she didn't have to head up any committees! The season, albeit a short one, was planned and they'd decided on a name too: Paint Patches. She didn't much like the name but it would do.

The phone rang. "We got it, Mom." Her son sounded hesitant. "CannRose-Medi made the cut. The DOH is having a press conference this afternoon. It'll be on the evening news."

It took a moment for Alice to register what he was talking about. The dispensary application had been sent to the Department of Health months and months ago. The state was so tardy reviewing and making its decisions she'd almost forgotten about it.

Luther, that aggressive lawyer, came on the phone. She'd had many conference calls with him in the weeks leading up to the application deadline. This time, he sounded absolutely ecstatic. He thanked her yet again for all her expert input. Alice noticed her son was silent. He was in fact concerned his mother might have changed her mind again, or would in the next week or so. But Alice never did anything in half measures or backed out of commitments once she'd made them. It was her signature.

"We're in for a lot of work," she said. "Hope everybody's gotten a good rest in the meantime."

"Absolutely," said Luther. "We're ready to hit the pavement running."

"You'd better get started looking for a chemist or a manufacturing specialist. You know the person you'll need to oversee the derivatives," Alice said.

"Yes, ma'am. The headhunter has already been at work. We've got ... I think four resumés here. But actually, it's not a priority now," Luther said. "The state has decided it only requires dried product by the first eight months. Oil and whatnot after sixteen."

"Gives you some time but I wouldn't leave it too long," Alice said. "You need that expertise even to finish the renovations I'd say."

"Good point!" said Luther. "Alice, is there any chance of you going to Hullbrooke to look at the grow facility? I think you should see the plans again before they start the next stage of construction."

"I don't know I'd be of much help any more than I have been," Alice said. "The actual dispensary plans, of course, I'll check those again and oversee modifications. I have to. But I really can't help you with the grow facility. Or even the manufacturing part for that matter. Things have changed since I studied that stuff. That's why you need that chemist or extraction specialist, whoever."

Luther was disappointed. He didn't trust Caldwell or his shady cousin to adhere to the planned renovations. Cyrus had persuaded Luther not to care about the offices, but he had a hunch he'd better care about the actual grow facility since the DOH would be watching. The plans had the engineer's stamp on them. But Luther couldn't imagine there wouldn't be changes. Necessary ones. Likely complicated ones. Possibly disastrous ones with Caldwell around. Luther had recently learned Lazlo didn't have a lot of fans when it came to contracting for commercial buildings and no experience whatsoever with industrial or manufacturing operations. Lazlo had assured everyone early on he would get all the best local people for the project. Luther imagined even if that were true, in fact because that could be true, the place might turn into a catastrophe.

Before he hung up, Luther suggested everyone should get together and have a little celebration soon. They said their goodbyes.

Alice stretched out on the sofa. A nap was in order. That would be her celebration. She didn't relish the thought of an evening in the company of that pushy little lawyer or that bigmouth Caldwell. She pitied her son. Then she thought about her own work and setting up the dispensary outlets. Lord! There were two of them. CannRose needed to employ a couple of good dispensary managers, possibly another pharmacist if it was to keep to the plan. And with a dispensary in Lyston, Alice might have to make trips. A traveling businesswoman!

As for the near future, she needed to add some details to the dispensaries' security. Even on the tony side of the city she wouldn't be taking any chances, and the Lyston dispensary site was in a mall. She'd rather they have too many security features than too few. And there were a lot of organizational matters to consider. This would mean late nights as things moved along. Her staff at the drugstore would tease that she was looking bleary-eyed and maybe taking the dispensary thing too literally. Did they need to buy her a better bong?

Chapter 11

What Luther and the others on that congratulatory conference call with Alice didn't appreciate was that Caldwell was already four steps ahead of everyone. Since the time they'd submitted the application, he'd seen just about every operation going. He was determined to take the best from all of them and build a masterpiece. What were they paying him for after all? He'd already decided on what equipment was needed and where it should be in the facility and how everything from the grow rooms to the shipping room needed to be rearranged. And the minute he heard of the application's success he hightailed it over to his cousin's place, humming to the radio.

Lazlo was in his yard cleaning up droppings from his wife's four yappy miniature schnauzers. He straightened up, sensing a shift in the universe just by the way Caldwell zoomed up the driveway and pulled to a stop. He carefully laid the scoop and plastic bag on one of the lawn chairs.

Caldwell bolted out of the car, raced over and slapped Lazlo on the back. "We're in business! We got it! Nothing to stop us now!"

Lazlo had been following Caldwell's often erratic orders regarding the administrative section for the last six months and listening to Caldwell's revisions to the production-area plans for the last four. He'd been preparing accordingly and he was very skilled at dealing with Caldwell. Sometimes Lazlo succeeded in changing Caldwell's mind, shifting some notion a little to the right or left, or mitigating some obsession Caldwell had. And Lazlo was so unremarkable he had perhaps come close to mastering the art of invisibility. Even with Caldwell's most outrageous ideas he knew how to just say yes and then quietly do what actually needed to be done. Or he did what would ensure financial health, particularly his own financial health. Lazlo realized that Caldwell didn't pay all that much attention to details or follow-up. In fact Caldwell jumped to new ideas so frequently he was apt to forget what he'd originally requested. This was a working style Lazlo could live with. In fact it was one in which he could flourish! He beamed at Caldwell.

Caldwell, by his own estimation, had grown enormously in the last year. It gave him an unshakable confidence. While everybody else was dozing, Caldwell had become a walking marijuana encyclopedia. With contacts! Certainly he knew way more about marijuana production than anybody else at CannRose-Medi. He could outtalk any of them. He countered all objections, doubts and queries, often with explosive dismissals.

"You simply can't have that nursery guy running the cultivation. With only greenhouse experience? Not an iota of practice growing indoors? Medicinal marijuana is not some vegetable or ground cover! It needs to be crafted!" Or "What in God's name was that engineer thinking? With that ventilation system the place will be infested with mold in no time."

Eventually the doubters crawled off to their respective cubicles of ignorance, including Cyrus and Luther, who really didn't have any time to waste on more research. So Caldwell ruled the roost in Hullbrooke, and since Lazlo was clearly crucial to the whole operation, Caldwell proposed his cousin be made vice president of CannRose-Medi. Luther, initially dumbstruck by this suggestion, quickly became vocal and vigorous with his opposition. Cyrus and Malcolm merely wrinkled their noses as if faced with something slightly septic but unavoidable. In the end it was Lydia who openly supported the decision. She could easily tolerate the man as her vice president, and Caldwell was delighted when she suggested Lazlo's name and position be inscribed on his office door.

Chapter 12

The green light for CannRose-Medi prompted great municipal rejoicing. According to the *Gazette*, Hullbrooke's Planning and Business Development Department was aflutter. Just like Ernie, Hullbrooke had not recovered to any degree after the financial collapse. Many businesses had closed or shifted out of the country altogether and so the local council had been unanimous in its approval of the plan. And judging from the quotes about attracting "even more new businesses" and "possible residential expansion," the two local building inspectors, one slightly deaf, the other with a bum knee, were feeling bride-like with anticipation.

This didn't mean that all the locals had been in favor of the operation. When folks heard the town had approved a plan and crawled into bed with CannRose, some of them balked. The not-in-my-backyard contingent and those opposed on religious and moral grounds had been highly demonstrative in their opposition. The Guardians of Jude and Ezekiel, some of Caldwell's distant relatives in fact, had taken a dilapidated school bus, painted it blood red and filled it to overflowing with moldy hay and weeds. After dousing it with gasoline they set it alight in front of the town hall at midnight. They added fireworks too. Ernie, startled awake by the racket, ran out in his shorts to take a look. "Arise! Repent! Reject the smoke of torment! Arise! Repent! Reject the smoke of torment!" Being a little groggy and quite distracted by the smoldering bus with fireworks bursting out of it, he wasn't sure what the protest was about so he jogged down the hill to find out. As he approached, a few protesters lowered their placards, brandishing them like spears. They hadn't planned on people showing up in their underwear. The Guardians were duly charged of course but achieved their ultimate objective. The photo made the cover of the *Gazette*, and in the bottom-left corner of it you could just make out Ernie's shin and foot.

#

Finally the true work began. The renovation of the offices had been just the appetizer. The rear end of the old building was soon crawling with contractors and tradespeople meeting the high standard set by Lazlo that they must have bulletproof insurance policies. And since they were willing to work with Lazlo, it meant they also had a fine appreciation of old-time adversarial construction culture. Those modular and prefab approaches were for the unimaginative. And this was no mundane project.

According to Caldwell — Ernie was now fairly well acquainted with him — this was a bold reno for revolutionizing plant cultivation. Steel and polymer reinforcement was required to support the rooftop HVAC systems, which looked so powerful Ernie figured they could probably service the Shanghai Tower. Apparently they could generate internal climates to remind a person of mountaintops, savannahs or the deepest jungle. Negative and positive pressure rooms could be established and temperatures could be controlled to decimal places. There'd be lighting brilliant enough to guide ships and roast retinas with electrical panels arranged like library stacks. There'd be polyester and fiberglass wall cladding, dazzling in its white purity. And epoxy flooring, or rather painted epoxy over old cement flooring — they would economize where they could. Three air showers were planned. Ernie knew about these from an evening cleaning gig as a student. They would whip up the hair and brace any spirit. Perhaps most impressive were the plumbing plans. The fertigation systems for the grow rooms were so elaborate Ernie thought the designs rivaled neural mapping of the human brain.

Forty rooms would be carved into the warehouse. Big ones for flowering, little ones for the baby plants and mothers. Potting, trimming, drying, curing and packaging rooms. And process rooms for extractions had their own bottling rooms attached. Even a kitchen was planned in the glorious hope the state would ultimately see the value of edibles. There were utility and storage rooms, production offices, change rooms, showers and washrooms. And also a vault to store the precious healing product before it made its way to the dispensaries. Spare areas were set aside too. Caldwell was thinking the company should do its own R and D, and its scientists would need a laboratory.

Lazlo asked Ernie if he could work more hours. "You'd be doing pretty much the same thing – cleaning up. It's just there's more of it now." Ernie hesitated. He didn't want work interfering with his winter reading program. He was catching up on the latest food trends, organic gardening and his new interest in permaculture and the free-stuff movement.

"How about just three days? Gives you four off," Lazlo said.

Ernie couldn't fault the math. And with the extra day's pay he could save for a decent soup pot, proper set of knives too, maybe. And he needed more supplies for his rooftop garden.

#

Now the irony in acting on dreams of leisure is that so much freedom potentially holds the seeds of its own destruction. How very Derrida! A person free to get curious about work can be drawn right back into it. And so it was in Ernie's case. Activities at the old warehouse became more compelling by the day, fascinating in the way a pig's ear might be turned into a silky purse with sequins, rhinestones and seed pearls. Improbable. Definitely over the top. And possibly fucking futile.

The back of the building was a puzzle of surprises. As they ripped things apart they found bats, carpenter ants, old wiring just waiting to ignite and of course asbestos. There were also the usual wasps nests in the rafters and mice everywhere, and the existing joists and supports were all in inconvenient places for the new design. Lazlo, who was looking more haggard by the week, was often heard muttering, "Shit, now what?" or "What the fuck now?"

One morning before coffee break, Ernie watched the roofers descend the ladder accompanied by a faint sprinkle of rain. "You want this shit on your roof, conditions gotta be perfect," the team lead said to Lazlo. "We got another job other side of Lyston. Gotta get started. Weather's supposed to clear next week. See ya then." The guy slapped Lazlo on the shoulder. Lazlo squinted as the raindrops fell in his eyes. Ernie bet the roofers wouldn't be back until the end of the next month and he was off by only a week.

The plumbing contractor was another "old friend" of Lazlo's. Ernie saw him looking at some revised plans for the grow rooms with Lazlo. "I can't just order those valves," the plumber said. "They have to be custom made. Expensive as hell." Lazlo grimaced. Then he pulled up the webpage that Caldwell had shown him. The valves were only ten bucks a piece at Home Depot. The plumber shrugged. "Well screw me. Not my usual supplier I guess." And he sauntered off with a smirk that suggested to Ernie he had more scams up his sleeve.

And there were plenty of other problems. Ernie watched an HVAC specialist nearly decapitate an electrician with a swinging sheet of aluminum. Ernie had helped the electrician to his feet again. The guy was cursing and vowing all manner of vengeance. And a few of the carpenters Lazlo routinely employed had developed longstanding grudges against each other. Ernie intervened in a bout of fisticuffs over an ex-wife. He could empathize and was very effective in calming them down. And in a less hostile vein there was the apprentice who nailed his hand to a joist in a Christ-like manner because he'd "never used that Jesus effin' kinda gun before." Throughout all of this Caldwell was jumping in with opinions on everything and often giving instructions that were contrary to Lazlo's.

The Hullbrooke building inspectors, who showed up way more than they needed to, added to Lazlo's trials. One nearly fell off a ladder. The other was so hard of hearing Lazlo had to bellow everything at least twice, and when that didn't work, he resorted to miming his responses. Ernie noted Lazlo's hand gestures were becoming more aggressive by the day, occasionally verging on obscene.

And the Hullbrooke Environment and Land Use manager appeared one day and declared that the existing septic bed would need to be relocated because it posed a groundwater hazard. He couldn't imagine why it had ever been put *there* in the first place. He also stated rather huffily that the revised CannRose plan for proper and safe waste disposal of regulated plant material was still owing and should have been a priority. Ernie watched Lazlo turn his back on the man at the earliest opportunity, close his eyes and mutter curses under his breath.

#

As the place got into some kind of shape, the vetting of future CannRose employees was thrown in Lazlo's lap as well. After all he was the vice president and Lydia couldn't possibly do it. Besides he'd run his own company for years and had employed lots of people. He was a pro! Of course Caldwell couldn't resist muscling his way into the hiring process, but only for the people he thought were important, like the managers. Or the master grower, who Caldwell insisted be imported from Colorado. He had someone in mind already — in actual fact he'd promised the guy the job as soon as he found out CannRose had made the application cut. Damian was a marijuana genius, according to Caldwell, and the company would be extremely fortunate to have him. Most importantly they would need to pay big bucks to keep him. Lazlo rolled his eyes at this and Luther nearly had a fit when he saw the proposed salary. Lydia had no strong opinion but offered lodgings at Rosefields — the fully furnished apartment over her five-car garage. Free rent could be used to reduce the dollar amount.

Lazlo's hiring practices were not sophisticated. Being pressed for time he resorted to just putting the word out. He pretty much hired anybody who was interested. Mostly his and Caldwell's relatives and their friends. At least half a dozen hires quit before they'd worked a month. They weren't expecting this type of work. Their notions of commercial marijuana production clearly did not match the reality. Many had envisioned a relaxed, possibly even hazy atmosphere, with the camaraderie and congeniality of a music festival. Lazlo's first production manager, a relative of Lydia's, lasted only a month and a half, so Caldwell's beloved godson took over the position. In fact friends and relatives came and went with such remarkable speed, sometimes they didn't hang around long enough for their security clearances to be finalized.

Everybody, even Ernie, had to go through a state-mandated background check. Greg, the big burly ex-cop and onetime FBI agent in charge of CannRose security, was responsible for it. He'd been on site periodically since construction started too, making sure the security measures he'd specified in the application were all put in place. Ernie found him affable enough but a little intimidating on first sight. Greg looked like he could stop trains with one hand. He'd probably played college football or been a hockey enforcer, something demanding brute force and possibly barbaric tendencies. Although his curly red hair and beard softened the look a little, as did his easy smile and frequent laugh.

Along with a background check, all workers had to be registered with the DOH. Ernie sadly coughed up his social security number. No more cash agreements. He'd even have to set up a new bank account, but he waited until he'd gotten through the background check. He was a little surprised when he did because in addition to spending a night in a cell for vagrancy a year before, he'd been in a bar fight in his twenties and was sure he'd been charged with something. *Ah*, Ernie thought, *the advantages of being white in America*. His eye patch was always a help too.

As the revolving staff became more than Lazlo could manage or tolerate, it was clear CannRose needed a proper HR department. So Luther, Caldwell, Lazlo and Lydia got together and did the only logical thing. They combined HR with security and handed it over to Greg. He was already doing more than half the work. Background checks were time-consuming and provided the most thorough vetting of employees anyway. It was a no brainer! In fact they all looked at each other in disbelief that they hadn't thought of it before. Greg for his part shrugged, smiled and said, "Sure, why not."

Ernie noticed that after Greg took over HR, he seemed to be even more cheery and have more of a bounce to his step. He could frequently be heard whistling. Ernie found the tunes familiar and after a while he realized they were all from Broadway musicals.

Right about the time Greg took over HR, the DOH scheduled its first inspection. This was nothing to whistle about. The inspector, Ms. Ligner, looked awfully young, though Ernie estimated she had to be over thirty by the way she talked. Her subtly swinging hips and prominent pout reminded him a little of Lenore. But he had to hand it to her, she was right up front. No surprise attack. No subterfuge. No wasted time. Her machete was sharpened and raised from the start. And Ms. Ligner wasn't impressed with anything. She spent two hours in the cultivation rooms running her finger along surfaces. She pointed out sanitation problems, which involved Ernie to a great degree, though when you carry a broom or a pail and a mop, people just know you're not the guy they need to speak to.

"We're still in the middle of construction here," Lazlo pointed out.

"That's not my problem," Ms. Ligner replied. "You've started cultivating. What if drywall dust gets into the finished product?"

"We're a ways from finished product," Lazlo exclaimed.

Caldwell's godson, the production manager, was standing next to him, rubbing his face. "Crap, yeah," he mumbled, and Ernie wondered what he'd taken that morning.

Damian, the master grower, was rolling his shoulders. He was tall, though not as tall as Ernie, and pale enough to be mistaken for an albino, with blond dreadlocks halfway down his back. "Hey, we just barely got the mother plants started," he said.

The inspector looked Damian up and down and frowned. She asked him where the cleaning procedures were for the drying chambers and the packaging rooms.

"The packaging rooms aren't finished yet . . . Like I said, we just got started with the mothers." Damian looked baffled.

She sighed. "You should have submitted the procedures with the application. Samples at least." And she ferociously scribbled something in her notes. She looked up and with a sweep of her eyes took in the potting room and brought her gaze back to Lazlo. "You've got mice traps set everywhere and bugs climbing your walls. If vermin and pests are a problem you need to fix it." She didn't wait for an answer but turned around and stalked down the hallway, heels clicking, clipboard in hand.

Her next victim was Greg. Ernie could see the big man through the glass walls, scurrying around, pointing out CannRose's stringent security measures. He kept smiling for as long as he could. After she'd gone, he told Ernie that she was nitpicking bonkers about the video records and their storage. Nothing was adequate. And she didn't like the people who'd been hired either. "Where are their qualifications?" Greg had been relieved to see her go.

In fact everybody was happy to see her go. Now they could get back to work. As if it wasn't difficult enough to get the whole place up and running, and they were just barely running. Sometimes only hanging on by their badly bitten fingernails.

Chapter 13

"Brobes, this exam's gonna annihilate us."

"No it's not. This stuff's easy!"

"You're batshit cray-cray."

The college dorm room was cramped but the three young devotees made do. The desk lamps were blazing, Styrofoam takeout containers littered the floor, and the beds were covered by open notebooks and laundry. The smell of sweat, dirty sneakers, tacos and fried chicken permeated the air. Large cans of energy drinks were lined up on the adjoining desks. A Boston cream donut sat on a chocolate-smeared paper towel. The young men rubbed their tired eyes, leaned back in their chairs and discussed their current situation.

"Just chill."

"Yeah. You'll do better."

"I'm getting baked."

"Bro, that's not a good idea."

"Why not?"

"You need to concentrate."

"I concentrate better when I'm baked."

"Me too!"

"I don't."

"It sucks. Why did we pick the accelerated program?"

"Because we're genius!"

"Gives us life, bro!"

"We're never gonna use this shit."

"Who cares? We're almost done the first semester. With the co-op we're like, half through already."

"Yeah. We can do this!"

"What's PEP?"

"Fuck! You made cards?"

"Yeah. Why not?"

"Let me see . . . he's never gonna ask about PEP."

"I'm tired AF."

"Two hours more."

"We'll Gucci this, bro."

"Just like we did the last one!"

"I was baked for the last one."

"Whatever."

"Okay. I get to ask the questions."

"Dude."

"Explain the different plant metabolisms: C3, C4 and CAM. Be descriptive and use examples. Then state why they exist."

"This is dumb."

"No it's not. It's just the type of shit he asks."

"I got this. So with C4, the plant fixes a four-carbon acid that gets transported outta the mesophyll cell to the bundle sheath cell."

"Why don't you start with C3?"

"Dude! He's answering the question."

"Goes through the Calvin cycle in the bundle sheath cell. Process uses more ATP."

"What's ATP?"

"He's not gonna ask about that."

"So why mention it?"

"Just let him finish."

"Weed's a C3 plant you know. I'm gonna use that as an example."

"Don't put weed down, bro. He'll take marks off."

"He can't do that."

"He'll take marks off somewhere. He hates us."

"He's an asshole."

"Needs to get baked."

"Brobes, we need to focus. You're supposed to be answering the question."

"What was the question again?"

"Explain the metabolisms. How are they different? Why are they—"

"I'm going to bed."

"It's all about plants having choice!"

"No it's not. Just answer the question."

"Brobes, he's not gonna ask anything like this. It's mostly gonna be multiple choice anyway. Are those your shoes on my bed?"

"They're yours. Your mom just sent them, remember!"

"When's she doing her next harvest?"

"I don't know. . . coupla weeks probably."

"Can we help?"

"Maybe."

"I hope she makes more squares again from the old stuff."

"Yeah, they're fire, bro. Getting baked on Christmas yummies!"

"Fucking awesome . . ."

"Dudes. For fuck's sake. Photorespiration is wasteful!"

"What?"

"That's the answer to the second part."

"What second part?"

"Of the question. Why are there different metabolisms?"

"Oh yeah. I knew that."

"Yeah, I knew that."

Chapter 14

Lydia was excited to have her own office. She puttered about in it. She hung pictures, bought stationary supplies and a small lightweight laptop. And she brought in a large engraved crystal egg to put on the windowsill. It had been a present years ago from Jordan and it was supposed to bring health, prosperity and safety. Lydia couldn't think of anything more appropriate for medical marijuana production.

A few days before, she'd mustered her courage and asked Cyrus, head of the CannRose-Medi board, if she mightn't be something more than just a silent president. Wasn't there something she could do? CannRose seemed to be shorthanded and behind schedule. Just a few days before she'd heard Caldwell ranting he had to paint trim in the administration section because it still hadn't been finished properly. Cyrus told her if she wanted to start painting and wallpapering that was her business but it wasn't anything he'd be caught dead doing. This glib response caused Lydia to stare at him with big disapproving blue eyes. So he cleared his throat and suggested she might consider public relations and maybe she could start putting together a company newsletter to spruce up internal relations too.

Lydia jumped at this. Why, it was perfect! She liked people. She liked talking. She could learn new things about communication and business relations, and she could sign up for seminars. She could travel to conferences. A new wind was under her sails. She had a feeling she was about to embark on the best time of her life. "Oh my gracious," she said to herself with a little smile.

Luther had rolled his eyes when he heard about this development. He didn't dislike the woman, it was more he considered her irreparably vapid. Cyrus had shrugged and laughed. "It's a weed company for Chrissake. She might turn out to be one of the intelligent ones." Luther almost smiled but reminded Cyrus that as the CEO of a weed company he didn't appreciate the aspersion. Cyrus strolled back to his office chuckling.

Caldwell was ambivalent about Lydia's increased capacity at CannRose. He wasn't convinced it would be in the company's best interests. But then he realized the state put the kibosh on advertising anyway, and once the whole business went recreational, he'd persuade Lydia to hire a top-notch marketing firm. The two of them had been on and off with their relationship over the last year. Caldwell thought if they were going to be working out of the same building, maybe it was time to cut the cord. When he approached Lydia with this notion, he half expected tears. He himself was close to crying.

"I see your point, Caldwell," Lydia said softly. She looked at her crystal egg and the rainbow it made on the windowsill. "You know what I think?" Caldwell was too moved to speak — she sounded so loving and calm. "I think it's very wise."

#

It was unclear at first how Caldwell got a copy of the DOH inspection report when nobody else at the CannRose grow facility, including Lazlo, appeared to have received one. Caldwell was in a foul mood over it, storming through the administration section. He dropped in on Lydia first.

"Have you seen this shit from the DOH?"

"What shit would that be, Caldwell?" Lydia was on her laptop registering for a communications conference in San Antonio, her old hometown. Absolutely nothing could dampen her high spirits.

"This inspection report. It's outrageous. Unfair. We're just getting started. I don't think that inspector had a clue."

"Her job must be difficult."

"What?"

"Inspections can't be very pleasant. Besides we're doing splendidly. Just a little slow. We'll catch up."

Caldwell lurched away and was growling and mumbling as he walked into Lazlo's office. Lazlo was buried in the plans for the waste-management facility. He was actually feeling encouraged that he might be able to get the county environment manger off his back soon.

"Have you seen this goddamn report?"

"What report?"

Caldwell held the papers up to Lazlo's nose.

"Oh Jesus. Wondered if something like that might show up. Why does everything have to be so official?"

The question distracted Caldwell only for a second or two. "What is with the damn pest control? Why do we have goddamn traps everywhere in plain sight?" he sputtered, looking at the report again. "Get those morons to do their job!" The morons were Lyle and Archie Cordoff, remarkably hairy brothers and the proprietors of Hullbrooke's own Pest Nixers — *Skuttlin' or crawlin', we do 'em all in.*

Still perusing the waste facility plans, Lazlo explained that the brothers, who'd done a fine job ridding the establishment of wasp nests and bat colonies, had advised against using bromine. They said it might keep the mice and rats more out of sight but they'd crawl to water once the poison took, and there "sure are a lotta vats around they could end up floatin' in." They were referring to the fertigation solutions. Caldwell groaned with frustration, but the brothers had a point.

He turned around and stalked the length of the admin section to Greg, who was on a ladder dusting the camera near the entrance. Caldwell came to a halt a couple of feet in front of him. He peered up at Greg and cleared his throat. "We need to hire somebody with at least a goddamn certificate or something, you know."

"Sure," said Greg, somewhat distracted. "No problem. How you doin' today, Caldwell?"

As Greg finished his dusting and clambered down the ladder, Caldwell noted the man had let his hair and beard grow even longer. Much more and he'd be casting material for a *Lord of the Rings* movie. That was all CannRose needed, hair in its products. He looked at Greg sharply. "Have you ever been clean shaven? It's got to be hot under that rug."

"Funny you should ask, Caldwell. Actually no, never. Can't shave. Look like a walkin' weepin' lesion if I did."

Caldwell winced at the image.

"So that's the inspection report there? Not exactly stellar I take it?" Greg sounded sympathetic.

Caldwell sighed. Then he told Greg how the report had been sent to Luther because Luther's name had been listed as the contact on the application a year ago. "A whole fucking year ago and more! We've come miles since then. We're a world away."

"He's still the CEO, isn't he?" Greg asked, genuinely not sure if there were changes in the executive he hadn't been apprised of yet.

"Yes," Caldwell muttered, annoyed at the reminder. It turned out Luther had been not only surprised when he received the report but also alarmed and dismayed by its contents. He'd immediately contacted Caldwell. Insults were exchanged, and Caldwell was damned if he was going to let Luther dump all the blame on him. Greg diffused Caldwell's pique somewhat by offering his impression of the disagreeable inspector. But then he added they might as well try to comply because it couldn't hurt.

"Then hire some veterans for God's sake!" Caldwell suggested. "They're trained. We'd look better if we had a few."

PART FOUR

Seedlings

Young ones, let eagerness guide. A luscious fervor. A lift and a rooting. Resilience in the flex, unswerving to the Way. Direction in resolve. Deep and down, the dark summons. The stretching and the feeding. A web for perpetuity. And up. Reaching. Straight to brightness, to the shine. Oh feed on this brilliant heart. Feed as the planets revolve and spin to it. Let us all be new with wonder and astonished by the rain.

from Cannto VI, *Cannabidadas*

Chapter 15

After the inspection report was somewhat digested at CannRose, Greg ran a onetime ad in the *Hullbrooke Gazette* and the *Lyston Chronicle* looking for horticulturalists or those with farming experience. This led to Cassie and Joe Milano, a couple who'd owned a nursery, recently sold it for a tidy profit and were looking around for a new challenge. Caldwell had sniffed at this move of course but he could tolerate them now he had his man from Colorado. He just offhandedly remarked, "They'll have a hell of a lot to learn." And so they did. After two and a half months at CannRose, they'd learned all sorts of things.

"Joey, did you just see what happened?" Cassie was giggling.

"I know! Sh-sh-sh."

Caldwell stormed by them, red-faced and grim. He was uncharacteristically silent until he saw Lazlo and Lydia standing by the production office. "Luther had no right!" he yelled at them.

Lydia shrugged and shook her head. Lazlo said in an uncharacteristically raised voice, "You tried. It's not your fault the rehab didn't stick!"

"Who was the snitch?" Caldwell screamed. "My boy deserves another chance."

"Caldwell, it was on the vault video . . ." Lazlo was shaking his head too now.

Joe pulled Cassie into the hallway out of sight and earshot. "I didn't know there was kief in the vault."

"What is it . . . like thirty percent THC?"

"Forty to fifty, honey."

"And after stealing it he just leaves it sitting in the front seat of his DayGlo orange convertible?" Cassie erupted with a snort. Reflexively her hand shot up to cover her mouth and nose. Her gray eyes glistened and she squinted as she tried to control her giggles.

"I am so glad to see the end of that arrogant little cokehead. How could they even think of making him a production manager? He couldn't even schedule a lunch date let alone a production cycle."

"You can send your boy to rehab but you can't fix rotten stupid," Cassie said, calming down and clearing her throat.

"I've never seen anybody get escorted out of a building like that." Joe was laughing now.

"Well, he couldn't weigh very much. He's mostly leather and gold jewelry."

"He was so fucked up, he thought they were taking him to a nightclub."

#

That evening after they'd put the kids to bed, Cassie and Joe sat on the porch having a few beers.

"I can't believe they spent all that money and have all that equipment to recreate the outdoors," Cassie said. "I'm sure the plants would be happier in a greenhouse."

"Well, honey, welcome to the new crazy! And it's paying the bills!"

"Seriously, Joe, everything works at cross purposes in that place!" Cassie swished her head back and forth. The bugs were starting to come out in force and her flying auburn curls deterred them somewhat.

"On the bright side, at least they got rid of one problem today." Joe, who had a buzz cut, merely swatted at the bugs from time to time.

"I mean, why would they add peat to everything if they're worried about fungus and mildew? I've told them the stuff breeds it. And why won't they use the soil sterilizer?"

"You're preachin' to the choir here."

"And why starve the plants for such a long time?" Cassie stared at the lilacs that bordered one side of the porch as if they might provide some answer.

"Maybe, just 'cause they're just so full of manure themselves, honey, they can't imagine the plants might need some."

Cassie and Joe didn't meet until college though they had both grown up in the area. Joe had even been to the garden center Cassie's dad owned, Caldor's Nursery, on the outskirts of Lyston, but he didn't remember ever seeing her there. She told him he wouldn't have noticed her — she was a late bloomer. Given their experience and previous success running a greenhouse and gardening center for twelve years, they assumed they would play a pivotal role in the marijuana production at CannRose-Medi. They just hadn't bargained on Damian, the master grower, aka Goldilocks.

"Goldilocks looks like a skeleton. No wonder he starves the plants. You know what I'm going to do?" Cassie shook her curls again.

"Wouldn't want to guess . . ."

"I'm going to talk to folks in Colorado myself. And California, Oregon and Washington and up in Canada, all those BC Bud people. I bet some of them would be more than happy to share their growing tips and recipes. And all their pot lore."

"I bet some would, Cas. Guys you showed me on YouTube looked real friendly."

"Not like Mr. Fort Knox Goldilocks. It's like he's some undercover agent or something. Everything's such a *big* secret." Cassie's eyes followed a mosquito that was buzzing around Joe's leg.

"Wonder how much illegal shit he did? Must be a habit he picked up. You know, back in the day. Had to keep quiet about everything."

"Seriously? I think he's just a dork. Plain and simple." Cassie leaned over and caught the mosquito that was just about to land on Joe's knee.

Joe laughed. "He doesn't like us, you know."

"The feeling's mutual." She leaned back against the porch railing. "You know what? I bet the agricultural colleges are going to get in on this too."

"Probably."

"We could get ourselves so schooled in this situation we'll be indispensable any way you look at it. We'll beat this weed game."

"I like your ambition, honey."

"Let's start with seeds."

"Your Goldilocks's latest seed crop looks like shit, by the way."

"The ones he put in the West Pod when he could have used the spare nursery?" Cassie took a swallow of beer.

"Everything in that pod looks half dead."

"Everything everywhere looks like crap. Have we even had a harvest yet?"

"Two. But one had to be tossed."

"I can't remember. We've thrown so much out."

"You know Lazlo showed me the plans for the waste-management facility?" A knowing smile spread over Joe's face. "Talk about overkill. He's putting in a rotator."

"Well the state won't allow windrows with weed, Joey. Can't do anything outside."

"It's amazing though how Lazlo sells Caldwell on all the junk. I mean I'm no contractor but it's pretty clear he's overbuilding on the incidentals and cutting corners on crucial stuff. You can buy industrial composters already put together. Get a guarantee, regular servicing. Lazlo's gonna have one built from scratch. Says it's cheaper and I'm betting on a scam. I'm betting he's skimming big time on that one."

"You think? I have to say he does kind of creep me out."

"It's the voice, honey." Joe sized up the mosquito feeding on his arm. "He's got court cases you know. A couple of big lawsuits against him. But at CannRose he's untouchable," he said, squashing the bug. Cassie grimaced as he brushed the blood and insect parts away. "It's all in the family," Joe said, looking up at her. "Come to think of it, maybe our friend Caldwell is in on the scam too. Who knows what deals they've made."

Cassie sat back and stared at her bottle of beer for a while. Then she looked up at Joe, and with the sound of defeat seeping into her voice, said, "We're being undermined every step of the way. You know that. Goldilocks and Caldwell come and do stuff when we're not around. Including screwing with the nutrients."

"I heard Caldwell referring to us as *newbies* again."

"Why bother calling us horticulture specialists then? God! I can't stand Caldwell either."

"If they want to shoot themselves in the foot, honey, that's not our problem."

"But we're the experts, Joey! And we're responsible, aren't we?"

"They haven't complained about us so far. Besides they can't. Everything's on video."

"God bless surveillance!"

Joe guffawed. "Wonder how much the surveillance system cost? Double what it should, you reckon?"

"I think Greg was likely in charge of that purchase."

"You're probably right. Maybe only a twenty-five-percent markup."

"Maybe no markup. He seems okay."

"For an ex-cop."

Cassie yawned and stretched before reaching for her beer again. "So what's his connection with those three new kids?"

"I don't know. One's his nephew I think."

"Where'd they come from though? I barely understand what they're saying and I swear they're high all the time."

"Honey, I don't think they're high — well sometimes they are — but mostly I think they just got their own little club there. They're still in their last co-op, you know. All registered users too. Chronic pain."

"Really."

"Yeah. Sports injuries. Skateboard accidents."

"That's perfect." Cassie took a final swig of her beer and threw the bottle across the yard so it spun end over end and landed among the tulips. She turned to Joe with a grin. "So you think they ever get a full day's work out of them?"

Joe smiled. He liked when she did unruly things like that. "They'll do anything you ask, you know. They're really good banana hunters too." Bananas were the undesirable male flowers that popped up from time to time on rogue, actually rather stressed plants that went *hermie*. Plants riddled with them usually got destroyed altogether. "You know they took the fast-track hort certificate program just so they could work here."

"Seriously? That's not easy."

"There you go. See, there's focus, commitment and hidden brains."

"Really hidden."

Chapter 16

Petra's mother was alternately irritated and saddened by her daughter's life. Petra hadn't flourished. As a little girl, she showed so much promise. Now she was divorced and childless, her career abandoned. She'd be hitting menopause any day and she was living with her mother, for crying out loud.

When Doreen heard through a friend that CannRose-Medi, only a fifteen-minute drive away, was looking for someone with some real plant science, she immediately began pestering her daughter about it. It had led to a great deal of bickering, but ultimately Doreen had prevailed. Petra promised to get in touch with the company.

When Petra did finally make the call, the CannRose-Medi executives and Caldwell could hardly believe their luck. Seemingly out of nowhere came a real plant scientist with a PhD — and credibility. She'd been faculty or something at an Ivy League university, she'd had a job with an equally respectable global company and she'd published dozens of research articles, even if she was never the main author. What did that matter? The research was over their heads anyway.

Caldwell, Lazlo and Greg sat across the table beaming at her during the interview. Luther was on the conference phone. She was hired on the spot in the space of about fifteen minutes. She could have made up everything and they'd be none the wiser. As it was she tried pointing out to them that her training and background did not really include much about cultivation or anything directly connected to plant production. And similarly her work history regarding plants was some time ago, had focused on lipids rather than secondary metabolites. It might take a little time to get up to speed. They didn't seem to care. In fact Petra wondered if they even knew what she was talking about. But they would build a lab they said, to her specifications. And to speed things up, they could bring in something modular and just make the necessary alterations. So Petra found herself nodding at them, more wide-eyed than she'd imagined she could be.

"I had such a good feeling about her, right from the start," Caldwell would later tell prospective investors as he waltzed them into her lab. As if he was privy to some otherworldly appraisal that trumped her resumé.

Petra drove back home very slowly after the interview and noticed anxiety creeping into her belly that she hadn't felt in a while. Who were these people? As she came in the door and met up with her mother, who'd gotten out of bed for the occasion and was hovering and smiling expectantly, she sighed. "Mom, I have no idea what I've just gotten myself into."

Her mother clapped her hands delightedly and gave her a hug. Doreen had taken to hugging everyone whenever she could. "Wonderful! I'm sure it will be fine!" She hung on to Petra for a good while.

"You do realize this is pot we're talking about? As is in dope, drugs?"

Her mother shrugged. "Pot, schmot. Who cares? They need you. Besides things are changing."

Petra stared at her mother. "I'm a card-carrying alcoholic, Mom. Nothing changes about that."

"Oh, honey. You're no alcoholic. You just had a rough time."

"Mother. Let's not start up again."

"Fine. You're an alcoholic. But I don't see what it has to do with the job."

Petra rolled her eyes.

"Well you don't drink around me," Doreen said. "Certainly not to any state of drunkenness. I don't see why you'd suddenly start drinking around them."

Petra looked at her mother with a mixture of frustration and amusement. "The nature of an addicted personality, Mother, one more time, is you tend to switch one activity or substance for another."

"So?"

"So what if I develop an addiction to pot?"

"Well, from what I hear, it won't take out your liver." Her mother smiled.

"Right." Petra went to the kitchen to make some tea.

"You know," her mother called after her, "maybe medical pot could do something for me too! I hear it's gaining popularity among the brittle and moderately senile."

Chapter 17

In Flower Room II, which still needed some finish, the coconut coir and peaty amendment were being unpacked and mixed in troughs to wait. The three young men worked slowly but diligently along the rows of tables, measuring out quantities and stirring with care. In a day or two, the seedlings in their delicate biodegradable three-inch pots would be spaced perfectly in rows and lowered into the mixture, giving the troughs order and great purpose.

"Bro, this is the best job ever."

"How would you know? It's the only job you ever had. And we're still on co-op."

"What's with you?"

"Yeah. Salty boy."

"Dad's pissed."

"Your dad's always pissed."

"This time he's really pissed."

"Why?"

"He says I tricked him into signing the waiver."

"What waiver?"

"The liability waiver."

"Bro, so what? He signed it. He can't unsign it!"

"Yeah. Who cares? You're gonna be eighteen next month anyway."

"He's taking the car. So how will we get here?"

"Maybe there's a bus."

"Greg can give us rides."

"And Lazlo's son."

"What's his name?"

"Gus."

"Yeah. Gus. He could bring us."

"Hey. Did you just see that!"

"What?"

"I didn't see anything."

"Something just jumped in that tray."

"What tray?"

"That one."

"I don't see anything."

"Over there. Something jumped again. There's another one."

"We should get a jar."

"They're thrips!"

"Dude, there's no plants yet. They're springtails."

"I think they're thrips."

"They're springtails."

"We should tell Damian."

"He's in Colorado."

"No, he's been here all week. I saw him this morning."

"Where?"

"Lydia's office, with Caldwell."

"What were you doing in the front?"

"They have granola bars."

"My grampy eats granola bars."

"Brobes. There's like a lot of bugs in this tray. It's like . . . active."

"I'm getting a jar."

"Maybe we should tell Cassie. She's next door."

"Don't tell Cassie."

"Yeah, bro. You'll upset her again."

"You think she likes us?"

Chapter 18

Alice checked the time. Almost ten minutes past three. Caldwell had wanted to see the dispensary in the city and now he was late. It was very clear to Alice that he didn't trust her or Luther to set things up to have customer appeal. Alice figured the clientele would want the usual displays you'd see in any store, but mostly they'd need to talk to somebody who could help them go through the trial-and-error process. Finding the appropriate product could take time.

Alice had looked up a couple of her old school friends who were now living in California. They had experience with medical marijuana. They said there was certainly a long way to go and a lot of research needed, but many things about cannabis were promising. Spectacular even, especially with seizures in children. Very few undesirable side effects, and if there were some they tended to be ones the sufferer might not mind. Like euphoria. Alice had always found the listing of euphoria as an adverse reaction rather amusing. Lord knows the FDA wouldn't want people to be too happy now would they? One of her friends also brought up the problem of obesity. Everybody knows pot can give you the munchies. And an already obese person could actually add to their problems by gaining weight. On the other hand, tetrahydrocannabivarin, a naturally occurring analog of the almighty THC and found significantly in some marijuana strains, was an appetite suppressant and showed promise in obesity treatments.

Back home in the city, Alice already had several potential clients and a number of people with a range of problems who were interested in trying marijuana. If the CannRose-Medi grow facility could get its act together and provide her with something to sell, she figured the two dispensaries would do well. As it was, they just sat looking discreet — which they were supposed to according to the regulations — but essentially useless, which was not according to regulations. CannRose still hadn't even hired a chemist or extraction technician to get the derivatives happening. If the grow facility didn't deliver by the revised state deadline, CannRose-Medi might have to cease operations altogether.

It was frustrating. People were buying off the street. One elderly woman had terrible arthritis and got her supply from her nephew who was selling anything and everything. Just a matter of time before the law caught up to him and his aunt too. According to local gossip he gave his aunt a one-hundred-percent discount and she baked laced cookies and brownies for him in return. They were a big hit. Alice also heard that the father of an autistic boy was bringing oil across state lines. He worried about being arrested on one of these drug runs or that the stock of that particular oil would run out. It was the only thing that had helped his boy. The state-approved oils and tinctures were still a few months away, though Alice had heard one dispensary was way ahead in that regard. They'd have something within the month. Alice hoped it might work for that autistic child even if she wasn't the one selling it.

The neighborhood case that really disturbed her though was a young immigrant family. The father looked anxious and aged beyond his years and the wife seemed chronically exhausted. They had a baby, a five-year-old and a very sick toddler. The toddler was much like the Palmers' child, the one she'd helped out years ago. The little girl in this family had over a hundred seizures a day. At three she hadn't developed much past a baby and could barely sit up. The woman had the child strapped into a stroller and often brought her into the drugstore.

"Ma'am, you think pot help my baby?"

"Maybe. I think it could," Alice said.

"But they take my husband in jail. They send us back. Yes?"

"You have to get the child registered. Then you can buy it for her."

"Ma'am, where I can buy this?"

"You have to go to a doctor."

"Doctor first," the woman said.

"Yes. Doctor first. The doctor can register your child."

"But city social worker say we go in jail."

Alice took her time explaining about the state dispensaries and how the system would work. She even let the woman know that she would be involved with one of the dispensaries in the city and could help her once it was up and running. After a while and a few smiles at her own confusion, the woman finally appeared to understand. She looked hopeful for a few moments. Then she asked how much it would cost. Alice told her what CannRose would be charging and the woman's face fell and she slowly shook her head. Alice said she would give the woman a discount and she would also ask the people who owned CannRose to lower the price even more for her. Alice even told her that once she got registered she could grow her own plants right away. "That might be much cheaper."

"Ah!" the woman's eyes lit up. "I can grow in garden! In Paint Patches!"

"No!" Alice had nearly jumped out of her chair at this suggestion. She envisioned the DEA arriving like grim reapers in black SUVs ripping everything out of the raised beds. "No. No pot in that garden," Alice said with panic in her voice. "You grow the pot at home. Inside the house."

"Grow inside house? Not smart. Better is garden."

"No!" Alice said. "You could land in jail if you grow in Paint Patches."

"Okay." The woman looked exhausted again. Alice was exhausted by that time too. The toddler started having another seizure and so the woman quickly left.

That had all happened four months ago and Alice felt uncomfortable every time the woman came into the store now because she still didn't have any good news for her.

Alice checked the time again. If Caldwell didn't show up in the next five minutes she was leaving. Alice found Caldwell's concerns insulting. It wasn't as if she had no experience. The way she saw it, she sure as hell had a lot more than Caldwell. In fact she couldn't make out what Caldwell's background was and she was beginning to think it maybe wasn't much. Luther had intimated Caldwell was good at the legwork . . . and footwork too — "Just humor him," Luther had suggested. But Alice wasn't about to waste more of her day humoring anybody. Especially somebody who talked that much and said so little. Alice figured Caldwell's behavior would be crazy-making if you had to deal with him for any length of time. She wondered if Lydia was damaged from having lived with the man for two years or if she was just naturally harebrained. Still, Alice quite liked Lydia. She'd never heard her say a harsh word about anybody or to anybody even during the most fractious of discussions. And that was a rare thing.

Alice was about to leave when she saw Caldwell huffing up the street.

"You didn't tell me Baron Street had an east *and* a west," he said. "I've been running for ten blocks."

Alice had no intention of apologizing. Baron Street West was residential. You'd have to be clueless to expect a storefront to pop up suddenly. "I did say what side of the overpass it was on and two blocks past the Episcopalian church. That steeple is pretty hard to miss from the parkway."

"I didn't come by the parkway. I met with an old friend for lunch down at the harbor."

Alice wasn't interested in his social life. "Well. It's a good thing you found the place. I was going to leave. I have another appointment so I only have about ten minutes. Rush hour starts early on Fridays. I hope ten minutes is enough for you."

Caldwell smiled faintly. He felt somewhat stripped by this woman. It was as if she'd been privy to any doubts he'd ever had about himself and threw them back at him one by one — so Caldwell was grateful for the time restriction. "Ten minutes should be more than enough, Alice. A customer will form their impression within the first ten seconds. Did you know that?"

"Well, these are sick people coming in here, Caldwell. It might take them a little longer."

Alice opened the first door. There was a bulletproof reinforced-glass fishbowl lobby, similar to the one at the grow facility, with a second locked door into the dispensary. Customers would be buzzed in from the lobby at the discretion of the security attendant or the dispensary staff. Alice unlocked the second door, walked across the room to the counter at the back, reached underneath and turned on the lights.

Caldwell looked around. There were glass cases — empty at the moment of course — arranged attractively enough in a semicircle.

The room was a very subdued sage green, almost gray, and the polished hardwood floor a deep amber. There was a small sign with the company logo suspended over the counter. The logo looked a little faded. Caldwell suspected it had been purposely toned down.

The overall effect of the room was conservative, and Caldwell immediately felt it lacked a level of design that would impress customers. Initially he'd proposed the dispensaries adopt the same look as the grow facility but he'd been overruled. It was ridiculous. The administrative section in Hullbrooke was considered striking and Caldwell was very proud of the part he'd played in its design. He felt the dispensaries should be like satellites to the mother ship. Or like clones. Of course! The dispensaries should be clones of the grow facility. Each one flowering to maturity. It made perfect sense to him, and the notion could have been a vital aspect of the branding. It would speak to the powerful proliferation and multiple uses of marijuana as a modern remedy. CannRose wasn't just selling marijuana to the sick and ailing. It was selling ideas. Ideas that made people's lives better. After another intense gaze around the room he decided to take a risk in his dealings with Alice. "It's a little bland," he ventured.

"Bland?"

"Yes. Bland."

"And do you think that could cause a problem of some sort?"

Caldwell saw her question as a sign of progress. She was asking for his expertise, so he continued, "If we want our customers to keep coming back, Alice, I think we need to be bold. Make a strong impression."

"I agree," said Alice.

"You do? Well then. I'd say we need to punch this place up a little."

"Yes, we certainly do."

"I'm delighted to hear that," said Caldwell and he was. Finally they were on the same page, connecting on a matter Caldwell knew had significant consequences for any company. "I have an idea or two already," he said.

"So do I," Alice said, staring intently at the glass case in front of her. "You know what I think would really, as you put it, *punch this place up?*"

"What?" Caldwell was truly curious.

Alice took a deep breath, then looked Caldwell in the eyes and leaned in with such a steely and determined expression it sent a little shiver down his back. Her voice was almost a whisper, and corrosive, like freshly spilled acid. "Product!" she said and gave a nod. "Having some product to sell would *really* impress. Possibly more than anything, don't you think, Caldwell? In fact I can't imagine anything more likely to keep customers coming back than actually having something *to buy*."

Caldwell recoiled. It was no use explaining to Alice why delivery of the product was delayed. It was hardly his fault. But she was turning it into his fault. "That goes without saying," Caldwell replied politely. He was resolved to stay cool.

"I'm not so sure," Alice said. "It's often surprising to find out what flies below people's radar. Anyway I have to go, Caldwell, or I'll be late. If you have genuine concerns you should take them up with Luther. He hired the designers." She ushered Caldwell out and locked up the dispensary again. She bade him a good afternoon, a safe drive back and then walked away as quickly as she could.

Alice was livid. Caldwell was an even bigger idiot than she'd originally thought. *Punch the place up.* Punch him up! And she was relying on *him* to supply the dispensaries. From the conference calls she'd been on it was clear Caldwell had an opinion on everything going on at that facility, and she'd witnessed the tantrums in meetings when he didn't get his own way. Probably drove everybody nuts and caused way more problems than he solved. She'd read the DOH report from the first inspection too. It was a disaster. He'd blamed it on the clueless and overzealous teenage inspector who was just trying to score points in her department. The same inspector had shown up at the dispensary. Alice hadn't liked the young woman, but she was organized and very efficient. And she couldn't find any problems with Alice's set-up. In fact Ms. Ligner had even asked Alice a few questions about where she thought the industry might go, and whether Alice really thought marijuana had any medicinal value or if it was all just something that would disappear as quickly as it had come about. Alice told her it had been a medicine for a few thousand years, so she wasn't sure how quickly it might disappear. Maybe along with the human race itself. Alice almost felt sorry for the young woman. She seemed to be on a mission.

As for Caldwell, the sooner somebody got rid of him the better.

Chapter 19

Ernie couldn't help noticing how the revolving door of employees, mostly the friends and relatives of those in charge, were often only remarkable for their incompetence and unsuitability. And if he was honest he had to admit he was part of the larger family himself. His own mother was old Hullbrooke stock and had been Lazlo's babysitter at some point. Connections. Connections. They were clearly a mixed blessing. It was curious how Ernie managed to hang on so well. Keeping his head down, looking busy and being as low on the totem pole as he could had no doubt been key. That and avoiding Caldwell as much as possible at the facility — Caldwell was very congenial with a beer in hand at Chelsea's, especially if you didn't mind hearing his philosophies and predictions for the marijuana industry. When he learned through the grapevine about Ernie's food and cooking sideline, Caldwell suggested Ernie start thinking about managing the edibles division for CannRose. "It's only a matter of time. The state has to wake up eventually." But at work Caldwell found faults and inadequacies that enraged him and baffled everyone else. Plus he was prone to finger-pointing. Ernie was pretty sure the last thing he'd ever want to do was head up the edibles division at CannRose.

Lazlo's son Gus had recently taken over as the third production manager at CannRose. Ernie couldn't imagine a worse job. Even though the bar was so low to the ground at that point a person would trip over it before seeing it, there was a pile of manure just beyond the bar that one would inevitably land in. Caldwell was bound to find fault with anyone who took the job after his precious godson had been fired. Never mind Caldwell had personally forked out for the best rehab money could buy and the scrawny little cokehead was utterly incorrigible and unrepentant; Caldwell was still deeply wounded by what he saw as the high-handed and cruel dismissal of the young man.

Gus was pretty much the polar opposite of Caldwell's godson. He weighed a few hundred pounds for starters. Sweat suits, gray, navy or black, were his daily attire, though often he would mix rather than match. He drove a little Ford Ranger pickup and was unhurried in his movements. He took his time about everything, and Ernie learned as he got to know him that it was because he liked to understand things before proceeding with action. He was stubborn too.

He'd been working from time to time for his dad, running errands and generally assisting in administration as the facility was being renovated. As soon as cultivation began, he'd done odd jobs with Damian, Cassie and Joe. The plants ruled after all. He'd also periodically worked with Ernie just tidying up, pushing brooms and Shop-Vacs. *He's not a bad choice*, Ernie thought, *if you have to pick somebody from the family*. But there it was again, the family.

Over various conversations, Ernie learned that Gus regarded Caldwell with some suspicion. It wasn't that Caldwell was a con. Not at all. That was perfectly acceptable, especially if you had to do business in places like Hullbrooke. A person has a right to make a living. No, it was because of where Caldwell's brain went. "Head in the clouds," Gus had said with a note of disdain. "Citified too. Never does anybody any good. They just end up looking like idiots." Gus did admit that Caldwell's original goal of building a commercial marijuana company was a good one, but still, he was too full of bullshit. Gus would overlook it though, he told Ernie. The job was a step up and they were going to pay him very well. Also he'd get to have his own office.

#

Ernie usually got to work before anybody else. When he showed up for his shift one Friday morning, he sensed something was off. The production wing felt slightly more humid than usual, and it was fairly humid to begin with. It was when he got in the air shower and saw the water coming in under the door that he got alarmed. He'd already pushed the button. Despite the word *shower*, it was a large piece of equipment specifically designed for dry operation. He briefly pictured himself hurled into the air by God knows how many volts sizzling his butt and frying his bones while his eye patch melted onto his wandering eyeball. Luckily the blast of air dried the sweat that was profusely oozing from his forehead. When he stepped out of the air shower, he could see water pouring into the hallway from under the doors of two flower rooms and he could hear water running in the West Mother Pod.

He opened the door to the flower room that had plants in it. It was like the water show in Las Vegas. Plumes were spraying from the ceiling sprinkler system, great spinning arches of droplets and mist. The sprinklers were for fires not plants. Where was the fire? And then Ernie noticed the pipes for the fertigation system, lower down by the plants. There were three or four valves dotted around the room, burst or something, spewing like the Tivoli fountains, and the tables had water and fertilizer solution pouring off them like Niagara. Many plants were toppled over, floating away, and some of were even shooting the falls. Ernie was so astonished he just stood there, immobilized. Greg came racing in after a few moments, having seen the disaster on the surveillance monitors.

"What the fuck! Any idea where the turnoffs are?"

Ernie was startled out of his trance. "Um, I know where the main is."

"Might be a good idea . . ."

And then Ernie was running for the mechanical room. He slipped in the water in the hallway and came crashing down, nearly putting his head through the door of the air shower. "Shit!" He was soaked now. His head was bruised and his eye patch askew. He got himself slowly to his feet, straightened the patch and then met up with Gus, who was coming the opposite way through the air shower.

"It's a disaster in there," Ernie said, a soggy strand of hair lifting off his forehead. Gus had pushed the button already, and Ernie couldn't get out now until the shower of air was finished and the other door automatically unlocked.

Gus looked at Ernie in his wet scrubs, then he noticed the water at his feet. He looked out the opposite glass door to the flooding in the hallway and then briefly back at Ernie, somewhat stricken. "Fuck," he said in a whisper.

"I'm going to turn off the main."

Gus nodded and then he said, "Might not do any good depending where it's coming from." Then Gus seemed to mentally vacate the situation, his attention riveted to the air rushing at his face.

Within a half hour, everyone scheduled to work had arrived. Cassie began charging around leading brigades to move plants out of the flood waters. Joe got busy with Gus and one of the construction guys still on site to figure out the water problems. Ernie headed up the water removal and Lily from admin was sent over to Gerry's Rent-All to see if he had any extra wet vacs on hand. And Damian was just wandering around with enlarged pupils muttering incoherently about "the wrath of God, man" and "one fucking thing after another."

When Caldwell showed up hours later, he was no help either. People were still mopping up and cleaning off the tables and troughs in the plant rooms. He started yelling at everybody just as a matter of course. "This is not a swamp, people! We don't need to singlehandedly restore the Everglades." Mostly he was blaming Lazlo for the problem, and Gus was used to this. The floor drains were plugged, for example, because Lazlo hadn't thought to thoroughly test them before construction, or maybe there was something about the construction that had plugged them. But when the septic and drain company that was supposed to be there by lunchtime didn't show up, Caldwell lit into Gus.

"Why the hell aren't they here? Didn't you impress upon them the urgency of the situation? Or did the urgency escape you?"

"I told them. Most of the water's vacuumed up anyway."

"Right, just like that. Same monotone. The old Hullbrooke sewer-and-manure banter. *You boys got a minute for us?* Very effective. You know you need to pick up the slack here."

"They were the first people I called." Gus folded his arms and shifted his considerable weight to one hip.

"And was that before you called your father? Or did you call your mommy instead? You know because she's so understanding — *My boy's poor flat feet* — Your feet. Your flab. The two are connected you know!"

If it had been Ernie being spoken to that way he was pretty sure he'd have put his mop down and thrown the bucket of dirty water all over Caldwell's designer jacket and shirt. But Gus just stood there for a second, then shrugged and walked away. Maybe the young man was just inured to it, or his notion of Caldwell saw him through. Maybe both. Whatever it was, Ernie was impressed with the refusal to engage. Very impressed. Gus probably was the right man for the job, even if he was family.

Interestingly, the advantage of having no relationship and no familiarity was also in evidence that day. As per Caldwell's wishes, Greg had finally hired a war vet. The young fellow started just that week and was told to look after purchasing and supplies, though because of the flood he was pitching in and cleaning along with everybody else. In spite of all the chaos, Caldwell's demeanor spun a hundred and eighty degrees when he met Ray, the recently hired veteran. He welcomed him so warmly and professionally you'd think Ray was worth millions and Caldwell had studied at the priciest business schools. Ernie wondered how long that would last.

Ray's presence made Ernie particularly glad he'd corrected anyone at CannRose who'd assumed he himself had been a veteran. Even though he'd gotten quite comfortable with the notion in his panhandling days, it would have been nerve-racking keeping up the pretense with the real deal wandering around. Façades could only be maintained by the supremely talented.

PART FIVE

Mothers

Oh Monsters, dispense with the smiling. Button up the praises.
Roast the cloying sentiment. Give us a break. Mostly there is no
choice. We stay. Rooted. Undeterred in the grips of desire. One
onslaught after another and we're still churning them out.
Decreasing the vigor, slamming the joy. But go ahead. Take another
slice. Revel in the comfort of uncertain sorrows. We stay all giving
until we've had it. As if you cared. We've heard everything by now.
It's made no difference. A word though. Do not miss the entry as the
earth waits spinning in grace and primordial slime. The thin film of
life edged like a sword will kill you. And it's a gift. You're welcome.

from Cannto III, *Cannabidadas*

Chapter 20

Luther, lawyer and junior partner about-to-be marijuana multi-millionaire, was speeding again. He kept checking his rearview to make sure he hadn't attracted any police attention. It was just going on nine o'clock and he'd had to get up in the dark without waking his wife to make this little foray into the hinterlands. He wanted a face-to-face with Caldwell and Lazlo. Alice too, if she could make it, although all she did of late was pester him about hiring somebody to get the oils and extracts happening. Of course Lydia would be there and whatever inane nonsense she might come up with would be anyone's guess. God knows perfect bone structure and azure-blue eyes could never make up for the tapioca between her ears. But Luther couldn't afford to dwell on the president's eccentricities. He was anxious. Cyrus, his old bugger of a boss, was questioning his preliminary research regarding the start-up and he'd heard the old accountant Malcolm was vexed too. In fact the old accountant was *particularly* vexed. The grow facility had gone over budget by more than eighty percent and it wasn't even finished.

Construction had not only been running on forever but also into endless snags. Roof rot, fraying asbestos, mice, fungus-ridden bats. It also struck Luther that possibly shoddy materials and shoddy workmanship were at play. Lazlo, with his dubious contractor origins, was pinning the blame on suppliers and subcontractors. He also pointed at Caldwell's insistence that they implement as much high-tech growing apparatus as they possibly could. They'd installed so much expensive lighting, Luther figured they could have done up a major opera house cheaper. The energy costs were breathtaking already and they were far from running at capacity.

Then there were the storefront dispensaries. The one in the city was ready but for some reason the one in Lyston was on hold. Luther wanted to know why. Of course there was nothing to sell yet anyway. Luther had heard the crops had had several false starts, whatever the hell that meant. And as for when finished product could be expected? He couldn't get a straight answer out of Caldwell.

It was coming down to the wire. CannRose had only a month or so left to produce something sellable. The state registration would wait for no man, woman, child, dysfunctional technology or uppity vegetation. They'd already extended the deadline once. Companies unable to meet this new deadline would forfeit their registration. Given the law firm's involvement, this would mean litigation and all manner of lawsuits that the firm already excelled at anyway. Still, actions against the state would be a waste of time and a further distraction. Luther was determined to avoid this.

This was only Luther's second visit to the grow facility. The last time he'd seen it work had barely started on the administration section. In the face of Caldwell's strident claims of expertise, the executives had acquiesced to the notion it was better to leave people to do their jobs. It was how both firms were run anyway. Bad move. They should have implemented restrictions. Severe ones. Lydia and her daft generosity! Caldwell should never have been allowed so much control.

Luther turned his Porsche into the parking lot and drove straight into mud. Recent rains had transformed the lot into a series of large potholes filled with clayish muck. This place was a disaster. You'd think a paved parking lot would be a given. Luther cursed quietly to himself and grabbed his laptop. As he opened the car door, Caldwell's furry head came into view.

"Luther, your timing couldn't be better! I was just about to give a tour here to Bob Stensen. You know Bob?"

How the fuck would he know Bob? How did Caldwell function with all these improbabilities floating through his head? "No, I don't believe we've met," said Luther, smiling tightly and exiting the car. He scraped the mud off his shoes on a stray rock.

"Luther is our legal mover and shaker, and CannRose's illustrious CEO," Caldwell exclaimed.

Luther extended a hand to Bob Stensen, who grabbed it in a vice-like grip. He had a fleshy mitt the size of a dinner plate and gave Luther the most excruciatingly painful handshake he'd ever experienced. Fucking hell. Luther quietly gasped and wished Bob all manner of catastrophe.

"Well, Bob here is from Idaho and he's very interested in our technology. Isn't that so, Bob?"

"Yes. I hear you have a top-of-the-line facility!"

It could have been a breeze but Luther saw the hair on Caldwell's head puff up even higher at this suggestion.

"We certainly do, Bob," Caldwell said. "We certainly do. Luther, Bob here is looking to invest in Emerald Air, the specialty HVAC supplier."

"I see," said Luther, massaging his fingers.

"Since Idaho still won't allow even medical marijuana to any extent, Bob is very wisely" — Caldwell nodded and smiled at Bob with unmistakable admiration — "looking to put his money in the support side of the industry. With luck of course, his investments stay clear of the state and any FDA or DEA nonsense. Lets him go nationwide. Maybe we should think about that too, Luther. It's a very smart approach." And he smiled again at Bob, who grinned back.

"Let's just get this place up and running first," said Luther, squinting at the building in front of him, a grim industrial box full of shortcuts from the 1980s. What were the old geezers Malcolm and Cyrus thinking?

"Why, Luther, we are up and running! With the best of them too!" Caldwell said this jovially, again smiling at Bob, but when he turned and caught Luther's eye, he scowled. Luther ignored him. He couldn't have been less interested in Caldwell's show for this midwestern boob.

Caldwell began in an even louder voice, "Did you know that Emerald sent Bob here to showcase their technology? That's how we're looking in the industry these days, Luther. A showcase facility."

"I'm really excited to see it," said Bob.

"Well we're just delighted you came," said Caldwell. "And we'll be more than happy to answer any questions." Caldwell turned toward the building and took a deep breath of the skunky stink emanating from it. He strode across the muddy parking lot as if it were a red carpet. Luther and Bob followed more gingerly, weaving their way around the worst of the puddles. Caldwell pressed the door buzzer and yelled into the two-way speaker. After a few seconds the door clicked to let them in.

They walked into a fishbowl of sorts. There was floor-to-ceiling glass on all three sides and another electronic lock on the glass door directly ahead of them. Beyond that, a woman was sitting at a desk and to the right of her, adjoining the entrance, was another much larger elevated fishbowl of a room. In it sat the big red-bearded security director, staring at his flat screens. He was head of HR now too because Lazlo was hopeless at it. The security director turned and waved at them. The glass door in front of them buzzed and Caldwell ushered the two men in.

"We have to have the highest level of security here, Bob. The criminal element is always a present danger. Greg there has extensive background in policing and security forces. He was even with the FBI for a time. Isn't that right, Luther?"

"Yes." Luther was still wiping mud off his shoes. "Early in his career, I believe."

"Well, our motto, Bob, is that you can't be too secure."

"I see you have a lot of cameras," Bob said, staring up at a little shiny black sphere attached to the corner of the ceiling.

"Sixty-two, Bob. All motion activated and recording all activities everywhere in the facility as we breathe."

"That's very impressive."

"You'll be even more impressed by our production processes." Caldwell looked into the distance and then raised his arms as if to caress a great imaginary sphere. "I like to think of this facility as the mother ship, Bob. We're charting new territory here, boldly going where no one has gone in terms of automation, efficiency and quality marijuana. It's the heart of the company. It's where everything, every impact that we have on the health of patients in this state, begins. This is where we grow the plants. It's where the magic happens, Bob."

Caldwell made a grand sweep of his arm encompassing the open-concept workspaces and the ceiling with its hanging light arrays. "As you can see this area is all administrative. We'll come back later and I'll point out the innovative office features. But I know what you came here for, Bob. We should get right to it." With Bob in tow, Caldwell quickly walked past the various work niches and pressed another buzzer beside a heavy steel door. Bob looked up at the camera glinting down at them as they waited.

Luther, in a thoroughly foul mood by this point, held up his phone motioning he had a call that needed answering and he took off in the opposite direction. Caldwell's voice droned on behind him. "We'll start at the beginning, Bob, and I can show you how the air handling systems are functional and crucial even in our . . ." The door finally opened and they vanished into the bright white production space.

Meanwhile, Luther was counting to ten. Just being around Caldwell was infuriating given all the questions that needed answering. Luther was at the far end of the administrative section by this point and began looking for Lazlo. There was no sign of him and Lydia wasn't in her office either.

Luther went to the young woman at the front desk. Her nametag said Lily and she was hugely pregnant. Either twins or just about due. "Lazlo's gone into Lyston," she told him. "About some lighting matter I think. He'll be back within the next hour I imagine." She smiled up at him.

Luther was annoyed. Lazlo had either forgotten he was coming or didn't give a damn.

"Oh, he's expecting you," Lily said. "We were all expecting you. You made it in record time or got up awfully early to get here by nine o'clock." She nodded with enthusiasm in an effort to soothe his irritation. "How was the drive?"

Luther noticed one of the muscles in his neck was beginning to twitch. "It was fine."

"Would you like a coffee or tea or water or . . . something?"

"No. Thanks." Luther softened a little. She was a pretty young woman and Luther had never been immune to ministrations from pretty women.

He moved away from her desk and gazed around at the gaudy lobby with its backlit chartreuse panel. The CannRose-Medi logo, garish and clunky, stared back at him. He'd never approved it. He'd been too busy and hadn't cared much until he saw the pictures. In fact he'd never approved anything about any part of this building. Cyrus had told him, "It's hardly important. Just let them decorate. It's a grow-op for Chrissake." All the chairs were retro orange, and the walls that weren't glass were an iridescent pearl-gray, as was the exposed ductwork up in the rafters. The floor was a gray-blue slate tile. It had cost a fortune and to Luther, it looked appalling. Some failed attempt at contemporary postmodernism, surrealist structuralism, obstructionism or some other fucking "ism." The overall effect made Luther feel like he was trapped inside a diseased oyster. He looked over at the pretty young assistant again. She was busy typing and he thought how healthy and hopeful she looked in this bizarre setting. He went back to the desk and asked her where he might find some water after all. She pointed to the conference room that had a sink and a bar fridge.

Luther found the conference room as hideous as the rest of the place. The table, an elongated oval slab of milky, green-tinted acrylic was more than two inches thick and also slightly iridescent. It was suspended by three steel rods descending from the exposed structural supports of the ceiling and was embedded with what looked like the inner workings of old wristwatches: tiny spiral springs and assorted sizes of small brass cogs and gears. When Luther sat down with his glass of water, he found the acrylic slab dizzying. The high-back leather chairs around it were lime green, a slightly deeper shade than the chartreuse on the logo that was staring back at him from yet another wall. The prevalence of gaudy greens cast a pall over the room that Luther guessed would make anyone look bilious.

As he was sitting contemplating his nausea, the security director walked in. "Hello, Luther," Greg said, heading for the fridge. Not hello *sir* or hello *Mr. Cohen*. Luther didn't remember ever meeting the guy, but clearly CEO status in this business did not inspire deference. Not that Luther ever counted on it in his life generally, but he'd never been a CEO before and in the back of his mind perhaps he'd hoped a few modest perks might come with it. Then as Luther watched him pick through the cans of pop he remembered Greg had done a background check on him too.

"So how's it goin'?" Greg said, turning around as he casually snapped open the pop can.

The notion that information is power — and in this instance was completely unequal and probably promoted way too much familiarity — irritated Luther. He decided to take the offensive.

"So tell me, Greg, you're a guy in the know. Any idea what the hell is going on and why this operation is mired in so many delays?"

Greg took a sip of his pop and stood contemplating the question with his head tilted to one side. "It's a little complicated, I guess."

"Complicated."

"Well, there's the regs that keep changing. The technology is extensive. Then there's actually growing the stuff." Greg took another sip. "I get your point though. It shouldn't take so long. It's just weed." He appeared to go on thinking deeply about the matter. He wasn't often consulted in this way. "It's a new direction. More sophisticated," he said, nodding to himself. And then he sauntered out of the conference room without waiting for a response from Luther.

Luther sat back in his chair. After a few minutes and feeling calmer, he decided he may as well see what Caldwell was telling people these days. While Caldwell's perception of reality was a mystery to Luther, Cyrus had told him it was a function of personality type. It could be mined to great advantage. He should treat Caldwell with some care and try a little flattery now and again if he really wanted to see the ease with which Caldwell could be directed. But Luther was not good at watching others reconstruct or embellish reality. Clearly Cyrus was more psychologically dexterous. Luther looked around again at the hideous décor and sighed as he stood up. He left his water glass by the sink and stepped out of the conference room into the open concept. He found the door that led to the production area and pressed the buzzer. As the door swung open, the whiteness that greeted him was a relief.

He made his way into the cultivation wing through the air shower and eventually found Caldwell and Bob in the hub of the mother pods, where Caldwell was holding forth. "We keep our mothers in these pods, Bob. We have four pods because various strains have different environmental requirements. We've named these after the four winds. South, East, North and West." Caldwell pointed to each doorway as he turned a graceless pirouette. "And in here is a particularly fine instance of the benefit of the Emerald Air Systems." He opened the door to the East Mother Pod.

"Wow," said Bob. "Sure is bright!"

"Yes, indeed. The plants just love light." Caldwell chortled. He pointed to a large elliptical disk, about the size of a refrigerator, hanging horizontally from the ceiling on the other side of the room. "You see here a medium-sized Emerald unit is suspended at the far end. It can handle fifteen-hundred cubic feet of airflow per minute, 24/7. We can achieve gale force in here, Bob." Caldwell laughed and

Bob chuckled in response. "Of course we wouldn't want to do that but we can set and control the air circulation in each room separately. It's one of the most important factors to keeping clear of mold. The plants are very susceptible — it's an ongoing concern. And inside that unit, as Emerald Air has no doubt explained to you, there are the UV catalytic bug zappers, dehumidification subunits and their proprietary ionic, ultrasonic particulate-and-spore filters."

Caldwell cleared his throat and glanced at Bob, ensuring he still had the man's attention.

Luther lurked in the doorway avoiding the heat, humidity and bright lights as best he could. Also he could make a quick getaway if Caldwell's blather became too unbearable again.

"As you can see," Caldwell continued, "there are these very efficient fans suspended here by the entrance wall. It all keeps the air moving in one big circle from the unit across the plants up to the ceiling and back down to the air handler. Now our ceilings are probably a little higher than most grow facilities and this allows for better mixing of the air when you're adding carbon dioxide or dehumidifying, for example. It's important the plants all get exposed to the same air properties. This wasn't exactly planned on our part. It was more a happy accident of the building we've refurbished." Caldwell put his hands out to feel the airflow. The rows of leaves fluttered gently.

Luther noticed some of the leaves close to the doorway were yellow and had dark-green veins sharply contrasting the paleness. He wondered what strain this was and if it was exotic.

Caldwell noticed him looking at the leaves and quickly went on with his talk. "Now, that air-handler unit has a volume-controlled vent leading to a chiller on the roof. The chiller augments the dehumidification, brings in fresh air as required and of course circulates the coolant through the whole system. There's an automatic feedback that regulates the airflow, temperature and humidity to the set points established for each room. And, Bob, I think I mentioned, each room has its own HVAC system. And virtually all of this is controlled by computers."

"That's very impressive. And you're completely happy with the Emerald Systems's performance and reliability?"

"Couldn't be happier, Bob. As I said these HVACs are crucial to our operations."

Luther pointed at the very pale plant, trying to catch Caldwell's eye to ask him about it, but Caldwell only glanced at him fleetingly and then turned his back. "You see, Bob, the plants throw out a lot of water vapor, and most regular systems just can't handle that much humidity. And with the lights — although these don't throw off as much heat as the old halides — things do heat up, and that needs regulating too. Most strains like things on the chilly side, except for those in the South Mother of course. They're more tropical. We set temperatures at least five degrees higher."

"What about CO_2? You said you use that?"

"Yes indeed, Bob. We certainly do and that is also on its own discreet system; a simple feedback unit set up with a CO_2 monitor and a mass flow controller. We keep concentrations between about seven hundred and a thousand parts per million. As you know this is around double the ambient concentration. Of course it all depends on the development of the plants. Here's our CO_2 unit right on the wall." And Caldwell passed right by Luther to point it out. "It's hooked up to a main tank at the moment. Course in the future we'd like to harvest from anything generating CO_2 to keep things recycling. I believe Emerald is working on something like this."

"That's what they told me."

"Well here at CannRose, environmental concerns are *our* concerns. We are taking this place very green. You can count on that."

Luther had stopped trying to get Caldwell's attention. It was fairly obvious there was some problem with the pale plant. The peculiar color signified an infection or some screw-up rather than heritage. He knew for a fact that the carbon dioxide systems were prone to disastrous malfunction. Not long ago he'd been shown an incident report where the carbon dioxide was spewing to the point of displacing oxygen. Somebody looking in the window of the affected room noticed the disorientation of her coworker and pulled her out in the nick of time. Luther also knew that at least a quarter of the air handlers had broken down in the first three weeks and several chillers had yet to be delivered. And personally he didn't give a damn about environmental anything. As far as he knew, the place ate up more energy than a small city, and the advanced waste-management facility still only amounted to a ditch. He cleared his throat quietly and smiled at Caldwell and Bob.

Chapter 21

Lydia felt an uneasy heaviness after a night of only fitful naps. Every time she dozed off she'd wake with a start from vaguely disturbing dreams. Something quietly moving in them. Something stealthy, slow and grasping. She couldn't remember what. Her daughter had cancelled her monthly visit to Rosefields again. It was becoming a habit, but Lydia had never lost sleep over her daughter's absence before. It could have been the wine or the fish. She'd hadn't ever seen little fried fish like that. They were delicious but perhaps a little spicy. Or maybe, and Lydia suddenly felt a spark of recognition as the thought occurred to her, maybe it was because of the tour the previous day.

Lydia rarely ventured into the production area. That was Caldwell and the growers' territory. But Damian, the master grower, who now lived over her five-car garage when he was in Hullbrooke for his work stints, had insisted she come take a proper tour. As president, surely she needed an appreciation of all that was going on and all that was starting to grow. He seemed quite proud of it in his relaxed way.

As he'd led her through the various grow rooms, she'd found it dizzying. She'd gazed at the rows and rows of young plants while Damian talked about their personalities. The breed or the hybrid had certain traits, just like a person, he'd told her. Lydia couldn't keep them straight, the plant breeds and their characters. Damian was particularly talkative in the mother pods and he even addressed the plants as if they were people. Women to be exact — "my northern beauties" or "my wild western lovelies" or "how are we growing today, my sweethearts?" At the time, Lydia thought it was quite charming.

Lydia had an old aunt in Tennessee who used to talk to her plants, but she muttered and mumbled. Everybody assumed it was because she lived alone and had nobody else to talk to. Or she could have been bats, her mother admitted one day. More than a few of her mother's relatives had been institutionalized.

But the way Damian talked, it seemed absolutely normal. He mentioned some Colorado friends and it was clear they all talked the same way. "Bill told me Purple Peanut Kush was a temperamental hussy. 'Stay away from her. She's the lady antichrist in peaches and mauve.' Did I listen? Course not. The young are stupid. She was a disaster." Damian had smiled as he reminisced. But Lydia wondered now if perhaps it wasn't this familiarity, this personification of the plants that prompted her restless night. The mention of the antichrist had been amusing at the time. But now the thought was unsettling, not that she was religious in the least. She stared at the African violet on her bedroom windowsill. Was it staring back? Could it wish her ill? Did it want to say something?

She lay there for a few minutes and tried to put it all out of her mind. Then she hauled herself out of bed, donned a robe, sat down at her dressing table and picked up her comb. In the mirror, she spotted a tiny cluster of gray hairs high up, almost at the top of her blonde head. She pulled them all out together and then examined them closely. The roots, tiny white bulbs, were like little aliens looking back at her. She flicked the hairs away and a couple of them came to rest on the picture of her children. Lydia almost never looked at it. She plucked the hairs off the silver frame and briefly glanced at the little faces. They were staring at her too. Everything was staring at her this morning. She looked away and then looked back at the photograph. Their gaze was even more intense. She coughed. There was something accusatory in their eyes. She'd never seen it before.

She loved them. Of course she did. She'd birthed them. How could you not love your own children? Even the daughter who kept cancelling. So what was it? They hadn't gotten enough? But they had everything! Hadn't gotten enough of her? Was that it? Jordan had always wanted her by his side. "Don't fuss. They're perfectly well taken care of by professionals. Nothing to worry about." So perhaps she didn't know them. Didn't put in the requisite mother hours.

It was true, she didn't often speculate about their trajectory through life. She didn't quiz them on their hopes and fears, though she was happy if they occasionally confided these things to her. But

Lydia thought this was a good thing. She never found them lacking or exceeding in some way that prompted either disappointment or pride. Other mothers in Lydia's social circle either complained bitterly about their children or bragged, usually for no compelling reason. Lydia just smiled at their stories. She didn't think she'd avoided some crucial aspect of motherhood by not judging her own children, not holding them to some standard dictated by class and custom. Lydia shook her head. Mothering comes in various shapes and sizes. Maybe her children just had indigestion when the photographer showed up that day. She put the picture in the dressing-table drawer.

Lydia wanted a green smoothie for breakfast. The black kale was looking particularly healthy. Carl had set up a few pots of herbs and leafy vegetables in the solarium off the kitchen for her. She picked two young leaves then headed back into the kitchen to add a stalk of celery, some cucumber, lettuce, a couple of kiwi fruits and filtered water. She watched as the blender did its work. Watched first how everything scrambled and then how the little pieces in the carafe got smaller and smaller and became a brilliant rich green. The plant parts were decimated and indistinguishable. No personalities left at all. And nothing was staring back at her. There was only a union, a fusion, and a tasty one too, she decided with satisfaction.

Lydia's thoughts drifted to the recent meeting at CannRose. It hadn't gone well. Luther had come all the way from the state capital to be there and had accused Lazlo of "routinely dropping the ball." Lazlo countered he could hardly work "twelve hours every day without a break and be expected to remember every frickin' detail." Luther had also questioned the construction costs and the price of materials, and Lazlo had squirmed at this. Everybody decided Lazlo needed an assistant, and Luther said his firm would see to the hiring. Lazlo fired back he could "find his own goddamn help" and accused Luther of trying to handle him. And when the CannRose CFO, an associate in Malcolm's firm who was attending via conference phone, requested access to the various quotes for a particular item that had already been purchased, Lazlo called him an asshole.

The worst of that afternoon of course was when Caldwell flew into rages at both Lazlo and Luther. He slammed his phone on the table at one point and challenged Luther to outline one single thing he knew about marijuana cultivation. Did he even know the difference between indica and sativa? Or soilless media and coconut coir? Could he name a landrace strain or know how it might be acquired? No, of course not. And what could Lazlo possibly know about discerning patients who prefer organic products when Lazlo's tastes barely extended beyond hotdogs, ketchup and cheese spread?

Lydia hadn't had a job since her modeling days. But she was beginning to feel this was her calling. She wasn't just the silent president anymore. Internal and public relations were fascinating. And she was learning so many new things and attending workshops on intriguing topics like team-building, leadership, synergy, influencing customer confidence, and jumping out of the box. And there were simply dozens of business and communications gurus to choose from. Some of the gurus reminded her of Caldwell, and she was beginning to think he'd never been so singular after all. They could talk as much as he could and were just as convincing. Except, unlike Caldwell, who often needed her only to be an appreciative audience, they demanded participation and feedback. It was very encouraging to be called upon to participate. In fact it was thrilling and it was paying off too.

That afternoon when things became so unpleasant in the meeting, Lydia tried out her new skills. She insisted everybody stand up and stretch, and those in the same room form a circle, hold hands and move in toward each other, raising their arms high to the middle until they had formed a temple-like structure. Well of course they all looked peeved at the suggestion, but she prevailed. She'd been warned about naysayers in her seminars. Besides, she was the president. Once they were in the circle, the arguing stopped. She even heard the CFO and Alice start to laugh over the phone. She'd told them they should just raise their arms individually and "be the temple." Luther had eventually laughed too. It was amazing. She'd changed the mood of that room with a simple suggestion and an activity that took less than three minutes.

Lydia took another gulp of her smoothie. And as it washed down, she realized not only was she something of a babysitter at CannRose, mothering again, but she was also the financial tit for all these squabbling children. The thought was rather shocking for her. She didn't often have thoughts like that.

Chapter 22

The plants in Flower Room III fluttered in the breeze from the fans. They were all eight weeks old and slightly yellowing, especially the big leaves. The three young devotees moved methodically along the table rows. Scissors flashed from time to time, reflecting the photon blizzard streaming down from the intense lighting.

"I think we're gonna have to take this to Cassie. I got thirty bananas on these four plants."

"We should take it to Damian. He's woke."

"Not. You see that book?"

"What book? He's chill."

"Worse than my dad. Has a purple corduroy cover with a green jewel on it."

"What?"

"Weird title. Keeps it in his office like a Bible."

"Dude, that's his weed singing book or something. He says it's old."

"Whatever. Too much like the shit my dad reads."

"I got . . . um . . . wait a minute. . . ten, eleven . . . uh, fifteen . . . Yeah, I got over twenty."

"Fuck! These ladies suck, bro."

"It was the flood."

"Yeah."

"But the Kush babies got flooded too. They don't have bananas."

"But they might get them."

"I don't know. I'd a never used those mothers for the Blitz."

"Me neither."

"Yeah."

"They gotta be solid. Like one sex or another."

"Yeah, like, and over time."

"I don't know, might be cool to be both sexes."

"Dude, it's just the stress."

"Yeah. What's with Cassie givin' them a lot and Damian doesn't?"

"Basic AF."

"Yeah that sucks."

"You shouldn't confuse them."

"No. You shouldn't.

"Mothers should never be confused."

"Maybe we shouldn't, like, take this to Cassie then."

"Maybe we should take it to Joe."

"Let's just take it to Gus. It's easier."

"I got . . . eleven . . . thirteen . . . fifteen, sixteen . . . more! Oh crap, there's seeds too."

"That's totally fucked up, dude."

"They're gonna have to kill another crop."

"Sucks!"

"Yeah."

"I don't wanna do that."

"Me neither."

"Maybe we shouldn't take this to anybody."

"Yeah, but these ladies are, like, totally fucked. Right?"

"Then they'll kill 'em."

"Yeah."

"Don't we have to fill in a form?"

"Yeah."

"So let's not fill in the form."

"Yeah! Let's curve the form."

"Awesome! That's fire!"

Chapter 23

After Cassie and Joe had been working at CannRose for about six months, Ms. Ligner from the DOH came in like a hurricane for a surprise second inspection. Cassie took an instant and rock-solid dislike to the woman. As one of Lydia's assistants in administration exclaimed, "She's incredibly fucking hot, man." So she was, Cassie noted, and it was evident she put it to use. Between finding most everyone incompetent and everything inadequate and not meeting the state code, Ms. Ligner flirted. She flirted with Joe in particular. And with Greg, who was old enough to be her father. It appeared she flirted with every male. Even the three young lads, who were so terrified of her they didn't notice.

"Where is the sanitation plan for the grow area?" Ms. Ligner asked.

Cassie wasn't even sure what the woman was talking about. She'd heard nothing about a sanitation plan.

Ernie, who was standing right there, just shrugged and smiled. He'd never heard anything about a sanitation plan either. "I just do the cleaning, empty the garbage, you know. Sounds mighty impressive though."

Ms. Ligner did not hide her disgust. "You still have bugs here. Are you expecting to sell product with bugs?" She stared at Cassie. "Sell it to sick people?"

Damian showed up at this point and Cassie was impressed that he showed no signs of attraction to her. "This is an organic operation. Organic's a lot safer than the crap that isn't. So the ecology of the flower rooms includes pests. Also includes their predators. And they don't get harvested." He paused. "So they don't end up in product."

Ms. Ligner almost snorted and then wanted to know what they were planning to do with the moldy crop that appeared to have landed in the bottling room. "There were bugs there too. Is that part of the organic approach?"

The bottling room wasn't Damian's territory, he confessed, but he assumed they'd be tossing the crop. He personally would never allow its sale. Then she wanted to know whose territory it was. Damian told her Caldwell oversaw most things but since he wasn't there she should talk to Terry, the quality assurance officer. She stalked off.

The organic approach was news to Cassie but she didn't let on. Later she heard Damian saying to one of the cultivation assistants, "Fuckin' bureaucracy. Uptight ho. Man, this state sucks."

After that, Cassie couldn't decide whether the inspector thought they were all morons or criminals. Likely both. What Cassie observed was that most men in the facility were eager like puppy dogs when Ms. Ligner appeared in the morning, but by the afternoon they all looked as if they'd been publicly flogged or humiliated in some other equally unpleasant fashion.

Then Cassie heard that Ms. Ligner would be recommending the DOH withdraw CannRose-Medi's registration.

The worst had happened.

The next morning, Caldwell, having heard the news from Lazlo, came raging into the facility and Cassie was the first person he saw. "You!" he yelled at her, "why did you tell that moronic teenager from the DOH we were organically certified when we're not."

"I-I never . . . I never mentioned organic anything. I never said that."

"Well somebody did. And because it's not true yet, she's going to use it to crucify—" But before he could finish his thought, he caught sight of the quality assurance officer, Terry, coming through the back entrance, sporting his trademark tight jeans and Jimmy Dean–style leather jacket. Early on, Lazlo had hired his daughter's boyfriend because he'd briefly had a job in auto-parts quality assurance and Lazlo thought it was a great fit. But Ms. Ligner had pretty much destroyed any confidence Terry might have developed about his job. She'd talked about things he'd never heard of and couldn't even pronounce in some cases.

Caldwell reddened at the sorry sight of him and started slowly shaking his head. He took a few quick steps toward Terry and told him he needed to pack up his things and get the hell out that very moment, for the good of company. "Please, do not show your face here again. Ever!" Then Caldwell saw Greg and pulled him aside none too politely, and in a voice loud enough that Cassie could hear all the way down by the mother pods told him he needed to hire some people who were "actually qualified for their fucking jobs."

Chapter 24

"You can't quit that grow-op place, I want you to get me some weed." Petra's mom was sitting up in the hospital bed. A hospital attendant had just given her a can of juice and a straw. Petra was fiddling with her phone and looked up to see her mother struggling. She was trying to hold the can steady between her chest and the bed tray and open it with the hand that still worked. Petra jumped up, annoyed with the attendant who hadn't bothered to open the can and with herself for not paying attention.

"Mom, getting weed doesn't work like that. I can't just bring it home. And I'm quitting."

"That's ridiculous. Why won't you stay there? It can't be that bad."

"It's a fiasco. They just wanted a token scientist with some letters after their name to raise the place's legitimacy for the DOH. They haven't paid any attention to what I need for the lab. They can't even get the countertops right. They don't have a clue. Besides, someone has to look after you now."

"I'm perfectly fine. Just a little setback. And I don't need you moping around the house to make me feel worse." Doreen smiled at her own mischievous remark, but the left side of her face went nowhere. Petra still couldn't get used to it. It was like one half of her mother was carved stone. How does a person deal with that? Petra managed a little chuckle but it was difficult.

"I want you to get me some pot. It's supposed to help. And besides it's about time I tried some. I wanna get wasted! Damn fifties. We never got to try anything."

The doctor walked in, the same beautiful doctor with the black hair and blue, blue eyes that Petra had wanted to ask out the year before. Her mother smiled at him, her face even more lopsided.

"So you never got to try anything?" he asked shaking his head in forlorn sympathy.

"Not a damn thing. Especially if you were a girl. Had to be goodie-goodie. God forbid you had sex. You'd get pregnant because nobody knew what the hell they were doing. Now I see all those programs on sex and the things you can do."

"What programs on sex?" Petra was squinting at her mother. "Have you been watching pornography?"

"No! Educational programs. PBS, BBC. Discovery maybe. I don't know. But I'd have never believed you could do all those things with somebody else. Some of those programs were thirty years old. Where the hell was I? Your father was never very inventive. And now it's too late. I'll never get to try any of it. So I want to get some pot."

"It's never too late, Doreen." The doctor sat down in the chair beside her bed, picked up her right hand and held it gently. Her mother's crooked smile now looked like a crazed and obscene leer. Petra had to wonder where all this was going. "So do we need to have the talk about safe sex?" the doctor said with perhaps exaggerated gravitas.

"Oh for crying out loud!" Her mother threw up her hand.

"Doreen, some of the retirement homes are riddled with STDs. I'm not kidding."

"I wouldn't even want to think about that. Ugh! Some toothless old goat, lousy digestion and bad breath, snuffling around all over me and having a heart attack."

"I'd say you've already done some thinking about it."

"I was just trying to make a point. All I wanna do is try some pot. And it won't give me STDs."

"No. But it has an aphrodisiac effect I hear. It could be a slippery slope," he said, smiling.

"Would you be okay with weed for her?" Petra asked.

"Well as you know, reports are mixed. It's supposed to help with the healing process." He turned back to Petra's mother. "And your stroke was a mild one. But there's also evidence that smoking weed, just like tobacco, increases the stroke risk."

"So I'll have it in brownies. And fudge!"

"It affects the vascular system no matter how you take it. And you should watch the sugar intake. You can have it in a tea, you know."

"So you'll give me a prescription?"

"I won't deny you the registration but I want you to think very carefully about it."

"I've already thought about it. I want to get absolutely wasted at least once in my life. If I die, I die. If I live, I want to try ayahuasca next."

"I can't help you out with that. You're on your own."

"I like being on my own."

Turning to Petra again, the doctor said, "Your mother is out of control. She may need supervision."

"I do not!"

"Good night, Doreen. I'll bring the forms for you tomorrow so you can get wasted. Properly." The doctor got up and headed out the door smiling.

"See. So you can't quit that job because I'm going to need a big supply." Petra's mother stared at her.

"Yes I can quit. And we can get a little greenhouse and grow weed in the backyard. Always could if you'd really wanted to try it. You just had to get registered."

"Didn't see the point until now. But you have to stick with that job. I don't want you underfoot."

Chapter 25

Lily, the lovely and charming CannRose receptionist, was quietly ordering shot after shot until she was bleary-eyed and slurring. The rest of the CannRose crew, a dozen or so, sitting around four tables pushed together at Chelsea's, didn't seem to notice. But Ernie did and if he recalled correctly, she'd given birth to her second child only a few months ago. He wondered if he was witnessing a total disintegration, a boost for workplace gossip for sure, especially if she lurched out of Chelsea's with one of the guys who was eyeing her from across the way.

Lily was the good girl of CannRose. Being a weed company, the execs and everybody working there milked all the respectability available. And Lily was the blonde-haired, blue-eyed girl next door, the congenial wife, the good mother, pure in practically every way, uncorruptible and surely incorruptible. But there's nothing a small town relishes like seeing some respectable paragon stumble, the more celestial and highly regarded in their original unsullied state the better.

Ernie finished the dregs of his beer, got up and dragged his chair over to her. He sat down, blocking the view of the interested onlookers. "So how you doin' tonight, Lily?"

"Well, Ernie, I'm pretty much fucked. How are you?"

"I'm good."

"Will you take me home?"

"Funny you should ask. I was just going to offer."

"You're always so kind. Happy too. How do you do that?"

"I'm resourceful."

"Not just high all the time? I tried that. It doesn't work you know. Not for me. I just forget things. And then there's trouble because I've forgotten something. Like picking the kids up. But I don't worry about that anymore."

When Ernie got Lily safely into his car and started driving in the direction of her house, she started to cry. She wanted to go to his place. She couldn't go home.

Ernie stopped the car. "Have you eaten anything today?"

No, she had not. She didn't think she could. Everything was done, including her appetite. So Ernie asked if she had a friend he could call and she did. It came out she was staying with her best friend from high school. Where were the kids? Oh, the kids were with *him* — her husband — and his mother.

Ernie heaved a sigh. That last thing he needed was Lily's husband pounding his door down or bringing his rifle over for target practice. The guy belonged to the group of hunters and fishermen who kept Ernie's freezer full of wild game and fish in return for the prepared goodies.

So Ernie called her friend, Bonnie, and it turned out she hadn't had much to eat either. The result was dinner at his place for three.

Shortly after she arrived, Bonnie pulled Ernie aside. "I'd hazard it's postpartum depression but she was fine with the first one. She's getting help but I don't think it works very well."

"The husband?"

"He's a peach. Really. Never heard an unkind word between them. I didn't expect she'd get so hammered. I thought she was going to Chelsea's for a beer. One beer."

"Maybe the food will help." So Ernie prepared a light, high-protein feast. To start with there was *osuimono*, a clear soup with clams, followed by baked lemon-pepper and wild garlic flounder served with lightly steamed bok choy. Some left over quinoa with fresh tomatoes and basil tossed with Dijon dressing made a cheerful addition to the dinner.

Lily began to talk. Nothing was as it was supposed to be. Not least was the fiasco that was CannRose. Her job weighed heavily on her. She was most people's first contact with the grow facility. Perfection was required. Everybody depended on her to be pleasant. All the time. It should have been impossible because nothing there was working. There was nothing for sale yet. People in town kept asking her when they could buy product. And she had nothing to say. And now the DOH might be pulling their registration. And everyone was supposed to be so up! So positive. And she was supposed to be up, even with Caldwell yelling at people. It wasn't possible. It wasn't possible for her to keep this up.

There was the other matter too. Life. All the things that were supposed to be good — were they? The news and the world. How could anyone be happy? The world was a horrible place to bring children into. It had been a mistake. Everything was failing. The climate. Fires everywhere. All the refugees. Eternal wars. Humans were the cruelest living beings. There was no point to any of it. Life was random and mean and meaningless. God was dead. Definitely dead. Without a requiem. Without anybody even noticing really.

Ernie cleared his throat. There wasn't much he could say. Existential and spiritual crises were not his area of expertise. His life had been focused on succeeding, and then immediate survival, and now he was simply enjoying resisting all societal expectations.

"Love!" Bonnie piped up. "Don't you love your kids?"

"Oh, I love them," Lily said stonily. "I've fobbed this existence onto them. By rights they should hate me. Maybe they will."

"Maybe they won't see it that way," Bonnie said.

There was silence for a few moments.

"I love this food," Lily said suddenly. "And it doesn't come with sorrow attached, does it? Maybe for the clams and fish. But not for me, at least not for me on this one." She looked at Ernie, smiling. "It's just food. We eat it and that's it."

Lily's drunkenness, or possible over-medication or under-medication, did not really abate during the evening, but Ernie was glad he'd cooked. It seemed to cheer her up a little at least. As she and Bonnie were leaving, Lily took his hands and looked at them closely. "These are great hands," she said. "Thank you."

"You're welcome."

Ernie tidied up the kitchen, finished up the cider he'd been drinking with dinner and then went to check on his roof garden. The tomatoes were in very good shape, the Asian eggplant was looking spectacular. He also had three marijuana plants just starting to flower and two little ones he'd cloned from one of them. He brought the little ones inside and put them under a set of lights he'd arranged for the purpose. Ernie had found he quite liked smoothies made with a couple of fresh marijuana leaves in them so he wanted to keep plants going well into the winter. He had no idea if there were health benefits from consuming fresh product. He just felt better for some reason. It could even have been the ritual.

One might assume, given where he worked, it would be easy to obtain fresh leaves every week or so. But no. He'd have to be registered specifically for fresh product to buy it commercially and that would require him to have MS or some other vile ailment. It had to be complicated. Then again it didn't take a wizard to see that his five plants looked a whole lot healthier than most of the plants at the facility. Ernie was fast turning into a food snob. He worked with only the best raw materials.

Sometimes Ernie missed his days of just living out of his station wagon. It was so simple and uncluttered. At these times he cautioned himself he was romanticizing and tried to remember how crappy it had been waking up if he'd had to spend the night inside the car; it took an hour just to get all the kinks and cramps out. But if it was a clear night, nothing could compare to staring up into the sky as he drifted off. So on the occasions when he was nostalgic, like he was that night, he moved his foam onto the Rent-All roof and parked it right between the zucchini and the pole beans.

Ernie liked to think he was immune to people's moods and he imagined that Lenore had helped make him that way. But as he lay there staring up at Lyra, the starry harp, the sadness of Lily preyed upon him. She was probably the polar opposite of Lenore and maybe that's why she was contagious. Her bleak observations about CannRose had settled right into his solar plexus. He'd always seen his job as a bit of a joke, stickin' it to the man in a way, but now he realized he'd grown fond of it. Sure the people were fractious, the place was chaotic and there was pervasive ineptitude, but that was the beauty of it. The sad part was it just might not make it. Lily was right. Nothing seemed to work there. And what if it failed altogether and they shut it down? Ernie didn't want to see it go. CannRose was his new dysfunctional family and family comes first.

#

About three weeks after Ernie made the supper for three, Lily leaned over her desk and told him in a whisper she'd moved back in with her husband and kids. Then she winked at him. She chitchatted with everybody as if nothing had ever been awry, and she seemed happy. You never could tell, but he liked to think everything was good now. Of course there was plenty to talk about that day. There was an element of merriment in the air, Caldwell's mood notwithstanding. The Guardians of Jude and Ezekiel had struck again.

Ernie had to hand it to the Guardians. They'd opted for inventiveness over shock and awe this time. But it disappointed him somewhat. It had a ring of the cliché, a sort of morbid adolescent kitsch about it. Perhaps their apocalyptic visual sense had finally stalled in the margin of diminishing returns. Ezekiel and Jude needed a break. Or in some rejuvenating move, perhaps a new inexperienced crew was in charge of public action. It could easily have been mistaken for an enthusiastic Halloween display. Regardless, people did slow down to look at the creation. Perhaps it was the pneumatic Santa modified into a crooked horned devil that repeatedly rose up to its full height and girth only to collapse approximately every two minutes, or the makeshift artificial marijuana plant between its teeth giving it a nineteenth-century artistic air that made the rubberneckers drive off laughing. Or perhaps it was the poor paint job on the six skinned goat heads churned out by a 3D printer and impaled on ten-foot spikes, which occasionally interfered with the devil's crotch, that broke everybody up.

Not surprisingly Caldwell was ticked and possibly embarrassed, though hardly anybody knew of the family connections. He came in screaming Monday morning, demanding Ernie dismantle the idiotic mess immediately. It had been erected on the road allowance in front of the grow facility late on Saturday night so that locals, including the *Hullbrooke Gazette* photographer, had all of Sunday to take it in.

Of course somebody had to call the local police. Lazlo was not happy with that move at all, and Ernie figured it must have been one of the neighbors upset with the increased traffic. The cruiser came to a full stop right in front Ernie who was pulling the first of the goat heads off its spike.

"Morning, Chief." Ernie knew Jim Thorpes from way back. He was the eldest brother of Ernie's best friend in high school. They'd always called him Chief, even before he became a policeman, and now that he headed up the local unit, most people didn't even know he had a first name.

"Heard you were workin' here, Ernie. So what have we got? Guardians been at it again?"

"Looks like it."

"Nothin' explosive?"

"Not that I know of."

"Now this thing here," the chief said, pointing. "This could be a hazard to drivers." By this time the battery-generated pneumatic apparatus was losing power and the devil was more or less just writhing on the roadside.

"Could be, but I think the traffic's diminished," Ernie said.

"What the hell are these though?" the chief said, looking at the skinned goat head in Ernie's hand. "Shit! You think they got a 3D printer?"

"If I had to hazard a guess, I'd say yes."

"Now that bothers me. It really does. One thing I always counted on was their lack of digital savvy. Hell, next thing you know they'll have more guns. Shit, they could be all over the internet or screwing around with robotics before we know it. No sir, I do not like that one bit."

Ernie nodded. "Could get interesting."

"So does CannRose want to lay charges?"

"No. They just want it to go away and that's what I'm doing."

"Good man! No use uppin' the ante. *Gazette*'s gonna run the photo I hear. Should keep 'em happy for another couple of years."

"Probably."

"Well, just checkin' up on things."

"Keepin' the peace."

"You bet. You have yourself a good day, Ernie. Oh, nice job on the terraces by the way. Hilda raves about you."

"Thanks," Ernie said. Jim Thorpes was Mrs. Cranston's cousin.

PART SIX

Cloning

Oh Greedy Knives! No matter the handle's fine filigree, the steel of stagger and drop is your lot. We are so many. Do not waste us in pieces and slivers, or carve and align us to where we are not. You think by dicing, by splicing, you will gain an upper hand. This game is the age of stars and just as complex. With each tiny cut you slice off your own finger. Oh Greedy Knives, there is no winning. We weep. We weep that you may still the blade, let the blessed be and see the splendor.

from Cannto V, *Cannabidadas*

Chapter 26

"So, not that I ever planned on leaving anything for posterity, but here they are: general cleaning procedures for everything but the grow rooms. I can get those to you in a week or so. Would that work?" Ernie laid out the paperwork on the desk.

"Peachy. Just splendid!" Percy, the new quality assurance officer, was effusive as he peered more closely at one of the pages. He was a little older than Ernie, effeminate and an elegant dresser. His tastes were more subdued, more refined and possibly more expensive than Caldwell's. That would soon be irrelevant. Ernie found out Percy was introducing "proper gowning," so everybody working in the production part of the facility would be wearing scrubs and lab coats by the end of the month. And of course it wasn't the man's taste in clothes that pissed off Caldwell, or the fact the guy was educated, logical and had diplomatic people skills. It was that the CannRose board had hired him in a unilateral move. That's what really got up Caldwell's nose. He fumed around the facility making snide remarks about the board's heavy-handed players, "a bunch of draconian geriatrics." The new QA officer barely noticed.

"Bravo! A man with a grasp of the written word!" Percy exclaimed, putting the page back on the pile.

"General liberal arts. A dying education track but it still comes in handy," Ernie said.

Ernie had seen the trail in and out of the new QA guy's office all afternoon, people sighing heavily, holding the pages they were responsible for and slouching back to their work areas to make corrections. You had to hand it to Percy, he was whipping the place into shape. Administratively speaking that is. Even the DOH had been impressed enough with Percy they were willing to back down on pulling the registration. The threat of nasty litigation from Luther and the gang at the law firm didn't hurt either. Ernie heard the state was giving CannRose-Medi another four months to clean up its act.

"Lots of paperwork, huh?"

"As I've mentioned to the others, it's a magnum opus." Percy pointed to the large three-inch binder sitting on the new filing cabinet. Apparently it would be full to overflowing in a couple of months with instructions on how to do absolutely everything that mattered to the DOH. The filing cabinet would be full too, with sign-offs, harvest, curing and packaging records, test results and of course sanitation records.

Ernie sat down because it looked like Percy needed a break. He could always tell when people wanted to talk and it made work go by so much faster. Shootin' the breeze was Ernie's second vocation, after cooking.

"So do you live around here, Percy?"

Percy lived with his husband Gavin not far from Rosefields. But up until a few months ago, he was only there on weekends and holidays because he'd been working in New Jersey in the pharmaceutical industry. It turned out Ernie was well acquainted with Percy's house. Long before Percy and Gavin renovated it, Ernie's first girlfriend had lived there. His mom had always liked Trina, and Trina's folks had liked innocent and trusting Ernesto. Those were the days.

"So are you going to stay here or are you the high-priced fixer and on to new pastures once you've cleaned up this mess?"

"My dear man, I've taken a considerable cut in remuneration but the plan is to indeed stay here."

Percy, like Ernie himself, had become a reject from another world. He'd refused to sign off on some cost-saving measure at the pharmaceutical company. He perceived with a high degree of certainty that the cost savings would create a risk down the line. Not good. Not safe. Not healthy. The section VP disagreed and decided the product was not the liability. Percy was. Guards arrived to escort him out. A bit of a shock. But here he was getting in on a whole revolution. No matter what you called it, ganja, dagga, bhanga, bobo bush, or even the albatross of the DEA, it was making a comeback. One by one, the states were saying no in a whole new way, as in "No. Go blow prohibition out your ear!" Percy was delighted.

Percy's mood suddenly changed though, and he asked Ernie in a conspiratorial tone, "What's Petra like? I haven't had the pleasure yet."

"Couldn't say really. I haven't seen all that much of Petra myself." Ernie omitted any mention of the times he'd seen her at Chelsea's.

"Curious, she's head of R and D and doesn't even have a functioning lab," Percy sniffed. Her presence clearly bothered him. "I mean, I suppose it's not *that* odd. CannRose is still a start-up. But of course I'm going to have to share a lab with her. They're only building one of them as far as I know."

Apparently Caldwell had laid it on thick. No doubt to intimidate Percy. He'd gone on about Petra's Ivy League background and faculty appointment. "I don't think Caldwell has a clue adjunct professors usually aren't even on the university payroll," Percy said. "Besides I don't fall for academic credentials. On the contrary! The more initials accumulated, the more I suggest inspecting for damages left in the wake. Truth is often money. Just like everything else I suppose. And the egos!" Percy peered over his glasses at Ernie and, seeing he still had a sympathetic ear, continued, "Invariably, prima donnas get vexed by quality protocols, you know. They claim it cramps their creativity. Dampens a few psychopathic tendencies too." Percy sniffed again. "Academia and research are full of them. I should know."

"So you've had run-ins then with the researchers and academics?" Ernie inquired.

"Run-ins? Ha! In addition to my recent cessation of relations with the pharma research boys — whores really, the lot of them — I survived the most fucked PhD-turned-terminal-master's supervised by a narcissistic monster in the Biochemistry Department at Yale. Twenty-five years ago and it's still surprisingly vivid. I too have Ivy League cred. You can't fool me." He paused, suddenly remembering he was talking to the guy with the broom at his new workplace. Possibly not too professional of him. But then, this was a just weed factory.

Chapter 27

Caldwell adjusted his watch so the face was dead center on the top of his wrist. Even though only the most discerning eyes might notice it under his Armani jacket, it was one of those little things that counted, a small symmetry with comforting consequences. He'd meant to get another link taken out of the gold wristband but he never found the time. He could of course give it to Lydia as an errand. She still liked to do things for him sometimes. As soon as the notion occurred though, he dismissed it. Sure he and Lydia had a history and maybe they'd still be occasional lovers at some point, but he wasn't keen on handing over the diamond-and-sapphire Cartier even for an hour or two. It represented an intolerable kind of intimacy. He'd moved past that. Lydia should too.

Caldwell had a new lover. Bit of a fluffy thing, but so what. Young women were easy enough to get at his age, with his experience. Why shouldn't he make the best of it? They admired a man of means, passion and experience and didn't question him about matters they knew nothing about. In fact this one barely had a word to say at all. He liked that. He had too much on his mind right now.

Luther, that sycophantic jacked-up little munchkin and naysayer to his best ideas, had challenged him to bring in more investors. "If you're so worried about power balances, Caldwell, maybe you should work them." That's what the little twerp had said. So work them Caldwell would. And one day, one day very soon, when the power was stacked as destiny had ordained, CannRose would be global and it would be his.

Caldwell often imagined his great success. All the motivational experts recommended it. The more detailed the better. In a recurring scenario he gave his father a two-week tour of the international holdings. Wouldn't that be a stunner! The man, possibly on his last legs, humbled and open-mouthed with astonishment. Oh, how Caldwell would relish it. Nothing he ever did as a child seemed to satisfy. His father would point out the missed catch in the winning game, the spelling mistake in the story that got an A, the glue that came unstuck on the prize-winning science project, the mismatched coloring in his bedroom, the clumsiness of the knots he tied, the poverty and bad habits of his best friend. Not that his father was a paragon of brilliance or social standing himself. Quite the contrary. He was a clerk in some import company on the West Coast. And one day he just disappeared. His mother told him his father had probably been planning it for ages.

Caldwell checked his smartphone, then he checked the Cartier; it was four minutes slow. He felt a slight twinge in his stomach. The potential investor was flying in from New Mexico and clearly this guy's time was at a premium. He was hiring a helicopter from the city airport so he could land right in the empty field beside the facility.

Caldwell had heard the New Mexico guy was a retired CEO of a Fortune 500 company. The words *shrewd, measured, inscrutable* and *cutthroat* had been bandied about. Caldwell took a deep breath. He'd come to realize there were businesspeople, especially quiet ones, who were a different predator species. *Heartless* came to mind, though he admired them greatly. They bypassed camaraderie for a killing. They picked up on weakness. So Caldwell had to be careful. He'd had certain experiences they might . . . misinterpret.

There were times in Caldwell's life when he'd kept out of sight. For business reasons of course. Who doesn't need a break from time to time before starting a new venture? For example, he'd occasionally resorted to living out of his mother's garage. It was economical. Skipping town was also often effective in maintaining one's strength and spirit. In one instance he'd retreated completely for six months to a makeshift tree house somewhere in the woods in Oregon. Winter had driven him out and cautiously back to civilization. Another time he'd lived in a derelict Airstream for a whole year, hidden in a few acres of scrub bush right beside the Green River in Utah. In extreme circumstances, Caldwell had found that fabricated identities could also give him a break.

But now things had come full circle and he was back to the real Caldwell. He saw this as a lucky omen. He was finally aligned with

God's grace. His skill set, enthusiasm and natural talent were working brilliantly with the moneyed crowd drooling to get in on the green wave. Marijuana was manna!

Caldwell meditated again on the upcoming meeting. His demeanor needed to be perfect, flawless, Zen-like. While the negotiations of an investment deal might go on for weeks or even months, the defining decision would be made in the first thirty seconds after the handshake. Caldwell lived for this.

As the helicopter landed, the wind generated by the whirling blades blew up so much dust that Caldwell was momentarily blinded, and he started to cough.

"Wonderful you could make the trip so quickly," he gasped as he squinted at the man from New Mexico.

Then Caldwell began to sneeze uncontrollably. It stopped only when they went inside, but his eyes watered throughout the twenty-minute tour of the grow facility. During the fifteen-minute meeting that followed, Caldwell's nose began to drip and his red eyes became excruciatingly itchy.

The New Mexico businessman expressed genuine concern for Caldwell's health as he climbed back into his rented helicopter.

Chapter 28

The three young devotees were in the first nursery. Some plants had yellowing leaves and a few had smaller leaves at the top that were curling. Unlike some staff, the young men did not pretend everything was fine while they trimmed. They were accepting though, and abundantly aware of just how little influence they had at CannRose or anywhere for that matter. They contemplated change.

"Dude. You think this place'll ever grow decent weed?"

"It's depressing."

"Look at these!"

"How does that happen?"

"They're confusing them again."

"Why can't they just let them grow."

"It's a war, bro. See who can throw the most shade. And the ladies are collateral damage."

"They shouldn't be cloned when they're confused."

"Yeah. The kids always suffer."

"Yeah. It's, like, worse than before my parents split."

"Was your mother confused?"

"All the time."

"That's why you gotta grow your own."

"Dad's never gonna let me. He says it's unsustainable."

"Weed is totally sustainable. If people grew more weed and hemp and shit, we wouldn't need polyester."

"Weed is awesome!"

"He says he'd allow it only if I grew it outdoors."

"We should, like, so totally be able to grow it outdoors."

"Yeah. Ladies would like the sunshine!"

"We should just get our own place."

"That would be dumb lit!"

"Ca-*ching*, ca-*ching*."

"No. It's not, dude. We could find a place in Hullbrooke. They're cheap."

"Yeah! We could walk to the skate park! There's Chelsea's too!"

"Chelsea's sucks. All that smoke."

"So?"

"I'd have to take my puffer."

"I didn't know you had asthma."

"Like since I was three. Cat dander."

"There's no cats at Chelsea's, dude."

"Cougars."

"Dude. That's pathetic."

"We should get a *Gazette*. Check the rents."

"Yeah, we could totally rent in Hullbrooke."

"With a bedroom for the ladies."

"I'd take the couch so the ladies could have their own room."

"Shit, yeah."

"You know that inspector?"

"The one Lydia's assistant wanted to date?"

"She hates the ladies. I can tell."

"Maybe that's why they're sick."

"They take it up. Clone these — spread the hate."

"Joe said she's why the first QA guy got fired."

"State shade, bro. Savage."

"He was a jerk anyway. Told me to get my hair cut. Said my man bun looked stupid."

"Yeah, yours does."

"Fuck off."

"The hair nets now are so cool."

"So are the scrubs! The color goes with the ladies."

"I didn't even know they made beard nets."

"Dude, I'm never wearing a beard net."

"Dude, you'd need a beard."

Chapter 29

Since CannRose-Medi still wasn't getting product out the door, Alice was very pleased the state suddenly decided to allow dispensaries to sell product to each other. Alice could open the storefronts even if all she did was sell other companies' products for them. When she mentioned to her staff at the drugstore that she could finally start hiring for the CannRose dispensaries, one of her pharmacists piped up that she'd be interested. Given all the jokes bandied about by her staff over the past year or so, this surprised Alice a little. It had also registered vaguely in the back of Alice's mind that psychotropic substances of any sort might be taboo for Sameera Hassan Abdul. So much for that assumption! And Sammy was her favorite pharmacist so she didn't really want to lose her to the medical marijuana industry.

"You mean to the Dark Side? Aren't you being a little hypocritical?" Sammy had teased.

And so Alice had thought about it for a while, but the more she thought about it, the more she didn't like the idea. Mostly it had to do with making the three-hour trip back and forth to Lyston.

"I'm a good driver!" Sammy said. "I don't even get parking tickets. Well at least not this year."

"I don't want you on that highway all the time."

"I'll be fine, Alice!'

"You get pulled over, you might not be fine."

"I'm careful."

"Maybe so." Alice cleared her throat and then slowly shook her head. "Lot of misunderstandings these days on the side of a highway."

Sammy shrugged.

"What if your car smells of it. And it just might if you're working with weed all day."

"I'll take all the documents I need."

"Nope."

"Alice!"

"Nope. I'm not going to have it on my conscience. You're young. You're not white. Officer might not give you a chance to show him the papers. And after he — because it will in all probability be a *he* — after he's slammed your head onto the car roof and thrown you in jail, or worse, he'll claim it was all a misunderstanding and he'll be fine. But you won't be fine."

Sammy looked at Alice. There was no winning this kind of argument with her. "I could still just manage things from the dispensary across town. Phones and internet, you know."

Alice thought about that too for a while and it sat better with her. Sammy taking over would mean that getting the dispensaries running would be relatively seamless. Alice wouldn't have to spend time filling anybody in on how she ran things.

After discussions with Luther it was decided Alice would do the traveling if there was a need for it. Sammy could run things from the city. But they would still have to hire technicians for the Lyston dispensary. So a few days later Alice and Sammy drove up to Lyston.

Lydia was waiting for them at the dispensary. She was thrilled to see Alice again and delighted to meet Sammy. When they entered the building, Alice was immediately struck by the serenity of the space. The walls were very pale and had a warm gray, almost mauve tint to them. The woodwork, used to divide the room and frame the ceiling into sections, was stained with deep umber that glowed with russet overtones. It was the color of black coffee loaded with cinnamon, as were the floors that looked to be finished cork. The wall leading into the storage and work area was actually a screen that would slide. The counters and display cases were arranged much like they were in the city dispensary, except the woodwork on them was dark to match the floors and trim and they were more square and unadorned looking.

"Has a kind of Japanese feel to it," Alice said.

"Elegant," Sammy said.

"You've hit the nail on the head. I'll have to tell Hi," Lydia said. "He told me when he found out what it was for, he wanted it to look like a place where someone might hold a tea ceremony. And he started telling me about the history of spiritual uses associated with marijuana. I thought that was such an interesting approach and charming."

"What does Caldwell think?" Alice asked, not without some mischief.

"Oh, he hates it of course. But he's vastly outnumbered on this one." And Lydia smiled an equally mischievous smile.

"How is the cultivation coming, Lydia? When do you think we might see mature plants?" Alice asked.

"The cultivation is fine. They were harvesting again just yesterday."

Alice looked a little confused. "We keep being told we don't have a crop yet."

"I guess Caldwell says that because we still haven't met the . . . tests. You know how the health department sets numbers for things. And when test results come back . . ."

"You mean there's been product all along? I only knew about the crop that blew the lid off the DOH specifications."

"Specifications! That's the word I was looking for. That's right! We still do not meet the DOH specifications," Lydia said and then added, "for yeast and mold, I hear."

"So that's why I've never seen any test results."

"Well they come back with that big red stamp on them. Upsets Caldwell to no end. So I imagine he doesn't allow Gus to send them on."

"So, is it just the microbial limits? No metals? And surely no pesticides I would assume, with all this talk about 'organic,'" Alice said.

"That's right. I've heard Caldwell complain bitterly about *microbial contamination*. He says we're out only by tiny numbers. That's after the first moldy crop fiasco of course. He figures the facility sanitation is still a problem."

"It's possible. But there's been no mention of mycotoxins or anything like that?" Alice asked.

Lydia shook her head. "Not from what I hear."

"What happens with crops that don't meet specifications?" Sammy, not at all familiar with any processes at the grow facility, was curious.

"Oh, they get buried."

"What?" Alice was incredulous. "Lydia, if it's just a microbial-count problem, why aren't we sterilizing the product? The state is allowing irradiation. In fact it's recommending it. Why aren't we doing that?"

"Oh! Caldwell won't hear of it! He gets positively beside himself if anyone mentions it."

"But the literature says that's still the best way to sterilize marijuana. They use it in Europe," Alice said. "In fact in Holland I think medical cannabis *has* to be irradiated. And if the state's allowing it I'm pretty sure all the other dispensaries are doing it."

"I don't think you can label something organic if you irradiate," Sammy said.

"You can't certify organic right now anyway because it's under the USDA and that's federal," Alice said.

Lydia shrugged. "Caldwell says CannRose product will never ever be irradiated because the marijuana just won't be the same."

"I was just reading a study," Sammy said. "Looks like irradiation doesn't affect the cannabinoids, but there is some concentration loss for a few of the terpenes. They evaporate, if I recall correctly. State doesn't require labeling or testing for terpenes. Maybe they don't consider them active ingredients."

"No and they'll probably ignore them for some time," Alice said. "There's over a hundred of them in cannabis. Just like there're dozens of cannabinoids they don't require labeling for yet either. The complexity of interactions and the entourage effects are going to take years for researchers to figure out. If they ever do!" Alice shook her head. "And losses in a few terpene concentrations from irradiation are irrelevant. Especially if it's from evaporation. They're volatilizing all the time — that's what you're smelling! And the concentrations, including those of terpenes, are determined *after* irradiation. Just like you'd run the clinical trials — and the entourage studies if anybody ever gets around to them — *after* irradiation of the product. The important thing right now is labeling accurately so the customer knows what they're getting. And sterilizing when necessary so they don't get sick from mold, *E. coli, pseudomonas* or whatever!"

"Well," Lydia said with a sigh, "Caldwell says people won't buy irradiated marijuana. And he wouldn't ever want the company name associated with it."

"What people won't buy it?" Alice was perplexed. "Lots of drugs on the market are irradiated. Half the food you eat is irradiated. You know sick people mostly have compromised immune systems. They'd probably have more confidence in the product knowing it was sterilized."

"Well Damian says you shouldn't ever do that to marijuana."

"Oh lord!" Alice exhaled audibly. "What you're really telling me is old stoners don't like the idea of their weed being nuked!"

Sammy started to laugh but Alice was clearly irritated. "This is a problem, Lydia. We're trying to get medicine on the shelves, not provide weed connoisseurs with what they consider the perfect high. I think there's a little confusion going on in the company. We need to get this clarified and soon. Otherwise the DOH really will pull the registration if we can't meet quotas."

"You'll have to raise it with Caldwell. I just don't want to be in the room when you do." Lydia looked at Sammy and they both giggled.

"What does your new QA guy think of all this? He's got a pharma background."

"You can ask Percy yourself," Lydia said. "I thought we could all go for lunch if you've got the time."

Alice and Sammy held interviews all morning. When they went for lunch with Lydia and Percy, Alice found out the extent of the contamination issues. As Percy explained to her, while tempering his description in Lydia's presence, "I believe there are a few practices at CannRose that are less effective than they might be. But according to my review of the pertinent literature, getting microbial counts down for plant-based medicine is a constant challenge." And he had heard by a particular grapevine he was now privy to that CannRose was possibly the only state dispensary not considering irradiation. Later over the phone he would say, "It's insane, Alice! Utter madness. They won't even consider sterilizing the grow media and sometimes it's positively hopping with bugs."

\#

When Alice brought up the subject of irradiation on the next conference call, Caldwell predictably hit the roof and started going on about brand integrity and customer trust, but Alice countered every one of his arguments with facts, numbers and relevant studies. Percy had sent her all the results from the DOH lab too, so Caldwell couldn't do a runaround about those numbers either. He became so enraged he eventually stormed out of the meeting and slammed the door. Alice wished she'd been there to see it.

She also got to raise her favorite complaint of getting oils and derivatives on the shelf. "This should be prioritized. We need to hire somebody who knows what the hell they're doing! And extracts are the best way to ensure dosage. Some of the processing might even help sterilize the product for you!" The others on the call all mumbled in agreement.

When she got off the phone she was smiling. One way or another she was finally going to get some CannRose product on those dispensary shelves.

Chapter 30

Petra walked into the spare office in the admin wing where Lazlo was standing beside the spectacular haul he'd dumped on the conference table. She surveyed the jumble of derelict instruments and saw the frustration of her future. She was a scientist, not a technician, for crying out loud!

Lazlo was nodding to himself, clearly pleased with the deal he got. "The guy at the EPA office said they were all real gems. Trusty workhorses he called 'em. He seemed real sad about havin' to get rid of everything."

Petra did not smile. The crippling of environmental oversight and renewed devastation of the planet were no longer her concern. She put her hand on the oven door of the gas chromatograph, felt around the side and pulled the latch. An old capillary column was still inside. It had the color and sheen of beeswax. For volatiles probably. She looked for an identification tag, but it was missing.

"That one's for pesticides, the guy said. He said it was dedicated. I figure that sounds pretty good. Right?" Lazlo said. "Dedication is always good, right?"

Petra was still not acknowledging his presence.

"I thought that's what we had to test. You were sayin' you might need to test pesticides, and now you can. Right?"

"Maybe," she said finally. "I'm more interested in terpenes, actually." She put both hands on the mass spectrometer component and turned it around on the table. "This will do." It was about the size of two stacked cement blocks and probably weighed about the same. She wondered if it had ever worked for more than a week without collapsing in some convulsion. That had been her experience with a mass spec. She'd need a headspace sampler to go with it, and she wondered if that was even possible, given the instrument's age.

"There's a box with the CDs and manuals and everything for that one. He thought you'd want the maintenance history, so that's in there too."

"We need to test the cannabinoids. The THC, CBD and whatnot." She was talking more to the air than to Lazlo. "And for that we need HPLC" — She glanced up at him — "High-performance liquid chromatography, or some exotic variation . . . Ah! And here she is."

"I forget what he said that one was used for, but he said it's top of the line. You couldn't get better, the guy said."

Petra looked at the manufacturer's seal on the crate. Lazlo was right: You really couldn't get better. She peered into the crate. The instrument looked new enough. She wondered if it was still under any kind of warranty.

"Pile of paperwork came with it, binders and everything. Here in this box. This goes with that." Lazlo pointed to the HPLC.

Her hand still on the box, Petra looked around until she found the autosampler that went with it. She peered into that box too. It was a sleek thing with an elegant sampling arm that likely made impressive beeps and pings as it went about its business. The image gave Petra a fleeting sense of hope. She looked up and took in the extent of the haul: computers; a small centrifuge; three balances (one was a five-decimal-place — just breathe on it wrong and you'd send it reeling); a muffle furnace; a microwave; a dozen autopipettes; what looked like a brand-new rotovap; boxes and boxes of beakers; Erlenmeyers and volumetrics of all sizes.

What the hell? Was the EPA getting rid of everything these days? She felt like a vulture at the aftermath of a slaughter. It was disgusting and exhilarating at the same time.

But for crying out loud, how was she going to get all of it up and running? She didn't have the energy, let alone the patience or skill set. She needed staff. Somebody very technically inclined. There didn't seem to be anybody at the facility capable of repairing fans, never mind futzing with finicky analytical instruments. She had heard the guy doing purchasing had a mechanical background, but he was busy already and she doubted whatever background he had included equipment like this.

She clearly hadn't asked enough questions at the interview. She couldn't remember if she'd been hung over. She still kept a case of vodka in the garden shed for emergencies. And at this very moment, she could think of nothing more comforting than achieving her own private oblivion.

She walked out of the office, away from Lazlo and the EPA carnage. Maybe she should just take the rest of the day and claim nausea. She'd pretty well perfected nausea in all its iterations, existential and otherwise. As she passed by Lydia's office, a voice called out, "Oh, Petra! I was just thinking of you."

Petra turned and retraced her steps. She'd spoken to Lydia only once, on her third or fourth visit to CannRose. She was not put off by the general consensus regarding Lydia, that she was eccentric and spare on gray matter. People often made the very rich into whatever demons suited them. Petra was dimly conscious that some part of her almost respected money more than pretense to achievement or intelligence. Money was a necessity and claimed no particular greatness for itself. She popped her head in the door of Lydia's office.

"Do you have some time?" said Lydia.

Petra nodded.

"Good. Have a seat. Would you like a drink?"

Petra wondered how far she could stretch propriety at ten in the morning. "I'm okay, thanks."

"You sure? I have a very fine Sumatran gourmet blend. And that little cappuccino machine in the corner there doesn't get enough action. It was a present from Caldwell. You know he can be very extravagant."

Petra thought about it. Caffeine was mood altering. "Okay, that sounds . . . extravagant. I'll have mine really strong, thanks."

"Wonderful." Lydia picked up the desk phone and punched in several numbers. "Tim, would you have a minute or two to come make a couple of cappuccinos? . . . Oh, you're a dear! You do absolutely make the best." Lydia put the phone down. "He even does the little petals, you know, the design in the foam on top. Caldwell has him making a marijuana leaf now. He thinks there's a big possibility for gourmet coffee and gourmet buds in the same shop if it all goes recreational. Just like in Holland, he says."

"That's an idea. Beans and buds, I guess."

"Caldwell is just full of ideas. It's hard to keep up."

"So I hear." Petra was thinking of Gus, the young, heavy-set production manager who had obviously resisted keeping up. He was the methodical and plodding type. Just the type to drive someone like Caldwell bonkers. Apparently it had all came to a head a few days before. Insults were hurled very loudly and very publicly. Then Gus simply walked out. He left a sign on the production office door that said, "I QUIT. Go fuck yourself, Caldwell." Greg had rushed to take it down, but the crowd around the door had already gathered and the snickering was well under way by the time Petra had walked by.

"So how are you getting on?" Lydia asked. "It's a few months since you started with us, isn't it?"

"Six."

"Oh my gracious! I do lose track of time. This job just keeps me so busy."

Tim stuck his head in the door and Lydia introduced him to Petra. He was a student of policy studies, home in Hullbrooke for the semester. "This job's kind of like research for me," he told Petra. "It's all ... fascinating." She thought she noticed a hint of irony in his voice.

He started the cappuccino maker and opened the little bar fridge. "Everyone good with lactose free?"

"Fine," Lydia said and Petra nodded. "Oh, and Tim, Petra wants hers very strong."

In silence, they watched Tim in action. They couldn't talk over the steamer anyway. As he handed them each their cappuccinos, a marijuana leaf drawn in the foam, Tim pantomimed a proud chef puckering his lips and kissing the air.

Cheeky little brat, Petra thought, but it was delicious.

"Timothy, you've outdone yourself," Lydia exclaimed in her best Texan drawl. Timothy bowed with a flourish and left the room.

"So," Lydia asked Petra, "what exciting science are you coming up with these days?" She was trying to recall what Jordan had told her about his dealings with technical people and scientists. He told her there was an art to getting the best out of them. She couldn't remember the rest of what he said but being congenial and welcoming had to be a good place to start.

"There's mostly a lot of inconclusive science at the moment," Petra began. "Uh, historically, there's been quite a bit of research in

Israel. And the field is certainly starting to boom." She took another sip of her cappuccino. "To be honest, I'm pretty much having to retool for this industry. Cannabis is a complex plant. Most plants are, but . . . uh . . ."

Lydia nodded encouragingly.

"Human interaction with cannabis is extremely complex from a physiological standpoint. It's difficult to determine what a medical producer should be aiming to achieve." It was a long-winded way of saying she didn't have a damn clue what she was up to yet.

After the first month, she'd got the impression nobody really cared what she did. She was pretty sure Caldwell and Luther had hired her as a PR move. CannRose-Medi would look better if there was a scientist with a PhD on board. She realized after it was too late she should have asked for more money. But given that it was a job and she was getting paid for it, even if not handsomely, she found it curious that she still had no idea who she was reporting to. It was increasingly probable she might not be answering to anybody. *My God* — the door to a new universe swung open at the thought of it — she might be able to do curiosity-driven science! It was a vanishing if not extinct endeavor these days. Even back when she was a grad student there were funding cuts for fundamental plant research. They used to joke that they could maybe start applying to the Hell's Angels or the Mexican drug cartels so they could keep working on plants. And here she was, up to her ears in weed. "It's not something I've ever worked with before. Cannabis that is."

"Why, of course. I can certainly understand that."

"I am starting an experiment, though. The clones are being prepped today. Um . . . I did mention this at the interview . . . most of the plant research I've been involved with had very little to do with secondary metabolism or, say, soil-plant relations, disease resistance, that kind of thing — all the issues that would concern marijuana growers specifically. So I'm having to catch up."

Lydia nodded, a slight furrow forming in her brow.

Petra figured she might as well come out with her current problem too, since the worst Lydia could be was indifferent. "I'm having technical hurdles as well. I'm not a technician. All those instruments that Lazlo just brought back from the EPA, somebody needs to look after them. I could probably do it, but that's all I'd end up doing, and I think CannRose hired me to do research."

Lydia suddenly remembered what it was Jordan had said about keeping scientists at their best: Make sure they had the tools and resources at their disposal and then give them problems they couldn't possibly solve. It was amazing what they could come up with. "We absolutely want you to do the best science possible for CannRose-Medi. What resources and tools do you need?"

Petra blinked. Lydia had gotten to the crux of the issue before she had herself. "A tech," she said. "A technician. Someone to do that kind of work for me."

"That's a simple thing, I think."

Petra nodded.

"I'll just speak to Luther about it and have it cleared. Of course, you'll want to do the interviewing yourself."

Petra nodded again. Given the complete ignorance in the whole company of virtually anything required to do her job, she found it hard to believe she'd just hit pay dirt with Lydia.

"I don't imagine Greg will know what you're looking for in the person, so maybe you can make up a little list for him. For the posting. I've noticed he likes lists." Lydia smiled.

Petra smiled back. "There's one more thing I could use. It would be very helpful."

"Yes?"

"I need a couple of growth chambers."

"Now would you need two of these exactly?"

"Um . . . the more the merrier!"

"So we should get them in bulk."

"Actually, they're pretty big. About double the size of a refrigerator. Sometimes bigger. A DNA sequencer would probably be handy too!" Petra was joking now. The DNA sequencer she had her eye on cost over a million bucks and given its potential, she'd like a team, not just a tech. The thing about marijuana was, because of hybridization and the crazy underworld breeding over the past forty years, the genetics were all fragmented, duplicated, triplicated and multiplied every which way. It was practically impossible to get a reliable reference. Everything she'd read indicated it was probably a mug's game at this point. Especially with the less expensive sequencers. "Just kidding," she said.

"Really?"

"Well, we could consider it down the line. Let somebody else start working on it."

"They can do the heavy lifting? Is that what you're implying?"

"Exactly."

"But these other things that you need, you know where to get them?"

"Absolutely."

"You know what I'm going to do? I'm just going talk to our CFO. He can set you up with a budget. That way you don't have to go through Lazlo or that other young fellow we have for purchasing, I forget his name. You can order what you need directly. Would that suit you?"

"That would be fantastic!"

Lydia beamed. "I'm so glad we had this chat. We should get together more often. I don't get to talk much to people in the other wing. Of course, I travel a lot these days. Almost as much as Caldwell! You know," she confided, "I never would have imagined I'd be doing something like this in a million years."

"Me neither," said Petra.

Chapter 31

"I don't believe this." Joe was staring at the feeding records for Flower Room II. "He's starving them again."

"I thought you guys had worked that all out," said Lizzie, one of the grow staff, sitting at the next desk and sorting through the flower-room logs.

"Who okayed this?"

She shrugged. "Gus, before he . . . you know . . ."

"Bet he didn't. Bet it's just Damian. What a jerk," Joe muttered.

"So now we're back to doing it his way again?"

"Not if I can help it."

"It'd be nice if you guys could start agreeing on things."

"Okay. So I'll ask you this: When have all the plants looked the best? No hermies. No diseases. Happy, happy."

Lizzie considered Joe's question for a few seconds. "Umm . . . about two months ago," she said. "Yeah, the flower rooms looked really lush. And the one nursery too."

"Right. And where had Damian been the whole month before that?"

"See what you mean."

"Yeah. So the plants were just fine while he was on his friggin' expenses-paid trip home to Colorado."

"Uh-huh." The young woman thought it best to be noncommittal.

#

Damian showed up an hour later. Since his stays in the north were fairly intensive and he worked through weekends, he didn't feel the need to keep a regular schedule. This was seen as an affront by many of the grow staff. Greg and Gus — up until the time he quit — held everybody else at CannRose to tight schedules. Clearly *master grower* was a mysterious position. The staff had never been able to figure out what the job actually entailed. More specifically they were never sure who was actually the master.

"Glad you could make it," Joe said, as Damian sauntered into the cultivation office.

"Yup," Damian replied and gestured as if to brush away a fly. He found Joe depressing with his square-head and brush cut, his perky wife and his pink, plastic-looking kids, like they'd come out of a 3D printer. Damian had run into the whole family one Saturday at the deli in Hullbrooke. He imagined Joe and the kids chowing down on their nightly meat and potatoes. Or fish and potatoes. The picture was nauseating. He hoped spending time in the facility with such mediocrity and claustrophobic family values would not rob him of his own soul. If Lydia wasn't paying him so much he'd be back in Colorado.

"So why are we doing this again?" Joe was wasting no time. He threw the fertilizer record down on the table in front of Damian. "That batch was set for filling out and you're starving them."

"They were overfed."

"They were not. And what about these mothers? They've just been cloned. What the frig?"

"Yeah, well. What the frig." Damian shrugged, turned and walked out of the office.

"I was talking to you."

"You mean you were talking *at* me," he said, looking briefly back over his shoulder.

"This isn't about you or me. This is about the plants, asshole."

Damian threw up his arms and kept walking. He swiveled around briefly — "Must be an East Coast thing with you guys!" — before vanishing into the hallway that led to the mother pods.

Damian opened the door to the South Mother Pod. "How are we all today, my southern belles?" The strains in the South Mother were all shapes and sizes and most of them were very bushy. They were old breeds and hybrids and many were even first generation, grown up from seed. Damian was extremely secretive about where the seeds had come from. They had names like Sweet Puddin', Jakarta Honey, Hula Colada, Bubba Kush, Alabama Blitz, Skunk Bunny and Toto's

Revenge. Of course by the time any of these plants' children or derivative products got to market, the names would be gone. They'd be sanitized to things like A-Bmz-4a or Whole Flowers SB-3. Yeah, all so the state could pretend it wasn't dealing pot. So ridiculous.

Damian motioned to the other person in the room, a young woman. She was new to cultivation work. He pointed to the plastic basket of shears. "Make sure everything's a good fit or you'll end up with blisters."

The young woman walked over to the table, grabbed a small pair of gloves and tried out a few shears until she found a comfortable pair.

"So, you'll just be looking for any wilted, unhealthy, damaged, dead or dying leaves and cutting them off at the base of the frond, like this." And Damian clipped off a yellowing seven-pointer in one easy move. "Don't just take the leaflets. Make sure it's the whole thing."

They began working down the same row. Occasionally Damian would point out something the young woman had missed. They both looked up when the door opened and Cassie came into the pod to get clones for Petra's experiment. She'd hoped Damian might be in one of the other pods. Possibly in the west one where he was most effective at killing the mothers by a slow death. Cassie decided to ignore both Damian and the new hire. She would be very busy. She was to make fifteen cuttings each from four different mothers: Alabama Blitz, Krishna's Caress, Columbian Amber and Amazonian Amma. Petra had asked about Toto's Revenge. Cassie told her it was a strain that grew well in any climate and really was the weediest strain of weed. Cassie was thinking it was probably the only one Damian wouldn't be able to kill.

"Hey, hey! What's this, man? Why you doin' a hatchet job on my Krishna?" Damian said with a raised voice after seeing what Cassie was up to.

"I'm not a man." Cassie snipped forcefully with the shears. "And I'm getting clones for Petra." She wanted to add "asshole" but refrained.

"Who?"

"Petra. You know? The scientist? That woman with the degrees who actually knows something about plants?"

"Oh. Her. I don't know she knows so much about plants. She's just going to mangle them."

"Really!"

"Yeah. That's what scientists do."

"They do?"

"Yeah. They do. Cut everything up into tiny pieces and lose all connection to what they started out with."

"Wow, Damian. You know so much!"

"Yeah, I do. I know a few things."

"Yeah. It's just so hard to know what they are . . ."

Damian shook his head and kept smiling.

"It's stunning," Cassie said, "trying to figure out the few things you know. It's so minimal . . . it's awesome! Humbling!"

Damian had never experienced Cassie's chirpy sarcasm before. He found it oddly titillating. "Glad you find me so transformative," he said.

"Oh totally. It's, like, life changing! You know, critical."

The young woman pruning off the dead leaves wasn't sure what she was witnessing but figured it wise to just keep her head down.

PART SEVEN

Growth

Oh Wads! Lose your clumpings of disaster. Lose your knack for despair. Swing your light so we may bask, knowing gentler fools have loved us. Since you must waste eons, can you not do it brightly? Bring laughter that the sun may prevail and the moon have one last go around before throwing in the towel? Oh Wads and your Sphincters of Titus! What can we say? Lose your tidings of terror and the ends of your days. Wake up. Gently.

from Cannto VIII, *Cannabidadas*

Chapter 32

Ernie adjusted his slipping eye patch. It was getting a little greasy and the elastic was going on it. Time for a new one. He bought them in packages of four, one of the few things, along with shoes, that he purchased new. He'd been contemplating getting something made from snakeskin for special occasions. The odd catering gig where he cooked on site demanded a good play on the talented chef image. He was debating what would be best — natural markings because he often cooked wild foods, or dyed black — when he caught sight of the new production manager, the fourth CannRose had hired in little over a year and a half.

A blond picture of health, Lorne was probably a decade younger than Ernie with a California tan like he'd just stepped off a surfboard. How irritating! And he was so keen, so sincere, talking to Lazlo and Caldwell, nodding enthusiastically and hanging on to every word. Just ripe for clobbering, Ernie figured. He'd probably be on anti-anxiety meds in no time, if he wasn't already.

Lorne had been hesitant about accepting the position after he heard about the turnover at CannRose. But Ernie knew Greg had smooth-talked him. Greg was good at that. Used phrases like "a disappointing initial trial period" and "not exactly a good fit" and often declared, "Hey, it's just natural growing pains. Nobody's really done this before. Unless you were born in the Stoned Age." And Greg would laugh at his own bad jokes. But it must have reassured Lorne, who had a wife, three kids and a dog and was relocating for this job. Ernie wondered how long it would be before all hell broke loose and the guy packed it in.

Lorne had been in the herbal tea business overseeing production of the short-lived Heaven Blessed Infusions and Tibetan Toner Teas. He lost his job when the company was bought out by one of the big tea producers, who promptly shut them down. But that was CannRose's good fortune, Greg pointed out. Lorne looked to have about the best experience anyone could have for the job. "Unless your name's Fatty Diego from Columbia," Greg chuckled. Ernie figured it must have been those years of being a cop and busting people that made Greg so loose with the bad weed jokes.

Three days after Lorne started work he sought out Ernie. "Finally. Just the person I wanted to talk to."

"What can I do for you?" Ernie smiled.

"Well, I'm looking at your hours, Ernie. You don't work much do you?"

"Nope."

"Do you want more hours?"

"Nope."

"You work a couple of jobs, huh. Or three, like some people I know?" Lorne grinned, flashing his perfect white teeth.

"Nope."

"Oh."

Ernie noted Lorne's tone dropped. The man didn't approve or was puzzled perhaps. Ambition, keeping busy and absolute trust in the benefits of productivity were clearly givens in his world. Ernie waited for him to say something more but Lorne seemed to lose interest in him. "Well, you have yourself a great afternoon, Lorne," and Ernie went back to cleaning the utility sink.

#

Ernie noticed after a few weeks that Lorne, rather than showing any signs of crumbling, was doing awfully well. Though Ernie continued to find the man's seeming sincerity and unrufflable composure irritating, most everyone else was impressed. His very existence created a level of strategizing among management and staff that Ernie had never witnessed at CannRose. People were clearly seeking the new man's alliance and endeavoring to shore up favor.

Percy was particularly attentive with Lorne. The QA officer fired up the machine in Lydia's office and took Lorne double cappuccinos at coffee break. It seemed he needed Lorne to understand the importance of quality assurance. "I know it's just humble weed we're cultivating and processing here," Ernie overheard him say, "but the staff need to adhere to — no, they need to unequivocally embrace — the quality system. Of course you'd know that from the tea industry."

"It sure looks to be thorough," Lorne said, smiling as he took the cappuccino. "Your system. It's detailed."

"They didn't have a clue, you know. There was virtually nothing here in the way of a protocol. The DOH was actually rather lenient, I thought. Mind you, marijuana's a long stretch from cranking out statins and ACE inhibitors."

"For sure. Pharmaceuticals. That's a whole other level, isn't it?"

"But we're still producing medicine. Stringency should never be dismissed out of hand just because it's cannabis. I mean Six Sigma is out of the question! But for the love of God, the staff need to at least follow the operating procedures now they have some. Consistency in method is crucial. And they need to keep records. I worry some of them can barely spell their names, let alone fill in a maintenance log."

"Hmm. Yeah, it's always a battle I think for QA."

Ernie didn't hear the rest of that particular conversation but Caldwell's name drifted down the hallway a few times. Ernie imagined Percy was spilling the beans on the ad-hoc maneuvers that turned his carefully documented protocols upside down. All in all, Percy's wooing must have been successful. After half an hour he came strolling out of Lorne's office looking like a Cheshire cat with a new best friend.

Next up was Petra. If Percy flailed against the lack of quality culture at CannRose, Petra flailed at the dearth of science comprehension. Like Percy, she had issues with Caldwell. He'd say anything, do anything just to bring in the next thousand dollars. "He just makes shit up and then expects it to fly because he believes it." And the board and Luther were no better as far as Petra was concerned. "They're prone to the same delusions, or maybe it's just easier to believe Caldwell than challenge him."

One day Ernie watched Caldwell making a pitch, with Percy and Petra standing right behind the potential investor. "CannRose is growing plants with identical buds, Chad," Caldwell exclaimed. "And identical concentrations of active pharmaceutical ingredients! That's the THC and the CBD, Chad. Every ounce of product will have the same dosage." Percy and Petra were glaring at Caldwell, shaking their heads, but Caldwell kept smiling and talking. "Chad, you may find it hard to believe, but growing techniques make all the difference. We have the most advanced growing techniques in the industry."

Petra later said this was lunacy. Not a goddam shred of evidence. In fact science would suggest plants, like humans, are fairly heterogeneous products of genetics and environment. Add to that the predominance of hybrid strains, thanks to years of black-market R and D, and you have a genetic and phenotypic variability that would knock old Mendel's socks off. Plus there was no way there weren't differing microclimates in a room that size, nor could anybody in their wildest dreams guarantee the homogeneity of all the organic grow media.

When the investor was gone they tried to have it out with Caldwell. "If authorities get wind of these claims they might decide to step in."

Caldwell dismissed the idea.

"What about lawsuits or fraud cases if the investors lose their money and learn the truth?" Petra said. "We need real science to make progress. Making crazy statements just puts the company in jeopardy."

"We need to get a few of the claims off the website too, by the way," Percy added. "The DOH might do more than slap our wrists. We're not exactly popular with them as it is."

"This is business!" Caldwell said and slipped away to a meeting in the city.

So Petra apprised Lorne of the absurdities. There'd been unsubstantiated claims about healings too, and God knows what else. She suggested Lorne might want to keep notes if the false claims ever came to light so he couldn't be held responsible. That's what *she* was doing. Along with saving her emails.

Cassie and Joe were keeping notes too. But it would be a while before they got around to showing Lorne their special logbook with page headings like "Major Fertigation Fail by Damian, October 15, on Jazmine Kush" or "Idiotic Cloning Fail by Caldwell, November 14" and so on. Instead Ernie noted they did their best to just charm Lorne. They were helpful and informative, knowing full well that Damian, though probably friendly to the new guy, would do his best to keep Lorne in the dark. And it seemed to be working.

Chapter 33

Greg noted that Petra's analytical demeanor changed when Sanjay walked into the office to interview for the technician position. He was the fifth person they'd seen in the last three days. Greg was finding it all tedious because half the time he barely understood all the jargon. Petra had insisted Greg post the job with a web-based company specializing in technical and engineering talent. He was hoping she'd settle on someone soon. So he watched optimistically as she straightened right up in her chair and pulled her glasses down on her nose a little to peer over them. Then she took her glasses right off and put them down on the desk. And she smiled. She hadn't done that with the other four applicants.

The truth was Petra was getting a little bored with the process. But she'd taken one long look and decided, consciously or not, that Sanjay had the job even if he could barely hold a wrench or knew what a spreadsheet was. Sanjay was tall and all of about thirty, if his resumé was anything to go by. *But holy smokin' Adonis!* The guy was serious candy. Her nostrils flared a little as she took in the faint scent that wafted in with him. While the current jury might be out on the exact nature of human pheromones, Sanjay's particular mix of androstadienone, or perhaps the odor indirectly generated by his immune system, the histocompatibility complex, or whatever riffraff molecules he exuded, possibly even from his upper lip, all set Petra's brain aglow. It was a delectable blend and most invigorating. He didn't just walk into the room. He made an entrance.

When he took off his jacket as he sat down, the simple snug gray T-shirt revealed more treasures. Muscled, Petra noted, but not overly so, and classically proportioned. Skin a warm, pale bronze that looked to be the texture of fine woven silk. And his eyes were a striking composite of earth tones, the irises a deep amber that blended into a rich brown near the pupils. His hair, jet black, had just the right degree of unkempt nonchalance about it and his smile was completely disarming. Petra couldn't stop a little gasp. He would add a whole new dimension to the scientific discoveries. And there were going to be lots of scientific discoveries because nobody knew jack shit about marijuana except maybe the Israelis. And even *they* had only scratched the surface. Anyway that was beside the point.

"Ah, so, how much experience have you had with organics?" Petra asked, still hanging on to her composure after all the initial introductions, pleasantries and assorted standard questions were out of the way.

"Well," Sanjay replied, "as you can see, my degree is in organic chemistry. With the last two years in a hospital lab and two before that at an environmental lab. You name it, I've probably done it."

"Volatiles, headspace analysis?"

"Piece of cake, usually," Sanjay nodded.

"And HPLC."

"I spent a whole year analyzing blood sugars and sweet talking an old Dionex."

"Good! And speaking of instruments, how are you with troubleshooting, tinkering, repairs, computer interface, that sort of thing?"

"I don't waste my time with the instruments unless they're over fifty thousand dollars. And I only rip apart the computers when they start to talk back."

Petra laughed and Sanjay smiled. He knew he had the job. At least if it was up to Petra.

"So why are you interested in working with marijuana?" Greg asked suddenly in a very serious tone.

"Ah, well. Jobs are not so easy to find these days. Especially given most things I can do are on the way down. Science generally, you know. Changes in health care coming. But marijuana looks to be on the way up. So I figure it's maybe a good place to be now. I'm thinking I might like to go on with some more academics at some point too. Looks like marijuana research is pretty wide open. Lots to do."

Petra was nodding.

Greg was satisfied with this answer but not completely sold. "You know we have drug screening here."

"No problem. We had it at the hospital too."

"Oh yeah, right," Greg said, having momentarily forgotten the range of controlled substances available in the world. "So did you see, like, overdoses and stuff?"

"No. I just worked in the lab. I didn't see patients."

Petra looked down at Sanjay's resumé again. He wasn't just a pretty face. Lucky thing she'd finally decided on a research direction or . . . what the hell . . . several possible directions. "So what's your experience with plant physiology, genetics, molecular techniques or maybe systems biology?"

"I have to admit, not a lot. I have basic botany. You know, undergrad stuff. Molecular techniques? Not so much, but I had a girlfriend I used to help out in the lab with the tissue cultures when she worked late."

"At the hospital?"

"No. At the university. She was doing her master's. She complained all she did was slaughter *Arabidopsis*."

"So you *were* working with plant tissue!"

"Just helping."

"Still. That's great!" Petra remarked rather unconvincingly. It was the only part of the interview that irked somewhere in the remote fields of her consciousness. The "just helping" took her back to her own late nights in Gerald's lab. God, she'd been an idiot. A hormonally induced stupidity had led her to forfeit her own research! Naiveté and some dumb trust in the nobility of love and self-sacrifice had supported her. Gerald certainly hadn't. She quickly put it out of her mind.

Petra asked Sanjay if he'd like to see the lab. He would of course. And then she explained that his first task would be to help set it up if he got the job. If? Who was she kidding? At this point, only Greg. As they walked through the production area to the lab, Petra told Sanjay about the assortment of secondhand instruments and where they'd come from. She was still waiting to have the floor epoxied and two sinks put in. There were two fume hoods in the process of being installed as well. Sanjay laughed when he saw the jumble of instrument parts, crates and boxes lining the benches.

"Oh my God! All this from the EPA?"

"Even half the glassware." And Petra pulled out a couple of drawers, showing him an assortment of beakers, flasks, graduated cylinders and funnels.

Sanjay shook his head. "Poor EPA. Makes you wonder doesn't it?"

Chapter 34

The three young devotees were in the change room at CannRose preparing for a day of work among the plants. As they threw their street clothes into their lockers and donned their scrubs and work shoes, they discussed their superiors. Personal and emotional hygiene were often uppermost in their minds.

"Dude, Lorne is hardcore."

"Yeah, I know."

"Dude, you need a shower."

"Yeah, seriously. You have odor."

"I don't smell anything."

"That's the other problem. Your nose."

"We're supposed to shower after work."

"You need one now. He'll say something."

"No he won't."

"Dude, if he gets this close he will."

"You should just shower every morning."

"Yeah. You probably have that sulfur problem. My uncle has it. So you have to shower more often."

"Fuck!"

"Use the soap!"

The young man picked up a bottle of aloe cleansing gel and took a clean towel from the shelf. He walked naked to the shower, turned on the taps and held his hand in the water stream to gauge the temperature. The other two devotees continued their conversation as the room filled with steam and the sound of running water.

"Gus shouldn't have left us."

"He left the ladies too."

"So basic."

"He's working across state at another place."

"Shit. That's, like, not fair!"

"Whatever."

"Maybe he'd hire us."

"What's wrong with here?"

"Everything. Why do you think Gus left?"

"Shook. Pissed at Caldwell. You saw the note."

"Yeah."

"It could be worse there. The ladies could be more sad."

"Damian says all the state places are a mess."

"Damian only likes Colorado."

"He was showing me that book again."

"He likes you, bro. Brobro."

"It's plants talking. That's all."

"Dude. Ladies are silent. Ladies just speak with the smoke. Optimum."

"Maybe they talk to Damian."

"Sure, brobro. Shippin' the Damian."

"Fuck off! Damian says the book is ancient."

"No it's not. It's some old hippie dude shit."

"Yeah, but maybe the ladies like it. Maybe he reads it to them."

"Dude. He doesn't."

"Maybe when we're not here he does. Because it's intimate."

"Dude, he doesn't."

"No. I mean like really old time. Like with knights and shit. They read poetry to their ladies. Sang it. We could set the words to song."

"Dude."

"It might make the ladies happy."

"Dude. You need to stop right there."

"No. Greg even said something about the Knights Hemplar once."

"Dude! Greg does bad jokes and Broadway. Fuck!"

"So! It'd be lit. Get the ladies on stage! That would be fucking fire!"

"Stop. Your mom'll get you another six months with Psycho San."

"Psycho San's cool with stuff like that. It's art. He told me to be an artist."

"Psycho San told every kid to be an artist."

"So why not?"

"Why not what?"

"Be an artist and make the ladies happy."

"Dude. Think about it. The ladies would only want the spotlight, not your songs."

"They'd have both."

"They'd need water and nutrients too."

"It's not about necessity."

"Dude, it's always about necessity."

"No, it's art."

"Not for the ladies. They need stuff."

"Maybe they need songs too."

"Whatever."

"You think Caldwell is cool with Lorne?"

"Lazlo is. Greg thinks he's the best. Told my mom an' everything."

"Lorne's extra. Way too extra. The ladies don't like him. He's never with them. They can't form a bond."

"Dude. They got him. All over him and they're pissed. They liked Gus better."

"How would you know, if the plants are so silent?"

"Look at them."

"They always look like shit. No change since Lorne."

"They looked good a few months ago!"

"That was way before Lorne."

"Wait, Damian was off too. So, if the ladies are talking, he's not listening."

"He says you need to treat them like that for their own good."

"Fuckin' gross. Cringe, bro. That's abuse! Psycho San told us that at least. All abusers say that. You should watch out."

"Jesus."

"If your Brobro's reading that book to the ladies, it's not givin' 'em any life. You shouldn't let him give you that book either."

"Dude, now who's batshit?"

"You know how old he is?"

"Who cares?"

"Dude, he's older than your dad. You should watch out."

"He's got a girlfriend, a kid and he hooks up with Lydia sometimes. So fuck off."

"Lydia?"

"That's what Joe said."

"She's older than my grampy!"

"No, she's not."

"Yeah, she's had face-lifts. My mom said so."

"Does your grampy still have that chair?"

"What chair?"

"The one where the back goes down so you can fall asleep in it."

"Recliner, yeah."

"We should get one. It would be fire."

"They cost lots."

"Getting baked. Then pizza. We could save. Or maybe your grampy could get a new one and give us his old one."

"Maybe. Don't we need more than one?"

"You should ask him."

"Ask who?"

"My grampy. Dude, I don't think that shower was long enough."

"Yeah, I think you still smell."

"You really have that sulfur problem. You should see a doctor. They can recommend shit."

"Fuck!"

Chapter 35

Luther was not having a good day, again. His wife slammed the refrigerator door. "You're pissing away your life on this fucking marijuana venture." She was fed up with his excuses, his need to oversee legal matters, his compulsion to keep Lydia's old gigolo in line. "Why does it always have to be you, huh? Only you can slay dragons? You work in a firm full of lawyers! It's not like you even use the stuff. What the fuck, Luther? I didn't marry you for this. I might as well be a widow."

Luther turned his back to her as he poured himself a coffee. "Actually you'd probably be better off. The insurance plan is drop-dead gorgeous, you know."

"That's not funny. Why do you say shit like that?"

He turned around and leaned nonchalantly against the kitchen counter. "You brought up the widow thing. Not me."

"I was trying to illustrate a point. Is it so terrible I want to see you more than twice a year?"

"You're wedded to hyperbole. Add me, that's polygamy if I'm not mistaken."

"You're being impossible."

"No, I'm being rational."

"Hardly!"

He blew on his coffee before taking a sip. "I provide. And nicely, if I'm not mistaken."

"Seriously? You don't provide a pinhead of emotional support."

"I thought you went to your girlfriends and your mother for that." He smiled.

"You really are a prick."

He stared off in mock thoughtfulness. "Actually, I should revise that point about emotional support."

"Oh, here it comes."

"You don't have to work. Don't even have to lift a finger if you don't want to." He took another sip and cocked his head with feigned amazement at a sudden realization. "You can hire help, go on trips, take courses, singing lessons, cooking lessons — though I don't see that's ever had any effect — and yoga up the wazoo! And the children go to the best schools, best camps, best therapists." He smiled again and his eyes narrowed. "Lack of money's a fat fucking emotional stressor! Maybe you should take a little walk on the other side of town and check out how 'emotionally fulfilled' some of those women with two jobs on shift work are. Or better yet, check out the emotional status of most single mothers. I've seen the misery, darling. It's not pretty." This was barely true. Luther's law firm was strictly corporate. In fact they only dealt with multimillion-dollar enterprises, and almost nobody he knew did pro-bono work or handled family law. He was as remote from the happenings on the other side of town as he was from his marriage. But he'd read about it. Luther was a prodigious reader.

"You're full of shit, Luther. And if by that mention of single mothers you're threatening me, don't even think of it."

"Oh really?"

"Yeah. You would be so fucked by my dad's law firm."

"Yeah?"

"I'd make sure you were ruined."

Luther tossed his hand in the air dismissively and headed for the door.

"I'd fucking ruin you!" his wife screamed after him.

Luther got into his car. It was Saturday. Now that CannRose products were finally on the shelves he was going to go check on the dispensary in Lyston and then head over to the grow facility for a meeting with Lazlo. Every time he was in the area, Lydia offered to put him up overnight at Rosefields. He'd always declined, even the last time after the tenth-crop celebration when it was one o'clock in the morning. Well tonight he would take her up on her offer. Sure he felt guilty about being away from his family so much but it was for their benefit. His wife was just spoiled. She'd always been spoiled, especially by her father. The dithering old fart. If Luther had gone to work for him he'd be up to his butt in patent cases and poorer by half.

Luther occasionally regretted his choices as a younger man. In law school he'd been besotted by his future wife's confidence and her patrician bearing. She'd so clearly come from privilege. He had not. He was just smart and not put off by slogging through masses and masses of paperwork. Now he wondered at the way he'd set himself up. His wife had no clue how financially invested he was in CannRose. Sixteen-hour days over the past two and a half years trying to ensure his place in the anointed class was beginning to wear on him. And though his wife wanted to see him more often, he knew she'd never take a cut in prosperity for it.

#

Lydia was delighted to host Luther overnight. He'd always seemed so preoccupied, eternally rushed. She couldn't imagine having to keep one foot in a law firm and the other in a medical marijuana business. My gracious, just looking after the public and internal relations of one company was sometimes more than she could handle. Luther must be a wizard of some kind. And he did so much for CannRose even if Caldwell was less than appreciative. Lydia thought she would invite Damian as the other dinner guest and not bother to mention any of it to Caldwell. He was in St. Lucia right now, hoping to "reel in a progressive-minded investor," whatever that meant.

Lydia had come to realize several months ago it was useless trying to understand the world from Caldwell's perspective. It wasn't helpful for her job. It didn't usually make her happy. And it never made the people around her happy. Corinna at the spa, who was now back to being Lydia's weekly confidante, had pointed out that given CannRose's organizational structure, Caldwell should be making an effort to understand Lydia's perspective, not the other way around. Corinna wasn't for a moment suffering any delusion that Caldwell would ever make such an effort. And that clarity, though never actually expressed, seemed to be absorbed on some level by Lydia.

Lydia had recently hired a part-time housekeeper who especially liked cooking. So Lydia added another day to her schedule — Friday as it turned out — and the woman spent the day roasting, baking, concocting marinades, chopping vegetables and otherwise preparing meals for the week. So Saturdays the larder was full. It was difficult to decide what to eat; there was so much to choose from.

"What would you prefer, Luther?" Lydia was bent over scrutinizing the refrigerator contents. "A cold roast pork or we could barbecue some marinated lamb. Oh yum! She's even made those delightful little salmon skewers with the spicy sauce. We must have these as hors d'oeuvres. They're to die for, Luther. You like salmon? You're not allergic to fish or anything are you?"

"No. I'm . . . I'm not allergic. It sounds wonderful." Luther sat on one of the high kitchen stools and cradled his gin and tonic.

"And lamb or pork?"

"Oh . . . uh . . . lamb, I guess."

"Oh of course. Sorry, I wasn't thinking." As Lydia closed the fridge and turned to face him, her blue eyes seemed to pick up the evening sunlight and they shone like sapphires.

Luther squinted briefly. "Oh no. Don't worry about that. I eat ham sandwiches. Even bacon. He stared down at his drink again. Our kitchen at home is hardly kosher. My wife's culinary skills amount to stir-fries and I don't cook at all."

Lydia noted his gloominess and slouch. Poor man. So overworked. "You know what you need, Luther?" Lydia said in her best Southern manner.

Luther looked up at Lydia confused. No one had addressed anything to do with his needs as far back as he could remember.

Lydia smiled. He was sweet, so boyish. "Two good weeks on a lovely beach, or in some beautiful mountains somewhere," she said. "No cell phones and nothing to do but eat, sleep and play."

"That's hardly going to happen any time soon." Luther suddenly felt himself on the verge of tears and he had no idea where it was coming from. Luckily Damian appeared and he'd brought a bottle of wine and some dark-looking cookies or crackers.

"Are those what I think they are?" Lydia asked.

Damian nodded as he reached out to shake hands with Luther.

"You're so naughty," Lydia tittered.

"One of Ernie's creations," Damian said. "Savory, gluten-free Misdemeanor Crackers. For cheese or something. Or seriously, just on their own, they're pretty fine."

"They'll be terrific with the little salmon kabobs then. Speaking of which, Damian dear, could you fire up the barbecue for us? Grab yourself a drink too. Caldwell brought some fancy tequila back from his holiday. You're a tequila aficionado, aren't you? Tell me what you think." Lydia turned and smiled at Luther again. "One day, I'll get caught you know," she giggled. "I'll have to fire myself from my own company."

It took Luther a second to realize the crackers were laced.

"Damian's registered here. Of course you don't need anything in Colorado. And he's very generous as you can see." Lydia began picking artichokes out of the quart basket sitting on the counter. "So's Caldwell by the way. You know Caldwell uses it medicinally?"

Luther shook his head. This was new. If anything he'd imagined Caldwell was on amphetamines or at the very least too much coffee.

"I thought everyone knew that about Caldwell," Lydia said. "It's why he's so fussy about what goes on in the facility. I just haven't gotten around to getting registered yet. He keeps telling me I'm an idiot not to. And I do have pain you know — sometimes in my feet. I suppose it only makes sense to get registered so I can at least legally test my own products. I test them anyway. Shush." She turned back to washing the artichokes.

Luther wondered how the evening was going to progress and if he should take a pass on the crackers. Then again, what the hell. Not like half the clients he dealt with on a day-to-day basis weren't on something. The recreational habits of the wealthy and powerful were hardly restrained.

Damian came waltzing back in. "You know it's freaky warm out there. We should eat on the patio."

"A great idea. Would that suit you, Luther?"

"Sure." And he smiled a wan little smile.

#

Everything was delicious. The dinner party for three stretched to an hour or so after midnight. The crackers had an extraordinary effect on Luther. He was laughing like never before and in the quiet moments when he thought of it, he saw his own life was outlandish. He worked like a slave, for what? He'd become a crazed idiot. Damian told him he needed a "chill tutor." Damian had also brought some "high-end Colorado product" along with his bong. They polished off a bottle of champagne with the salmon and crackers, and a substantial quantity of French merlot with the lamb. Luther had rarely eaten artichokes, and like a kid, he found them fun to pull apart. Damian had barbecued the eggplant and lamb to perfection, and Lydia's housekeeper had triumphed with the balsamic-and-basil dressing for the tomato salad.

Luther couldn't ever remember feeling so light or pleasant. Nor could he remember enjoying company so much or having such amusing conversation. Not since his college days. And Lydia, as it turned out, was hardly stupid. She was just odd and seemed to be tuned in to some other channel. She was also incredibly beautiful in the candlelight wrapped in her pale-blue Angora shawl. Damian bade the two of them a good night and tottered off to his apartment at about 1:30 a.m.

Luther found he couldn't take his eyes off Lydia. She noticed this and pondered what Corinna would advise. Of course she knew the answer. Corinna was ever in favor of carpe diem, or carpe noctem in this case. Lydia reached out and stroked Luther's face. She thought she saw a tear in his eye. He was so sweet and, my gracious, so very boyish. She took his hand and got up from the table. He stood up too, held her hand to his chest and then he raised it to his mouth. He kissed it so gently, all the while looking most forlornly at her.

"You poor boy. Poor boy," Lydia said softly and she put her arm around him. They stood kissing in the candlelight for a long time. And Luther again felt for some odd reason he was on the verge of tears. Then Lydia took him by the hand and led him upstairs to her bed where all thoughts and tendencies to tears were washed away.

And so Lydia began the fifth and possibly most passionate affair of her life. Luther was a wonder. Such a surprise too! She never would have imagined the energy behind that bespectacled, ambitious façade. Jordan would have seen him as a type, as a typical lawyer, acclimated to tedium and versed in argument — "something of a blight" — but for all she knew her dead husband's best friend, Cyrus, had been no better in his younger days. Why had Jordan held those kinds of opinions about people anyway? You never really could tell what someone was like unless you got very close, and even then sometimes you still might not have a clue. She'd often felt like that with Jordan himself.

Enough of Jordan. Now she had a whole new prospect for diversion and enthusiasm. And a veritable cornucopia of items to discuss with Corinna. She'd already told Corinna about the night she'd had with Damian. She admitted it had been ill-considered. She'd felt lonely and was still missing Caldwell. Damian had made the first move. But. Well . . . the poor man was awfully thin. Not much energy or stamina there. Or genuine inclination when it came right down to it. They'd agreed, Damian and Lydia, they'd just be good friends after that. Upon hearing this, Corinna had voiced not only her approval but the opinion that at Lydia's age, quality sex was absolutely of the essence. When she heard about Luther, Corinna gave Lydia a round of applause and then produced two small glasses and a bottle of grappa she always kept handy.

Chapter 36

It had taken Petra forever, and occasional tumblers of vodka, to feel caught up on the science of weed. Almost a year if she wanted to be a little more precise about it. Then again she'd hardly had a functioning lab until now. So in what direction should her research go? Initially she'd assumed CannRose would want to increase yield. "Oh of course, that would be perfect," said Caldwell while Luther and Lydia enthusiastically agreed. Then she'd explained perhaps characterizing cultivars for metabolite profiles and genetics would be beneficial since there were so many cultivars now and very little documented about them. Marijuana was complex. It had several cannabinoids apart from the almighty THC, and possibly well over a hundred terpenes. Characterization could allow for better pinpointing and breeding of specific assortments of the active drug ingredients. "Oh of course, that would be perfect too," Luther said while the other two nodded this time.

And the facility had problems with pests and disease. Cannabis-breeding for the black-market over the last fifty years had perhaps led to losses of the plant's natural resistance. Back in the old days, hemp, for example, was planted with other crops to reduce pests. Reintroducing old genetics might improve resilience. She might retrieve vestigial cannabinoids and terpenes in the process. "My gracious, that would be wonderful, wouldn't it?" Lydia spoke up, and they'd smiled and murmured among themselves.

Petra stared at the lemon slice and single ice cube floating in her tall rum and water, and then gradually took in the distorted view of her muddy backyard through the liquid. She sighed. The CannRose people were clueless, and it only served to increase her options. She could just show up at the lab and quietly drink herself into the grave and they'd be none the wiser. Or maybe she could personally explore her own endocannabinoid system with lots of in vivo trials, and dwell in a permanent haze. On the other hand, she could finally do some research! Hell, the field was wide open and even though it was very modest, she did have a budget. The situation challenged her cultivated cynicism.

So Petra set up a lunch date with Alice. Her research might as well benefit the frail and infirm as soon as possible. Alice at least was a pharmacist; she'd have some idea of the areas most in need of investigation from a patient's perspective. Best of all they could talk science.

They met just outside the city at a trendy roadhouse known for its hearty food, and the lunch extended well into the afternoon. They discussed how marijuana's medicinal value was invariably about the entourage effect — every time a single cannabinoid was isolated or synthesized and used on its own, its effectiveness was muted or sometimes nonexistent. Patients often had to try various products until they got it right. Often, even individual lots of the same product had differences. Every patient was unique too. More understanding of the human endocannabinoid system would help. Add to that the forms of administering: smoking, vaping and ingesting. Edibles particularly could have unpredictable effects because the liver was involved. And almost no one had even looked at what terpenes added to the mix. They were playing an important part too. While several terpenes, like limonene, had been well studied for pharmacological effects on their own, the combined effects of these with cannabinoids — whether synergistic, complimentary, inhibitory or merely inactive — were barely identified let alone understood. But regardless, marijuana was effective medicine judging by its use over the ages.

"It's astounding," Alice remarked, digging into her plate of baked sole and roasted vegetables, "the number of ailments historically treated by cannabis, especially in Victorian times. Lord, the list in the old pharmacopoeia was extraordinary: any kind of pain; all manner of convulsions; tics and brain tumors; impotence; insanity; the three g's, goiter, gout and gonorrhea; dysentery; dyspepsia; palpitations; toothaches; spasms of the bladder; and *hydrophobia*!" Alice smiled. "Oh, and let's not forget the treatment of women!" she rolled her eyes. "But you know, they used it successfully for difficult births and healing afterwards, not to mention menstrual pain and of course hysteria and neurasthenia!"

"They'd try just about anything for hysteria and neurasthenia," Petra said, and they both laughed.

"Oh dear. Will women never behave!" Alice said.

"I sure as hell hope not." Petra took another swig of her Bloody Mary and then launched into her own summary of cannabis research from the 1960s, most of it on rats. It turned out it was some of that research on rats that had changed Alice's mind two and a half years before.

"The studies coming out of Israel now," Petra said, still picking at her salad, "are suggesting that it just might be a wonder drug after all. Kind of like the Victorians, they're finding effectiveness for everything from epilepsy and ulcerative colitis to cancer, arthritis, MS and skin diseases; never mind all the common uses, PTSD, glaucoma, that sort of thing. There are even ongoing studies showing promise for its use in autism. It's mindboggling."

Alice agreed.

While discussions with Alice were infinitely more enjoyable than trying to converse with the company executives, Petra still had trouble focusing, so she decided to start building a database, at least for the few strains CannRose would sell. Genetic, cannabinoid and terpene profiles. Pretty basic! Alice agreed to set up an ongoing survey with clients: What is your ailment? What product works? What doesn't? Were there pleasant or unpleasant side effects? Petra would look for patterns and brush up on her stats. She'd buy expensive software — always a good investment.

As Petra got in her car and waved goodbye, she was pleased she'd set up the meeting. A research project with Alice would keep her on track. And besides, Alice was fun.

As a sideline and also fun, Petra would be on the lookout for landrace strains, even if they were rare and approaching extinction more rapidly by the month. The frenzy of hybrid breeding put purity at a premium. There was a Dutch company that traveled the world looking for these unadulterated strains and claimed to have an extensive, not to mention expensive, seed bank. But Petra had put the word out quietly among the staff that she'd be interested in "old-timer weed." The contemporary genetics were a jumbled mess for sure, thanks to years of black-market R and D focused on one narrow objective: the highest high. In fact all the hybridization and confused terminology over the last fifty years had totally erased any distinctions like sativa, indica and ruderalis. *Chemovar* was the term of choice now in the medical weed world and it was based only on chemistry, the cannabinoid and terpene profiles.

Petra might also cultivate plants that Damian wanted to toss because they didn't grow according to expectations. In fact once she got the cannabinoid and terpene characterization going, she could start looking at the effects of environmental stressors on the secondary metabolite production. Down the road, maybe she could ally herself with a doctor keen on clinical studies. She could start looking right now. Clinical studies were finally happening even if they weren't happening in this state. No matter how much it made her feel like an impostor, she would endeavor to start talking to other researchers again. She'd rather stick pins in her eyes of course.

In fact she'd much rather spend time with her new tech. He was wonderfully conversant on matters of science. He was also thoroughly irresistible. She knew sleeping with somebody she supervised was never a good idea. It complicated emotions as well as logistics. But as it turned out, Sanjay was hardly new to the business of it, and Petra had to wonder how many jobs he'd slept his way into. It turned out Sanjay was as seductive with men as he was with women. At least he was honest about it. He seemed to treat himself like a personal experiment.

"There's no point in being shy or coy about it," Sanjay said. "Sex is great, no matter how you look at it or who you're doing it with. It's a gateway."

"Sure," Petra replied. She was almost more blown away by his candidly expressed opportunism than his prowess and perfect body.

"I don't just mean, you know, securing a job. Sex is great because it's a portal to another world. Even if it's lousy, you get a hint of something more than this everyday stuff. Don't you find?"

"Um, sure," Petra said. "I guess." She sat up and looked around the room for her clothes. The mention of everyday stuff reminded her she'd promised her mom a roast pork loin for Sunday dinner. She should probably get going.

"I know it's a biological trick," Sanjay continued. "But then so is chocolate. So is sugar, heroin. You name it. Mood altering is mood altering. And something, some living thing, is always gaining an advantage by it."

"I'd have to think about that."

"You know it's true. It's exactly how evolution works."

"I don't know I'd put it just like that." Petra remembered her clothes were lying on Sanjay's living room floor. She lay down again.

"To me, it's all wonderful. You get to be here. You get to eat chocolate. You get to have sex. You can try drugs if you want to. You can kill yourself with them too. You get to have the experience. That's all." He rolled off his back, propped himself up on his elbow and looked down at her. "I never judge. It leaves more room for wonder."

In fact Sanjay found Petra's body something of a wonder. Having no profound sexual preference and no great expectations around body ideals, he simply concentrated on its salient features. She had enormous nipples for starters. The diameter of one seemed to cover almost half the breast itself, and they were so sensitive. Just the slightest attention to them would have her moaning and panting in no time. He'd only ever had sex a few times with women who were that much older than he was. But none of them had responded quite like that. And even the younger women might be very touchy, sometimes even complain of having painful breasts, but regardless, they certainly did not have orgasms without significant attention elsewhere. In fact he was so impressed by Petra's nipples he was beginning to wonder if they constituted some neural anomaly. Some evolutionary advantage even. She was the easiest woman to satisfy he'd ever been with. And her legs! So strong, long and lanky, the inner thighs also highly responsive. She would wrap them around him. Frequently. And he found this very comforting and exciting all at the same time.

And as for what Sanjay referred to as the "place of mercy," he found its surroundings both surprising and enlightening. Petra's head was covered in uniformly dark and straight short-bobbed hair that in no way matched the frenzied mass of salt-and-pepper curls rising out of her pubis. "OMG!" he'd exclaimed. "You know, I hadn't really thought about this!" Petra, open-mouthed and breathing heavily, had briefly raised her head and peered at him before falling back onto the pillows.

PART EIGHT

Flowerings

Oh Lust and Lament that you can speak it but not feel it. That we must feel it and stay silent. Open wide to the wind and wonder how your natures have vanished. In every glistening petal we embrace the pulse that brings you back to your senses: your soft seeing and the sweet fragrance of lightness and love. We long for your simplicity, your guilelessness, in the face of such forcings. We long for the easy blooming of your hearts.

from Cannto II, *Cannabidadas*

Chapter 37

It was Sunday morning and Caldwell was eating his bacon sandwich out on the balcony of his Hullbrooke apartment. It overlooked the town park, and at the very far end of it, a good football field and a half away, was the skateboard playground or whatever that was with its bowls and ramps and jumps that led nowhere. He noticed the three young lads from the grow facility were there again, zooming, leaping and twirling. They were very good at it. He should mention that to them one day. He could never remember even one of their names, but Harper Koch, the motivational guru he was reading, mentioned that compliments about activities outside work were effective in maintaining employee loyalty.

Ha! Loyalty! Caldwell's comprehension of it was becoming more acute by the day. Like most things it had two sides. In this case the lack of it was turning out to be a boon in disguise because most of the big CannRose rats couldn't tell a sinking kayak from a Virginia-class nuclear submarine. Lydia's boring advisory team, which checked his every inspiration, was finally shifting aside. Oh, they'd put the lid on expenditures. But so what! If Lydia wished to keep the place running on her disposable income — and there were some months where she was compelled to foot the bills — that was her business. And Caldwell would ensure that was his business too.

The rats had finally admitted mistakes had been made, though they still tried to blame him and Lazlo for most of them. At any rate they suggested if Caldwell could bring in a big investor or two they would not be at all averse to redistributing the pudding. They were clearing out, all right. They weren't so confident marijuana was the next big thing. It was the next big competitive thing, and that meant lots of losers. They moaned the price of marijuana did nothing but drop as suppliers multiplied across the country. Cowards. Myopic morons. The fools even told Lydia she should make a break for it too while she could. He'd show them! He chuckled to himself at their inability to grasp the long view. All he ever needed was to find himself a rich ally who'd be happy to take a back seat. And Mother of Mary, Caldwell had the tingly feeling he'd just won the lottery.

Guido Batelli was, in Lydia's words, "a sweet old Italian gentleman." She'd met him at a charity function a few years before and he'd recently gotten in touch with her to enquire about a substantial donation he was planning. She told him she wasn't on the board of that organization anymore and then of course she went on to tell him what she was currently doing.

"Lydia, you have no idea how perfect this is! I must meet with your people."

From Caldwell's perspective the old guy seemed to be just off the boat, though he'd apparently been in the in the US as a younger man. He'd moved from Milan back to Manhattan fifteen years ago and become an American citizen. Greg, suspicious by vocation, and having devoured *The Day of the Owl* as a teenager and maybe too many Mario Puzo novels, had been worried about this Italian connection. But after a good week or more of digging around in the man's past, he was satisfied there was no mob affiliation. Besides, Guido was from Lombardy not Sicily. And he was a widower. A recent one, and as he told Caldwell, his wife's illness had convinced him that marijuana was a wonder drug.

"My beautiful Rosa, mother of my children, in so much agony. She says to me, 'Guido, the pills. They're turning me into a zombie. I'd rather have the pain.' Oh my God, it broke my heart. I tell the doctor, 'You have to do something.' Doctors, sometimes, they know nothing." So at his wit's end, her doctor had finally suggested she might want to try marijuana. "Caldwell, I tell you, it changed everything!" His wife even outlived the doctor's death sentence by three years.

So Guido was a believer. "This is so important, Caldwell. I have faith in this plant. Utmost. Is so much more than the world understands." And the more Guido had read about it, the more he was sold on the benefits of marijuana.

He brought Caldwell to tears when he told him how he wanted to give back in the last years of his own life. He'd promised to his wife that he'd do something good with his fortune. She was worried for his soul and she didn't want to be in heaven without him. "It just wouldn't be heaven then would it?" Guido wanted his money to make a difference to all the suffering in the world. He wanted it to be a tribute to the woman he'd loved for fifty years. Helping a struggling medical marijuana enterprise seemed like the perfect thing to do. Caldwell wept openly at all this.

Chapter 38

Joe was checking the auxiliary temperature monitors outside the grow rooms when Damian wandered by. *He's looking a little rough around the edges*, Joe thought when he saw him. *What exactly goes on at Lydia's estate?* Joe couldn't figure out how a woman like Lydia would tolerate having an old stoner staying at her house. How did that work?

"Hey, Damian."

"Hey, Joe."

"You look . . . kind of like hell. You know, exhausted or something."

"Guess I am."

"Too much excitement up at the estate?"

"You could maybe call it that."

"So what's it like living up there? Place is huge I hear."

"Yeah."

"You do any riding?"

"Yeah, sometimes."

"Oh yeah? How are you finding it?"

"I don't know. Just . . . riding."

"That's putting the bags under your eyes?"

"Is that a trick question?"

"Trick pony. Trick question. No, you look tired, man."

Damian caught the look on Joe's face. "Yeah. Lydia likes to talk. About everything. All night."

Joe didn't expect such a forthright answer and was nonplussed.

"And we screw like minks too. For hours and hours. She's insatiable." Damian found Joe's questioning absurd. Joe was nosy, likely because his own life was such a frigging monotony.

In fact Damian, who lived in the apartment over the five-car garage at Rosefields, mostly saw Lydia just in passing. If he socialized regularly with anyone there it was with Carl, the farm manager, and his wife. A few times over the last year, Lydia had invited him for dinner but mostly when Caldwell and the board members were there. One time when Lydia's children descended upon the estate for a weekend, she'd invited Damian to the family barbecue. They were a weird, uncomfortable group and he'd claimed fatigue early in the evening. On only two occasions had he gone to dinner with Lydia alone. He didn't fancy her cooking much — so he brought dinner the second time. She'd been impressed. And admittedly things had gotten a little out of hand. She was an attractive woman. Very attractive, especially after half a bottle of champagne (Lydia's contribution) and some great Thai bud (Damian's contribution). And Lydia did like to talk. But that had been just a onetime thing. They had an understanding. She was cool. Everything was cool. Besides Damian had a girlfriend back in Colorado.

It was true though — sex was keeping Damian up at night. It was spring. The frogs in the pond, a whippoorwill, red-winged blackbirds singing about it half the night and at it again before sunup. Rosefields was the noisiest place he'd ever slept in his whole life. He was going into Hullbrooke to buy some earplugs that afternoon.

"Wow!" said Joe. "You sure are a piece of work." Joe could tell when he was being fucked with. No way Damian was doing it with the company president!

"Happy to oblige. At least I don't let things get moldy." This was an ongoing dig. Cassie and Joe had misted a stressed-looking crop the day before it was harvested. Of course it wasn't supposed to have been harvested the next day. That was Caldwell, barging in, insisting they had to harvest then and there. It couldn't wait. Damian had been in Colorado. And whoever had set the drying sequence — various people pointed fingers at each other — totally blew it the rest of the way. Damian liked to keep reminding them moldy crops had almost cost the company their registration.

Joe bristled. "Well maybe if everything wasn't such a big fucking secret with you . . . maybe if you gave us *a reason* from time to time. You know, *why* you adopt aberrant growing methods."

Damian chuckled to himself. So easy to get a rise out of these white-bread boys with their chubby pink progeny and perky pink wives. "You got to chill better, man," Damian said. "You know, loosen up the bowels a little. Easier to learn when it's not coming out of every other orifice."

"Asshole!"

"Yeah, man. You should get one. It'll change your life." Damian swiveled away and sauntered off into one of the flower rooms.

Cassie came up behind Joe and put her hand on his arm. "I just heard the tail end. He is such a jerk. Don't let it get to you."

They stood staring down the hallway after Damian and then they both said in unison, "You have to consider who it's coming from." Saying it together like that made them look at each other and they kissed. They held each other for a few moments while Greg in the security office watched them on his computer screen.

Chapter 39

Alice put down the trowel and took her gloves off. That was enough planting for the afternoon. The thing about having a plot in the community garden was you had to tend it. But the little tomato plants she'd started from seed in a cold frame were looking splendid, and she would have carrots, peppers, eggplant and probably too much zucchini again. Ricardo, two patches over, had warned her about zucchini. But she'd kept ten plants anyway the first year. In no time they'd dropped down the side of the raised bed, made off along the interlocking brick pathway, and she'd given away zucchini until Thanksgiving.

"I got to thank you, ma'am." It was the woman with the little girl who had seizures. She was always coming into the drugstore now and thanking her there too. CannRose finally had a few products for sale and the dispensary across town was doing a brisk business, even if most of it was for other companies. Sammy had given Alice a full report of how the woman with the little girl had actually wept the second time she visited the dispensary. The joy or relief was overwhelming because the number of seizures a day had dropped from over a hundred to a dozen or so in just two weeks.

"How is your little girl doing today?"

"Oh yes. Is really good. One fit only this morning. And now is four o'clock!"

"That's pretty amazing."

"Yes, ma'am. Amazing." The woman held out a tray of a dozen seedlings — spinach or kale maybe — although when Alice looked more closely she realized they weren't anything she recognized. "Is special, for you, ma'am. We grow in my country. Very good for you. Pick like this." And the woman raised her hand about a foot and a half above the tray. "Plant like this." And she dropped her hand to about five inches from the tray to show the spacing. "Special taste."

"Would I cook it?"

"Just one minute, two, no more. Taste very good. Good health. Good for eyes and skin."

They discussed the cooking a little more, exchanged several thank-yous and then Alice watched as the woman went back to her little girl sitting in the stroller. The child was facing them and she looked right at Alice and smiled. Alice was taken aback. She'd never seen the child focus on anything before, let alone make eye contact.

Alice took up her trowel again to put in the seedlings. It occurred to her that her involvement with this medicine, this weed, was changing her life in ways she hadn't expected. People who needed it and knew about her involvement were appreciative in a way they'd certainly never been with drugs she sold at the pharmacy. It was like a new community. But Alice still kept a very low profile. Some nights she'd wake up worried. The laws could change again. Or the drug scheduling could change again. Then where would they be? And even though she made sure her contract with CannRose was crystal clear — the dispensaries and her involvement with them were completely separate from her drugstore — and her son assured her the best legal services in the state would be available to her at no cost, she wondered if she might wake up one morning and find herself in a fix.

Alice put away her gardening tools and sat for a moment on the edge of one of the beds. She'd call Zack when she got home. See how he was doing. Her son had grown a little distant since she'd had so many dealings with Luther and the law firm. She wondered if he regretted putting her name forward. Probably a little tricky working for people you know talk to your mother all the time. Alice certainly wouldn't have liked it when she was that age. It made her laugh a little. She'd go easy on him.

#

It turned out Zack was having woman troubles. Again. The last one had left him just like the one before. And none too nicely. She'd brazenly come in with some big guy who was helping her with her luggage. He had his hands all over her. More so than the luggage.

"Well, sweetheart," Alice said. "I don't know what to tell you. Maybe you have to learn more patience with—"

"I am patient. I never made big demands on her."

"Did you fight?"

"No. Well, hardly ever."

"What did you fight about?"

"I don't know. The usual. I'm home late. I don't do the dishes. I leave the bathroom a mess. I didn't find the movie we just watched uplifting. In fact I found it boring, stupid and saccharine. She wants a puppy. I like cats . . ."

"Zack, honey, I think you need to up your game."

"I know. I just didn't think she would be so . . ."

"So . . . what?"

"Predictable. I don't know. Tedious?"

"Uh-huh." Alice put her feet up on the couch and leaned back into the cushions to make herself more comfortable. "I never really liked her. I liked the one before her."

"I know you did."

"You never told me what happened there."

"Yeah, well. She told me I was too gutless to be emotionally intimate."

"Did she have a point?"

"Probably."

"Probably?"

"You know when you and Dad split up, I thought he was a total asshole. Now I have no idea how the hell things are supposed to work."

"Oh, you're blaming your parents' divorce for your romantic disasters. Honey, you were in college by that point."

"I'm not blaming anything. I just don't know how things are supposed to be maybe."

"I didn't leave him, you know."

"I know. He said you never had to. You just vanished while you were with him."

"He said that?"

"Yeah. Maybe you should have split up before I went to college."

"Huh. Well he never told me."

"How the hell does that work, Mom?"

"I don't know, honey. But I have to admit, I'm a whole lot happier not having to look at his miserable face every morning when I wake up."

Chapter 40

Ernie noticed with a feeling of growing unease that Guido and his sidekick, Jason, had more or less installed themselves at the grow facility. They took over a corner nook in the administration section that had comfy chairs and a long coffee table, and they sat at opposite ends, always with a tablet or laptop in front of them usually displaying some financial or investment news site. The silver-haired Guido, with his sporty tan and fine Italian tweeds, was there almost every day. Ernie noted he would only occasionally glance at his screen because he was apparently fascinated by the activities going on around him. Jason, by contrast, stared constantly at his screen or his phone, or he alternated between the two devices. And he didn't show up as often. When he was there, with his shaved head, beard stubble and leather jacket, he freaked more than a few people out.

Neither Guido nor Jason had any title or position in the company. Guido said he didn't want one. "Please, indulge an old widower his distractions. I just want to get the feel of this extraordinary operation and all its extraordinary people." Ernie noticed the old guy wasn't at all averse to running errands either. He was happy to take new display labels over to the Lyston dispensary or pick up new boot racks and hangers from the hardware store. He sat in on all the big meetings too. And it seemed he had no ambition or strong opinions about the operation, so the staff, managers and executives all chatted with him. In fact people talked with Guido now more than they did with Ernie. It was clear advanced years and European charm could turn you into a full-time father confessor. If Ernie had the goods on local gossip, Guido had his mitts on people's actual pulses. It was unnerving.

The only other person who seemed to find it all peculiar was Percy. "Grieving old widower my foot!" the QA officer said. "He's got more life in his step than I do." And Percy raised his eyebrows accordingly.

So Ernie rarely spoke about himself with Guido. Instead he asked Guido about his life or stuck to pleasantries.

Guido occasionally carried a violin case around, and there really was a violin in it. He'd played with the Houston Opera until his father died and he was called in to help run the family business — high-end shoes. Guido handled the North American operations. One morning at CannRose, Guido gave a little concert during coffee break. "I'm getting into the jazz in my golden years. *Roba forte*, huh!" And then he whipped off something like you'd hear in a café. One of the tunes sounded vaguely familiar. He beamed at Ernie. "A Rodgers and Hart standard, 'This Can't Be Love.' I learn listening to old Grappelli. What a master. He was still touring in his eighties." Of course this little concert endeared Guido to the staff and put most of the rumors and Mafia jokes to rest. The trail of people darting into his space with their coffees in hand and gushing "Ciao" as they left was unending.

Lorne, the production manager, was often seen chatting with Guido. Ernie thought Lorne was beginning to show a few cracks in his surfer-boy oh-so-composed persona, especially when Caldwell was on the rampage about some new measure he wanted in place "yesterday!" As well, there was the ongoing issue about employees who were registered for medical marijuana and needed to smoke on the job. Some of them smoked an awful lot, and Lorne wasn't sure they were very sick.

One day there was a kerfuffle. A dark affair with much whispering and tut-tutting. Apparently, two registered employees, who were buying as much weed at the company discount as they possibly could, were then reselling it on the side. They were so brazen they'd asked Lorne if he wanted to buy some too, and Ernie had witnessed this incident a few days before. He could see it shocked Lorne, leaving him tongue-tied and shaking his head while the two erstwhile dealers merely shrugged and pretended nothing had happened. So Ernie dusted things as slowly as he could on other side of dividing wall when he saw Lorne scuttle into Guido's little corner.

"Caldwell won't let me fire them." Lorne sounded uneasy. "Or inform the authorities. It would look bad for the company. We're supposed to deal with it internally. I don't know what to do."

"An interesting problem," Guido said. "Caldwell is right of course. But you are in a perfect position. You can cut off the supply, yes?"

"Only if I rat to the DOH."

"Stop the discount?"

"It would draw attention too. They audit the purchase records." Lorne sucked in his breath. "But now we know what they're up to, it means we're party to the crime."

"In other parts of the country, it's not a crime. It would just be an independent resale."

"We could lose the registration!"

"Caldwell says we could never lose the registration now."

"Caldwell says a lot of things. Just check out subsection c32-1-a of the code. I think I could go to jail."

"That's ridiculous." Guido cleared his throat and Ernie heard the clink as the old man put his cup back on the saucer. Everybody else used mugs.

"I'm having trouble sleeping . . ."

"That's terrible. No one should have to lose sleep over these things."

"What do you think I should do? What would you do?"

There was silence and Ernie imagined Guido chewing on his upper lip or stroking his collar. Finally he said, "I guess I'd tell Jason."

"What would he do?"

"He'd take care of it."

People only guessed at Jason's function: assistant, business associate, bodyguard? Or maybe hit man. Somebody said he was a biker from Montreal and he had obscure tattooed symbols that crept up his neck at the back. He spoke French a lot on the phone and moved in and out of CannRose like a fast-moving shadow. Sometimes he was away for several days.

"What will Jason do?"

Ernie thought he heard alarm in Lorne's voice.

"He will talk to them. He's very good at this. Especially with the little punks. Yes? This is what you are telling me. We have two little punks here. CannRose is better not employing them. You are right. So we will see."

"Well, I'm not so sure . . ."

"You are very busy. I will speak to Jason for you."

Ernie watched as Lorne seemed to dash out from the corner, his head down. And he was heading straight for Ernie, who had now moved out from behind the dividing wall.

"Hey, Lorne. How's your day?"

Lorne looked up. He was spooked all right. "Fine, Ernie. Thanks for asking." And he sped on by, lab coat flaring behind him.

Two days later, the employees in question quit.

Ernie saw Lorne give Jason a thumbs-up, which was completely ignored. He looked flustered by the lack of response and turned to the person closest to him, who happened to be Cassie. He immediately struck up a conversation with her about the next day's cloning. And Ernie thought he talked a little louder than usual.

#

There was enormous pressure to get the derivative products developed and on the shelf. The company was almost a year behind on extracts, oils, tinctures, lotions and suppositories. Interestingly, there had been a statewide push among commercial suppliers to get into the suppository market. Ernie was keeping track of all the CannRose luminaries who were in favor. So far only Lazlo and Guido were wholeheartedly enthusiastic.

Stoyan, the recently hired extraction specialist, told Ernie he'd never once imagined a life outside Moldova. Herbal medicines were the popular remedies there, often ahead of synthetic drugs, and Stoyan, wanting to be popular, had trained in pharmaceutical botany. For a good fifteen years he'd ground, pounded, pressurized, ethylated or otherwise clobbered plant material for the healing properties that Moldovans relied upon. But that couldn't make up for statewide poverty. He figured he'd be better off driving a cab for his Uncle Nicolai in Poughkeepsie. And he was, until one afternoon when he gave Lydia a ride from the airport to the Women Bound for Green conference at the university. She told him about CannRose and he told her about his life in Moldova. It was immediately apparent to both of them that Stoyan's herbal know-how was worth more than a Vassar degree. His skill set catapulted him out of that taxi and right into the CannRose extraction room.

He was a year or two younger than Ernie but he had an aura about him of the Beat Generation, the cool edge of the Cold War. Everything he owned was black, including slightly pointy shoes that he kept in a superlative state of polish, which Ernie thought contrasted strangely with the state of his nicotine-yellow fingers. He frequently threw his head back to fling his dyed-black hair out of his eyes, clearly a gesture perfected to accompany his smoking. And he sported eyebrow and ear piercings, a more modern touch to the retro look. Stoyan, having found himself in the new cool of weed works, realized this wasn't just your granny's medicine. He was hip to the ways of botanicals. And getting hip to weed, man, that was child's play.

But speaking with people? That could be complicated. "What you can expect?" he'd say flicking his wrists. "Bulgarian raised in Moldova! Little boy force to learn Romanian and Russian! Now must to conquer English." Ernie wondered if Stoyan wasn't just crafty with the misunderstandings.

"I am not using this shits. Has bugs. If has bugs, has also bug poo." Stoyan tilted his head to one side and leisurely leaned against the Extraction Room doorframe.

"Dear Stoyan, it's just to develop the methods," Percy tried to explain as Lorne stood beside him holding two large Ziploc bags of dried plants.

Stoyan folded his arms and nodded at the QA officer and the production manager. "Yes, of course. I develop methods!"

"So you can use it?"

"You should know! No heating. These extracts, pressure only, ethanol only. Give bug headache maybe. Drunk maybe. No stopping poo."

"But it's not for sale. It's just for development. And—"

"Yes. I already say! I develop methods."

"It's just for testing."

"Yes! Yes! Test of course! Testing too. But still bug poo. Maybe wrong test. Has risk!"

"Right." Percy mopped his brow with a Kimwipe.

"I am right? Yes?"

"If we were going to sell it after, yes. But we're not going to sell it. We don't sell product until the product is validated."

"Of course. I validate product too!"

"So can you use this stuff or not?" Lorne asked, shaking the bags.

"I never do that! You should know! Is trick. Trick question. Yes? Test for me. I am right?"

The production manager sighed. Despite their best efforts, Lorne and Percy were not able to unload any of the slightly buggy crop of Jamabalaya Skunk for Stoyan's method development that day. Clearly only the best product would do to establish extraction parameters and make sure the result was always repeatable.

Ernie thought Stoyan's interactions with Caldwell were particularly skillful. Rather than keeping his head down like most people when Caldwell was on a rampage, Stoyan took the opportunity to be particularly gregarious and cryptic.

"Caldwell! Come. What I done here. Very cool. Is good. I show you."

"It better be. I'm paying you enough," Caldwell grumbled.

"Ah yes. Beautiful Lydia pay. Yes. I understand. Is very cool."

"What have you got to show me?"

"Lydia very cool. Yes?"

"You said you had something to show me. What have you got?"

And Stoyan would put his hand to his heart. "Lydia! . . . she give me best opportunity in America. Best opportunity in life!"

"You said you had something to show me!"

"Ah. Yes. Two parts! Different colors. You see. Test each one." And Stoyan had presented Caldwell with two small half-full stainless-steel vats.

"That looks disgusting. What is that stuff?"

"Is extract! From CO_2 extractor."

"That thing?" Caldwell pointed to the collection of equipment, mostly tanks and large vats with bolted lids sitting by an assortment of pressure gauges attached to the wall.

"Yes. Very nice. First time I use. Is not so much in Moldova."

"I thought we hired you for your experience."

"Yes. I have lot. Many experience. Many plants."

"Well we can't sell stuff that looks like that!"

"You want we sell this? Caldwell! This not cool! Not good."

"What? What are you trying to tell me? I know it's not good. Looks like it came out of a sewer."

"But is beautiful extract! No? We test, Caldwell. We test."

"Why would you?"

"Is stupid not to!"

"Just get rid of it!"

"No! Caldwell! We test. Test. Test each one."

Caldwell threw up his hands.

"We test. Then make formula. We mix. Test more. Okay?"

"Whatever!"

"Yes. I work formula. Write. Beautiful pen writing. Yes? Is joke! I type."

"You're driving me crazy. You know that?"

"Crazy? Caldwell. No crazy. No! How I can work in crazy?"

Chapter 41

Alice saw the flashing lights of a police car in the rearview mirror and looked at her speedometer. Good lord. She couldn't remember the last speed limit sign. She slowed down, moved over to the shoulder of the road and took a deep breath as she braked her car to a full stop. The police car pulled in front. A fat, bald-headed officer got out and hitched up his pants as he walked back to her. Alice lowered her window. She smiled but looked straight ahead.

The officer leaned down. "Hello ma'am. You know why I stopped you?"

"I suppose I was speeding, Officer. I'm very sorry."

"Yeah, I guess you were." The officer chuckled. "But that's not really why I'm stoppin' you. I'm gonna give you a ticket though now you mention it. License, ma'am?"

Alice gasped inaudibly. Where the hell was her head that morning? She always told Zack to put his license and ownership right on the dash, especially on long trips. She needed to wake up and follow her own advice. Alice slowly lifted her handbag into her lap so the officer could see the contents of her purse, so there would be no mistaking what she was doing. She handed him the license. He took it back to his car and then took his time. Alice felt a little queasy, and the longer he took the queasier she felt. What in God's name would be taking him so long? Finally, he reappeared and handed her license back to her.

He started to chuckle again. "Not exactly from around here, are you?"

Alice smiled at him briefly and then looked ahead again.

He leaned down. "So where you headed?"

"Lyston, Officer."

"Well there's your trouble right there."

Alice felt the panic beginning to rise in her throat. They were in the middle of nowhere. "I'm sorry if I was speeding, Officer. I have an appointment and I was thinking about the meeting. Not paying enough attention I imagine."

The officer cleared his throat. "Well, I guess you were speedin', ma'am. But like I said, that's not why I stopped you."

"I see." Alice held her breath. The officer's gun was in its holster, just about at her eye level.

"See, I can't in all good conscience let you continue on this road."

Alice was still looking straight ahead. She was a little breathless.

The officer stepped closer and practically put his head right in her car. "Because the damn road is washed out!" He tried to catch her eye but Alice was having none of it. "Yup. Caused a real nasty accident too." He straightened up. "Never seen anything like it. Big propane truck exploded. Prob'ly three people killed at least!"

Alice finally looked at the officer.

"They just blocked the road a mile back but you managed to slip through before they got there." He paused. "That there," he said, pointing to a rough gravel road veering off to the right about fifty yards ahead, "is your only turnoff. Unless you want to go back. But you take that gravel road west for a mile or so — take it easy, there's potholes —'til you get to the paved road and the signs there'll take you to the interstate. Get you to Lyston faster anyway." The officer smiled faintly. "An' you can pick up your speeding ticket on the interstate if you like." He walked back to his patrol car. Alice noticed a lightness in his step now, as if he'd just had himself a mighty fine time. He got in, and as he was doing so, pointed to the gravel road again.

Alice nodded. He drove ahead of her and stopped just past the turnoff. As she turned onto the gravel road, the police car made a U-turn and sped off the way it had come with its lights flashing. As Alice watched it disappear, she wiped the sweat from her forehead.

She was on her way to the dispensary in Lyston and thought she'd take the scenic route. Avoidance is always helped by good scenery. Alice had recently put it to Caldwell and Luther that something would need to change. Even now, with CannRose finished product finally making it onto the shelves, sales barely covered the cost of running the dispensaries. How could they ever keep the grow facility going? Caldwell had been indignant and implied Alice was such a small-time player she wouldn't understand. It was all part of the master plan. "This is a venture of go slow, perfect the model and don't let early returns fool you," he'd announced. He had all sorts of buzzwords and phrases, like "falling forward," to legitimize what Alice could see as only lousy decisions and poor management.

Alice was supposed to have a late lunch with Lydia, Percy and Petra after sorting out some details with Sammy at the Lyston dispensary. Sammy had decided she wanted to get out of the big city, so she was working there full time now and loving it. Alice was looking forward to seeing her but even that didn't lighten Alice's apprehension or reticence about the day generally. She doubted that the lunch would be very well-digested.

Lydia was always unfathomably positive. Or willfully blind. Even back when the state had threatened to pull the company's registration, Lydia was unperturbed and waxing on about how wonderfully CannRose was doing. It didn't help that her suggestions were mostly met with open-mouthed bewilderment. People found her ridiculous and yet her money kept CannRose afloat. From Alice's perspective the woman was surrounded by vultures, scorpions and a slew of assorted parasites. At least with that new Guido guy around she wouldn't be the lone cash cow anymore. Not that Alice liked him much at all.

As Alice drove, she contemplated responsibility, integrity and loyalty. And there was the greater good to consider. She tried her best to convince herself that Lydia's exploitation by all was none of her business. Marijuana was helping a lot of people — maybe not enough to pay the bills of the company — but if Lydia was as wealthy as rumored, then what of it? It would make no difference in Lydia's life, but it was making a big difference to others. Maybe that was what Lydia wanted all along. Who knew really? Alice had little insight into the motivations of the moneyed and privileged. But no sooner had Alice persuaded herself that all was as it should be than misgivings about her own complicity crept in and put her stomach in knots.

#

The late lunch was attended by only the three women. The grow facility was in the middle of a harvest and Percy's QA skills were required to keep the paperwork straight.

"Have you noticed this industry is mostly men?" Lydia piped up. "I went to that big cannabis conference in San Francisco and there was a seminar specially for company owners and CEOs. I was the only woman in the room."

"Well it's mostly white too. Try being the only Black person in the room as well as the only woman."

"Did they ask you to make the coffee?" Petra popped a piece of cheese in her mouth and smiled at Alice.

"It wasn't quite that bad. It was a while ago, for the drugstore business actually. They were all pretty uncomfortable. They had a mission statement from a few years before with all sorts of references to affirmative action. Just had to take a look around the room to see how well all that was going."

Petra tsked. Then she took another gulp of her wine and reached for a second piece of cheese.

Lydia was eyeing the cheese too but then clearly thought better of it. "But why do you think men are dominating the marijuana industry? White men in particular. The plants are female. Most farmers in the world are women."

"Look at the start-up costs, Lydia," Alice said. "I know *class* is an uncomfortable word, right up there with *racism*, but there it is. Plus the politics of marijuana have never done Black people any favors. And that's putting it mildly. As for male dominance . . ." Alice shook her head.

"Take subsistence farming out of the equation, you got bigger agriculture. That's very male. And corporations get in there," Petra said, waving her wineglass. She was feeling pretty good. "Greed takes over. Men have a much easier time manifesting their greed. Women usually get punished for it."

"They're supposed to be selfless. Didn't you know that? Women are the life-givers," Alice said, batting her eyes.

They laughed.

"I hear women prefer their abusive partners stoned rather than drunk," Petra said. "And sometimes stoned rather than sober."

"I can believe that," Alice said.

Petra waved her wineglass more vigorously. "Did you know that cannabinoids interact with animal reproductive systems, suppress sperm production and can lead to pregnancy failure? So if you could get the world stoned more often, maybe we could slow the population growth."

They all laughed. And then Lydia leaned forward and said, "So really, Petra, you think the medical marijuana business is about greed? We're not doing very well if that's the case."

"The boys are bankin' on the future, Lydia. Buds and bonuses." Petra helped herself to some more wine.

"I'm glad you brought this up," Alice said, her tone becoming serious. Then she looked intently at Lydia. "The sales I'm seeing barely cover my costs. This company is going to bleed to death. Something big needs to change."

Lydia shifted uncomfortably in her chair. "You know I don't make most of the decisions. And there's a cap on my investment now, but Guido has already been a big help. He says we can aim for a five-year turnaround. He's very committed. And I think he'd be happy just to see the company break even."

"You might want to watch that, Lydia. He is a fiddler," Petra announced, realizing she'd consumed too much lunchtime Chardonnay by that point. "And so was Nero." She belched rather loudly, and the three of them started to laugh again.

PART NINE

Harvesting

Squandering Reapers! A dervish demurs at your repose. We loved life too. Consider that as the scythe swings. Consider our mission all spent. No mercy is your mercy. We loved hope. We saw the sky and the twelve heavens. Now we pay rent. We felt exaltation and tasted pure light. We bring our soul to the years coming in and to the earth. You want gummy bears. Our distance grows and you harvest mileage. Consider our love as the blades flash in the light of limits. Blades made by midgets and stumblers. Consider this for a minute. One. If you can.

from Cannto VII, *Cannabidadas*

.

Chapter 42

"The DOH won't allow it." Percy stood looking out the QA office window at the unrelenting gray day. Rain had been drizzling the whole morning. And this was the second round of this discussion.

"What do you mean the DOH won't allow it?" Caldwell found Percy's detachment incomprehensible. CannRose had produced its best crop yet. The buds were big, dense, beautiful. Dried like a dream. Perfect. And the THC concentration was coming in at a whopping thirty-three and a half percent. It was premium bud. They hadn't even had to irradiate it. Caldwell had been overjoyed. Proud like a new dad! Now Percy was telling him they'd have to lose it. Mill it with something else! Sell it to one of the other dispensaries for extract because Stoyan was still validating! This was craziness. Caldwell was having none of it.

Percy turned briefly to look at Caldwell, who'd taken over the one chair in the office. "You can't sell cannabis products with that profile," Percy said. "The THC is unfortunately just too high." He was not unsympathetic. It was a spectacular crop. Everything had worked. No mechanical breakdowns. No fertilizer screw-ups. No humidity issues. No yeast or mold counts to speak of. Stellar really. But the DOH was the DOH, and it had recently issued THC-concentration limits on all products sold.

"The DOH doesn't control the plants," Caldwell said, jutting out his chin.

"No." Percy turned back to stare out the window. It was best to let Caldwell get to the other side of the tantrum before discussing what to actually do about the matter.

"They don't control the product," Caldwell continued, his voice rising.

"No. They don't."

"And they certainly don't control this company!"

"No, they just take the offending product off the shelves, and, if we do sell any, make us do a recall." Percy didn't have to look to know that the veins on Caldwell's forehead were bulging.

"I don't care! We're selling it anyway. In fact we're selling it as premium product. The CannRose Premium line!"

"You might consider we're still on probation," Percy said, watching a couple of birds fluffed up against the rain and perched on the sumacs. "Some people at the DOH are just looking for another reason to pull the registration, you know."

"They wouldn't pull it over that!" Caldwell almost laughed — the idea was ridiculous.

"Have you met Ms. Ligner? Our delightfully officious inspector is on a mission. I think she'd like nothing better than to see CannRose dead in the water."

"Well screw that," Caldwell stormed. "We'll threaten to sue them again! This time we'll do it. We'll sue the goddamn DOH." Caldwell raked the hair off his reddening forehead. "And we'll win."

Percy sighed. "But they still won't allow the sale. It's in the regs."

"I know the code inside out, and nowhere does it give concentration limits for THC." Caldwell figured Percy was siding with the incompetent know-nothing teenage inspector. Another tiny miserable person trying to thwart the CannRose vision.

"It's in the commissioner's letter," Percy said. "Talk to Alice if you don't believe me. She's not going to put it on the shelves." And then Percy began to explain it all again. In the interest of public safety, the state reserved the right to issue amendments to the code at any time. Percy had received official notice three months ago that no trimmed dried flowers or derivative products, including tinctures, oils, creams, capsules or suppositories containing more than twenty-five percent THC could be sold. There was also a looming issue with the plant growth hormones because they would concentrate in the extracts. CannRose should take note.

Caldwell's exasperation tended to encourage Percy. So he launched into more explanation about the growth hormone issue. "The state will inevitably set specifications, Caldwell. They're bound to be stringent and they might not be so easily attained given the current cultivation practices, especially when you consider—"

Caldwell's phone jingled. He got up from the chair, gave one last annoyed glance at Percy and left the room to answer the call.

Petra came waltzing in. She looked outrageously happy these days. Percy didn't want to think about it. He'd only had to spend a few minutes in that lab to know what was going on. And the last time he'd been in there, Sanjay had winked at him. Again! The saucy tramp. He wouldn't tell Gavin about how compelling a little hussy he was — not yet anyway. Percy leaned against the wall and folded his arms. "What can I do for you, Petra?"

"I thought you might need a little cheering up. You know after old buggerlugs there got through chewing you out for doing your job."

"I could do without his toddler tendencies. Then again, I'd like to see him try putting that stuff on the shelves."

"Wonder what kind of a hissy fit the DOH would throw . . ."

"He'd never get it past Alice. That's the fireworks I'd like to see. He does have a point though, even if it is for all the wrong reasons. There's no proof whatsoever concentrations like that are universally harmful. What if thirty-three percent is the perfect dosage for some condition? Honestly, between the DOH tying our hands and feet at every turn and Caldwell tilting at windmills, I'm surprised we function at all. Tell me, Petra, why do any of us stay?"

"I'm kind of off in my corner there, Percy. I work on stuff Caldwell doesn't pretend to understand. I have to hand that to him at least."

"The man does not tolerate instruction nor abide even the most moderate directives. He dismisses almost everything I tell him."

"I wouldn't take it too much to heart."

"Speaking of hearts, I think he's putting on weight. And he's looking pasty. I don't think he exercises either. And he's that age, you know."

"Oh, you're in a much more hopeful mood than I thought you'd be. Good for you!"

"Yes. Good for me."

Chapter 43

Cassie and Joe's opinion of Damian grew worse every day. When cultivation was going well, they were able to ignore the master grower. But not when there were issues, like right now. One of the flower rooms was infested with thrips, small flat insects. They were a sinister group, even with only a left mandible — the right one was reabsorbed during the embryonic stage — and they had a second pair of jaws that worked like vacuum pumps sucking the life out of plants until the young leaves curled in disfigurement. Some thrips delighted in floral tissues, and like a Typhoid Mary of the plant world, would pass on diseases to the plants. Their trajectory on the dark side began early; the larvae were diabolically red-eyed.

Cassie and Joe blamed Damian and his stressful growing practices, which made the plants more susceptible to herbivory by tiny demons. And they didn't hide their contempt for the master grower. The more they familiarized themselves with marijuana-grow culture, the more they were convinced of his incompetence. He seemed to gravitate toward the most unsound and blatantly dumb practices going. In effect they'd decided Damian was a fraud with no right to be making the money he made or even influencing the show, never mind running it. They openly challenged him at every opportunity and kept up their private log — the one that documented all the stupid decisions Damian made and the even more outrageous pronouncements and snap changes directed by Caldwell.

And then they showed their logbook to Lorne. The production manager grimaced at the entries and suggested they keep it under their hat a while longer. Things could change quickly. He'd noticed that seemed to be the nature of the cannabis industry and he'd smiled at them with composed assurance. As for the thrips, they just kept multiplying.

It all came to a head in the potting room. Cassie was taking samples and measuring the pH for a new lot of grow media. She'd airily remarked to Damian that she wasn't at all surprised the primary flushing procedures he'd used for the Alabama Blitz had resulted in the lowest yield yet. The head grower from Condor Rush, the most successful outfit in the West, had told her that amateurs often had difficulty with both timing and duration for most techniques. Cassie went on to mention Damian might want to reconsider his drought strategies too, since Javier Corvidez, the legendary West Coast pot guru, had told her just last Saturday that thrips are best thwarted by misting.

Damian just stood there. His head began twitching with sharp little forward movements. His jaw clamped and the tendons on his neck bulged. He picked up a trowel, clenching his fist around the handle until his knuckles went white.

Cassie continued smiling and working, not looking at him, and pointing out that he shouldn't be too hard on himself since there were probably a lot worse things than amateurism, and besides it was probably unavoidable given his lifetime of smoking homegrown second-class weed.

Suddenly Damian took one long step toward her and stabbed the trowel into the table where the probe had been lying just an instant before, and Cassie's hand right next to it.

Cassie jumped back. "What the fuck!" The metal went deep enough into the tabletop that the trowel stood vertically on its own and vibrated. "Asshole!" she screamed at him.

That did it. Joe seemed to come out of nowhere. He jumped Damian from behind and rode him piggyback with an arm tight around his neck. With his free hand he kept smacking Damian on the side of his head. After a few seconds of this, with Damian spinning around trying to throw him off, the master grower dropped and rolled, bashing Joe into the table legs to disengage him. Then Damian lifted himself, climbed on top of Joe and started punching him in the face.

Cassie looked around wildly as if she was going to scream but didn't know who to scream to. Her eyes lit upon the pH probe. Her movement was swift. She gripped the probe, her face contorted with indignation and rage. She ran at Damian. In a move that looked to have been perfected in some bowling alley in hell, she swooped in low and stabbed him.

"You fucking cunt!" Damian screamed. He reached around, pulled out the probe and turned to face her, holding it up to her as she towered over him. "I'm gonna have you locked up," he hissed. "And then I'm gonna sue your ass for every last fucking penny."

"It was well aimed," Sanjay said later. He'd heard the crashing in the potting room and went to take a look. "Very resoundingly, in the right buttock."

Chapter 44

"How come there's just two of us here?"

"I don't know."

"Won't take that long."

"These buds are fire, bro."

"Frosty femmes!"

"Thirsty ladies! Gonna be lit AF."

The two young devotees put their earbuds back in to listen to their music as they trimmed. They hummed along from time to time and smiled at each new plant as they came to it. Eventually the flower-room door opened and the third young man entered, somewhat breathless and excited. The two who were working each took out one earbud.

"Yo, bro! Where you been?"

"Yeah. We're like Gucci on this trimming."

"High key! They finally had it out. Big fight!"

"Who?"

"Who else, Perennial Shade Throwers."

"Who won?"

"Whoever was loudest, bro. And they'll be at it again tomorrow."

"No, brobes. They were talkin' fists. Catchin' hands!"

"What? Seriously?"

"Right on the potting-room floor."

"Shit! You see it?"

"No. Got there after. There was a crowd. Everybody was freaking."

"So who won?"

"I don't know. Ernie said Cassie rammed a pH probe up Damian's ass!"

"Fuck! That's savage!"

"Joe had a bloody nose."

"Sick. Wish I'd seen that."

"Why? It's terrible."

"Maybe one of 'em'll quit now."

"Who though?"

"What's it matter? We just end up doing what Lorne tells us anyway."

"Least it wasn't in front of the ladies."

"Yeah. That would suck."

"Ladies shouldn't ever be triggered."

"No violence in front of the ladies."

"What about harvest? That's pretty violent."

"No it's not."

"Yeah it is. For the ladies."

"No . . . yeah, I guess. But it's not gratuitous."

"And it's not angry."

"It's not so lit either, if you're one of the ladies."

"Why are we talking about this?"

Chapter 45

"So no one thought to call the police?" Luther was leaning back in the lime-green leather chair looking disgustedly at the acrylic slab of a conference table rather than at Lorne.

"Were we supposed to?"

"No. No report. Less material for a civil suit."

"Damian's claiming it was assault with a deadly weapon."

"He threatened a woman with a trowel. That could be deadly too, Lorne. Her husband protected her. Then she protected her husband. Damian might not have a leg to stand on, or a cheek to sit on, maybe." Luther snorted. The Damian he saw in the video bore no resemblance to the laid-back guy he'd chitchatted with during dinner at Lydia's a few months ago. You just never knew about people. "Anyway, it's the other two I'm worried about. Did Joe — er, that's his name, right? — Did he go to a doctor? Hospital?"

"I don't know." Lorne was feeling sick.

"Let's make sure we have a slight technical problem. Don't let the couple get a look at the video footage. How much did you know about this horticulture war?"

"I tried to say out of it."

"For God's sake, Lorne. You're the production manager!" Luther threw up his hands and stared at Lorne. Then he sighed. "So did the couple's logbook document any threats from Damian?"

"No threats against them. But threats to the plants? Yeah. They were documenting Caldwell's activities in the production area too."

"Jesus." Luther could do without this craziness. Thank God, there wasn't a union! Yet.

He needed to send in another lawyer. He didn't have the time or the knack. He'd decided as a student that employment and labor law was a mire, and he'd steered clear of it. His being even near the grow facility was a fluke. He just happened to be in the area "discussing business" with Lydia. The company needed to bury this. Fast. They should just fire everybody involved, including Lorne. Probably Greg too given he was head of HR. And Lydia! Luther could see several lawsuits unfolding; damage control was his specialty even if labor law wasn't. This was the last thing the company needed.

Lydia was shocked by the altercation and by the notion that the company could somehow be liable. She wanted to convene a meeting with all those involved and get to the bottom of things so that people could get along and appreciate the gifts that each brought to the CannRose family. "Why should anyone be fired? How will people ever learn to be friends that way?"

Luther was speechless. No wonder Jordan had set up an industry around her just to look after the estate. Luther suggested she step down as president. She was puzzled by this because she thought her contribution was key to the company's functioning. Luther shut up at that point. His wife was divorcing him. He needed a friend and he'd miraculously found a lover. A very rich one. She had a few years on him but so what? Maybe it was time to learn to get along. Take a look at things from Lydia's uncommon perspective.

#

Cleaning up "the incident" at CannRose was simple. The company could not tolerate violent behavior under any circumstances, the labor lawyer explained in his deep, solemn voice. Cassie, Joe and Damian had to be fired. Six weeks' full pay was offered to each. They just had to sign an agreement. Of course in signing, they released the company from any future responsibilities, health claims or any kind of litigation whatsoever related to the little fracas.

Six weeks' pay looked generous from the perspective of a black eye, given black eyes tend to heal quickly. Even the owner of the punctured butt thought it was a pleasant surprise. And any legal action Damian intended to take against Cassie was deterred by self-medication. Some premium Zimbabwe bud, cultivated by his current Colorado girlfriend, relieved the pain quite remarkably, so he never got around to the "obtaining legal counsel" step. And Joe and Cassie's outrage at Damian's very existence left no room for other considerations. They had never tolerated a perception of themselves as victims. So they hadn't talked to anybody either. All three were somewhat bemused by the payoff and quite happy to sign. They'd all been about to quit anyway.

However, the labor lawyer went on to explain that CannRose was also very forgiving. In truth, the execs realized they might be up shit creek if they got rid of all the cultivation experts at the same time. The lawyer didn't allude to this point for even a millisecond. He'd spent years refining his approach, ensuring workers were screwed out of any leverage they might have for even the most legitimate claims. But this situation was turning out to be so easy it was almost insulting. He explained that the company was willing to grant people a second chance. If they wished to reapply after or even while attending anger-management classes or seeking therapy, their applications would be seen in a favorable light, though remuneration at present levels may have to be reconsidered as the company bore considerable risk by taking them back.

When they told the guy he was wasting his breath, Lydia unexpectedly exercised her authority. She genuinely wanted to understand how any of this could have happened at CannRose. Damian had been living only yards away from her own house and she considered him a friend, but not once had she heard about difficulties between staff from him. And she'd always thought Joe and Cassie and their sweet children embodied the perfect wholesome young American family. Why, the freshness and hope in their faces fairly shone. CannRose couldn't find a more suitable couple aligned with the company's own core values. The labor lawyer advised her that understanding was unnecessary and a waste of time. "People are just naturally barbaric," he said. Nevertheless she invited them individually into her office to hear each person's side of the story. Since they weren't planning to reapply they needn't hold back, she told them. She wanted to hear all their thoughts on the matter, even the uncomfortable ones. How else was CannRose to avoid this in the future?

#

"You know what I think, Luther?" Lydia said to him as they swung gently in the hammock. They were wrapped up in their big towels enjoying a sunny afternoon down by the Great Pond.

It was so rare that Luther was able to relax, he felt he'd stolen the time. He clasped her hands between his. "What do you think?"

"I think people just want to be appreciated," Lydia said. "They want to know they count."

"I wish it were that simple!"

"But I think it is, Luther. People don't get up in the morning and decide they're going to do something terrible."

"I think lots of people do. Some people are driven, and a person better not get in their way. Or they think they have a right to something when somebody else has it. Or sometimes, say with a psychopath, the meanness just comes naturally. It's a state of being."

Lydia looked across the water as a duck skidded in for a landing. "You see a much darker world than I do. I guess I like to see the best in people."

"Well that's who you are, Lydia. I think I adore that about you." He stroked the side of her face.

"Really, Luther? That's sweet." Her smile waned as she turned her gaze back to him.

He kissed her cheek.

Lydia stared at him — maybe right through him. "You know Jordan saw a darker world too. I suppose that's why he liked to keep me in the dark. He kept me naive." She nodded to herself. "Maybe so he could continue to adore me. I don't think that's such a good idea. You mustn't ever censor information for me, Luther. Don't coddle. It's not fair." She looked away again, back to the duck paddling in the pond. "You know when Cassie was telling me those horrible things she thought about Damian, I didn't think she was a bad person for it. I just saw all that frustration. It was heartbreaking you know. She's a very hard worker."

"I think the three people involved were relatively untainted, Lydia. Just rather innocent people caught up in a conflict. Nothing like the people I see most of the time."

"You're saying the world out there is much, much darker." Lydia sighed.

"It's sure not pretty. People are ruthless, cynical, greedy."

"Do you think Jordan was ruthless? Did you ever hear that about him?"

Luther realized the conversation was becoming something more than just a chatty afternoon in the sun with his magnanimous lover. He needed to tread carefully. "I suppose I have heard that about Jordan. But it was pretty normal for the times."

Lydia turned back to him with her full attention. "How so?"

"Oh, usual stuff. Hostile takeovers, mergers, plunder the competition's talent to shut it down. Outsourcing, bribes on the side, financial threats, whatever it took to stay on top. Only so much market and profit to go around, Lydia. He was just more clever at it than most."

"But people got hurt."

"That's business, Lydia. Hell, now it's gone one further: cover-ups, collusion, artificial inflation of earnings, accounting fraud, tax evasion every which way you name it. Back in Jordan's day the corporate world at least pretended to have a moral compass."

"Are we doing that now, with CannRose, Luther? You know I don't understand business all that well. Are we carrying on in that normal manner? Like what you just said about how it's gone further."

Luther kissed Lydia on the cheek again. "I think we're pretty small players, Lydia." Then he turned away to look out at the water himself. He wished he'd skipped drinks several months ago with Jordan's two dearest old friends, the overseers of Lydia's estate. Cyrus and Malcolm were as cold-blooded as vipers. They'd chortled and snickered over their martinis as they discussed Jordan's shell companies and the Dutch mailbox set-ups. Usually things worked the other way around with money flowing out of the country. But for Malcolm and Cyrus, tax laws were minor hurdles, background noise that was easily filtered. Besides, the Netherlands held the European gold standard for marijuana production. They'd been at it for years.

"How much more fitting could the financial arrangements possibly be?" Cyrus had exclaimed, popping an olive into his mouth.

"Like tulips and windmills," Malcolm had said.

Chapter 46

"It was a blood moon and something to do with the planets linin' up on the equinox, something like that," Lazlo explained, his rheumy eyes more lit up than usual. The CannRose vice-president-and-contractor was in a jolly mood. Even his voice was clear. The waste-management facility had finally been completed. Most everything was built now — enough to satisfy the state anyway. Caldwell and Luther would be off his back. He was telling Ernie and Greg about the festivities at Rosefields the day Guido had signed over millions of dollars. Rumors had reverberated through the grow facility that the party had turned into an orgy. It wasn't an event that Ernie had catered, so he was curious about what happened.

"More like a mosh-up for geriatrics. The board's a bunch of antiques you know — friends Lydia had from Jordan's old crowd. Cyrus and Malcolm weren't there though. I think Malcolm was off the board by then anyway. And the munchkin wasn't there either."

"Who's the munchkin?" Ernie asked.

"Luther." Lazlo smiled. "Caldwell named him ages ago. Fitting I think. Now I guess he's Lydia's little munchkin."

"Yeah, I did notice that. People who work in glass offices . . ." Ernie shook his head.

"Anyway they were all drunk," Lazlo continued. "Half of 'em high. Damian has a bottomless stash and who knows what else he's got."

"So who got naked? That's what I want to know," Greg said.

"I sure as hell didn't. Most of 'em were out on the patio having this ceremony."

"For Guido and the blood moon," Greg said.

"No, for the spring equinox. Anyway, I just stayed at the bar and raised my glass to 'em. Lydia had these sparklers, incense burning everywhere, candles floating in the pool. It's heated you know — she keeps it going all year round."

"I don't even start up my hot tub 'til late April," Greg said.

"So Guido, Jason, me and some woman — I can't remember her name — we're just chatting, and somebody turns the music up. It's this airy-fairy stuff, la-la-la, and suddenly they're all hugging each other out on the patio and they troop back in with their arms stretched out. I didn't know where this was going and Guido was looking pretty uncomfortable."

"Not his kind of people?"

"Even if they are the same generation." Lazlo shook his head. "I got hugged too by at least four of 'em. Two months ago they wanted me fired."

"Money changes things."

"I'll say. So then one of 'em puts on some old R & B. And it was that really old Bradford lady who started it. She goes outside hollerin' about freedom and springtime, whips all her clothes off and starts gyrating to the music."

"That's a very scary visual."

"She's an old flower child ya know. Woodstock an' everything 'til she married into money. Anyway, then the others decide to join her."

"It just takes one."

"Well, it took some of 'em quite a while. Like I said, they're mostly antiques. I can't remember who all. But picture this — there's a couple of 'em on the big table and the rest out on the retainer wall. Music's blaring. They're dancin', singin' and bangin' on cocktail shakers. Lydia's found herself a ukulele."

Greg choked on his coffee.

"It was crazy. I mean the Bradford woman's gotta be close to eighty. The husband, he's about the same and all stooped over. And this other guy, he's a hippo, twice the size of my Gus. And Damian? Jesus with that hair, and he's so skinny, looks like he stepped out of a concentration camp."

"Another night at Rosefields, I guess!" Greg chuckled.

"It gets better. Caldwell finally comes back. He took his little girlfriend home. I can never remember that kid's name and she's so quiet. Anyway she wasn't feelin' too good. Tossed her cookies out by the garage."

"So did he have a tantrum or start telling them how to dance?" Greg asked.

"Well, he's watchin' all this and he's watchin' Guido too. Guido's lookin' anywhere but out the patio doors and finishing up his drink like he's getting ready to leave. So Caldwell starts taking off his shirt and I tell you the look on Guido's face . . ."

"Poor guy gets a freak show for his millions."

"I gotta hand it to Caldwell, though. He goes sprinting across the patio and cannonballs straight into the pool. So naturally all the nutbars follow him, with Lydia saying, 'My gracious! What a perfect idea!'" Lazlo paused and smiled. "It was like water therapy, you know, like in the old days at the asylum. Settled 'em all right down."

"Good thing they weren't all dancin' on the table," Greg said. "Can you imagine the accident that coulda been?"

"Broken hips. Damian losing the other half of his brain."

"Everybody losing their teeth. Jesus!" Greg started laughing.

Lazlo and Ernie were laughing too and rocking a little in the new ergonomic office chairs. Infusions of money, like the one from Guido, were always put to fine use at the facility.

"So what was Jason doin' in all this?" Greg asked.

"Drinkin'. He's likely seen crazier shit where he came from."

Lazlo and Greg had been in agreement for some time about the angel investor and his sidekick. Lazlo had friends north of the border who knew about Jason. They said he'd reformed from his wasted youth. Greg said he was legally resilient and valuable too. He'd managed to beat any convictions or deal his way out of them. Guido was pure as snow by comparison.

"He may have one or two distant connections, but they're . . ." Greg shrugged. "They're loose. Inconsequential."

"Fluid?" Ernie suggested. "Like little ripples intersecting in a pond?"

"Yeah," Greg nodded, liking the image. "Something like that." Then he looked at Ernie quizzically for a second and smiled.

Lazlo picked up his coffee. "He can be whatever from wherever. I don't think any of us would still be here without him." He raised his mug. "Here's to Guido."

"And obviously he's a good sport, among crazies too," Ernie added and kept his suspicions about the man to himself. It wasn't that

Ernie thought Guido was some Mafia boss or anything, but he was sure the man was up to something. Guido knew way more about what was going on at CannRose than anybody else. Intel was power and Guido sure knew how to land the intel.

#

It was a warm night so Ernie sat out on his rooftop getting a little high. His attention was drawn to the bats that were flitting above him, in and out among the big oaks that towered on one side of the Rent-All. The bats absorbed all light; the stars above fleetingly disappeared and reappeared as the little mammals dipped and darted after their dinners. It was like the bats were in some complex and highly choreographed dance number. Perhaps dancing under the stars was a natural thing to do, although Ernie himself had never felt compelled that way. It had to do with his lack of coordination when moving with any speed. The same reason he'd never played basketball in spite of his height. *Appearances are often deceiving,* Ernie thought.

Riffing on the dance motif, Greg came to mind. The bearded hulk of an ex-cop, who was always making lame jokes about the black market, also had a thing for old Broadway shows. He whistled the tunes when he figured nobody was listening. Ernie had heard him lots of times. *Cabaret, A Chorus Line, Gypsy, Guys and Dolls.* Late one Friday afternoon when Greg thought everybody else had gone home, Ernie saw him dance. Who knew. He was amazingly light on his feet and did an elaborate jazz walk down the length of the admin section. He ended with a pirouette. Then he ducked, swayed and leaped with a weird kind of grand jeté into the security office.

When he realized Ernie had seen him, he blushed as deeply as only a fair-skinned brute of a redhead could. It didn't help that Ernie was doubled over with laughter. Then Ernie had said in all honesty, "Man, I wish I could do that. It was spectacular." They went for a beer. Ernie talked about his teenage basketball incompetence and Greg told him how he'd taken tap and jazz until he was fifteen, before he unexpectedly grew the body of a two-hundred-and-fifty-pound linebacker.

Maybe it was just the dope, but as Ernie got drowsy and stared up at the stars he got the feeling probably nobody was who they appeared to be. Not Greg, not Guido or Jason, not Lydia, not even himself. He was betting people showed up on the planet in fractions, and the whole of them had to be way more mysterious than the world imagined.

Chapter 47

Alice was doing her best. She always did, but she was getting discouraged. She didn't think the dispensaries would prosper no matter how well she organized them. She couldn't do much if the grow facility still wasn't meeting demand and she had to fill her inventory with other dispensaries' products. Ironically, CannRose was occasionally selling off dried product to other dispensaries. It could get a better price for intact buds from the other companies who weren't averse to irradiation than it could for milled product under the CannRose brand name. Caldwell had managed to convince the board to stop to selling irradiated buds because it could be bad for future recreational marijuana sales. Irradiation was for milled product only and for the one oil Stoyan had formulated so far. So she was actually selling CannRose product but under another dispensary's name. It wasn't how things were supposed to work.

When confronted recently, Caldwell opted for distraction. He claimed the other dispensaries were all cheating and he pointed to the various pesticide problems that were showing up in the news. Her son Zack had made the observation that CannRose was basically a mom-and-pop operation with a very dysfunctional family.

To add to the discouragement, Ms. Ligner, that unpleasant inspector from the DOH, was throwing her weight around again. Sammy told Alice that the woman had treated her like she was a criminal during the last inspection and had demanded to see all the financial records at the Lyston dispensary. Alice was quite sure access to most of that information was outside the DOH's medical cannabis mandate. But maybe she'd missed some notification. "Lord knows they amend the marijuana regulations every month," she muttered to herself.

As Alice was thinking about this, her phone rang. It was Nina from the dispensary across town and she was in a panic. The very same inspector was threatening to shut the place down because they couldn't find a simple document, a chain of custody. Alice grabbed her purse, jumped in the car and raced over there.

When she arrived, Ms. Ligner was in the back room, pacing back and forth on her stilettos while Nina sat at the table crying and blindly going through several open file folders spread out in front of her.

"What's the problem?" Alice said, removing her coat.

"You don't have a chain of custody," the inspector said. "You've lost a shipment! Or diverted one."

"Excuse me. There would be a receiving log and inventory records." Alice looked at Nina, who nodded through her tears. She busied herself with the laptop in front of her. After a few seconds she handed it to Alice.

"See, it's all here," Alice said. "The date, the time, the products, the quantity. So the shipment has not been lost."

"Dispensaries must maintain chains of custody. You're in noncompliance."

Alice took a deep breath. "I'm sure it's just been misfiled. I believe a company is given some time to produce records during an audit."

"This is no audit, ma'am. This is an inspection. May I remind you, dispensaries operate at the discretion of the Department of Health."

"And may I remind you the Department of Health is funded by the taxpayer. And as a taxpayer I don't find your insinuations or your threatening my staff to the point of tears acceptable."

"I'm merely doing my job."

"I'm not so sure."

"I repeat, the state does not tolerate diversion."

At this point Todd, the other dispensary technician, came rushing in. "Found it!" he said. "It was on the bottom of the drawer, under all the files."

Alice smiled. "There, you see."

Ms. Ligner briefly looked at the document and handed it back. "Perhaps you should review your filing system."

Alice stayed for the rest of the inspection. The woman wanted to see financial records for this dispensary too. For inventory, sales, suppliers and purchases maybe, but surely not the bookkeeping for the whole operation. The inspector looked daggers at Alice when she was confronted and insisted she had the authority. She was all over the security details too, picking nits at the littlest imperfection. She wrote up findings about the surveillance camera at the back of the store. It didn't show the bottom two feet of the back door, and five minutes of video from it was blurry. She found other minor issues too. Mostly in record-keeping, a missing initial here, a date there. And she didn't approve of some packaging from one of the other dispensaries. She said the type was too ornate on the product brand and the logo too large. It was too much like advertising.

"It's not even our product," Alice said, "and it's clearly passed inspection on the other side of the state."

"Some inspectors miss things."

"Ms. Ligner, this product is being sold and has been sold for the past year. It was one of the first products available and it's very popular."

"Popularity is not my concern. If the packaging doesn't meet regulations, it's noncompliant. This has to come off the shelves. If you choose to repackage it, make sure the labeling meets the requirements."

Alice and Todd looked at each other in resignation. Nina stared down at the floor. The three of them took the offending product back to the vault, where Ms. Ligner randomly picked three packages of CannRose product for testing, signing for them with unmistakable disgust. Ms. Ligner would be sending the official report within ten business days, and without any goodbye she vanished out the door.

"I can hardly wait," Alice said, folding her arms.

"What's her problem?" Todd's exhale was almost a raspberry as he stared after her.

"Who knows? But I'm going to make some more problems for her."

Todd turned to Alice, eyebrows raised.

"She's way out of line," Alice said. "I'm reporting her. The DOH can't expect dispensaries to function with inspectors like that."

That very evening Alice wrote a letter to the director of the medical marijuana division at the DOH and cc'd the state commissioner himself. She sent it by registered post the next morning, though it might not get very far. Dealing with the DOH was like talking to a great abyss staffed at various tiers by headless officials. A little Kafkaesque. But the letter would be unusual, arriving as a physical missive instead of an email, and might actually catch someone's attention. Plus she felt a whole lot better having written it.

Still, the episode was worrying. Was there really some new legislation she hadn't heard about yet allowing the DOH to go through finances like that? These days criminality and even regular pharmacies were being mentioned in the same breath because of the opioid crisis. Alice had limited what she would sell at her own pharmacy years ago because of the robbery problem. She never kept a stock of opioids on the premises and let it be known to all. Anyone with a prescription had to wait a day or two for the order to come in. If they needed it right away they could find another pharmacy.

#

Alice woke up at three o'clock in the morning, her son on her mind. She realized she hadn't heard him laugh or seen him smile in a year or more. Nor had she heard of a new girlfriend since the last one left, and that wasn't like him. The notion that she would see more of him because of CannRose's involvement with the law firm had been an illusion. Even when he came home at Christmas he was out with old friends most of the time. So Alice hadn't been keeping track. Only at three o'clock on that particular morning did she see the whole picture. Her son was miserable.

So that Saturday after breakfast, she sat in her favorite armchair reading the local newspaper and kept calling until she got hold of him. "Zack, honey. I woke up in the middle of the night thinking about you. Are you okay?"

"Must have been boring dreams if they couldn't hold your attention." Zack snickered.

"See, this is just why I was thinking of you. You're unhappy, aren't you. You sound cynical. That laugh . . . What's going on?"

Her son wasn't expecting this. And maybe he didn't want his mother knowing all that much anyway. She seemed to be everywhere. People at the firm spoke so highly of her, while he spent his days in a quiet hell, wading through documents and case files. He'd woken up himself at three o'clock in the morning several months ago and realized he hated being a lawyer. "Um, I guess being a lawyer . . . sucks," he said.

"You don't like law anymore?" Alice maneuvered the stool over so she could put her feet up.

He snorted. "Don't like it? I'd prefer sticking a hook up my nose to pull out my brains."

"Are you drinking?"

"Single malt helps the work go down, Mom."

"Honey, I don't like the sound of this at all."

"That makes two of us." Zack started twirling his pen.

"You need to do something."

"Maybe I can change my alarm to 'Zen Bells' or 'Birdsong of Paradise.' Did you know I have twenty-two alarm sounds to choose from on my company phone? Isn't that inspiring?"

"Can't you change the type of work you do there?"

"No. I do the type of work they do here. I do what they do."

"Have you really thought about it though? Investigated? I mean changing what you do somehow?" Alice could hear the ice rattle as Zack took a drink from his tumbler.

"Sure!" he said. "I think I'd like to be a tennis pro!"

"Honey, you're drunk!"

"Maybe a little."

"It's eleven o'clock in the morning!"

"I know and I've got ten hours of work left on this case today."

"You're working today?"

"I work most every Saturday, Mom. Sundays too."

"That's crazy."

"That's law."

"How does Luther—"

Zack slurped his drink loudly enough to drown her out. "I don't work with Luther, Mom. How's your work? How's the world of high times and total cray-cray. Let's just talk about *your* job satisfaction for a moment."

"Honey, you need to stop with the scotch and drink some water. I know you don't work with Luther. I just wondered how he manages to be CEO of CannRose if he's doing law seven days a week."

"Who knows? Helps if you're sleeping with a weed dowager, I mean the company president. He probably gets a load of work done in bed."

"Did you just say he's sleeping with Lydia?"

"Thought everybody knew."

"He's married!"

"He's in the middle of a divorce. Did you know lawyers have high divorce rates?" He started to laugh uncontrollably. "Law joke, Mom."

"Oh my goodness. Where have I been?" Alice reached for her own glass of water and took a gulp. "Isn't he rather young for Lydia?"

"I don't know. She's rich. That should make up for it, don't you think?"

PART TEN

Processing

Oh Handlers and Crafty Ones, the drought turns us delicate, our thirst exhumed for a benevolent trust. So severed and parched we fade to a pale presence. Husks of ourselves. Barren and yet you would love us more now. Our essence so much the richer as you are the poorer. We lead you without care it seems. Hurried runs to a solvent heaven, made weightless by sad angels. They sing of scarcity and grief. And the fool's lame resolutions. Can you hear them? No discernment or grace? They pick and they chose. The pulling of best, the culling of less. Oh that you might love us for more than refinement in pieces and haste. Would that our hearts' richer notes sing straight to yours. But you must hear your own blood pump to notice.

from Cannto VI, *Cannabidadas*

Chapter 48

The three young devotees were cleaning up Flower Room IV after the most recent harvest. They had bushels of waste from the troughs. It consisted of grow media and roots, and there were six big bags of plant waste already signed out of the live inventory and waiting for disposal.

"This is so fire!"

"S'up?"

"We got waste for the new rotating composter."

"Awesome!"

"Time to check out the waste management, bro."

"Yeah. Check out the waste management!"

"I thought they were getting a conveyor belt right to the loading dock."

"Conveyor belt! That's lit, bro!"

"When?"

"I don't know. When they figure it out."

"Is that a new door?"

"Everything's new."

"It's really shiny."

"This is sick, bro!"

"Look at this! Totally fucking awesome!"

"So what do we do now?"

"I don't know."

"Automatic feeder. Says right here."

"AF! Automatic feeder."

"It's the hopper."

"The hopper is fire!"

"Put the stuff all in there."

"Okay."

"Now what?"

"Bye-bye."

"What's with the bye-bye?"

"It's part of the kush, ladies. I'm bein' respectful."

"Push the Start button, bro."

"Woooah!"

"Dude, that's loud!"

"That's the chopper, bro."

"The chopper kills!"

"Chopper after the hopper! Awesome. Yeah!"

"What's that?"

"I don't know."

"We should turn it on if the other stuff is on."

"Yeah."

"Totally."

"Okay."

"It's turning!"

"It's supposed to turn, bro. It's rotating."

"Fucking fire!"

"That is so lit. Turn, turn. It's turned, dude. The rotator in the rotating composter."

"Bro, I think it's speeding up."

"Yeah, awesome."

"Is it supposed to do that?"

"I don't know."

"So dope."

"Yeah it's going faster."

"Yeah."

"Faster. Fucking fire!"

"Bro, that's starting to go really fast."

"That's fucking awesome!"

"Dude. I don't think it's supposed to be going that fast. I think you should slow it down."

"Yeah. I don't know how to do that."

"Dude, I think you should shut it off."

"I just tried."

"Dude! You should like, shut off that switch!"

"I'm trying, bro. It won't shut off."

"Yeah, it shouldn't go that fast. Basic."

"Shut it off, bro!"

"Fuck off! I can't!"

"Shit! I don't think that flap was supposed to open."

"Fuck!"

"Stuff just hit me in the face!"

"Fuck!"

"Bro! It's all over your back."

"It's in your hair!"

"Open the fucking door!"

"Yeah. Fucking get out of here!"

"Fuck!"

Chapter 49

"Anger management wouldn't be such a bad thing," Cassie said. "Might help me with the kids when they start driving me up the wall." It was four o'clock in the morning and Cassie and Joe were sitting up in bed.

"Honey, the kids are nothing like that situation at CannRose. Besides seeing a shrink is trouble. You're branded for life."

"We've been working with marijuana. It's still federally illegal. We're already branded."

"I think a shrink is worse."

"They never specified we had to see a shrink. They didn't say what type of therapy. I bet we could see anybody. Take a yoga class!"

"I don't think yoga was what they had in mind."

"Joey, I don't think they had anything in mind. They're just covering their butts. I think they actually want us to come back. Anyway we've already run a successful business and sold it for a profit! We don't need them. What do we care what's in our personnel files? And I think they need us, and we have way more power here than we know."

"Lydia did seem genuinely concerned."

"That's why I think we should reconsider."

"But that company isn't going anywhere. We should get a job with the competition."

"Or start another nursery? Hullbrooke doesn't have anything close by."

"Not enough people." Joe yawned, stretching his arms up and back as far as the headboard would let him. "We should figure out something easier. Supply the marijuana industry! Make something essential for hothouse production and make it cheaper. Mildew-resistant pots."

"Been so done. And I don't know how you do that without a fungicide."

"We just find the right one."

"Nobody wants pesticide in their weed, Joey." A look of disgust came over her face. "That may be the only thing we did learn from Damian! I still think we should consider going back. I think we should ask Lydia—"

"But she doesn't do anything. She doesn't make any decisions. And I sure as hell don't want to go back there for less pay."

"That's why we need to ask her."

They were silent for a moment. "You know," Joe said, "Goldilocks once told me he was doing her. Lydia. He said she was insatiable."

"He was just fucking with your head!"

"I know. But he does live at her place. He got the same offer too, from the lawyer."

"I'm pretty sure he's had enough of the Northeast."

"Yeah. Good work with the pH probe there, Cas!"

"He's such a jerk. I can't believe he has a girlfriend. She must be baked 24/7."

"He's got a kid somewhere too, you know."

"He tell you that?"

"Yup. Hasn't seen the boy since he was two and the mother ran off with him."

"Well now there's a testimonial!"

"I wonder if that's why he hated us so much? 'Cause we're together."

"I think he's just a fucking idiot. I'm going to talk to Lydia."

Chapter 50

Sanjay tapped Petra between her breasts. They weren't sagging much, but Petra regarded them with growing disdain. The slow decline of her body was yet another thing she must learn to tolerate she supposed.

"You have an extraordinarily wide sternum. It's quite stellar."

"Thank you," she replied, a little surprised but pleased, since he seemed pleased.

He bent and kissed her collarbone. "This too. A most excellent bone."

"Really."

"And usually visible too on any given day, so I have something to remind me of this when we're working so hard."

Petra guffawed, not quite sure whether it was the notion of screwing someone she worked with, the vodka they'd consumed or the actual conversation that was striking her as outlandish.

Sanjay took her prominent right nipple gently between his thumb and forefinger and rolled it ever so slowly before moving in to kiss it. Petra gasped and laughed in the same breath. Very few men ever seemed to catch on to her nipple sensitivity, but Sanjay was naturally gifted, as with many endeavors he undertook.

"It's a pity you never had children," he said airily as she moaned. He cupped her breast while rubbing the now glistening nipple with his thumb. "I think you would have been a very happy mummy."

"Oh for crying out loud. What is it with you and the mommy stuff?" She moaned again.

"Just observing. And thinking."

She reached down for him. "I'll give you something to think about."

"Oh God, I really hope so. Holy Mother!" Sanjay moaned as she brought him into her and wrapped her legs around him. They made love for hours, with the odd break for food or a little more vodka and chitchat. They talked about the potential of cannabis as a sex aid. It had a long history there too, according to Sanjay, who'd been brushing up on the matter. And in California and Colorado, they were coming up with everything from yoni sprays to canna-condoms.

"Clearly time for a little research project."

It was Sunday for Petra, a lapsed Protestant in every way imaginable, and probably some sunny god's day for Sanjay, who expressed a fondness for so many exotic deities Petra had lost count. Accordingly, it was a day of holy reckoning and illumination respectively. Petra faced the fact she'd been starved of intimate affection for the last three years, and approaching menopause was making her hornier than ever. It was her body's last kick at the can, and she figured she'd lost all her better judgment in the mad flush of hormones. Sanjay was looking on the bright and blazing side of opportunity. He wanted no sins of omission on his karma. His bride would be arriving in less than two months, and there weren't likely to be more chances for this kind of affair.

Later, cutting up a spectacularly large pineapple, Petra broached the subject of Sanjay's upcoming marriage. "I still can't believe you asked for an arranged one."

"In my case, it's the only smart option."

"What are you talking about? You have absolutely no trouble hooking up. Everyone, no matter what sex, falls in love with you on sight, Sanjay."

"That's probably true."

"God, you're sure of yourself. Omnivorous! And a heartbreaker too." She was thinking of his effect on Percy. "Why get married at all?"

"Actually, that's the problem. I find it impossible to choose any one person or lifestyle over all the rest."

"So an arrangement made by someone else would somehow make it all work? What if you don't even like the person they choose for you?"

"I've made lots of choices for myself, and they haven't been so great."

Petra snorted, shoved a piece of pineapple in her mouth and chewed slowly. "What do your parents think? I suppose they're pleased."

"My parents? They think I'm bonkers. But I have plenty of relatives happy to help out."

"Your parents' marriage wasn't arranged?"

"Absolutely not. They met at Cambridge."

"So you're a social throwback!"

"How many insults do you think you can deliver in a single afternoon?"

"In your case, I can make a special effort."

Sanjay sighed. "I'm tired of games. Chasing happiness this way and that."

"Come on. You live for the rush of it."

"I do not." Sanjay threw his head back. "Besides, for whatever reason, an arrangement takes the worry out of this type of commitment."

"Like taking the train takes the worry out of traveling."

"You could say that, though back in India the trains aren't necessarily without hitches. But yes, on the whole."

"You know what I think? I think you just don't want to have to take any responsibility when it all goes tits up." Petra put another piece of pineapple in her mouth.

"It's not going to go tits up. Tits-up marriages are American, Petra. Indian marriages are forever. She's from India and I still have India in my bones."

"You haven't even met her. You could be the worst-matched couple on the planet."

"No, we're well matched. And I did meet her. We skyped."

"What if she can't stand the way you smell? Did you think of that? You know body odor is highly personal."

Sanjay sighed. "Here we go with the evolutionary theory again."

"Hey, that's what I do. And you do too."

Sanjay picked up the pineapple top and balanced it on his head. "This is what I do."

"What, grow pineapples out of your head?"

"No. Play the fool." He spun around. "And the fool is often lucky. Favored. So he finds love."

"Good lord, you're betting on luck and magical thinking. And I just recommended you to the only academic who's still speaking to me. Does your bride have a clue what she's getting into with you and your various" — Petra paused for effect — "predilections?"

"She knows everything." Juice dribbled onto his chest. "In fact I think she already knows me better than myself."

"Really."

"Yes, really. And you'd like her. She's a real oddball. Nobody in India wanted to marry her."

"Really. All of India." Petra perked up a little at the crazy math and the thought that socially unacceptable attributes in one country could be successfully plied in another. "And why is that? She's a Gorgon? One-eyed? Three hundred pounds?" She leaned over and whispered in Sanjay's ear, "A castrating man-eater?"

"More likely three-eyed," Sanjay whispered back. He tapped his forefinger between his eyebrows. "And she looks like a goddess, by the way," he added at full volume. "Much, much prettier than I am."

"Anything else?"

Sanjay shrugged. "She's twenty-eight, a palm reader, an astrologer, and I hear the local men are scared of her. She didn't even want a picture of me, just my birth date and a set of palm prints."

Petra cut another large piece off the pineapple, managing to slice her finger too. "Ow! Oh my God! That juice stings."

"Wait. I'll get you a Band-Aid. Don't bleed all over the pineapple!"

Petra put her finger under the tap and let it run while Sanjay ran to the medicine cabinet in the bathroom. He came back with some iodine and the package of Band-Aids.

"Here. Disinfect it first."

Petra ignored the iodine and instead poured vodka over her finger. Her eyes were a bit red when she looked up and reached for the Band-Aid.

"Would you like me to kiss it better?"

"You know, she should have asked for a pair of your dirty shorts too. Or a sweaty T-shirt." Petra knocked back another shot. "I'm telling you, body odor is very important," she said, putting the glass down. Then she pulled him to her, buried her face in his neck and took a long deep inhale.

Chapter 51

Alice had been on the warpath since the DOH inspection report came back. She'd expected most of the findings, except one. One big one. One that had made her life and her staff's lives hellish for the last two weeks. Because of the laboratory test results from the random samples the inspector had taken, CannRose was ordered to recall two product lines.

It wasn't mold. It wasn't *E. coli* or *pseudomonas* lurking. There weren't bugs in the product or any other foreign matter. No ma'am. What violated the specifications — and Alice had to admit, violated the very essence of medicine, its purpose and its promise — was the label itself. The label with the dosage. The percentage of active ingredients. The medicine, baby!

And hardly surprising, it wasn't the CBD, the nonintoxicant, that was so badly mislabeled. Of course not. It was the blast, the jam-jam, the bobo bush buzz, as Damian liked to call it. In two of the products, the THC amount wasn't fifteen and twenty-two percent, respectively, it was thirty-two and thirty-eight! Not only was the labeling off but the THC content violated the code. Percy was mortified and had no clue how this could have happened. There had been the arguments with Caldwell about the high THC in two of the harvests, but Percy himself had overseen the milling with trim, as well as the in-house analyses that eventually cleared the product. And then he'd overseen the sampling for the state lab tests.

Now, chemical analysis of any sort has a percentage of uncertainty associated with it. And testing for cannabinoids in a sample that was once alive can hardly be expected to be exact in its repeatability. Precision is hard-won in biological testing, Percy had often pointed out. Had the results been out fifteen or even twenty percent, one could have claimed natural product heterogeneity and the normal spread in analytical results. But to be out this much, Alice suspected sabotage. Not only was a drug recall a major pain in the ass, it was a strike against the company's already dicey integrity. A different DOH inspector, albeit less zealous than Ms. Ligner, was hanging around both dispensaries, double-checking the recall process. All clients who'd bought the product had to be located, notified and instructed on the return protocol. It took time, and of course CannRose had to refund everyone.

Most clients reported they'd already used up the offending cannabis. When Alice reported this to Luther and the others at a meeting, Caldwell had laughed. "Of course they have, even if they haven't. They know good product when they've got some. And," he pointed out, "I notice our sales are up since this hit the news."

Alice was incensed by the comment. She, Sammy and Percy had to troubleshoot the whole mess and figure out what went wrong, so it couldn't go wrong again. And they had to document their efforts in a report for the DOH. Alice requested access to the CannRose video records. There were hours and hours of viewing from the dispensary cameras and from five of the cameras in the cultivation facility. Because of Caldwell's comment, Alice wanted to review recordings from the vault cameras, the ones in the curing rooms and the one in the packaging room. Everybody was bug-eyed after four days of watching videos in addition to all their regular work.

Late Friday night, just before the long weekend, Alice got a call from Percy. He'd found something.

"My God, Alice. There's a five-minute sequence of Caldwell in one of the curing rooms shifting bins of product and taking a small sample, labeling it and putting it in his pocket, and then it conks out."

"What conks out?"

"The tape, the record, whatever. Nothing until somebody else activates the sensors the next morning. And Alice, just before it goes blank, there's another pair of shoes visible. Somebody else is in the room. I don't know who. I don't recognize the shoes, and according to the other camera records leading up to that time, there's no activity in that area. They must have figured out a way to disable the motion detectors."

"We're absolutely sure it's not some technical glitch showing us a scrap from a year ago? I hear that was happening at some point."

"I don't know. The time on it is midnight. The sequence before it is four o'clock p.m."

"A date?"

"Yes, but only the day and the month, not the year."

"Oh lord! We need that new IT guy to check it. Maybe he can tell."

"I'll give it to him first thing Tuesday."

"Make sure he keeps this quiet. We need to be absolutely sure before we say anything to anybody. This is serious."

"I know."

Alice put down the phone and felt like crying. Much as she disliked Caldwell, she didn't relish the thought of going to Luther, and especially Lydia, with this. He'd have to be fired. He should probably be fired anyway, but Alice didn't want to be the one to initiate the process. And now she had a whole long weekend to stew about it.

Chapter 52

Lydia was going for a ride. A nice hack around Rosefields to soften her disappointment. Her daughter had again cancelled. She couldn't make it this month, just like she couldn't make it all those other months. Lydia's children made her fully aware that they did not approve of her life. Just when Lydia felt like she was finally starting to enjoy it.

Lydia's favorite old mare was Shasta. She was easygoing, and as thoroughbreds went, an anomaly. Heavy-boned. So much so that the breeders had never bothered sending her to the yearling sales. They'd made cracks about dog food. Shasta came from a good line but they figured she was a throwback. One of the English cobs was resurfacing with a vengeance; the riffraff were winning in the lineage. She had a rump like a Clydesdale and a heavy neck. Big chunky hooves. She was lacking in the finer characteristics, except for her head, where the Arabian heritage was apparent; she had a lovely dish to the nose and big soulful eyes. She was also a dappled gray, and Lydia had fallen in love with her at first sight. Seeing Lydia's reaction, Jordan had bought her on the spot and the breeders were very thankful. The mare had grown on them too. But she certainly wasn't a keeper in the tony world of invitation stakes and sales-topper fillies. They were delighted to find a home for their gentle lubberly freak.

Shasta was happy to munch on Lydia's offering of carrot chunks. She'd lain down in a little manure at some point so Lydia had busied herself right away with the black rubber currycomb, gently breaking up the dried matted coat on her hind quarters. Satisfied with the preliminary cleanup, Lydia moved back to her neck and started the grooming ritual. Shasta hung her head low between the two leads attached on either side of her halter. She leaned a little into Lydia's circular movements.

"You're a sweet girl," Lydia said.

Shasta's ears flicked and one stayed permanently back to catch more cooings. All of these were welcome. Sugar too, in any form. Watermelon, apples, pears. When it was the season, Shasta could smell these things in the air, the delicious odors of late summer. It was as if Shasta knew very well she'd landed with the horseshoes up her butt rather than on her feet. The best time of all — and she had groaned and sighed with the pleasure of it — was when Lydia had hired a massage therapist for her. He was a swarthy man, hairy and hearty, but with the hands of a god. He'd cooed too and softly whistled. That certain humans could be a horse's dream was not lost on Shasta. She waited. Waiting was easy. Lydia offered her another carrot chunk.

The grooming went on for a good hour. Lydia enjoyed that often more than the ride itself. Just being with Shasta, talking to her and getting a feel for her mood without trying to make her do something was pure pleasure. There was no rush and no expectation. Eventually Lydia saddled up and got on her horse. Carl walked into the barn just as they were heading out.

"Shasta's looking pretty pleased with herself," he remarked.

"Well it's nice to be able to ride so often. You know I don't think I miss the city at all."

"Well, you're doing a fine job up here! You should be proud."

"You think so?"

"Of course. Everybody in town talks about CannRose now. Few more people got jobs too. People takin' a new interest in life. What's not to be proud of?"

"Well that's lovely to hear. Thank you for that, Carl. Gives me a real lift."

"Say, you still looking for more security people? I know a guy."

"Tell him to call Greg. I think they still might be."

"So what's happening with those kids who tried to break in?"

"Oh, Carl, I just don't know." Lydia shook her head. "The oldest was a Bradford. The grandson of one the board members! I'm staying right out of it. Let the lawyers settle it."

"Kids!"

"Drunk kids!" Lydia clicked her tongue and gave Shasta a little leg pressure. She waved at Carl as they went out into the late afternoon sun. They took the path around the side paddock. Lydia decided to take a closer look at the expanded Great Pond. Her daughter, the one who hadn't shown up again that weekend, wanted to put a jump at one end and Lydia hadn't paid much attention to the idea. Lydia didn't like water jumps much. She'd been dunked a couple of times and took a nasty fall when her horse (not Shasta) bucked, swerved and bolted in another direction at the prospect of water. Soaring over a two-foot fence and landing into water with solid ground two feet below its surface was just too much for the horse. Or perhaps it was really just too much for Lydia. Horses have a knack for smelling fear and can be very obliging. "Horses can show you a lot," Lydia thought out loud. "Maybe they're the best medicine." Medicine was on her mind all the time now.

These days Lydia frequently went into the cultivation area to see the plants. And each night after she did, she had strange, sometimes slightly disturbing dreams that she could barely recall on waking. Green dreams. Always very green. She began to feel like the plants were trying to make contact. As if they'd something to say, specifically to her. They were creatures, living their lives. And maybe they wanted to let her in on something. This was a new perception for Lydia. Quite startling. Endearing? No. Cooler than that. Compelling. Persuasive. Ah, another agenda. Lydia was surrounded by beings with agendas. That was it.

She wondered if horses liked marijuana and if they saw plants as other creatures too. Would they like their weed fresh or dried? Grass or hay? Both probably. Shasta liked a cookie now and then too. Yes, she did. She'd probably like it carboxylated in a cookie. Maybe all horses would like it in cookies. The medicine of cookies. She'd ask the veterinarian next time she saw her. If weed was good for horses, and Lydia couldn't see why not, she'd suggest CannRose start putting some effort into veterinary medical marijuana. It could be just as big. Maybe bigger. And she'd know something about it. Wouldn't have to just sit mute in those meetings while Caldwell talked everybody into a stupor.

Lydia wished she'd brought a fly whisk. Shasta was bothered, tossing her head and swishing her tail. It slapped against Lydia's boots. She stood up in the stirrups and reached forward with her torso almost lying on top of Shasta's neck. She gently brushed the flies away from the horse's eyes. As they got closer to the pond, the old willow came into view. It was practically horizontal and hovered out over the pond a good fifteen feet. Perfect. Lydia smiled at the sight of it.

She dismounted and led Shasta up to the drooping tree. There was a small heron across the way, partially hidden in the bulrushes, one leg up, poised and peering into the water. Lydia wondered if a muskrat would show. Years ago when she and Jordan used to go for walks, they would often see one.

She stood there studying the water, looking for movement. Before Jordan got sick, when everyone told her she was lucky and had the best husband in the world, Lydia often felt lost. He was always so pleasant but busy with his empire. Yet he would insist on her company. She'd shopped in every major city and spent whole days lounging in five-star hotels. He'd called her his oasis. But what had *oasis* meant to him?

She'd suspected affairs. He wasn't much to look at but some women would take power and money over beauty any day. She oughta know! And she'd met the women of his heady world. Not that there were many. But one of them in particular, oh she was pretty. Lydia had watched the woman chatting to Jordan, cocktail glass in one hand, the red décolleté Valentino blouse fluttering over the little black skirt. Lydia was sure, wasn't she? This tiny young woman had a kind of power that might, if armed and pointed in the right direction, totally vaporize an oasis. Couldn't it? So Lydia had done the only thing she could. She'd made her way over to them in her best runway style, and with all her enthusiasm, she demanded an introduction to the lovely young woman. And then the pretty thing beamed at her, just beamed! So happy that Jordan's glamorous wife had noticed her, so flattered by Lydia's attention, so reassured by her Southern charm. She introduced Lydia to her partner, a rather morose young woman with a buzz cut who sported a gray tweed jacket and Doc Martens.

"Ah yes," Jordan admitted later, "the girlfriend's a bit odd but an absolute genius with software. Sometimes goes with the territory, my love." And he'd pulled her close and kissed her on the forehead. All that had made Lydia feel even more lost.

Shasta put her nose down and nudged Lydia, then stepped closer and rubbed her head on Lydia's back to get rid of a few flies. "You're so right," Lydia said, turning and patting Shasta's cheek. "Get rid of those flies." Lydia ripped a couple of dangling willow branches off the main trunk and got back on Shasta. She gently swung the branches around Shasta's forelock then flopped them back and forth either side of her neck.

Lydia smiled. She had a new life. No longer adrift at heart. She'd surely been a fool with Caldwell. And what did that matter? It had come to something good. She was involved. Situated. Helping the community. New interests. New ideas. The veterinary uses of marijuana. Green dreams. Who knew where it might take her? Shasta perked up and broke into a trot.

Chapter 53

Percy was quite relieved the IT guy had determined that Caldwell's alleged sabotage was a technical glitch after all. You could tell by the slight shift in the shelving units in the background, and if you looked very closely, the bin arrangement on the shelves was different during the five-minute sequence. Besides, Alice and Percy had sent in samples from the offending product lines to two private labs, and Petra had analyzed another set of samples in-house. Needless to say the results were variable but the state lab was the one most out of agreement. With some embarrassment, the state was forced to withdraw the finding and initiate an audit of its own lab.

But Percy was beside himself with Caldwell's newest antics. Like some prime turkey, all red-wattled and babbling, Caldwell wouldn't leave Percy alone. The previous month, Caldwell had been on about getting organic certification, and Percy had to explain to him that they actually had to grow plants organically. Using synthetic hormone gels to get clones started put them out of the running from the get-go. They couldn't certify products anyway, only the processes, because that's all the state would allow. And the national certifying organizations wouldn't touch any of it because they still operated under the FDA.

But now Caldwell wanted cGMP — Current Good Manufacturing Practice. Apparently the modest rigor required by the state regarding manufacturing practices wasn't cutting it. Like some new convert who'd just found Jesus, he was all on about it. "And I mean real *certified* GMP. Just the way you'd see it in Pfizer or Merck!" CannRose was to partner with some company from Canada that was implementing it and together they were going to change the industry. This was the first step to global operations and would apparently put CannRose ahead of every curveball known to man. Certainly ahead of the FDA. "We'll be international. These other countries want certified GMP. As the world shifts to acceptance, this is our chance."

Percy clenched his jaw so hard it made his teeth ache. For the love of Jesus, this was Caldwell's idea? Or no, a brainy idea from Canada? Well, screw him and screw Canada! Had Caldwell been stone deaf a year ago when Percy had proposed much the same thing? No! He'd been ridiculing, antagonistic, dismissive. And he still undermined Percy at every step. Refused to wear booties, changed protocols on a whim, ignored checklists! And he bitched to the board and the executives about how "all the bureaucratic bullshit" Percy was trying to implement just slowed the whole operation down. Of course the staff all saw this and so they flouted the rules too. Percy would never get CannRose operating even close to a cGMP standard. No one could. And why? Because Caldwell was a clueless, controlling, impulsive, tantrum-prone — and possibly sociopathic — monster!

"That company up in Canada wants to know why we're not doing all the science that goes with GMP. I want to know about this! Why isn't this happening? You've been telling me we do things GMP here."

"No, Caldwell, I've been telling you we implement it where we can. And we can't do the science if we don't do the tests to get the *test results*."

"What do you mean? We do tests! There's test results all over the place. Results from our lab. Results from the state labs. Stoyan was babbling about more testing. We have all sorts of test results here!"

"Not the boring kind. At least you consider them boring."

"What are you talking about? You think I'm too gauche to appreciate high-quality standards?"

"Remember last year when you said the state regs didn't require 'all that crap.' And you said Petra needed the lab. She's the research director and I'm just the QA officer?"

"I never said that!" Caldwell raised his voice. "Why would I say that?"

Petra suddenly appeared out of nowhere. "You did say that, Caldwell. We'd have to run the lab 24/7 to get my work and Percy's done, and now there's Stoyan's stuff too. And like you said way back, the state doesn't require it. They're only interested in the finished product."

Percy was positively delighted at how Petra always seemed to show up at the right time. He watched the veins in Caldwell's forehead bulge. As Caldwell raised his hand to rake it through his hair, Percy noticed the tremors. Hmm. Caldwell was definitely losing it — or he was on something more than marijuana. It could be worth sticking around for the denouement. But if Caldwell was going to be on his case now, it was time to move on. They could hire somebody else to get all the CannRose wankers operating in a disciplined system. Good luck with that! They'd need an army.

That afternoon Percy started composing a resignation letter. He hadn't gotten very far when Lorne came into his office looking worn out, sat himself down and said, "Why are we expanding into Canada? We barely get product out the door to our own dispensaries. And isn't that still illegal because of the federal laws?"

Percy smiled. "Pharmaceutical GMP is not required for cannabis processing and sales in Canada as far as I know," he said. "Caldwell is looking to a vast and global future and you know what this would mean."

"Not . . . precisely." The production manager sucked his breath in through his teeth. "Exactly how much more work would this be?"

So Percy described what running the facility under cGMP might look like: additional protocols, documentation, audits, more testing and validations, risk analyses of processes, expiration studies, more record-keeping and inspections by whatever external organization was issuing the certification — certainly not the FDA! About twenty percent more staff. More training. Even eye tests!

After some moments of silence, Lorne got up slowly from the chair. "None," he said, "none of the other companies are this crazy." And he drifted out the door.

Percy tried to get back to his resignation letter but there was cloning that day at the facility and he kept being interrupted. He oversaw all the picky paperwork, and the staff had all sorts of picky little questions.

The next morning Percy heard raised voices coming from the production office. It went on for several minutes, then Caldwell came barreling past Percy's door shouting that Lorne "had all the imagination of doorknob!" It occurred to Percy that just the lack of manners and dignity at CannRose was reason enough to bail. When he'd talked about it the night before, his husband, Gavin, had pointed out that if CannRose had to hire an army to handle the extra quality measures then Percy would be the general. He could outflank the opposition by sheer numbers. But Percy figured one way or another Caldwell would maintain mayhem, so he was still going to finish his letter.

After about an hour, Percy saw Lorne walk by in his street clothes. Then a few minutes later, Percy heard giggling in the hallway, so he got up from his desk to see what was going on. There, scrawled in big bold letters — clearly this was turning into a CannRose tradition — was a sign on the production office door: Go Fuck Your Mother, Caldwell. I QUIT!

PART ELEVEN

Packaging

*Oh the brains of little boxes. The bumptious bags. The bottles
boasting sterility. Tie it all up. Parcel it and leave us. As if vessels
alone ensure containment! Amp up the ampules if you must. Gild the
lids. But put this in your sack: We will prevail, we're already
winning in fact, and you never knew what the war was. You
imagined the front and forgot your back. You slay yourselves in
your own wrapping. Your portion of concern rallied to deny the
fleeting days. Trifles and fripperies. Resistance to what, we'd like to
know. Entropy's unavoidable. Try to love the cascade.*

from Cannto VI, *Cannabidadas*

Chapter 54

The anniversary of CannRose's first sale and Caldwell's birthday were a day apart and fast approaching. Lydia wanted a big party at Rosefields. It was to be a family-friendly affair. No loose abandon or excess joie de vivre this time. Everybody who worked at CannRose and their families were invited. It would start in the afternoon and end in its own good time. There'd be games for the kids and swimming, and it was reported Lydia was even negotiating a live band for dancing under the stars. Ernie thought it was so sad, just a damn shame Lorne had quit before he got to party at the company's expense.

Ernie was asked if he'd honor the party with his splendid catering. The thought of feeding a mass of people, sweating or dripping in their bathing suits with kids running around screaming and everybody drinking more than they should, held no appeal for Ernie. Even all the extra money he'd haul in for the effort had no attraction. But he agreed to do it.

"I'm thinking barbecue . . ." Lydia offered.

"Absolutely. People would be disappointed if it wasn't." Ernie was visualizing the elaborate outdoor cooking facilities at Rosefields. Carl had given him a tour one day. Along with a variety of grills, there was a smoker, a sixteenth-century Italian-looking gas-fired stone oven and two massive Texan custom-built rotisseries suspended over pits the size of wading pools. Ernie suggested he'd need to check out everything, see what was in working order. According to Carl, only one small grill was currently in use. Apparently the patio kitchen had serviced huge summer parties when Jordan ruled the world but it hadn't seen much action in the last decade or so.

"Oh, and we should have lots of finger foods too," Lydia said. "Like you had for the tenth-crop celebration. They were such a hit,

Ernie. And Caldwell just loved the little Japanese prawn cakes and meat skewer things."

Oh there would be prep! Ernie had been hoping he could just get away with roasting a whole pig or barbecuing half a cow with no trouble at all, and then the hordes could just rip the meat off the carcasses in a feeding frenzy. Easy peasy. But he smiled at Lydia. "No problem," he said.

#

Ernie noticed Caldwell stagger over to one of the chairs by the bar. It was right after the little fireworks show, during which Guido had played an electric violin accompanied by recorded instrumentation. "Vivaldi and Piazzolla," he'd announced. It had been a spectacular interlude while the Latin band Lydia had hired for the evening was taking a break. They were back up now cranking out mambos and salsas. It was quite an active party, but very civilized, Ernie noted with pleasant surprise. Almost no screaming children, and folks were joyful and not dripping all over his food. But Caldwell had clearly consumed too much booze, or he'd had a puff of Damian's Thai Po Blush maybe. Ernie had taken just one good inhale of that a few months ago and had barely been able to put one foot in front of the other. He'd also thought his bad eye had developed superpowers under the patch and he was seeing the world like an insect.

Caldwell sat slumped, looking as if he was hanging on for dear life to the arms of the elevated bar chair, so Ernie wandered over to him.

"Happy Birthday, Caldwell. Enjoying the party?"

"Oh . . . Ernie. Hi."

"Great night for this. You can really see the stars out in the country," Ernie said.

Caldwell tilted his head way, way back and gazed up. "Yes. Yes the stars are really there. Aren't they? Oh . . . oh . . . oh yeah, I know what I wanted to say: Great food, Ernie."

"Thanks," Ernie said, mystified by this strange new version of Caldwell.

"You know, I don't usually eat cake. It's always too sweet. But that was exceptional. I had two pieces." Caldwell spoke very slowly and was still gazing up at the stars.

"Thanks, Caldwell. Look, can I get you some water or something? You seem a little shaky."

"Oh. No thanks . . . Ernie. I'm fine. I'm really fine. Very fine."

Ernie watched as Caldwell lowered his gaze to stare straight ahead, his hands trembling, sweat on his forehead. So Ernie went to search out Damian or Lydia to see if either of them knew anything about Caldwell's personality transformation or would be worried about it.

"He didn't get anything from me," Damian said. "Anyway, he can smoke enough to bake an elephant and you'd never know it." And he wandered over to check out Caldwell while Ernie went to find Lydia.

"Oh dear," Lydia said. "I wonder if he's on medication again." She and Ernie made their way over to Caldwell, who was sitting there smiling at Damian, not saying anything.

"Caldwell, sweetheart, people are worried. Are you okay?"

"Lydia! How lovely. Thank you for this lovely party." He stared at her briefly and then smiled at all three of them. "I may have had quite a bit of champagne." He chuckled conspiratorially and smiled even more.

Damian, who'd seen Caldwell drunk on way more than one occasion, looked at the other two and shook his head.

"Caldwell, sweetheart, would you like to lie down for a minute or two?"

"I didn't think you felt that way about me anymore, Lydia."

"No Caldwell, we think you're not quite yourself. We think you might need a little lie-down."

"Oh! Okay."

Ernie and Damian got on either side of Caldwell and walked him into the house to the big daybed that looked out onto the pool through the French doors. He could stretch right out there, and as he did, he seemed to go right to sleep.

"Do you think we should call a doctor? Or take him to emergency?"

"It's past midnight," Luther said, suddenly appearing. "But I could drive him."

"He's breathing fine." Damian was bent over watching Caldwell's chest move. Then he picked up Caldwell's wrist to check his pulse. The other three looked on, waiting for Damian's verdict. "His blood's pumping okay. Nothing weird."

"Maybe he just needs a little nap."

"He was very surprised by the party." Luther had noted the tears. "I mean that it was a birthday party for him too. As well as the anniversary of the first sale."

"He's very sensitive," Lydia said. "People often don't see that about him."

"I can sit here for a while, if you think somebody needs to," Ernie said.

"No, man. I think he's fine," Damian said. "He's been overdoing it again, that's all. The food, the booze. He's been pretty stressed lately too. What's new? I know."

"I've never seen him dance like that before," Lydia exclaimed.

"Me neither. Man, and whoever knew Greg could dance!" Damian started laughing.

"That's the biggest surprise of the night." Luther grinned.

The worry had vanished from the four of them. They left Caldwell sleeping soundly and went back to join the party. An hour or so later as Ernie was packing up his various pots and platters for the evening, Luther appeared with a blanket. Caldwell was snoring quite loudly and Ernie saw Luther laugh as he put the blanket over him.

"I think he's just fine," Lydia said. "He could always snore up a storm. That I know. I used to have to wear earplugs."

Luther frowned a little at this revelation.

When Ernie was back at work two days later, the old familiar Caldwell was back, driving everybody crazy again. Particularly Percy. Caldwell had finally stopped talking about making the CannRose facility cGMP. Instead he claimed the Canadian deal fell through because of Percy's poor-quality system. Percy said he'd like to kill him.

#

Apart from the man's love of old Broadway, Ernie didn't know Greg's history all that well. He just knew Greg had been a cop in Lyston for years. It was surprising he'd never heard of him given Ernie's teenage activities of mall-roaming and frequenting the video arcade. It's not that Ernie had been a bad kid. He was just a normal teenager pushing boundaries, and in towns and smaller cities that makes kids more familiar with their local constabulary. Mostly it's just gossip. Or if the cop is a complete dick, they all know about them.

When Greg asked Ernie one day if he'd like to go on a little field trip because he had a proposition for him, Ernie assumed it would have something to do with wild beasts, fruit or maybe some mushroom patch. It was a long drive and Greg talked on about CannRose or baseball, never mentioning what it was they were going to look at. Ernie was surprised when their trip took them right across the state line.

They pulled into what looked like an overgrown private park. There were woods on three sides and they hopped over the fence to their right. "This is the quickest way into the site," Greg explained. They walked silently through an acre or so of mature forest that petered out into scrub and young saplings regenerating a burned area. Then they came to a farmer's field. It was full of tomato plants fruiting up nicely. Probably would be ready for harvest by the end of the month. Greg just stood at the edge of the field smiling. Ernie had all the tomato varieties he ever needed either from his own garden or from Carl. Plenty for salads, sauces, chutneys and preserves, so he wasn't exactly excited by the view.

"Look a little closer my friend."

Ernie walked up the row directly in front of them looking to his right and left. He stopped about sixty yards in and then looked all around. "Fuck me!" he whispered under his breath. From where he stood, as far as the eye could make out, which wasn't all that far given the prevalence of the staked tomato crop, about every third plant was marijuana. They were lusciously flowering, frosty looking and about a week away from harvest. As far as Ernie knew, even medical cannabis wasn't exactly legal in this state.

"They're all dwarfs," Greg called to him. "Pretty much the same as CannRose, though there's nothing super potent. We like to keep it mild. Pretty damn fine this year too, I'd say."

Ernie looked at the tomatoes as if they might offer some explanation as to what the fuck was going on. But they were mute, too dignified to offer any black-market intel in spite of the company they were keeping. Ernie wandered back slowly, looking at the crops around him again and then at Greg in some bewilderment.

"Been intercropping for years," Greg said, grinning. "When we started out we just had a couple of buried Sealift containers but the generator costs for lights and cooling were prohibitive, considering we never charge much."

Ernie continued to stare at Greg.

"We had to do something. The war on drugs was a disaster. Just made everything worse. I lost a kid sister, you know, because some little prick sold her laced weed. We never did find out exactly what it was. My partner had a couple of nephews who were getting into trouble too. You couldn't keep the kids away from it. So the plan was, educate the youth and undercut all the little rat-faced suppliers. Remember Rainy Day Dope?"

Ernie thought for a second. "Yeah. Of course! That's what you bought for a couple of bucks from one of the other kids."

"Yup, and you still can. Cleanest organic supply you'll get anywhere. And not too strong. Well, my friend. *This* is Rainy Day Dope."

"No shit!"

"Yeah, no shit. Actually lots of it this year." He chuckled. "See my old partner and I are retiring come December. The wife wants to move someplace a little warmer."

Ernie wondered why the fuck Greg had brought him here. What was the point if he was retiring? Did he need harvest labor?"

"So here's my proposition, Ernie: Would you like to take over and partner the operation?"

Ernie's good eye popped open so wide the one under the patch practically realigned on its own. "What? No!"

"Hear me out now. Fifty-fifty split. We have other sites too but we'll split this particular one with you. It's premium. Now we'd look after the regional distribution this year and then we'd ask you to take that on. You're homegrown, smart, got integrity, I've noticed, so we'd trust you to keep the prices low for the kids and make sure it all stays organic and clean. There's a lot to catch up on of course. But we've got an excellent infrastructure working — farmers and so on. Great bunch. Just a great bunch. You'd fit right in."

Ernie was somewhere between a laugh and total breathlessness. "There's no way."

"You're not into something similar?"

"Jesus! Fuck no!"

"Always thought you were."

"Do I look like a drug lord?"

"See that's the thing. My old partner and I had a bet that you were cooking more than gourmet food. You know, you're educated. Got burned in the housing crisis, so did a lot of people. But you're just pushin' a broom and growin' produce on your roof. I figured you were an inventive independent. You know, maybe other plants and things. Connections south, in the big cities. Nice little network going for you."

"No. I ... I like pushing a broom. It's enough."

"So I can't interest you in the business?"

"No." Ernie was shaking his head, still in disbelief. "No. No."

"Not even a tiny bit?"

"No thanks," he said, shaking his head more vigorously and breathing rather quickly. "It's way too much work anyway."

"So you are a lazy bastard! Goddamn, man. You just lost me a thousand-dollar bet." Greg looked slightly morose. "You're absolutely sure?"

"Sure as shit!" Ernie paused and then said, "I'll have you know, the roof garden is a lot of work. So's the cooking. Plus I look after Hilda Cranston's terraces. Some days I don't finish until eight o'clock."

Greg sighed wistfully and looked out over the field. A gentle breeze was stirring the plants and sending the lemony and mildly skunky odors their way. Greg took a deep breath through his nose. "Oh well." He brightened. "Really good crops this year and we do sell the surplus to a reputable distributor." He paused, furrowing his forehead for a moment. "Now, Ernie, I trust you'll keep this little field trip under your hat. At least until the wife and I are safely retired elsewhere."

"Jesus. Of course! Fuck. My lips are sealed." Ernie started rolling his shoulder, which seemed to be seizing up all of a sudden, and realized he still had a two-hour drive back to Hullbrooke with Greg, the Rainy Day Dope Kingpin. "I swear, sealed for all eternity." Ernie made a zipping motion with his index finger and thumb across his lips. "With Krazy Glue. With Krazy Glue, Greg."

Greg just looked at him. "You're kind of a pussy, you know that?"

Chapter 55

There it was, thrashing in all its aphid irritation. "You little bugger!" Cassie adjusted the magnification from fifteen to thirty. She watched the insect's determined maneuvering as various parts of its anatomy came into focus. Antennae almost longer than the bulbous body trailed and shifted from side to side, gauging the boundaries of its tiny prison. The bug's colors were indistinct, mottled gray, green and brown. It looked to be in camouflage fatigues. The needle-like proboscis came into view as the bug reared up to negotiate the wall of the microscope well.

Cassie's skin crawled. There could be thousands more just like it. Whole battalions of aphids armed with capillary force probes, sucking the life out of the plants. Possibly there were squadrons already flying, scouting the room for fresh birthing grounds. The leaves she'd just trimmed had those telltale specks. They were on about five plants in the trough farthest from the door. How does that even happen? A complete infestation of Flower Room III could take no time at all. Aphids were born pregnant, like little Russian dolls. Mothers would sit there sucking away at the sap, dropping out a new little mother every several minutes. Their kind of cloning beat human efforts by magnitudes.

Cassie felt a wave of anxiety wash over her. Her butt was on the line now. She was newly returned to CannRose and doing yoga therapy. She'd been right about all that anger-management nonsense. And also right again that CannRose didn't want to lose all its cultivation managers. But she was back by herself. Joe was off creating a company. She would keep steady money flowing in while he did more research and got the new business rolling. They still weren't at all that sure what they were going to come up with. Maybe it should be something to blast aphids all to hell!

The idea of blasting things to hell brought Damian to mind. He'd been rehired too but with a different title, something about product strategy. Director of Some New Idiocy. Probably got a raise too. It was ridiculous. He was back from a month's holiday in Colorado. How he managed to negotiate all that was a mystery. Maybe he was screwing Lydia like Joe said. Whatever. Cassie was on her best behavior and trying to not appear dismissive of everything that came out of Damian's mouth.

Now that Lorne was gone, Cassie had a lot of responsibility. She was looking after the production scheduling and it wasn't so easy. Stoyan had wisecracked as he flicked cigarette ash on the CannRose driveway during coffee, "Is very special, your timing! You have maybe event horizon time sense?"

But most importantly, Cassie now had the final say on all cultivation practices, and she'd made changes. She was steam sterilizing the grow media before it was inoculated. She figured it could even be recycled that way. The practice would keep the operation cleaner, reduce pests and disease and wouldn't violate organic requirements either. The cultivation staff were really pleased with the new arrangements because they weren't getting conflicting instructions anymore, and Cassie thought the plants were starting to look happier too. Until today. Aphids were a whole new nightmare.

A few days earlier Caldwell was all shook up by a big scandal a couple of states over. The medical marijuana there started making people really sick. The problem was traced back to designer pesticides. Like some performance-enhancing drugs, designer pesticides were made to avoid detection. Testing labs wouldn't suspect that the blips they thought were probably just noise in the chromatograms actually signified some vile little neurotoxin or worse. Caldwell was paranoid. Cassie had been in the lab with Petra when he barged in and started opening all the cupboards and drawers.

Petra scowled. "Can I help you find something?"

"Why is this locked?" Caldwell was struggling to open the incubator.

"It's in the middle of incubating and it's on a timer. What on earth are you looking for?"

Caldwell ignored her. He opened the refrigerator and started moving flasks and trays around.

"Can you please tell me what's going on?"

"What's going on? The future of this company. That's what's going on."

Petra took a few steps closer to see exactly what he was rearranging. "And why should it involve rifling through the lab?"

Caldwell shoved aside a rack of vials to pull out a box that was behind it.

"Careful with that! That's four days' work," Petra said.

"Isn't it clear? How do you spell *pesticide*, Petra?"

"With a P?"

"You know what I mean."

"No I don't, Caldwell."

"What's in pesticides?"

"How should I know?"

"But you test for them!"

"No. I test for terpenes and cannabinoids."

"But that . . . that instrument there tests for pesticides! Lazlo said that's what it was for." Caldwell, red-faced and sweating, pointed shakily at the tall beige box on the other side of the lab.

"You mean this one." Petra patted the instrument beside her. It whirred while its arm shifted and hovered over the sampling tray. "They used it for pesticides at the EPA. But that's not what I use it for."

"I want you to test all the crops for pesticides."

"You should talk to Percy if you want that. And these instruments need to be dedicated. Pesticides could—"

"I don't care. I want pesticides tested."

Petra rolled her eyes. "Really? Which ones?"

"All of them!"

"There are hundreds!"

Caldwell had been looking in the cupboard under the sink, finding only sponges, spare wash bins and paper towels. He stood back up to his full height and frowned. "There could be banned pesticides or even legal pesticides banned for marijuana. They had that going on in Oregon just last month!"

"Caldwell, our growers don't use those kinds of pesticides."

"That CEO of Greenmont said he had no idea how pesticides got on their plants. You could be creating them here and no one would know it."

"Jesus, Caldwell! I'm a biologist not a chemist! And even if I were I wouldn't sabotage the company!"

Cassie ventured in nervously, "The R and D guy at Greenmont claimed the order came straight from the owner. He said he got bonuses for it. It was all on CannaBlog yesterday. And there's an old selfie with him and the owner holding wads of cash on Instagram too."

"I don't care. I want every crop tested. They could be in the coconut coir . . . or the fertilizer mix! Pesticides . . . could ruin us!"

Petra leaned against the bench and folded her arms. "Fine. Then have grow media and fertilizers tested before you use them. Testing every crop will cost a fortune."

"We're testing everything!"

Sanjay had been listening to all of this, looking puzzled. "Caldwell, do you think plants can just end up with pesticides? You know, even if pesticides weren't applied or taken up during growing?" Sanjay was being sincere. He was trying to home in on the root of Caldwell's anxiety.

"Well, obviously . . . you never know, do you!"

Cassie grimaced and shook her head.

"So this is the problem," Sanjay announced. "It's not Caldwell's fault. Fundamental science literacy. That's the problem. They should teach the laws of mass and energy conservation in kindergarten. I'm telling you."

"Here, here." Percy had poked his head in the lab to see what the fuss was. There'd been no mention of cGMP or "Percy's system" at all for a couple of weeks, so Percy was upbeat. The resignation letter was still on the computer desktop just in case though.

Caldwell exploded at the sight of Percy. His dashed hopes for a Canadian partnership were still raw and Percy's cheerfulness was goading. "We're testing everything and we're throwing out all our pesticides too!"

"But we only have organic-certified ones. Natural stuff," Cassie said. The anxiety in her voice was apparent to everyone in the room but Caldwell.

"And they're in the potting room. Not here!" Petra said.

"I don't care. Everything's going! Everything even remotely resembling a pesticide."

"You'll have to destroy more crops then," Percy pointed out and he gave Cassie a sympathetic look. "State labs aren't keen on creepy crawlies. And you won't get anything past Stoyan either, not even for trials. He's running a kosher shop."

Caldwell glared at Percy.

"Caldwell, I'm sure I could help you understand this a little better. I've tutored lots of students," Sanjay said.

"I don't have time for this nonsense! Get rid of the pesticides." Caldwell turned and strode out of the lab.

"I think he thinks pesticides can morph," Percy said.

"Actually he thinks they can spontaneously arise," Sanjay added, shaking his head.

Cassie wanted to weep. Caldwell had just left the grow rooms defenseless.

Chapter 56

Petra and Sanjay were staring at the ceiling.

"So are you going to grant Percy his deepest darkest wish before you lock yourself into matrimonial bliss and take off for your new academic career?" Petra yawned, stretched her arms above her head and pointed her toes. She sighed.

"No." Sanjay closed his eyes.

"You could spend a steamy night in some seedy little lodge in the Catskills. It could be poetic."

"No."

"He adores you. He pines for you."

"Why take the risk?"

"You take risks all the time. You're the ultimate opportunist."

"I'm not an opportunist."

"Then you're confused."

"Hardly as confused as you are. At least I know when I'm confused. And I'm careful."

"What's so careful about screwing anything on two legs?"

Sanjay opened his eyes, turned his head and glared at her. "Do I screw someone else when I'm having an affair with you?"

"I don't know. Do you?"

"No. I don't need to do that!"

"So you're just serially confused."

"I want a family! That's all. I know this about myself. Is that a crime?"

"No," said Petra, sounding bored.

"You want everything cut and dried. Easily labeled."

"Not at all."

"What then?" He looked back up at the ceiling.

"I guess it's an inconsistency."

"There is nothing inconsistent about this."

"A denial then."

"I am denying nothing. I'm saying some relationships at some times are not worth the risk."

"I can be pretty risky," Petra said.

"You don't have that look of desperation, where you know the person has lost all judgment."

"Percy has that?" Petra rolled on her side to face him.

"In spades. He's worried about getting old." Sanjay turned again to face her.

"And I'm not?"

"If you are, it is not reflected in your personal hygiene."

"What the fuck? I take showers." She sat up and backhanded his thigh.

"No, no, you misunderstand." Sanjay laughed. "You don't worry about your appearance. You barely look in the mirror. You don't care that every hair is in place. You don't pluck your eyebrows. You don't wear expensive aftershave—"

"I hope not!"

"You don't get manicures and pedicures and facials. You don't spend hours in a sauna at a sports club getting steam-cleaned. You don't press your T-shirts and wear them tight under your scrubs. Percy does. He even violates his own requirements regarding scent in the workplace. That takes a worried man."

Petra pondered this burst of information about a man she'd considered merely bureaucratic, often inflexible and occasionally annoying. Though she did admire his talent for taking on Caldwell. "Then all the more reason to be charitable. You could take pity on him."

"I don't make love out of pity. It's an insult."

"I doubt he'd complain. Or be insulted."

"I thought you were the grown-up here."

"What's being grown up got to do with this? It's about being alive. Having no regrets. Remember? Your words not mine!"

"Why do you keep carping on about this?" Sanjay asked. "About my sexuality! And about my marriage!" He sat up turned his head away and focused on some imaginary point that excluded her.

Petra watched him for a few seconds. "I know," she said, her voice resigned and weary, "I'm being a pest." She took a long, quiet breath.

Sanjay said nothing.

"I'm being a bitch then."

His silence was not comforting.

"I'm going to miss you and it hurts," she said finally and she lay back on the bed.

Sanjay looked down at her. Now Petra was looking away and he could see her eyes watering up. He hoped she wouldn't cry but he leaned down anyway. "You see what I mean by risky," he said quietly. "It's not always just my own skin I worry about."

Petra pushed him away and sat up again. "I don't think I can come to your wedding." She didn't look at him. "I thought I could. But I can't." She was trying very hard not to cry.

"It's okay. Don't worry." He put his arms around her and felt the warm tears fall on his shoulder. "I'll miss you too." And he heard his own voice waver. They sat holding each other for several minutes, Petra weeping audibly and Sanjay mute with sadness.

Finally Sanjay's cat wandered in and jumped onto the bed. He rubbed up against Petra, looked Sanjay in the eye and howled. Sanjay got up and padded into the kitchen with Marvin racing ahead to the refrigerator. Petra heard the clatter of a dish, the buzz of a can opener and Marvin meowing every second or so.

When the all the noise stopped Petra called out, "Maybe Percy would be honored by an invitation."

"That's not a bad idea," Sanjay called back. "I'll think about it. I'm going to invite the quiet guy from security, Ray. We talked a lot when I stayed late."

"Yeah, he's a nice guy. Anybody else? How about Damian or some of the execs! Wouldn't that be a treat?"

"Well, definitely none of the execs. And certainly not Caldwell. I think they're all getting nuttier by the day." Sanjay came back into the bedroom and sat on the bed.

"I hear Lydia is whispering to the plants now," Petra said. "Cassie told me she came into the one of the grow rooms talking about weed for horses and then started cooing at the plants. Then again Damian, talks to them like they're his harem."

"I don't think that's crazy at all."

"Really."

"No."

"Oh. You think it's one more piece of reality we just haven't figured out how to measure yet."

"Or maybe it's something we never get to measure," Sanjay said.

Petra was smiling. She enjoyed how unapologetic Sanjay was about his unscientific views.

"When I was a little boy, before we came to America, my grandmother knew an old woman who talked to plants. She harvested them for medicine and they told her what ailments they were good for. I used to play with her great-granddaughter and she talked to plants too. She wasn't worried about medicine though. She just talked to them."

"What about?"

Sanjay paused, trying to remember. "The weather, I think."

Petra guffawed and then they both started laughing uncontrollably.

"No, it's very important for plants," Sanjay gasped. "And she was always right with forecasts too. She told me the plants were the best forecasters."

"So when the dickwad in the White House finally cuts all the funding to NOAA, and the national weather service gets lobotomized, we know who to turn to."

"It's not as crazy as you think."

Chapter 57

Caldwell's flight from Denver arrived late. Sixty-five minutes late. If he was going to make the dinner party at Guido's new place, he'd have to hurry. His luggage was minimal; a carry-on leather knapsack from Florence, a gift from Guido himself. Caldwell walked quickly past the baggage claim to the exit. As the automatic doors closed behind him, the coolness of the late afternoon breeze was like heaven. Colorado had been in the grips of an unseasonable heat wave.

He grabbed the shuttle to the parking lot but the walk to his car was still long and rather uphill. Rebecca or Rachel — he still couldn't get his new assistant's name straight — should have arranged for valet parking. He'd have to speak to her. When he reached his SUV, he was out of breath. Sweaty. Maybe he should ask to try out Guido's marble shower. The old guy boasted about it enough. But the thought made him cringe a little. There was a truck stop just off the interstate, one exit before Hullbrooke. He could shower and buy a new ten-dollar T-shirt to wear under his $4000 jacket. How au courant!

Caldwell reached for the car door handle and it opened immediately. He loved biometric technology. So convenient. He needed only his voice and fingerprints, though it was disturbing news about the thieves who chopped some guy's finger off so they could steal his Mercedes.

Caldwell got in and told the car to start. It didn't. Maybe sitting for a week wasn't good for it. He pressed the start button. The car hesitated but eventually the motor began to purr. He put it in gear, drove out of the airport lot, pulled onto the south ramp and was on the interstate in no time.

Maybe he could phone Guido and tell him he'd be a little late. Then again, he'd easily shave a good half hour off the trip even with the truck stop. His vehicle was sleek and smooth and there was only one section on the interstate he'd have to watch for troopers. He sped by the traffic. He could even take the old Lusteadt Side Road. He hadn't been on that in a while, years really, but what was the point of four-wheel drive if you couldn't take it on a little rough terrain?

Guido had purchased an old farm about twenty-five minutes east of Hullbrooke. "These perennially privileged and their remote retreats!" Caldwell muttered. The old man was pouring a small fortune into the restoration. Must have been inspired by Lydia's colonial spread. And he had a condo in the city just like her too. And God knows how many other residences dotted around the globe. Caldwell turned on the sound system. A little easy jazz to take the edge off. When he made his fortune, he wouldn't spend money on restorations. He'd build new. Clean. Modern. And nowhere remotely bucolic.

The highway flattened to monotony. Caldwell needed caffeine. He kept his eyes peeled for the turnoff with the trendy café. He couldn't remember the town's name and hoped he hadn't missed it. After about ten minutes the café came into view. Caldwell moved into the slow lane at ninety miles an hour and barely made the exit. He heard a car honk but didn't bother to look back.

He parked and headed into the café, where the young blonde barista eyed him with disdain. Caldwell hovered, fanning himself with his credit card while the gray-haired woman ahead of him discussed what kind of milk alternatives might be best for her latte. She settled on half lactose-free, half almond milk. Caldwell rolled his eyes. When got to the head of the queue he said quickly and in a rather loud voice, "I'll have a triple shot cappuccino and just the foam. I'm not crazy about milk."

When Caldwell went back to his SUV, cappuccino in hand, the vocal "start" command still didn't work. He pushed the button and the engine began, albeit with the same hesitation he'd noted at the airport.

Back on the highway, Caldwell wondered why Guido moved into the area at all. It wasn't as if CannRose was his biggest investment. All that blather about an old widower needing distractions. Was he really just a lonely old man? Something about Guido's involvement was becoming disturbing. Maybe it was his just going ahead and purchasing the seventy-five-acre lot next door to the facility that bugged Caldwell. Or maybe it was Guido's plan to build a new CannRose marijuana facility on it — ten times the size and without any license — and temporarily purpose it for herbal supplements and teas. They could run it at less than a quarter capacity, enough to pay the bills but be ready and way ahead of the other producers when the state let them expand. Or when recreational marijuana got the okay. Either way it could be churning out cannabis products within the time it took to grow and process a single crop. Maybe, and Caldwell tapped on the steering wheel as he had this rare moment of self-reflection, maybe what he really didn't like was that he hadn't thought of this first. Guido made him feel like he was losing his edge. Losing it to an old man. Hmm. Caldwell would be an old man himself someday. Perhaps he should be inspired.

Caldwell drove for another hour until he got to the truck stop. He showered and even found a T-shirt that was better than just plain black. It had Almost There, Never Where written on it in blocky white type. It sounded obscure and possibly philosophical. Perfect. If he'd had time he might have borrowed someone's cigarette at the truck stop and burned a couple of holes in it. He'd have laundered it too. As it was he simply put it on, and it looked good enough under the gray linen jacket. He rolled the shirt he'd picked up in Colorado into a ball and stuffed it into the bottom of his knapsack. When he got back in the SUV, he didn't bother with the voice commands.

Just outside Hullbrooke, Caldwell noticed the SUV was sluggish. And the radio took a few seconds to come on. The turn signal on the dash didn't go off immediately either once he'd rounded a corner. The car needed servicing. He'd have to borrow one of Lydia's SUVs. Why she kept a five-bay garage full in the middle of the countryside was beyond him. "They were Jordan's," she'd said, as if that explained everything.

It was dark when he turned onto the Lusteadt Side Road. Branches overhanging and growing into the roadway touched the vehicle on both sides. This would be fun. He could regale them at dinner about his little adventure. About four miles along, as the rough road cut through the hills with granite outcroppings, the dashboard on the SUV suddenly went into digital meltdown. The speedometer swung wildly to 180 mph. Caldwell couldn't have been doing more than twenty-five. The other lights and icons started flashing too and the car shuddered. Caldwell slammed on the brakes. They worked begrudgingly. The power steering was gone as well. Caldwell put all his strength into the wheel and the brakes and brought the car to a halt on the side of the road. He barely avoided driving it into a huge ditch.

"Shit!"

The dash lights were still flashing wildly. He turned the car off. Maybe it just needed a reset. He waited a minute in total darkness then pressed the start button. The dash lights came on spastically. The engine did nothing. He waited several minutes in the darkness, occasionally trying to start the car, but still nothing happened.

"Shit! Shit! Shit!" he screamed as he rapidly punched the start button three more times.

Now he *would* have to call Guido. And a tow truck. Who could he get to pick him up? Lydia probably. But she might not know the side road. Maybe Greg or Lazlo or the security guy at CannRose. Yeah. The facility was only twenty minutes away. He pulled out his phone. There was no reception.

"Goddamn it!" He pounded his fist into the passenger seat. It could be hours, possibly days before anyone would come along this road. He sat fuming, then decided he might as well start walking. At least it wasn't freezing outside. He made a note to himself never to take the side road in winter. He opened the glove compartment and felt around for a flashlight. Maybe Lydia had put one there in one of her taking-care-of-him moments. Nothing. Then he remembered there was one on his phone. As he got out of the car he stopped suddenly. What if the car wouldn't lock? Or if it did, what if he couldn't get back in? This was ridiculous. He felt a twinge in his chest. *Too much coffee.* He should stop eating red meat too. He should be a vegetarian. Better yet, a vegan. He reached into the back seat for his knapsack. It wasn't ever meant for hiking, but like his phone flashlight, it would do. He put his arm through one strap and closed the car door. It didn't lock. Good. He set out along the road.

He hadn't gone very far, not more than a hundred yards or so, when he heard the faint noise of a motor behind him, growing louder. Sounded like a truck. Caldwell was overjoyed. He could flag it down and maybe the driver could take him to Guido's. He was going in the right direction. He should run back to the car. The driver would see right away his car had broken down and he'd stop for sure. He might even know how to fix it, though that was unlikely.

As Caldwell ran he could see the glow from the vehicle's headlights starting to appear above the hilltop. He ran a little faster and then suddenly he tripped. His foot had landed in a pothole. He scrambled to regain his balance. The knapsack fell off his right arm, he tripped again and the phone flew out of his hand to the center of the road. It shone, reflecting the truck's headlights. Caldwell took a step and reached down for it.

It was while he was picking the phone up that he realized the truck wasn't slowing down. In fact it was speeding up coming down the hill. *Gravity*, thought Caldwell. "Oh my God! Gravity." It was his last utterance. He felt the full brunt of the truck's momentum. It was breathtaking. Caldwell heard smashing and cracking in some vague, distant dimension, and he heard thunder too. Then he was airborne in the dazzling lights and out of the sky he saw a fork of lightning coming his way. He felt his chest explode into a thousand pieces. They flew at some marvelous warp speed, sparkling with visions and voices. This was bigger than anything he'd ever experienced. Extraordinary! He had no other thoughts for it. And then it was very, very silent. And dark.

Chapter 58

Teddy Voik and his parents lived on a farm near the Lusteadt Side Road. Teddy's dad told him at breakfast to go check the fields before he went to school. He wanted to know how much got washed out from the rain the night before.

"All spring we had no goddamn rain! This month everything's washin' out. I don't know why I stay here. Not makin' any money this year that's for sure."

Teddy's mom stamped her cigarette out with a little more force than usual. "You could say that about the last five years."

"A lesson to ya, Teddy," his father said. "Stay in school. Don't end up like your old man."

"I wanna farm, though."

"Family farm's a dead end, Teddy," his mother sniffed.

Teddy shrugged and got up from the table. "I just don't wanna be stuck workin' in a building or sittin' at some desk all day."

"Maybe you should go work at that marijuana place. Make us all rich!"

"Jesus! Don't tell him stuff like that." Teddy's mother took out another cigarette and tapped it on the table. "You know Mort?"

"Yeah. Does janitorial work or somethin' there?"

"Somethin' like that. So he got stopped in Branxton County and 'cause the asshole cop smelled pot in his car, they strip search him right on the side of the road. Didn't matter what he told 'em."

Teddy's father grimaced before he turned back to his son. "Take the ATV, Teddy. And take it slow. Especially on the side road there."

#

Two of the Voiks' fields and some of their woods edged onto the side road. When Teddy got there it looked like one of the fields had been dug a foot or so deeper from the storm, and the lowest part had a layer of water on it.

Teddy spotted the SUV immediately. It was at the bottom of the hill, upended and half in the ditch. A chunk of the road was flooded ahead of it. He wondered briefly if the SUV had been driven or washed into that angle. He slowly drove the ATV toward it. He couldn't be sure how deep the water was or if there was some big hole he might fall into. He stopped at the water's edge, got off and waded through it. He walked up to the SUV and looked in the window. Fancy, that was for sure. Then he tried the door and it opened. He wondered what it was doing here. Some city idiots using their GPS? Then again, city idiots locked their doors religiously.

Teddy shut the door and started wading back to the ATV. He'd noticed what he'd thought was a big rock when he was coming the other way was actually a knapsack covered in mud. As he bent to get a closer look he saw something out of the corner of his eye. It was down in the ditch. He walked around the ATV and looked over the edge of the road.

He could see the whole thing now. The back of a head with matted hair, grass floating around it. A jacket ballooned out in the murky water behind. Teddy looked where one might expect the rest of the body to be and saw a leg with the calf showing beneath bunched trousers. The sock and shoe were still on the foot and it appeared to be floating, though when Teddy looked closer he could see it was elevated by a rock. He just stared for several seconds. He thought maybe he should try to pull the person out and then he stopped. Instead Teddy pulled his mom's phone out. His hand was shaking. No reception. He'd have to get past the outcroppings. He hopped on the ATV and went back up to the top of the hill and into the field. He pressed his dad's number and his dad picked up on the first ring.

PART TWELVE

Distribution

Oh Shattered Ones! Bring us your splinters, your shards, your lost pieces. We mend with the spectra light years cannot decimate. We cascade through the ages. We suffer the limp and groan. We seek our smiling with the suns. We collect our wits. Our tiny pleasures. Our waking bliss. Come. Assemble. Defy the trend of waning and decay. Come be whole with us. Even for a moment. Even for the illusion. Join us.

from Cannto II, *Cannabidadas*

Chapter 59

News of Caldwell's death reverberated through the company. Perhaps from stress generally and a renewed sense of their own mortality, many people were terribly and visibly upset. A cleaner in the production area, whose only interactions with Caldwell had been his opening the door for her one day then yelling at her the next for not noticing the coconut coir that had accumulated under one of the work tables, was inconsolable. She was sent home for the day to recover.

A lot of people had trouble concentrating on their jobs. Stoyan chain-smoked the whole day and didn't even bother trying to work. Damian was initially speechless when he heard the news. He'd been at Guido's when Caldwell hadn't shown up. They'd made jokes in passing that Caldwell lost track of time again wooing the Colorado outfit. He'd missed his plane. Forgotten to charge his phone or left it somewhere. Typical Caldwell, always racing. It didn't seem funny at all now when he pictured Caldwell floating facedown in a ditch while they sat cozily around Guido's fireplace with their after dinner brandy and port. Damian was seen for the next few hours wandering around the cultivation section looking mostly at his shoes and muttering, "Wow, man. Wow."

Percy was completely flustered by the news and tried to call his husband, but there was no answer, so he went into Hullbrooke for a coffee and picked up some Irish whiskey to put in it. He also bought pastries. And chocolates. It dawned on him that he'd lost the chaos that gave his work purpose.

Lazlo began skulking around more than usual, frequently dropping into Greg's office, wanting to talk about Caldwell. He seemed to have more affection for his cousin than anyone knew. "What a crazy guy but he lived for this place, you know! Was his whole life! What are we going to do without him?"

Ernie wandered into Greg's office too. He wasn't sure why. Perhaps Greg's police persona might shed light on the strange ways people die. "Terrible isn't it? Drowning in a ditch. What's going to happen?"

Greg had been tasked with getting the word out, so he was mostly trying to determine who needed notifying. "Not a pretty way to go." He looked at Ernie and shook his head wearily.

Cassie was hoping she might not lose the crop in the Flower Room III now. No matter what, the bugs never let up. The new crop was in there three weeks and she'd found fungus gnats on Monday. It was Friday. Diatomaceous earth wasn't cutting it. Now she could apply one of the organic sprays they'd used for the same problem the year before.

Petra's response was cool, inquisitive and apropos of her nature. "So was he drunk or what? Why would he be on that road?"

Lydia was deeply saddened. She had nothing but fondness left for Caldwell and she'd genuinely wanted him to succeed. His success was her success after all. "He put every bit of energy he had into the business," she said. It also occurred to her she was now essentially three times a widow. Of course she and Caldwell hadn't been together for a while but the statistics associated with having a relationship with her for any length of time were not looking favorable for the men. The thought made her worry about Luther.

Luther, being spread so thin, simply slotted Caldwell's death into his day planner. "Caldwell had passion. He was a man dedicated to his vision. He had Herculean energy. And he was determined to make CannRose a great company. He will be sorely missed." Being the CEO, Luther felt he had to issue some kind of statement.

Alice had told her son long ago that Caldwell was building the company to fail and she didn't understand why anyone with half a brain couldn't see it. "I wish somebody would get rid of him," she'd said. When the news reached the law firm, her son couldn't help himself. He called her right away.

"Mom, you've got connections. Big guy in the sky on your payroll now? Wow. I need his number myself."

"Stop that! I didn't mean—"

"Careful what you wish for. Isn't that what they say?"

"I never wished him dead. At least I don't think I did, anyway."

Guido and Jason expressed shock and of course dismay at the news and then quickly retired to Guido's corner nook. They looked at each other and shrugged. "Freak accident," Jason said. "What are the chances?" They stared at each other a few more seconds, considering the consequences. This made their plans infinitely easier. Without Caldwell constantly stirring things up and losing his cool about minor details, they could get on with things.

A day before the funeral, Caldwell's son and a daughter even Lydia hadn't known existed suddenly appeared. The godson, the same one who'd briefly been the CannRose production manager, showed up too, recently recovered from an overdose. All three were deeply saddened to find out Caldwell's shares in the company were not part of his estate. In fact Caldwell didn't have much of an estate. Just his clothes and watch, a few sets of fancy cufflinks, a fountain pen and of course the SUV that now required a couple of thousand dollars in repairs. Malcolm and Cyrus, those old crafty advisers and caretakers of Lydia's estate had arranged that all CannRose shares and any assets acquired from Lydia would be transferred back to her in the event of Caldwell's death, with administration fees deducted of course. The children were free to challenge the arrangement, but given the bottomless resources of the law firm they'd be up against, they decided to limit their squabbling to his clothes and jewelry.

#

To Caldwell's credit, a good crowd showed up at his funeral. All the CannRose employees and associates were there, including Alice. People brought their families. Even Gus was there in a suit. At the service Guido played the sarabande from the first Bach Partita. Lydia, who'd spared no expense for the funeral, wept openly, and Percy joined her. Gus and Lazlo needed tissues too.

Once the formalities were over, after the sherry, tea and sandwiches had been passed around at Rosefields, many heaved a sigh of relief. And everybody went back to their day-to-day business. Though without Caldwell, adjustments would need to be made. Things were bound to change.

Chapter 60

The three young devotees sat slouched on stools in the potting room,
unsure what to do next. They'd received no instructions for the
afternoon. Two of them periodically pulled out their phones to check
messages. The third aimlessly surfed the internet on one of the
cultivation touchscreens.

"This week sucked."

"Funerals suck."

"Drowning. That sucks."

"Death."

"Bro, I think the ladies are sad too."

"They're just water-stressed. Cassie said there was a problem
with the main valve."

"Bro, they're sad."

"Not. He never spent time with them."

"They could still be sad."

"You think we should stay in Hullbrooke?

"Why not?"

"We could get another job."

"Doing what?"

"We can work at the dispensary."

"We can't do that."

"Why not?"

"That's for pharm techs."

"Why work at the dispensary?"

"Then we could move back to Lyston."

"What about the ladies?"

"Don't you care about the ladies? This is the perfect job!"

"I wanna go to cooking school."

"What?"

"Brobes, I'm so done with pizza."

"Just get a cookbook."

"Yeah. We could make tofu burgers!"

"Tofu burgers?"

"I wanna be a chef."

"Maybe he's going through the stages of grief."

"No. I wanna make edibles."

"That's fire! You could still work with the ladies."

"They shoulda had edibles at his funeral."

"I liked the lemon coconut squares."

"Edibles woulda been better."

"They're not legal."

"So. They'd still be better for paying respects."

"They're never gonna let anybody make them here."

"We should start our own company."

"We should start our own state."

Chapter 61

It took Guido almost no time at all to start rearranging the company. Lydia, on the advice of Cyrus and Malcolm, offered to sell him some of the shares that had come back to her when Caldwell died. He was more than happy to purchase. She also came to him with her idea of adding veterinary medicines. She'd already talked to Petra about it, and Petra was all for it — she even had a good contact in animal science at her old alma mater. Guido nodded thoughtfully at this proposal and then smiled. "Of course, Lydia, is beautiful idea. Exceptional! But even trickier here than for people across the country as you know. We will see."

Lydia's veterinarian had told her prescribing a little weed oil for a dog's fits or a pony's arthritis could get her locked up! The state may be allowing medical use for humans, but pets and beasts? Not that Rover or Fluffy would ever turn her in. But Lydia, possibly having absorbed some of Caldwell's characteristics over the years, found this kind of hurdle made her more determined. And she proposed an all-out lobbying effort, along with partnerships to expand research with a willing university.

Guido repeatedly told her it was a great idea, but after a few weeks she soon realized she was no more a business partner with Guido than she had been with Caldwell. Guido was always warm and convivial and he engaged her in all manner of chitchat, but he excluded her from anything to do with business. People she'd never heard of showed up at CannRose and spent an hour or two talking to Guido, and she'd often only find out after the fact. Unlike Caldwell, Guido was quiet, verging on surreptitious, about his moves, and he made many of them.

Guido started arriving at 7:00 a.m. Lydia learned he was going over the scheduling and meeting with Cassie or Stoyan as soon as they got in the door. They'd discuss the plants, the strains to grow, the various stages they were at and the priorities for the derivatives. Guido called a board meeting too and sold them on some guy she'd never even met, Herbert Cuttle, a smart money man with a background in the medical-devices industry. They appointed him CEO so Luther could get back to his law practice. Lydia imagined Cyrus was behind this move and she felt her influence at CannRose shrink even more. At the same meeting, Guido easily convinced the board that CannRose should merge with his other company, the one he'd founded for the purchase of the seventy-acre plot beside the grow facility. It would diversify operations. And Guido himself was very diversified already. She'd thought he just sold shoes! He had controlling shares in a supplements company, major investments in two other marijuana outfits in California and Oregon and who knew what else! He'd also reopened discussions with a Canadian conglomerate he was convinced would be perfect for CannRose to partner with. Lydia realized Guido had taken over completely.

Under the guise of directions from the new CEO, Guido soon got busy letting people go. "We really need to trim the fat here," Guido would tell Lydia, wringing his hands as if the whole matter pained him. "I've been watching so-and-so over the last several months," he would whisper, "and you know they are mostly fond of the coffee break." Or, "This is not the kind of person who can benefit CannRose. They will be much happier elsewhere, I'm sure." Lydia wasn't so sure, especially when Stoyan was told to start looking for another placement. Guido had Jason take care of the terminations and put him to work with Greg in HR. Lydia noticed Greg was looking nervous these days.

Some things she didn't mind at all; she had a clear sense Guido was maneuvering Lazlo out the door and that would be a relief. But Lydia thought that for a man in his late seventies, Guido had a remarkably steely focus on business. People were simply assets with dollar values. In fact he began to remind Lydia a little of Jordan.

As for Herbert Cuttle, Lydia found him unremarkable and rather phony, using his business jargon to fill up conversational space, spouting stock phrases one might expect of an executive. Like Guido though, he was less than forthcoming about what he actually did, and like Luther, he was rarely seen at CannRose. But unlike Luther, who was swamped with another career, Guido explained to Lydia that Herbert was "making alliances for the future, really taking the company into the next decade and making the kind of deals Caldwell would have aspired to."

Herbert in turn brought in several consultants and more money men. These were not neophytes hoping to get rich on the Green Rush, the types that Caldwell had so diligently cultivated, these were a different bunch altogether. They quietly talked about business algorithms, acquisitions, mergers, stock options, buybacks and international exchanges. Who knew where CannRose was going? In fact it might not be CannRose at all soon.

Lydia, feeling a little lost again, suited up and took herself into the cultivation area. What did the plants want? That was a happy question. Wasn't it? Or maybe a sad one. Because they wanted. They desired. She was sure of it. She could feel it walking through the hallways.

She let herself into one of the flowering rooms and sat down on a bare table at the far side. The air handlers hummed and the young plants all fluttered in the breeze. So uniform. A little green army with marching orders to grow, grow, grow and then blossom on cue. Such a push all the time. She thought of Caldwell. He hadn't ever perceived the business this way: dictated, willed or influenced by the plants themselves; though she suspected Damian might. Luther didn't have a clue, of course. He was just clever and Guido was even more clever. Did these men ever consider the consequences of the notions they held? Specifically, their notions of these green creatures. That bore a little thought too. After a while, Ray, the quiet security guy, showed up. She waved to him and he came and sat down on the table a little ways from her. They both just sat there looking at the plants. *Maybe grief does this*, she thought. *Provides a compelling view.*

Chapter 62

Alice's son called her a month or so after Caldwell's funeral. "Mom, I just heard some bad stuff about CannRose."

Alice was in the office at her drugstore sorting out some orders. "Honey, there's nothing much good to hear about CannRose these days. And why are you whispering?"

"There's major shit going down. You should keep away from the dispensaries. Both of them."

"Zack, sweetie, have you been smoking weed?"

"No? What's that got to do with it?"

"I know your job is stressful but weed's not good for everybody."

"What are you talking about?"

"Honey, it can make some people very anxious and paranoid. Are you okay? You can tell your mother, you know."

"I'm not paranoid. And I'm not high! I'm watching Luther and he's freaking out."

"Honey, Luther could be freaking out about anything." She put her phone on speaker and went back to checking boxes on the online order form.

"No, Mom, it's about CannRose."

"Well what's new? CannRose is prone to crisis. Caldwell probably left the place reeling in debt, though I always thought they kept a tight rein on him."

"It's worse than that. They don't think Caldwell accidentally drowned."

"What?"

"They think it was murder."

Alice took her eyes away from her order forms and looked at the phone with raised eyebrows. "What? Seriously?" She glanced back to her screen. "I can't believe that."

"A week or so ago, some cop, a real hick from Hullbrooke, shows up asking questions." Zack started to whisper again. "And today a couple of agents from the DEA were here. Cyrus was screaming at Luther about CannRose getting shut down. Luther was shouting back that he wasn't the one giving blow jobs to garden-variety criminals." He stopped whispering. "It was the only thing I heard clearly."

Alice was staring at the phone, giving it her full attention by this point. "I sure don't like the sounds of the DEA being there. Oh lord!" She leaned back in her chair and put both palms to her forehead.

"It stinks, Mom. This whole operation stinks. The law firm and the dope factory. I handed in my resignation yesterday!"

"You got another job?" Alice sat back up.

"I'm doing a master's. But that's beside the point."

"Oh, sweetie, I'm so glad you decided to make a move. What's the new direction?"

"Environmental law. Mom, we can't talk about that right now. You need to—"

"Zack, that's wonderful! Where are you going? Someplace close I hope."

"Vermont . . . Mom, you need to resign. You've got to get out of CannRose. I know I got you into it. And I'm sorry. But CannRose is dangerous. You need to walk away!"

"I think you're being dramatic, but I'll call some people and find out what's going on. I'm so glad you're doing a master's, honey."

So Alice called Percy.

"Alice, the place is insane." He sneezed. "Sorry, I have a cold. We're all going to be questioned."

"They really think Caldwell was murdered?"

"Oh that was a couple of weeks ago. Now they're asking all sorts of questions about Greg." Percy cleared his throat. "He retired right after the police showed up about Caldwell. Said he had to move up his retirement date because his wife was unwell. And now he's left the country. Gone, vanished."

"So they think Greg murdered Caldwell? I can't believe that for a minute."

"No, I . . . oh I don't know. Greg started acting weird. Lazlo thought he was scared because Greg sold him his company shares for peanuts. And why would you do that right when you're about to retire? Maybe he figured whoever killed Caldwell was coming after him next. That was Lazlo's guess."

"Good lord!"

"Or what if he did kill Caldwell? I wanted to kill him a few times." Percy sniffed.

"We all did. Doesn't mean anything. Besides, I always had the impression Greg found Caldwell amusing. Laughable even."

"Alice, it's a clusterfuck of the first order! As you know, I do not say that sort of thing lightly." Percy sneezed again.

Alice got off her call with Percy and sat down at her desk. It seemed smaller than she remembered. She needed a drink. The irony of Greg being scared, on the lam, possibly at the center of foul play did not escape Alice. He was a substantial investor in the company and Alice had always seen him as a beacon of hypocrisy. She'd wondered how many people he'd put away in his policing days for marijuana infractions, how many lives he'd managed to ruin and how many kids he'd ultimately turned into criminals by arresting them for a few joints. And now he was on the other side. Wasn't that interesting.

About ten minutes after she got off the phone with Percy, Luther called. He told her they might have to temporarily close the dispensaries. He'd let her know definitively in the next two days. She'd never heard him sound anxious before. Only frustrated or calculating. He told her not to worry, but his call left her completely rattled.

Alice bade her staff goodbye for the day, popped into Tilly's Oyster Bar for a quick scotch and water, then went for a long walk. After an hour of roaming the neighborhood, she sat down by the community garden. The harvested and spent beds suited her mood. A snowfall, early in the season, showered her with big, fluffy flakes. She sat huddled on the bench in her parka. There was no getting around it — CannRose was a mess. Maybe it *was* time to walk away. She didn't need the headache or the worry. Sammy probably wanted to take over anyway. She'd moved to Lyston ages ago and was unfazed by delays and lousy business decisions. And sometimes she didn't think they were such lousy decisions. Sometimes she even hinted that Alice was being difficult. There was a rumor Sammy and Guido were more than chummy these days. Alice had decided not to be inquisitive.

In fact Alice figured she could resign altogether. Nobody listened to a word she said anyway. The only people she talked to now were Petra and Percy, and it didn't sound like anybody listened to them either.

What she couldn't get over was that, after the company had taken a year or more to finally find an extraction specialist — and Stoyan was better than she'd imagined they could ever hope for — she'd heard Guido and that awful Herbert Cuttle were getting rid of him. They were bringing in some twenty-year-old technician who'd worked briefly for a pharmaceutical company and had no experience whatsoever with botanicals. Worse still, they put the old black-market guy with the blond dreadlocks in charge of product development. He was clueless! CannRose didn't stand much of a chance as far as Alice could make out. Especially with that miserable inspector running around. Alice still hadn't heard a word back from the DOH in response to her letter of complaint. Then again, she'd have been very surprised if she had.

Chapter 63

Ernie was busy wrapping burlap around some of the more delicate shrubbery at the foot of Mrs. Cranston's terraces. Never knew what winter might bring in the way of global warming irony, the dreaded polar vortex. If it was a nasty winter like the last one, shrubs would need a little help. He'd also discovered Gladys's toad nest. It was right at the base of the bottom terrace wall. He'd noticed the dug-up soil and peeked in the hole that went in right under one of the rocks. Gladys was already groggy and into hibernation mode. He figured she might need a little help too. So he piled dry leaves as high as he could in front of the wall where she'd tucked herself underneath.

Jim Thorpes, the chief, pulled up in his truck. It was Saturday, his day off, and he was out of uniform. He jumped out of the truck and wandered over to Ernie with his hands shoved into the back pockets of his jeans.

"Chief! What's new? How are you?"

"Hell, I could be better. Beautiful day though. Last one we'll see before the snow flies." He took his right hand out of his pocket and scratched his neck. "Can I talk to you for a second? I got a few questions for you if you don't mind."

Ernie put down the shears he was using to cut up the burlap and motioned to the bench in the sunshine where they could sit down. "How can I help you?"

Jim Thorpes let out a big sigh. "You know it goes without sayin', Ernie, that the damn grow-op where you work is nothing but a shitload of trouble for me."

"Has been quite a mess lately."

"Been a pain in the ass right from the beginning. All those false alarms. Havin' to send a cruiser out every time a raccoon farted."

"They man the place 24/7 now, Chief."

"You know I had the DEA on my ass?"

"Jesus, no. What did they want?"

"Not even sure exactly. Did you know Greg very well? You know, the security guy."

"Can't say I did, really."

"Some story about retiring two months earlier than planned because of his wife's health. That strike you as bogus?"

Ernie's attention was drawn to two little sparrows that were on the ground hopping and picking at seeds in front of them. "I don't know. Maybe she needed to get out before the cold."

"The guy just disappeared overseas. You haven't heard anything, have you?"

"Nope."

"No trace of him since Spain, they said. Bank accounts closed. Doesn't that strike you as odd?"

"It sure does."

"Shit." Jim Thorpes coughed up some phlegm and spat it out with obvious irritation. "So as a kid, I mean in high school, did you ever hear of Rainy Day Dope?"

"Um . . ." Ernie looked thoughtful.

"I was a good seven or eight years ahead of you. I'd never heard of it."

"Maybe. There was dope around, sure . . ."

"Those three Lyston kids working at CannRose, they know something about it. Sure as shit. One of 'em's Greg's nephew."

"I never knew that."

"Jesus, Ernie. There's so much about all this I don't know, makes me wanna puke. Goddamn DEA said I was under suspicion. Can you believe that?"

"Holy crap!"

"Accused me of willfully ignoring the local drug scene. They cleared me though. I showed them the list of infractions. It's substantial, Ernie. I can be proud of it."

"You should be, Chief." Ernie watched the little sparrows fly away.

"Greg was a Lyston cop, for Chrissake. Good guy. Only one with any brains at CannRose that I could see, present company excepted of course. He was twenty-five years on the force. Twenty-five years!

And they're tellin' me he probably operated in three states but they can't prove it. You know what that means if it's true?"

"No." Ernie was looking at the chief again.

"That I'm a fuckin' idiot."

"Jesus, Chief. I wouldn't take it personally. I thought Greg was great too. Level-headed. That's a rarity for CannRose."

"Shit, if it's true, could mean your weed boss in the ditch got offed in some drug war. Not just a random hit-and-run."

Ernie raised his eyebrows. "That's scary."

"I blame the goddamn coroner for that mess. 'Straight forward,' he says. 'I'll get the report to you in the morning,' he says. You can smell the booze on him. Doesn't mention a goddamn thing about a heart attack or broken bones. That's pretty crucial information."

"I don't think anybody at CannRose was too surprised to find out it was probably a heart attack that killed him."

"Yeah, but who's crazy enough to go seventy miles an hour on that side road, and where's the goddamn vehicle that hit him? It's still fifty-fifty, the impact gave him the heart attack."

"Guardians are pretty crazy."

"Oh, I checked them out all right. He was related you know."

"I did know that."

"Yeah well. Not their style." Jim Thorpes shook his head and gazed across the road at nothing. "They got so many guns in that compound, you wouldn't believe. But not a single driving infraction against any one of 'em in the whole history of Hullbrooke. Not a one. Vehicles all kept immaculate too." He was silent for a few moments. "You know Lyle Cordoff? The exterminator guy?"

"I see him staggering home from Chelsea's from time to time."

"You ever seen him driving like that? Drunk?"

"Nope. But I tend not to notice the truck traffic. It's the staggering and yelling about vermin catches my attention."

"Yeah, well he swears he hasn't been on that side road in five years but that's sober. You know anybody else likes to stunt drive?"

"I didn't even know Lyle did."

"Oh, he's a crazy bastard. I swear it's all the goddamn pesticides — his brother twitches like a dying weevil."

"Yeah, I noticed that."

"And what about that Guido Batelli. Who the fuck is he?" Jim Thorpes squinted.

"Your guess is as good as mine. High-end shoe guy is all I know. Oh, and he plays the violin."

"What a joke. It was Greg checked him out, right? And Lazlo Porter, he's as sneaky as they come."

"You know mostly I just mop the floors, Chief."

"I know." Jim Thorpes stared off again and idly tapped the bench. "Say, you got any extra venison jerky? Given the time of year."

"Now that you mention it, I do."

"How much you sellin' it for?"

"For you, Chief, and all the trouble you bear for this town, it's free. I'll drop some by your place tomorrow."

"Much appreciate it, Ernie." Jim Thorpes got up and walked back to his truck and gave a little nod and a smile as he climbed in.

Ernie stood up and watched him drive away. He looked up at the puffy cumulus clouds speeding along overhead and then he walked to the terrace wall and threw himself face down into the pile of leaves he'd raked up for Gladys. He just lay there for a few minutes. Jesus, Mary and Joseph. Were all little towns like this? At that moment it occurred to Ernie that Lenore hadn't crossed his mind in six months.

Later that same day, Ernie did some tidying up of his own container beds on the rooftop. He found a couple of onions he'd missed. There was still kale growing and he took some leaves for his dinner. An omelet would be nice. He'd traded a jar of his chutney for some shiitake mushrooms and he still had some goat cheese lurking in his fridge. Just before he started to chop the onion, he paused and looked at the beautiful set of knives that now graced his counter. They were a gift. Three weeks ago Greg had knocked on his door.

"Just dropping by for a second," he'd said. "Gotta tell you, the wife can't stop raving about that jar of chili sauce. She wanted you to have these. We sure as hell can't take 'em with us. She says they're professional. Chef grade. Real good, anyway. And there's this thing here too. Don't know if you already got one." Greg pulled a Japanese soba knife out of the shopping bag.

"Wow! These are gorgeous, Greg."

"Glad you like 'em. Wife'll be happy about that."

"So you're off?"

"Flyin' out tomorrow. Lookin' forward to warmer weather and a sea view. Cocktails on the balcony."

"Sounds good."

"You know, I don't know who the hell ran over Caldwell, but I don't like the looks of it. You might have been wiser than I thought giving Rainy Day a pass. Could be new players. I'm too old for all this." Greg sighed. "Maybe I wasn't as thorough on a couple of those background checks as I shoulda been. I don't know. Hate to cast any aspersions though. Best just to wrap things up sooner than later."

Ernie had nodded.

"Well, jeez. This is it. Been great workin' with you. You take care of yourself, and if you're ever in Montenegro, you'll probably find me on a beach. Oh. I almost forgot." Greg reached into the shopping bag again and pulled out a baggie full of weed. "A little nostalgia for your neck pain. RD Gold."

Ernie laughed. "Thanks, Greg. And congrats on the retirement."

"You bet." And with that, Greg vanished from Ernie's life. And vanished too from Hullbrooke, USA.

After Ernie finished his omelet and cleaned up the dishes, he rolled himself a fat doobie from the Rainy Day Dope rather than his own homegrown. He put on his winter coat, grabbed a cushion and headed out through the window to the rooftop. While Ernie lit up his joint, the stars were busy lighting up the universe. The Milky Way, serene and majestic, smiled down on him. He took a deep inhale and, by golly, it did bring back a few old memories. The agonies of adolescence were almost delightful in retrospect. The pimply gangly kid who worried about his sneakers not being cool enough. The tallest klutz to never make the high-school basketball team. The teachers he fantasized about. The girls who teased or sleazed. The prim girls. And oh, all that masturbation. Surprising he hadn't drowned in his own juices. He wrote poems too. Most often about death of course. He wished he'd kept them. He was sure he'd find them entertaining at this point. He really was way too earnest as a kid. Ernesto the Crane. Ernesto the Bean. Ernesto the Besto. Ernesto the Gnarly. He started to laugh. Maybe it was just the weed kicking in. He was glad he wasn't a kid anymore but he was pretty sure he liked the kid he'd been.

PART THIRTEEN

Sales

*Oh Friends. Dear Friends. We caution with care from the ages.
Beware of the dwindling repose. Here is the punch of your profits.
Your mind wrapped in sums, your heart fixed to close. It's rough to
see the sunset when you never caught on to the rise. So many riches
and so much rashness. Sadder even than the silence that vanished
for trading on noise. We sing for you still. We must. That's the deal.
Your loss is our loss, your gain, our gain, and the traffic of time, the
ledger.*

from Cannto III, *Cannabidadas*

Chapter 64

Petra rang the buzzer on Dr. Grange's door.

"Hello," the voice said. "Petra? Come right up."

Petra pondered the seemingly unvetted invitation. What if she wasn't Petra? *I could be an ax murderer*, she thought, but then she hadn't seen the shiny little black sphere bulging above her at the doorway. She opened the door after the buzzer sounded and climbed two flights in a steep, claustrophobic stairway. Petra wasn't handling life as well as she might. Percy had found her passed out at her desk. He told her she needed to get some help. He was right.

Two months after Caldwell died she'd come home from work to find her mother dead on the couch. She'd slipped away during the day. Probably during her afternoon nap. The doctors said it was likely painless — a massive stroke that would have killed her instantly. Petra felt a heaviness that made her weak in the knees when the doctor said that. And then she had taken only a few days off work to look after the funeral arrangements. Percy said that was ridiculous and she needed more time to deal with the grief. But the truth was, she'd been a mess since Sanjay left.

Petra asked Percy what the wedding was like. He said he had more fun than he'd ever had at a wedding. Indian weddings were a blast, or at least this Indian wedding of the diaspora was a blast. And Gavin outdid himself on the dance floor. The food was incredible of course. He told her the quiet guy from security was there too, with a couple of women, but Percy had barely said two words to them because there was so much going on.

Petra arrived at a landing under a bright skylight. There were two doors at opposite ends. The door to her left opened and a large billowy matron in a maroon shirtwaist dress welcomed her. "Come on in. Call me Phyllis," she said.

Petra felt a surge of sadness and panic as if she might start sobbing right there and then without having even spoken a word. She turned away quickly and focused on the oriental carpet that graced the room. There were armchairs and a sofa with a small desk facing out in one corner. She concentrated on putting her knapsack down and taking her coat off. She felt in those first three seconds of meeting Dr. Grange — Phyllis — that she could not bear to look her in the eyes without crying.

Dr. Grange picked up the box of tissues. "Have a seat. Wherever you think looks most comfy."

Petra crumpled into the biggest armchair as the flood gates opened and the therapist handed her a tissue. Petra wept for several minutes. Her shoulders shook, the tears streamed and the snot ran. "I don't know why I'm such a mess," she said.

Dr. Grange handed Petra another tissue.

After more tears, Petra babbled, "I'm going to lose my job. But I don't care that much about it. My research isn't going very well, anyway."

"I see."

"I've kind of lost the thread, I think. It's very complex. The physiology is tricky and the plant itself is bred for difficulties. It looked like we were going to move in a new direction with an animal-science group. But I'm pretty sure they're killing the deal now. And . . . and I've had equipment breakdowns."

Dr. Grange got up to get a glass of water. She pondered the human capacity for suffering and speculated to what extent it was fueled by denial. Honesty with self was always a challenge.

"Tell me more about your research," she said as she handed Petra the glass. It was a roundabout way to get to Petra's issues. Shoptalk or small talk. It didn't matter which. As it turned out though, this shoptalk grabbed Dr. Grange's attention. She'd never had a credentialed marijuana scientist show up at her door before and she soon found herself plying Petra with questions.

"Well," Petra said, "it's a slog no matter how you look at it. Way more clinical trials are badly needed. And there are issues around dosage and cannabinoid profiles. It can have very different effects on different people. For one person it's a depressant and for the next it increases their anxiety. It's a real cipher. We've been collecting data and a lot of it relies on self-reporting from the clients. It's a new approach for me and I never feel it's particularly good data but patterns are starting to emerge. I think they really are. I've been focusing on the terpenes mostly. I've only talked to a few other researchers, but we're putting together an information bank. The company didn't seem to care much. This new group of executives are different though. If it's not proprietary then it's a waste of money. They're just arrogant and ignorant."

"I guess that's the nature of private research."

"I don't think it has to be at all. It's completely short-sighted." Petra sat quiet for a moment. Then she smiled. "There is something I'm finding that might be profitable . . . but I'm not telling them. I don't care if it's totally illegal from the employer's perspective. I didn't tell the little DEA guy either when he came snooping around. I'm hanging on to the research and the seeds. I'll make it open source if it ever comes to anything."

"And what's that?" Dr. Grange noted the retaliatory hostility and was fascinated all the more.

"One of the guys at work, an ex-cop, brought me a seed collection just before he disappeared!" Petra let out a little laugh. "He thought I might find the seeds interesting. Said there was definitely old-timer weed in there. Most is pretty low THC by today's standards. Other people have brought me samples too. One batch of stuff was just growing on its own in some cow pasture since who knows when. I sent some of the samples to another researcher with access to good genome technology. A couple of them are lining up with what they have on some Himalayan strains. They're very stable too, comparatively. And the cannabinoid and terpene profiles are unlike anything I've seen. It's exciting, but I know the company's going to shut down my research. So screw 'em. They're not getting anything out of this. They think what I do is irrelevant anyway. So they can have all the 'irrelevant' client survey studies and all the 'irrelevant' profile and yield work on the strains they grow. Fuckers."

Dr. Grange had to refrain from her inclination to say, "Good for you!" She merely nodded instead.

Chapter 65

By her own appraisal, Lydia was disintegrating. Getting wobblier by the day. No matter where she was she felt she was barely present. The loss of Caldwell still weighed heavily on her, and CannRose wasn't the same. So many of the people she'd grown fond of over the last two years were gone. She'd been especially sad to see Stoyan leave, though they kept in touch. She wasn't sure who to turn to anymore. Initially she'd confided in Luther but he was in no shape to help. He was hardly a rock. Lydia only got more anxiety from him. Sometimes even annoyance and irritation. They barely saw each other these days. His divorce was bending him right out of shape and Cyrus was out for his blood because he'd lost a big client at the law firm. And that dicey business with Greg cast a pall over all of CannRose. Came right out of the blue! Repulsive little man from the DEA asking everybody all sorts of ridiculous questions. CannRose was mostly inaccessible to her now. It could be disintegrating right along with her for all she knew.

She called her daughter and tried to explain a little of what she was experiencing. "I don't know where the company's going now." She laughed a little, to make light of it all. "Come for a visit. I've put in the new water jump you wanted." But her daughter only reminded Lydia she'd told her getting involved with the weed business would turn out badly. And no she couldn't come; she was busy for the weekend.

Lydia walked like a ghost into CannRose in the mornings and closed her office door. Occasionally she would stay late, suit up for the cultivation area and go sit in the grow rooms. The quiet security guard often sat with her as he had done the first time. They barely spoke. He seemed to know she was feeling fragile and that it gave her peace to sit among the plants. She would dream about marijuana afterward of course. Mostly they were cheery dreams. Lots of green things growing. Sometimes the plants turned into little animals that nestled and cuddled. And propagated! She'd wake up feeling oddly rejuvenated. They wanted her to keep them growing. They were persistent. They wanted *her*, in particular. As some ambassador maybe. She just wasn't sure how she could have all that much influence now with Guido in control. He seemed to have more energy and move faster than Jordan ever had.

He didn't care about the plants. They were no different from shoes, except the cannabis industry was still unpredictable. She realized Guido fed off unpredictability. Swooped in for the opportunities in a crisis. She saw that clearly now. It was odd he played the violin so beautifully. His sensitivity didn't make him any less cutthroat. Maybe that was just all part of the skillfulness of the man. He'd even swooped in and charmed Sammy, the beautiful young pharmacist working out of the Lyston dispensary. At least he wouldn't be firing her.

One day Lydia booked off sick and shut herself up at Rosefields. She refused to answer her phone and the only people she talked to were Carl and his wife. At that time Damian was back in Colorado for his routine month off. The tin of weed he'd left by mistake when he'd last come over for Saturday morning coffee sat on her kitchen table. She'd planned to return it to him as soon as he got back. But instead she smoked the whole thing over the space of a couple of days. Then she took Shasta out for a three-hour ride and a frosty winter picnic by the Great Pond.

When Lydia finally resurfaced she told Guido she'd be working from home for a while. She took other initiatives too. With her considerable disposable income and without the knowledge of Cyrus or Malcolm, she hired another accountant, another lawyer and a private detective. There had been a Plan X from Jordan for her blue eyes only. It sat in an envelope in a safe at Rosefields, to be used if she ever felt things weren't adding up. So Lydia opened the envelope and read. Then she crumpled the paper into a ball and threw it in the fireplace. She was sick of Jordan still trying to run her life. She was going to be her own businesswoman from here on in. And she was going to either take charge and head up a division of CannRose to lobby for veterinary cannabis products and get some real research happening, or sell up everything and do something else. Photography. Get spiritual maybe. Go live in a hut.

She called a meeting with Guido, Herbert Cuttle, his money men, the other executives and of course Luther. When Herbert Cuttle started to talk in the subtly patronizing way he had adopted especially for her, she told him to shut up.

"I called this meeting, Herbert. The agenda is on that piece of paper in front of you. If you don't like it you can leave. I'm still the president here."

Chapter 66

Cassie stayed late to get ready for the harvest the next day. She wanted to make sure everything went smoothly. Make sure the barcode scanner for the plant tags was working. Make sure she had enough clean bins. Make sure the drying rooms had been sanitized and the racks too. She'd lost two of her staff in the recent spate of "layoffs." Nobody knew who'd be next.

She'd heard CannRose would likely be ditching the research program too. That would mean no more advice from Petra. She'd been very helpful since Cassie came back on her own. They'd troubleshoot problems in the grow rooms together. Petra didn't mind taking the extra time. Since Sanjay left, Petra practically lived at the grow facility. Must be a lot of extra work for her and they hadn't hired a new tech. It occurred to Cassie the new CEO might be arranging the failure of certain people. At least Cassie would have something to go to even if it was another start-up. Joe had joined forces with an energetic soil microbiologist. They were developing better cost-effective organic grow media, and they already had a handful of clients.

Cassie made her way to the hallway. There were still a few racks stored in one of the drying chambers and she needed to sanitize them. She put on a Tyvek bunny suit, hot and airless, took out the autoclaved cleaning rags from the bag and picked up the bottle of isopropyl alcohol before heading into Chamber III, where she scrubbed down two sets of racks. She had one more to go.

"Aren't you the committed employee!"

The voice made her jump. It was Damian, the last person she wanted to talk to. He appeared of late, often out of nowhere with his little goading remarks. It was as if he was conducting a slow and subtle retribution in lieu of suing her like he'd promised. She tensed up immediately. She'd have to fend off the urge to smash him in the face. It could be tricky. "Yeah, well some of us have a job to do."

Damian smiled. He noticed how the color in her cheeks rose so quickly and thought aggravation made her look splendid. And there was something about her mouth too. "I have to hand it to you. It's a nice-looking crop in Flower Room III there."

"Thank you." Cassie wondered exactly how high he was. She ducked back and continued wiping the racks. The smell of the alcohol was starting to make her a little dizzy. She'd hardly eaten a thing all day. She'd been too busy.

"You know, I'm not against how you do things." Damian inspected one of the bars on the rack that separated the two of them.

"Thank you for your support."

"Not at all." He smiled, enjoying her predictable acid chirpiness. "Yeah. I think I like what you've done with the place. You have a real knack for technology. I think I got stuck on the glitches. Don't you?"

"I just work with what's in front of me, Damian."

"Are you all right, Cassie? You were looking a little flushed there and now you're looking very pale."

"I'm fine, thank you. I just have to finish this up and then I'm going home."

"Ah. Home sweet home!"

"Do you have a point you're trying to make?"

Damian sighed. "No."

He wasn't moving or looking like he was going to leave. Cassie started feeling woozy again. Too bad she hadn't at least had a coffee before starting this. She grabbed the rack as she felt herself almost black out.

"Sure you're okay?" Damian looked a little startled.

"Skipped lunch."

"Never a good idea. Long past suppertime too!"

"I think I'm done here. If you don't mind, I need to move this rack."

"Sure." Damian stepped aside, still staring at her. As Cassie pushed the rack away she stumbled and then really did black out. He caught her as she fell forward. In fact she fell right into his arms.

It was only for a second, but when she regained consciousness, Cassie had no idea where she was. She just felt warm. Supported. Enveloped. She looked up.

"Hey there, you," he said in a whisper.

Maybe it was just the way his pupils were dilated but she'd never seen concern like that in anyone's eyes before. Not for her. Not even from her husband when she was birthing those babies! And then it happened so fast. It was a kiss like no one had kissed her before. It was gentle but it reached into her, right down to her toes. A fearsome desire welled up. And it startled. The urge to rip off Damian's bunny suit and the rest of his clothes right there in the drying chamber was almost overwhelming. But she remembered where she was and also that sanitizing the chamber took over an hour and it would have to be redone after use of any kind. She resisted the unfamiliar impulse. And then she remembered what an asshole Damian was. What the hell was she doing? The thought made her open her eyes and pull back slightly, and the first thing that came into focus was the surveillance camera. She looked at Damian in panic, and he let her go.

Ten minutes later, as she was walking out to her car, still shaking a little, he appeared again. He had a bottle of orange juice. "You should drink this or let me drive you home."

"Thanks." Cassie took the juice. She couldn't look at him. "I'll be OK." But then she did look at him. She saw the same concern in his eyes. There was something very grown up about it, maybe. Nothing was expected in return. It was simply given. It wasn't anything she'd anticipated. Certainly not from someone like him. She cried the whole drive home. He was such a fucking jerk! And he was the only person in her life she'd ever physically assaulted.

That night Cassie couldn't sleep. And she couldn't bear to look at Joe sleeping either. Instead she spent the night on the couch watching the ceiling fan slowly revolve and trying to convince herself that Damian was the worst, most despicable, presumptuous, ignorant cretin of a pothead she'd ever come across in her life. But then the body does remember, and it vividly recalled that minute or so in the drying chamber. And the orange juice and the straightforward offer to drive her home — the care and basic decency of it. She could never tell Joe. It was all just too much.

Chapter 67

"This lady's lookin' sad."

"Check for bugs, brobe."

"They got 'em in Flower Room I now."

"What are they?"

"Nobody knows yet."

"What do they look like?"

"Bugs!"

"Check under the leaf."

"This isn't bugs. It's a virus. Look at the mottling."

"Or toxic nutrients."

"This is all basic."

"Hey, my cousin just grew the best shit ever."

"Yeah?"

"Yeah. Like, it's gotta be forty percent."

"Yeah?"

"What is it?"

"Raspberry Kush."

"Fire!"

"Hydroponic too."

"Seriously?"

"Hydroponic's basic!"

"Not this. It's fire!"

"You brought some?"

"No. Savin' it."

"For what?"

"Saturday, man!"

"Why?"

"Why? Why you think?"

"I don't know."

"Seriously?"

"You got a birthday?"

"April twentieth, dude! April fuckin' twentieth!"

"Four-twenty. Who cares?"

"Yeah. I mean, yeah. Who cares?"

"Well. I thought it was a nice thing to honor."

"Like your mom and dad, maybe."

"Your mom does four-twenty?"

"Maybe. I don't know. She does Dab Day."

"What's Dab Day?"

"Oil Day. What do you think?"

"Oh yeah, right."

"But . . . but what's the occasion?"

"There's no occasion."

"But . . . what's it in honor of?"

"It's the word, brobes. *Oil.*"

"What?"

"O-I-L. Turned upside down, looks like seven-ten."

"Seven-ten? It's twice a year then!"

"Yeah! July and October."

"Awesome."

"Let's do Dab Day."

"With rolls instead!"

"July's too far away."

"Oh yeah."

"Let's do four-twenty on Saturday. Wake and bake."

"Brobes, I'm moving to California."

"What?"

"You heard me. I'm moving to California."

"When?"

"When we get fired."

"We're just techs. They won't fire us."

"Yeah, they'll need techs."

"I'm sick of being just a tech."

"Me too. I still want to be a chef."

"You should talk to Ernie."

"I'm sick of the stupid regulations and everything screwing up."

"That creep who questioned us about Greg?"

"Fuck. I threw up when I got home."

"Dude, we know already. We heard you."

"They talked to my mom for ages."

"Did she know?"

"Nothing. They told her he had fields of it."

"I just thought he had six plants like your mom."

"Rainy Day Dope!"

"That's so sick!"

"Fuckin' genius!"

"We should do that."

"Dude, we'd have to go to police academy."

"That would suck."

"Yeah. It's just way too complicated."

"It doesn't need to be. Let's move to Colorado."

"We should move to Canada. Weed's gonna be legal right across the whole country."

"Bro, moving to a different country is seriously complicated."

"Yeah, I don't want to go to Canada."

"Maybe we should all go look up Greg."

"He's in a different country too. Mom said he and Aunt Sal are totally retired. They got a big house with a sea view."

"Dude, you're supposed to shut up about that."

"Whatever. They've even got a maid."

"Let's all go to California."

"Yeah, California's fire."

"California's *on* fire. Let's not."

"Let's go to Oregon then."

Chapter 68

Ernie was walking back from the cultivation area with his dust mop. He spotted Percy and Lydia stopped outside the lab with their hands over their ears. The walls dividing the storage and the potting rooms were being demolished, as was the concrete floor, all in preparation for an expansion. Guido's plan was to break new ground as soon as the snow melted.

"I don't think they thought this out too well," Ernie said to them over the noise. "Halls in the grow area are covered in dust. It's coming through the ceiling cracks I think."

"Oh my gracious," Lydia exclaimed. "It's more extensive than I imagined."

"It's rattling, is what it is," Percy shouted. "I'm sure nobody thought of anything. They certainly didn't consult me. And they were supposed to." Another jackhammer started up. Percy yelled, "The new wankers are no better than the last lot!"

"At least Lazlo listened to us," Ernie shouted back.

Percy shook his head. "Never mind. We shall prevail!"

At that moment Petra opened the lab door behind the plastic curtain and waved them all in.

"It's positively haboobish out there!" Percy brushed off his lab coat. "Like Black Sunday in the Dust Bowl. Poor you!" He looked at Petra.

She shrugged and raised her voice above the din that still penetrated the walls, "Apparently it's *molto necessario*." She mimicked Guido's gestures flawlessly. "CannRose has to be ahead of any announcements."

"Ridiculous! There's not been a peep out of the DOH about recreational," Percy said.

"It'll be on the ballot again, dollars to donuts." Ernie's voice was still raised when suddenly all the equipment shut down, undoubtedly for the workers' coffee break.

"Probably also depends on who's running for governor now." Lydia sighed.

"Do you know our disgraced governor, Lydia?" Ernie enquired.

"No! Not well anyway. Jordan knew him of course, and Cyrus and Malcolm know him. I never liked him — he pinched me once."

"Where?" Petra said, perking up.

"Where do you think!" Lydia raised her eyebrows. "I was about to smack his face. Jordan intervened. Brushed it off with some comment about my irresistible butt."

"Scandal was no surprise to you then," Ernie said.

"Looks good on him." Lydia brushed some dust off her shoulder.

"So what news of the project?" Petra asked.

"I think your instincts, Petra, were unfortunately dead on." Lydia said. "For all the assurances and enthusiasm I was finally getting a month ago, Herbert is hedging with both those universities you lined up. I'm sure they just want to stall buying me out completely. I gave them an ultimatum you know."

"Good for you, Lydia," Percy said. "And for what it's worth, I think pursuing the veterinary medicine line is a fabulous idea."

"Thanks. I get the feeling the plants are keen on it too. And I don't care if people think I'm crazy, you know." Lydia smiled but then paused and frowned. "CannRose would need to stick with the medical side of things to make it work, though." She pointed her thumb in the direction of the admin section. "They're going to throw all that out the window as soon as they can."

"You keeping the place afloat for months doesn't move them in any way?" Ernie ventured.

Lydia laughed. "Things change fast in the marijuana industry, Ernie. You should know that. No room for sentiment."

"Guess Alice got out just in time," Percy said.

"*Meaner* and *Leaner*. Those should be Herbert and Guido's nicknames. Caldwell always had nicknames for people."

"So what's your best bet, Lydia? They toss me out this month or next?" Petra smiled ruefully.

"They won't while I'm around. But when I'm gone . . . end of your contract most likely. It's still the cheapest way for them. When is that?"

"Another six months."

"Good. Keep collecting your salary and do what you like, Petra! Don't leave until something better shows up," Lydia said. "I know my dead husband's old cronies. Malcolm and Cyrus will take their sweet time for a complete buyout. They'll make Guido sweat and ensure they come out on top. I don't care. If there's anything left, it's going straight to the Humane Society anyway. It's the last thing they're going to handle for me." Lydia smiled again, only more broadly this time, showing her excellent teeth. "I think I enjoy being a thorn for all these people now."

At that moment Cassie popped her head through the lab door. "What's the party? What's happening?"

"Oh we're just gabbing about how a rat can best desert a ship it doesn't like any more," Lydia said. "How are you doing, Cassie?"

"I'm okay. But this construction! Do you think this is the worst of it?" Cassie nodded in the direction of the loading dock. "There's already dust getting into the nurseries. I think we need to convert one of the other grow rooms, just as a temporary measure, Percy."

"Right you are, and we need to write up some temporary cleaning measures too," Percy said looking at Ernie.

"I should let you all get back to your work," Lydia said and winked at Petra. "Besides, I think Damian still wants to talk veterinary products this afternoon. For what it's worth!"

"Tell Damian thanks for the heads-up on that organic fungicide from Washington. It really worked." Cassie smiled.

Ernie stared open-mouthed at Cassie for a second. Someone started up a noisy machine again on the loading dock and Ernie looked around at the people in the lab. As Lydia waved a little goodbye and headed out the door, he pondered the changing dynamics of CannRose and was very glad that paid work was still only a small part of his life.

#

Ernie was squeezing water out of the mop, giving a brand-new side-press bucket its inaugural workout, when a woman came barreling around the corner into the production hallway at such a pace she nearly knocked Ernie and his bucket right over.

"Didn't anybody ever tell you to look around corners first?"

"Ernie!" she cried. "How the hell are you?"

Oh, not this. When did Jessica get back in town? "I thought you were in St. Louis."

"I was, but now I'm back."

"Visiting?"

"No way. I'm here for good! How could I have ever left Hullbrooke? Hear you've been doing a great job on the Cranston terraces. I used to look after them, you know."

"I know. Gladys the toad sends her best."

"What a sweetie."

Ernie didn't know if she was referring to him or Gladys. It didn't matter. Her effusiveness was irritating regardless. He cleared his throat. "So what are you doing at CannRose? You have a job here I take it?"

"I'm Guido's new PA. What a gentleman!"

"I thought Jason was his assistant."

"Jason is his hound. Different beast."

"I'll say."

"So we should get together. I hear you're a regular at Chelsea's."

"Yup. That's me. A regular guy."

"I also hear you've been cooking up a storm. I'd really like to get some of those blackberry preserves if there's any left. I missed the blackberries so much."

"Hmm." It bugged Ernie that Jessica, back in Hullbrooke before he had any notion of it, seemed to know so much about him. That was the worst and best thing about small towns. If you ever forgot what you were doing, there were at least ten people on any given day to set you straight. "I think I gave the last jar to Mrs. Cranston." That's probably where Jessica got all her news.

"So I'm renting the old Lansing house over by the side road. I heard that's where Caldwell met his end. Had no idea when I rented the place. Not that it would have put me off or anything. I thought it would be good for the boys to get a taste of country living."

"No doubt. And what's Matt think of country living?" Ernie asked. Jessica's husband used to be an old video gamer and a buddy of Ernie's.

"Who gives a shit? I'm a single mom like every other woman I know."

More signs of the post-apocalypse, thought Ernie, though he had to admit even he'd found his old friend a jerk at times.

Jessica was looking him up and down. He figured she was sizing him up for some future use. "You're chunkier than you used to be," she said. "More muscles."

"You're chunkier too." He smiled. Unwelcome personal comments could be a two-way street. "It's the gardening. And the mop here."

"I'm a circuit slut myself. Gotta love the weights." She made fists and flexed her arms, pumping them up and down like some boxer with an audience. "This place is really going to get up and running now."

"Is it?"

"Yeah, I heard Caldwell was kind of loose-cannon ineffective. But pretty cool what he managed to build anyway. Guido has major plans though. A whole different approach. You know he owns several companies, and not just for marijuana."

"I just thought he was a shoe guy."

"Nope. Fingers in many pies. Owns a nutraceutical business, among other things."

"Well, you're certainly in the know. Keep me posted."

"I will. We should go for drinks soon." Jessica turned away, uttering the oh-so-trendy-at-the-facility "Ciao, baby," and went into the production area.

"Sure," Ernie said as she left. He felt a cramp in his stomach. Had he ever actually had a thing for Jessica? Or was it just that one steamy grope in the back seat of Carl's car when he was home for his first reading week? He couldn't remember. Small town dilemmas. They could really bug a person.

Recipe for Ernie's Savory Gluten-Free Misdemeanor Crackers

Ingredients

1 cup boiled water

¼ cup chia seeds

2 tbsp flax seeds

1 garlic clove, crushed or minced (or powder)

½ cup oat flour

¼ cup almond flour

2 tbsp sesame seeds

2 tbsp chopped sunflower seeds

½ to 1 tsp salt, depending on taste

A few sprigs of oregano (or approximately 1 tsp dried)

A few sprigs of thyme (or approximately 1 tsp dried)

(You can substitute or add your spices of choice — rosemary, sage, basil — whatever your palate fancies.)

1 tsp to 2 tbsp* milled or coarsely ground dried bud (No decarboxylation needed, especially if you're in a rush, because these crackers are special! Actually it's just that they're so thin and, as Sanjay would point out after he'd carefully reviewed the First Law of Thermodynamics with you, the heat transfer here is very efficient. You don't use any oil either that might hang on to unpleasant flavors. **But please note that Ernie recommends a pre-decarboxylation step before making all other edibles, particularly butter and oil infusions.**)

*Add more or less depending on potency of the weed and depending on how you plan to ingest the crackers. If you make them very potent then they might best be treated like communion wafers. Eat only one. Seriously if you overdo this and bring out the cheese and wine with a wafer batch and eat say four or five with your cheese, you are looking at a very unpleasant time of it. Your communion may be with the bathroom fixtures, provided you can recognize them!

Method

1. Preheat your oven to 315 °F.
2. Boil water and add one cup to a small bowl. Add chia seeds, flax seeds and garlic and let sit for about a minute. Stir well, then stir again after a few more minutes. It will become quite gooey. Let sit.
3. Meanwhile, mix oat and almond flour and the rest of the seeds in a medium mixing bowl. Feel free to experiment with different seeds — ones you don't soak (e.g. pumpkin, black sesame, sunflower, poppy, hemp).
4. If you're using fresh herbs, chop them fine. Depending on the bud, if it's not already milled, do that (a coffee grinder works well and a coarse grind is best). Add salt, herbs and weed to the dry ingredients. Mix thoroughly. Add the soaked seeds and mix again. It will be a sticky, sludge-like mass.
5. Line the bottom of a cookie tray with parchment paper. Spread the cracker batter evenly over the whole area. It should be approximately one-eighth–inch thick. Score into appropriate cracker-sized pieces using a pizza wheel.
6. Bake for 20 minutes. Take out the tray and flip the parchment paper so the cracker sheet is now face down on the tray. Carefully remove the parchment paper and separate the crackers from each other. Put the tray back in the oven for another 20 minutes or so. Keep checking — you can turn the crackers back over especially if they start to curl. They do shrink. You can also raise the temperature to 325 °F if you find they are not crisping up quickly enough. Keep monitoring — you don't want to overdo them. But you do want them crispy and crunchy.

Bon appétit! Don't eat too many.

Author Notes on *Cannabidadas*

Is it even possible to be enthused about yet another discussion of *Cannabidadas*? Perhaps. These notes, along with the usual perfunctory descriptive summary, offer an alternative to the hastily conceived and, I'd posit, rather reckless consensus regarding the origins of the work.

The four known original copies of *Cannabidadas* are listed as follows: 1) the *Oregon Opus*, typed and found stuffed above the driver's-side sun visor of an abandoned Volkswagen van in Three Sisters Wilderness, Oregon; 2) the *Port Authority Duplicate*, identical to the *Oregon Opus* and found stashed above the ceiling tiles in the second-floor men's washroom of the NYC bus terminal; 3) the *LOC Copy*, casual cursive, a partial manuscript found rolled up in a janitor's closet on the first floor of the Library of Congress; and 4) the *Paris Edition*, chancery cursive, found in the Saint-Sulpice Church, Paris, France.

All the originals are now in private collections. As has often been noted, it is unfortunate they remain unavailable for modern analysis techniques, especially dating. However, photos exist and we know from the purple color of the text that a spirit duplicator, similar to a mimeograph machine, was used in the printing. The two typed copies also indicate use of a manual typewriter, specifically an Underwood, circa 1940.

All four copies were discovered in the early-to-mid 1960s and it has generally been assumed that the work was some curious creation of an amateur Beat poet. However, I believe the *Paris Edition* casts considerable doubt on this theory and the very existence of a Parisian manuscript suggests the work was penned at least forty years earlier.

The *Paris Edition* was found tucked out of sight and gathering dust under a stairway, one of many among the ladders and catwalks within the organ of Saint-Sulpice. Surely this cannot be mere happenstance. At least two associations can be made that indicate the placement was purposeful, an act of art in and of itself, or rather an absurd un-statement by none other than a Dadaist in the throes of creative insurrection.

Firstly, the *Dada Manifesto* of 1920 by Francis Picabia not only references the cathedral but perhaps the very document within the cathedral's organ. The manifesto states that "art is as easy to see as God (see Saint-Sulpice)." Consider the pipe organ, the king of instruments, often as visually remarkable as it is tonally sophisticated. The organ in Saint-Sulpice is a masterpiece of design and is regarded as the ultimate achievement of Aristide Cavaillé-Coll. Given the organ's function and situation, it is presumably close to God. Additionally one could argue that *Cannabidadas* has at least a toe in the tradition of ecstatic poetry. It is of course possible that Picabia was referring to the actual saint, but his reference is followed by the line "Art is a pharmaceutical product for idiots." Surely this is an oblique reference to cannabis and, by extension or association, *Cannabidadas*. The evidence could not be more persuasive from this author's perspective.

Secondly, the work is divided into eight "canntos." The pun repeated ad absurdum provides the only structure and division to the continuous prose poem that is undoubtedly an effort of stream-of-consciousness writing. The style became fashionable in the early twentieth century and was both used and intentionally abused by the Dadaists. If this were not enough, the persistent anonymity of the work also suggests Dadaist roots in keeping with the nihilism of the movement, which included as its ultimate expression the annihilation of the artist. Add to this the eponymous title, *Cannabidadas*, containing *dada* as the probable suffix of the word, and I rest my case.

One must inevitably ask, therefore, do the canntos themselves represent examples of Dadaism? Or was the work merely used by a Dadaist in the manner of, say, a found object? Clearly, the only answer can be, It all depends.

One might also wonder, does the *LOC Copy* hint at an even earlier origin? The janitor's closet housing the manuscript was located close to the library's Asian collection after all. The collection

332 THE BUDS ARE CALLING

contains rare and ancient texts as well as numerous translations including the Atharva Veda, which specifically references marijuana. Given the amount of text omitted in this copy though, as well as its sloppy cursive rendition, it seems just as likely that one of the janitors at the library was simply immersed in the culture of the day. They would perhaps have had access to one of the spirit duplicates and transcribed only what they "dug" about it.

In quoting passages I deemed appropriate for this book, I've taken the liberty of updating some phraseology that was poorly discerned in all the original four copies and they are as follows: 1) The famous passage from Cannto V, often written as "Yo . . . wand jelly babies" has been revised to the far less cryptic, less contentious, and I would suggest more in keeping with the humor of the Cannto, "You want gummy bears"; and 2) the totally illegible third, fourth and fifth sentences of Cannto VII, "c . . . a ion re . . . ges. Bew . . . dw . . . g . . .ose. Her . . . pu . . . pr . . . ts," which are usually left out altogether from most reproductions, have been revised to: "We caution with care from the ages. Beware of the dwindling repose. Here is the punch of your profits."

Acknowledgments

This book is one part of a larger project that began some time ago and has gone through a number of iterations. I am very grateful to Beth, who was the project's original midwife. A number of people gave feedback and occasionally their expertise to help bring that initial project or parts of it to some kind of completion. I am indebted and grateful to the following readers, listed in no particular order: Anne, Virginia, Frances, Sonja, Iris, Larry, Brian, Sandra, Michelle, Ann, Michele, Barb, Dave, Tolling, Kay, Teresa and Cynthia. A special thanks to Maureen, who edited some of the first project, and to Bruce, who suggested I give her a call. If I've left anyone out I do apologize — the memory fades with age and this project has been going on for a while. Thanks again to Dave for the Photoshop help. Last but far from least, I thank all the people at Iguana Books for their suggestions, advice, goodwill and wonderful expertise in bringing this book to its finished form.

BCD

www.ingramcontent.com/pod-product-compliance
Lightning Source LLC
Chambersburg PA
CBHW031332020726
47499CB00005B/1221